"The alien has not lodged outside,
For I have opened my doors to the
traveler."

~The Book of Job

The Legacy Continuum
Book 1

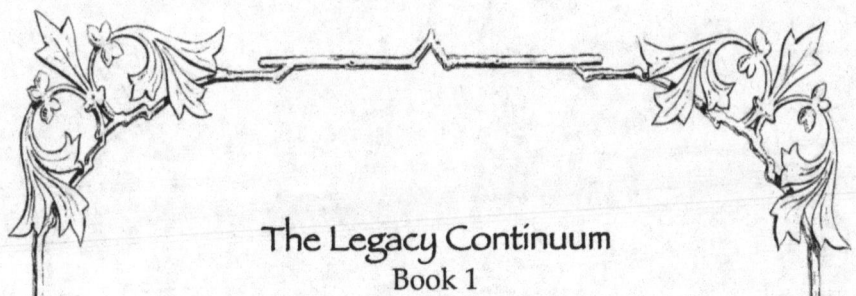

FADING STARLIGHT

Originally Published under the following
ISBN-13-978-1515036890
ISBN-13 978-0998667508
Case # 1-2498230171
Case # 1-4344929311

Final layout & cover art by Robert A. Foster
Printed in the United States of America
Set in 13pt. Palatino

ISBN-13-978-1737773313
Case # 1-12273151484

To my wonderful and loving wife, Kathy.

As well as Michael R. Carter,
to whom this project may never had started.
You are missed.

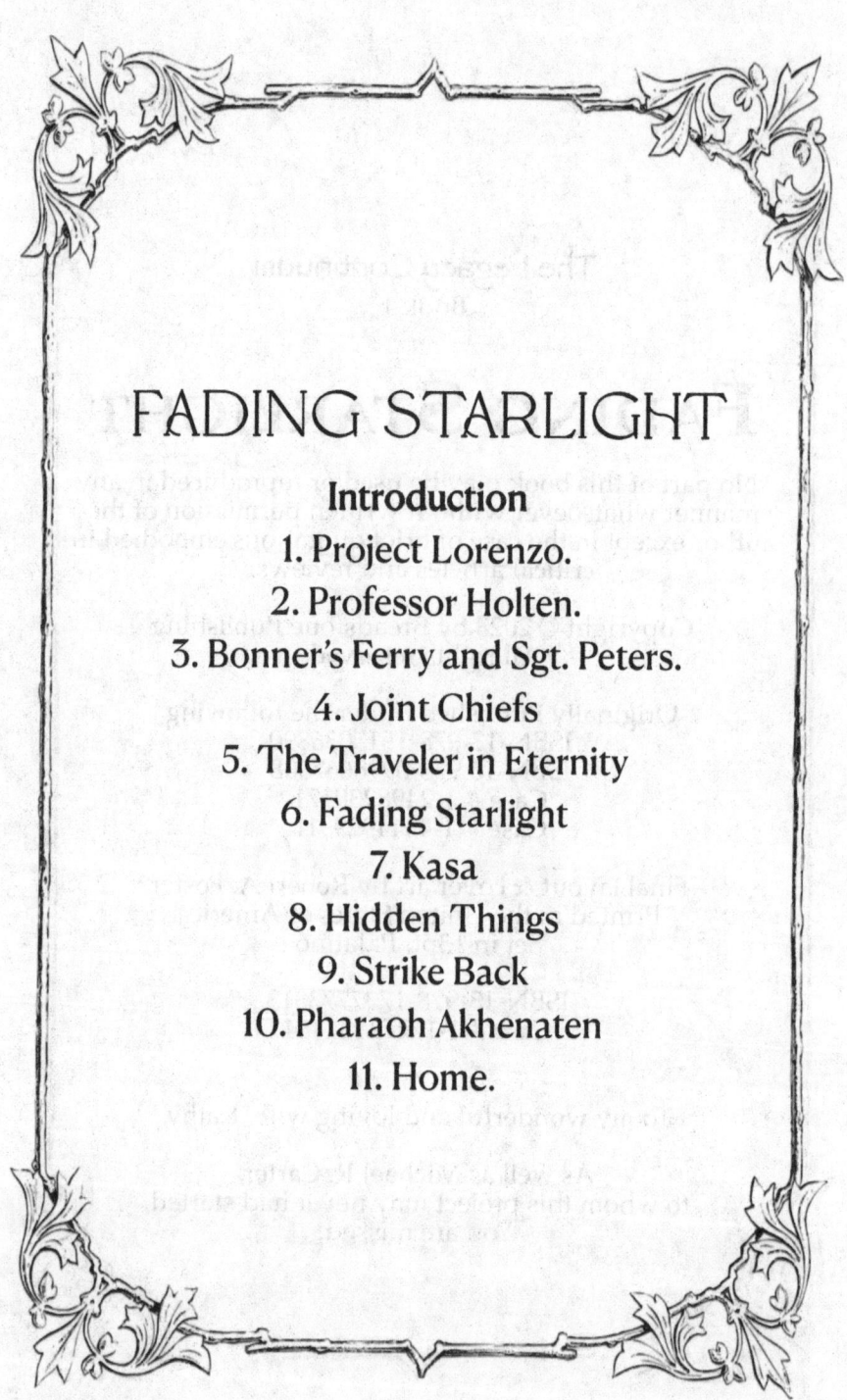

FADING STARLIGHT

Introduction.

Between the red stone canyon walls, a bit of dust kicked up in the dry, light breeze, making its way along the trail.The wind still felt a little cool in the early morning shade of the narrow canyon walls. The bits of sand twisting in the air formed a thin funnel as it worked its way uphill past a Jeep and a few tents in a small archaeology camp.

Watching it pass, a woman in her late thirties grabbed a hat off the seat of the Jeep to cover her red hair and fair skin. "It's going to get hot today," she thought to herself as she grabbed a canteen and a few hand tools. As she began to walk away from her older, late nineties Jeep, she put them into her backpack, only to find a hand in front of her offering a tube of sunscreen. "Becker, it's going to get hot today, you better put this on," exclaimed an older man who had just walked up to her.

His offer did not stop her, nor did it even slow down her walking, as she turned her head with a slight smile while raising her hand to the man with the salt and pepper hair, "No thanks."

Dave Shaver was the chief caregiver for her young son, Johnny, as well as a cook, bookkeeper, and flat tire fixer. Dave stopped walking and shook his head as he slipped the tube of sunscreen back into his chest pocket before starting back for the mess tent.

Megan Verity Becker, formerly Lieutenant Becker of the U.S. Army, widow, and single mother, was enjoying her early morning walk to a new archaeological dig site. Life was becoming better for Megan with her small but loyal crew of dedicated workers hired to help her with her work and caring for her son.

She could hear her child in the distance beating up some sage bush with a stick as if it was a sword. The sound of it made her smile a little, bringing forth a pleasant memory of Johnny's father. That thought slowly moved to the side of her mind as she walked while looking over how high the canyon walls were.

As the sun was pushing the shadows up the stone walls. She could almost feel the heat of the stone from a distance as she thought, "I should have taken his sunscreen." But she was never going to admit it to him.

After traveling around 50 yards or so, Megan stopped to look over the thick brush near the stone face. Pulling her backpack off, Megan removed the machete from her pack. Surveying the landscape for the best place to start, she started swinging the machete, hacking out a small path to the face of the sandstone.

Under the brush, the earth rose up at a sharp angle from the desert floor to the sandstone wall. Creating an earthen berm of fallen rocks, dead sticks, and gravel. Here is where she would start digging. Many old tribal petroglyphs had been covered over as the ancient Wingate sandstone gradually fell from above. In time, mixed with sandstorms and growing plants, the earth built up and covered the ancient artwork that she had come to record.

Within an hour Dave had sent two "younger" men up to help her. Josh and Andrew, who were only a little younger than Megan, had been by her side ever since her husband passed away. By midday, after the team cleared a small area, Dave was yelling in the distance that lunch would soon be ready. "Megan, don't you think we should head back for lunch? It's getting hot." Josh asked.

"I will join you and Andrew in a moment, go ahead without me. I just want to move a few more rocks and I'll be right there." Megan remarked as she wiped her brow with the back of her hand.

Josh gave a look of momentary concern as he looked behind himself to glance at Dave who was stomping up the trail with his apron on. Josh then looked at Andrew with a look of, "It's not our fight!" Pointing with his thumb over his shoulder Josh remarked, "Come on, we better go."

They pulled themselves out of the dust and sand and were about halfway to the trail when Megan put her shoulder on a large rock. As it finally rolled out of the way, she stopped to look at what she'd uncovered. After the rock stopped, she leaned backward as her butt slowly came to rest on the ground behind her.

Dave yelled at her from the road about the food and her need to come in. She barely heard him as she just sat there looking at what she had unearthed. Dave grew a little concerned and changed his message to just her name. "Becker, Becker, can you hear me?" She swallowed and finally spoke, not breaking her gaze at the stone, "Dave, do you have my cell phone with you?"

Confused by her question, Dave responded back, "Yes. Megan, are you okay?"

"Yes," she answered as she slowly raised her hand behind her as if he was about to hand her the phone "I think I need to call the General. Could you bring me my phone?"

Dave's eyes grew wide as he exclaimed, "You're going to call your father?"

**Fading Starlight
Chapter One
Project Lorenzo.**

Dave, Josh, Andrew, and Megan all sat around a table as they watched Johnny build a "rock house" for the lizard he had just caught. They said very little, sipping coffee as they stared at their dirty plates and scattered paperwork on the table.

Dave broke the silence. "How long till he gets here?"

"Could be any time," Megan answered as she watched her six-year-old son.

"Did he believe you?" Andrew asked.

"I didn't tell him," Megan remarked as she sipped her coffee. "Besides, would you believe it?"

The look on everyone's face agreed with Megan's statement. Slowly they all became aware of the sound of tires on gravel in the distance. Johnny could hear it also, and accidentally bumped his lizard's house that he was building. The side of it fell over like a tower of playing cards while his mother swallowed the last of her coffee in preparation for what was about to come.

A white truck pulled up to the tent in a cloud of dust as everyone rose to greet its passenger. The door opened and an older, dark-haired military man stepped out. Johnny realized instantly who it was and climbed over the table yelling, "Grandpa!"

The older gentleman took a step from the truck only to discover Johnny had suddenly grabbed his leg. Looking up from his grandson he gave Megan a look of "What are you up to?" Then, with a big grin, Lt. General Henry Mullins looked back at his grandson.

"Well hello, my little man. You're looking mighty healthy to me," Henry remarked as he picked up the squirmy little boy and held him to his chest.

Henry's inquisitive gaze at his daughter was quickly

interrupted by Johnny shoving his lizard in his face. "Look Grandpa, I've got Lorenzo and Lorenzo is a lizard." Henry cranked his head back in an attempt to focus on the lizard and keep it out of his mouth. There before him was a tired, over-played, half-dead-looking lizard.

Henry stood there for a moment, looking over his dirt-covered grandson with his lizard and a sparkle in his eyes. Unfortunately, that silent moment was broken by a long line of sentences coming out of the excited boy's mouth as he decided to tell his grandfather EVERYTHING that had happened in the last few months.

Dave walked up behind Johnny to gently took the young boy out of the General's hands. "Johnny, let's give your grandfather a moment or two with your mother." As Dave and Henry exchanged the boy, Dave continued to speak to Johnny, "I have a feeling they have a few grown-up things to say to each other right now."

Johnny conceded since he knew it was pointless to continue. Mom and Grandpa had many "talks," some nice, some not. And Johnny learned it was just better to not be involved.

Henry walked up to his daughter in a strong but reserved, fatherly way as the General's driver stepped out to greet Dave whom he obviously knew.

"I see my grandson is looking fine as ever," Henry remarked as he slowed to a stop in front of Megan.

A mischievous look in Megans eye grew as she addressed her father. "Yes, General, he is."

"Dad," Henry interjected with a little aggravation in his voice.

"Walk with me for a moment, General," Megan remarked as she turned to go up the road to the new dig site.

Henry stayed where he was. "I like it right here, Megan."

Megan did not stop but only turned to say, "Of course, General, but I think you would like it better if you walked instead."

"Will she ever change?" he grumbled under his voice as he began walking toward her in an effort to catch up.

Megan secretly loved this game she was playing with her father as she wrestled in her mind with how she was going to tell him what she had found. She looked around the flat canyon walls as she considered what to say. Her father was almost alongside her as he began to talk to her in his low voice.

"Why the false message, Megan? You hardly ever ask for anything and now you are using my grandson as bait? Where are we going?" Henry asked.

"Up here," Megan answered.

Henry turned his eyes away from Megan to look up the trail, "Why?"

Megan stopped at the entrance to her machete-hacked trail and turned to look at her father. "You should know that what I found is very old." She paused to look for any reaction in his eyes. Seeing nothing but puzzlement, Megan turned and walked toward the rock face.

Henry was not expecting that answer, pausing to watch her walk away, he finally put one foot in front of the other to join her. Finally catching up, Henry found his daughter sitting on the ground in front of the canyon wall. The surrounding brush provided a little shade as Henry joined his daughter, squinting he pulled his glasses from his shirt pocket to take a seat beside her.

Slowly, the same look of puzzlement and confusion came over his face that Megan had when she called him the day before. He sat there in silence until she told him once more, "It's very old."

Henry carefully looked over the ancient image crudely carved into stone, an image he knew very well. He counted the circle of thirteen stars above the winged eagle who was holding arrows in one claw and a branch in the other, with the whole thing encircled by the words, "United States Army" with an additional eight stars. It was the U.S. Army logo, about 18 inches wide, resting next to some American Indian petroglyphs

6

depicting warriors with bows.

Megan sat for what seemed like an hour waiting for her father to speak. Would he believe her? Would he say anything?

Finally, a light afternoon breeze began to pick up. The wind seemed to loosen his tongue from his thought as he asked, "How old, Megan?"

Relieved that he had finally spoken, Megan responded back, "Somewhere around two to three thousand, based on the weathering before the earth covered it."

"I have no idea what to say. Are you sure?" Henry inquired,

"Yes," Megan responded.

"Who else knows about this? And what else can you tell me?" Henry asked as he pushed his glasses further up his nose.

Megan took a deep breath. "Just my team. We stopped all digging in the area once I found it. I felt I should call you before disturbing any more soil."

He turned and looked directly at her for the first time since sitting down. "Why?"

Finally getting to the heart of the issue, Megan said, "Because to do a real serious job I will need to remove a lot of earth. My current permit will...."

The General interrupted her, "...will not allow you to remove more than a few yards at a time. So if you could get your old dad, the General involved, you hoped I could pull some strings," he remarked with a little aggravation in his voice.

"Yep." Megan quickly responded back.

Henry looked down at a bug on his pant leg. Flicking it off as he informed her, "I need to make some phone calls."

Megan reached the camp first as the General was taking his time walking down the trail talking on his phone. Dave handed her some cold water as she entered the shade of the tent. All eyes except Johnny's were on her. Taking a sip, she gave her team a smile.

Andy nervously asked, "Are we good to go?"

"He's working on it," Megan answered as she looked at the thermometer in the tent. "It's 97 in the shade right now. Get your tails up there and start removing the soil around the site. But do it slowly and bring lots of water."

"Boys, I think we are about to make history," Megan remarked with a smile with her left hand on her hip.

As Andrew walked up the trail past the General, who was still talking with someone on the phone as he came down, he tried not to overhear him saying that "he did not care if it landed him in court. He trusted the opinion of his daughter and he was ordering this operation to move forward." And that the person he was talking with, "would need to have a conversation with the National Park Service as to why our people were about to tear up the hillside."

Josh and Andrew's eyes widened as they looked at each other. "Operation?" Andrew quietly commented to Josh as they passed.

Josh returned the comment with the same puzzlement in his voice, "Tear up the hillside?"

Megan was giving her son a drink of water and encouraging him to eat his grilled cheese sandwich when she noticed her father was almost at the mess tent, still talking. He stopped in front of the tent, listening to the other person on the phone as his grandfatherly gaze drifted from Johnny to the sad-looking lizard who was now confined to an upside-down glass bowl. "Lorenzo. We will use the name Lorenzo," Henry said in a very formal way.

"Yes Sir, goodbye," Henry remarked as he ended his conversation. Putting his phone back in his pocket as he headed for the table to sit down. Megan half-heartedly tried to hold her son back as he wiggled toward his grandfather's lap. Soon Johnny was trying to feed his mangled sandwich to Henry. He was pretending to eat it as he began to explain to Dave and Megan what was about to happen.

"Tomorrow around 08:00, a small team will be arriving from Camp Williams to assist in the digging operations here," Henry informed them.

"Grandpa, you're not eating my sandwich." Johnny protested.

"Yes, I did. See the bite mark?" Henry told him, motioning toward the grilled cheese sandwich.

"I did that," insisted Johnny.

"Small team?" came the protesting voice of Megan. "From Williams? General, that's not what I wanted."

Henry looked a little concerned but tried to focus on Johnny. "Uh, Grandpa's not really hungry for a sandwich right now," as he tried to shake a soggy piece of it off the back of his hand. "What Grandpa could really use is something a little more solid like...."

"....a burger?" Dave interrupted.

Megan, whose voice was starting to grow a little louder with irritation, "General."

Dave took this as his cue to get up and move out of the growing line of fire.

"Grandpa, I like burgers. Can I have one?" Johnny asked.

"Sure, you can have one too," Henry responded back with a childlike tone in his voice while trying to avoid Megan's gaze.

"Two burgers coming right up," shot back Dave as he turned the grill back on.

Megan leaned in to move Johnny out of the way. "Johnny, you have already eaten. Dave, it will be one burger for the General only and I might be serving it to him raw." Pausing for a moment to look directly into her father's eyes, "You're ignoring me."

Feeling a little cornered, Henry defensively shot back, "Well now you know how it feels to be ignored. All this time I was willing to help you raise Johnny after Tom died. But you decided to ignore me and....."

Megan interrupted, "You're changing the subject and I did not ignore you. We agreed on a plan of action. I said I wanted your help to pull a few strings so I could dig up more than my permit allows, not to turn this area into an armed camp."

Henry tried to regain some composure but it slipped away quickly. "It was the only way, Megan."

"What do you mean?" Megan asked.

"A U.S. Army General can't call up a few people in Washington just to shoot the breeze and say, 'By the way, I want to dig up part of the Southwest desert out in the middle of nowhere.' Seriously, Megan, don't you think people are going to ask questions?" Henry informed her.

Megan sat back in her chair as the General's attempt to remain calm was failing. With a bit of irritation Henry's voice grew louder. "Seriously, you just showed me an old Army logo that, most likely (pause for a breath) predates even the building of Rome. You want me to get the Secretary of Agriculture out of meetings and tell him nothing? Seriously?"

Dave looked over at Megan, "He's starting to become repetitive."

"He does that when he gets flustered," Megan commented back to Dave.

That only irritated Henry as he attempted to repeat Megan's word, "flustered" but it seemed to turn sideways in his mouth as he only got, "fll.." out.

Megan leaned back, taking it all in as she began to realize the position she'd put her father in. Having spent a few years working for CECOM, the U.S. Army Communications-Electronics Command, she should have known better if she had taken the time to think about it. After a moment and a drink of water, Henry recomposed himself.

"What's next?" Megan asked.

"Megan, honey, in order to not tell the secretary anything, so that I did not sound like an idiot, I had to declare this a military operation and put it on a need-to-know basis." He took a deep breath and continued. "Then, I asked Watson to call my office to declare the same. A few phone calls later, as of 30 minutes ago, this area of rock and sand is now under my authority." Henry informed her.

Dave's eyebrow raised as he flipped the burger.

"And what about my dig, General?" Megan asked.

"Not a problem. Everyone here is ex-military, so you just became civilian advisors to the operation." Henry commented.

"Lovely," Megan sarcastically responded back.

"Lovely," echoed Dave from the grill.

Henry was feeling a little more confident now that he could see that she was beginning to resign herself to what was coming. Looking at his empty glass of water, Henry turned his head to look at Dave, "Where's the latrine?"

Dave was cutting slices of tomato and pointed with the tip of his blade over his shoulder, "About 20 paces behind you."

"Thank you," Henry responded back as he got up. Putting his hand on the door he heard Megan ask, "Johnny's not military."

That made Henry stop and look at Johnny with a smile. Taking off one of his General's stars, he leaned over to him at the table, and pinned it on his dirty tee shirt. "Don't ask and I won't tell," he responded back as he smiled and walked away.

Johnny ran to a mirror to announce that it was, "Cool!"

"Dad?" The comment made Henry stop in his tracks. "Now that this is a military operation, what's the name of the project?" Megan asked.

Henry's heart swelled a bit at hearing Megan finally call him Dad. He looked straight into Megan's eyes and said, "When Major Watson asked me that on the phone, the only name I could think of was the name of Johnny's lizard. Welcome to Project Lorenzo." Henry informed her with a smile as he turned and walked away with a bit of a swagger in his step. "Hope you got a place for me to sleep tonight," he announced before entering the latrine.

Bits of laughter and general good humor filled the long night of discussion and storytelling around the camp as everyone reflected on the past. They put Johnny to sleep several times but continued to find that he had slipped out of his sleeping bag to eavesdrop on the adults.

With the rolling of the hours, the early morning sunlight created the jagged canyon edges as Henry rolled off his cot to rub his aching neck. A night of sharing his pillow with his grandson did not work out well for him. Dave was also rubbing the sleep from his eyes as he attempted to grind coffee.

Before the first hours of morning light, Megan however was already awake. As the crisp red and orange colors of sandstone danced to life with the sunrise, Megan was now walking down from the dig site. Looking up as she walked, she could see from her vantage point, a small convoy of about four trucks kicking up dust in the distance drawing closer as they moved along the road.

The growing sound of the trucks grew louder in the ears of Henry's sleepy driver, Lt. Bill Cook, as he reach above his head to open the door of his truck. Seeing the small convoy arrive Bill rolled over to crawl out from truck seat where he was sleeping. Crawling out, Bill struggled to come to attention as the general drew near.

Grunting a gravelly "good morning, Sir" to the General as he wandered off to the latrine. Henry acknowledged his greeting with a head nod as he changed his direction to walk towards his daughter. They met each other at a small sandstone boulder near the camp trail. Raising her right eyebrow Megan stopped, sat down, and flipped one leg over the other as she took a drink from her canteen.

"Megan, I spent most of the night, well...when Johnny wasn't sticking his feet into my side, thinking about who might have made that image thousands of years ago," Henry remarked.

Megan screwed the cap back on her canteen, looking closely at it for a moment. "Yeah, so have I. Come to any conclusions?"

"You're the person with the archaeology degree. I was hoping you would have something?" Henry asked.

"Nope," she remarked as she put her canteen back in her pack. "The more I think about it, the more questions I come up with. I am long on questions at this point." Megan looked up at her father with her green eyes as she came to her feet next to him. "We are just going to have to keep digging."

Henry turned his head a little to the side to listen. He could hear the convoy stopping at the tents behind. He then looked back at Megan and asked, "Ready?"

"Oh, sure. Let's rock their world too," Megan sarcastically responded back as she got up and walked past her father.

Bill, who'd just exited the latrine joined Megan, Henry, and Dave who gave their greeting to Major Watson and his team as they stepped from the trucks. Watson who was a little younger than Henry shook everyone's hands, making Megans the last. "Good Morning, ma'am. Nice to see your still causing trouble where ever you go."

Megan gave a polite "thank you" while wondering what her father had told Watson on the phone.

Henry introduced each of the others as Josh and Andrew made their way out of the tent. Dave started to inquire if they all needed breakfast but was stopped mid-sentence by Major Watson, who politely told him that his men had eaten at four this morning before they left.

Watson, an older, black gentleman, glanced over the encampment and was motioned by a hand wave from the General to the shade of the mess tent, where he accepted a freshly brewed cup of coffee from Dave. Pausing a moment after taking a sip, Watson then spoke in a loud voice to a man who'd just walked up to him. "Buckings, have your men set up the tents, unload the gear, and post guards for the perimeter."

"Yes, Sir," Buckings responded back with a respectful salute. The Major gave a half-hearted return salute as Buckings turned to relay the orders to the men.

Andrew, who was standing near Dave, picked up his cup and quietly said, "Hmm, feels like old times."

Watson took another sip, looked at the General, and in a firm voice answered, "It's your show, General."

The General picked up his coffee and answered back, "Major, you will be in charge of security and your men. Megan Becker will oversee the dig. You will follow her directions on where and how. Have your men bring the equipment you brought up to the site."

"What are we looking for, General?" Watson asked.

"Something very old," Henry remarked as Megan nodded in agreement.

"Follow me, Major." Megan quickly added as she got up.

Megan, the General, and the Major all started walking up the trail. Megan began to explain the dig without telling him what they had found. "My men spent a good part of the day yesterday clearing out some of the underbrush and rocks. They could not dig any deeper without the sides falling back in so nothing new was found."

Watson was taking in the information in as he walked along looking at the sidewalls of the narrow canyon wondering what the General had gotten him into.

Megan who had paused continued speaking, "Major, your men must firmly understand that we cannot scrape the stone face or vital data may be lost."

"Seriously, Becker?" Watson responded back.

"Seriously, Watson. She means it," Henry quietly added.

Megan smiled as she turned towards the rock face. She loved it when her father backed her up. Soon, the Major was standing in front of the U.S. Army logo with the same stunned look on his face that everyone else had. Henry was going to give him a moment to adjust when Watson raised his voice and pointed at the logo with a serious amount of doubt in his voice. "This is actually real? This isn't some gag you're pulling on me?"

"It's very real, Major," Megan answered.

"How old, Becker?" The Major asked.

"Two to three thousand years, Major. Do you need me to explain why I believe that?" Megan asked.

The Major lifted the palm of his hand towards her. "No... no, I think I will just take your word on that." You could almost see Major Watson's mind processing the information as he took his radio out from his belt.

With a slight grin, Megan responded back, "Very well... if you will excuse me I need to talk to my team."

Watching her turn and walk away, Major Watson turned a little towards Henry, "Sir, I was ordered by the brass to remind you of the files on your desk you need to review."

With a slight sigh, the corner of Henry's mouth came up a little as he responded back, "Can I assume they mean that garbage from the Galton Assembly?"

Putting his hands together behind himself Watson looked once more at the canyon walls, "you could..."

"Never going to happen, Major, never going to happen," Henry responded back rather firmly.

"I thought as much," Watson responded back as he spoke into his radio, "Sergeant Buckings, you better get up here. I've got a project for you.

Johnny finally awoke when they started the engines of the heavy equipment. Red-eyed and still hanging on to his grandfather's star, he slid from his bed to lean against Dave's leg. Dave was holding a conversation with Henry as he cut some potatoes. The camp had just grown from six to sixteen, which meant he was going to have to prep all the food earlier than usual.

Johnny was listening to his grandfather's voice say something about the team and something called physics. He had no idea what all that was, but grandpa's lap was looking a lot better than Dave's leg.

"What do you think they're going to find out there, Henry?" Dave asked as he dumped another pile of potatoes into the sink to rinse.

"Unknown," Henry responded back as he paused to think about it. "There are not too many possibilities as to what this could all be." Reaching down Henry pulled Johnny up a little closer to himself as he was reflecting on something in his mind.

With a long pause and a distant, faraway look on his face it soon caused Dave to ask, "What are you thinking about, Henry?"

Henry jerked his head slightly as if he was coming back to reality. "I was thinking about a science lecture I was ordered to attend back just before I became a Major. A scientist was discussing the latest quantum physics theories. Most of it was way over my head, but some guy from New Mexico talked about a theory he had about breaking the time barrier."

Henry kissed Johnny on the head. "I am starting to wonder if he pulled it off."

Dave lifted the washed potatoes out of the sink. "Maybe you should give that guy a call."

"That's a lot easier said than done, Dave. I was so

bored in that meeting, I blocked most of it out including the man's name." Henry responded back.

Dave moved the washed potatoes to a cooler and began working on some carrots. "Do you really think it's time travel, Henry? What if some old Indian had a vision or something?" He remarked as he paused to wipe off his cutting board off into the trash. "This whole thing seems really far-fetched to me."

"As I see it, this could turn into one of two possibilities. One, nothing else will be found and I will have a lot of questions to answer in Washington with tons of paperwork ahead of me. Or we will find evidence to at least prove some measure of it and I will still be answering endless questions as this becomes one of the most classified projects in existence." Looking down at Johnny, Henry relaxed a bit. "Either way, I don't think I am going to get to retire next year."

Henry was thinking about changing the subject when Andrew walked into the camp. Taking his hat off as he sat down. Henry and Dave looked at him as Dave spoke up, "I thought you were going to work at the site today?"

Andrew shook his head, "Nope, Major Pain is starting to rip all the brush out. I think he would take the opportunity to run me over if I let him. Can I have some water?"

Henry's eyebrows narrowed, "Major Pain?"

Dave chuckled as he flicked some carrot peelings into a bucket. "Yeah, I forgot about that name. That's what some of the men called Watson when they were under his command back when Andrew was in."

"Yep, a well-deserved name at that," Andrew responded as he noticed Dave pointing to an icebox with his knife as if to say, "Get it yourself."

Henry smiled as he thought about it. "I can see it. Never thought about it like that, but I can see it."

Andrew was putting some ice into a cup while he told them about the Major's plan to blade off all the brush with a dozer to the other side of the trail. All the while, Megan is playing the over-protective mom with her dig, warning him about disturbing the petroglyphs on the rock wall.

"Personally, I think the only reason Major Pain is putting up with Megan is because she's your daughter," Andrew remarked as he sat down. "And . . . it's a bit of a pleasure right now to see someone else giving the Major a little bit of pain."

By noon, Henry decided to walk up to see how the project was progressing. Josh and Andy were both back at the mess tent so Henry decided he would let the Major know it was time to break for lunch. As he approached the worksite, a guard saluted him. Returning the salute, Henry strolled across the newly leveled ground that once held brush and rocks.

Megan saw him out of the corner of her eye, turned, and walked toward him. Major Watson was tapped on his shoulder by Sergeant Buckings to let him know the General just walked in. Henry noticed it all as he drew closer only to stop as Megan met him with Watson hot on her heels.

Before Megan got a chance to say anything Henry looked at Watson and informed him, "It's lunchtime, Major."

"Yes, Sir," Watson responded back.

"It's hot out. I want the men to return for lunch." Henry ordered.

"Sir?" Watson asked.

"You have your orders, Major." The General informed him.

Looking a little frustrated, "Yes, Sir." The Major responded back as he turned and yelled at Buckings to bring everything to a stop.

Megan stood silently next to her father as the men slowly filed out. When the last man left, Henry looked at his daughter and said, "You really should wear sunscreen out here."

"It's slimy and makes the sand stick to me. I can't stand the stuff. Besides, I have my hat." Megan informed him.

Henry just looked at her. He'd had the same argument

with her many times and it always ended the same. At this point, he realized her leaving the Army because she was pregnant with Johnny was a God-sent blessing.

"So did you find anything yet?" Henry asked.

With a grin and a raised eyebrow, Megan responded back. "Walk with me, General. So far they have just been getting the area ready but we ran into a snag."

"Oh? What's that?" he responded back as they neared the rock face.

Megan stopped just short of the wall. "Well, we are standing on a really big boulder," Megan remarked as she kicked the dirt and gravel aside with her boot to show him. "And if you look up," pointing with her finger to the edge of the upper rock wall, "that's where it came from. And now it's in our way."

Henry looked around at the size of it before he spoke, "And you can't just get the dozer in here and push it because?"

"It will mostly destroy the very evidence we are trying to find," Megan interrupted.

"So how do we fix it?" Her father asked.

Megan walked to the outer edge, away from the rock wall. "We dig a big hole on this side of it and roll it away from the wall."

Henry looked around and then at his daughter, "Sounds good. I hope this is all worth it?"

Megan's dirt-covered face smiled. "It is. Look at this." She motioned with her hand.

Henry followed her to the U.S. Army logo. They bent down and she brushed away the dirt and sand in the crack where the boulder rested itself on the wall. "What do you see?" Megan asked with a little glee in her voice.

Henry stooped down as low as he could while putting on his glasses. There in the thin crack between stone and rock wall, his eyes clearly saw the number "two."

"Two, I see the number two. Oh my. It's a two!" Astonished, Henry quickly looked back up at Megan. "And I think there's more down there, but I can't see what it is."

"I know," Megan confidently answered.

Watson's team worked hard all that afternoon clearing away the earth next to the boulder in an effort to roll it. It turned out to be larger than they realized and so were the smaller rocks that held it in place. Ultimately, General Mullins ordered them back to the camp before they were done. It was hard work and he knew they needed the rest.

Dave ordered Josh and Andrew to drive to town for more supplies. Megan oversaw the project and her dad spent most of his afternoon either on the phone or helping Dave entertain Johnny, who had a new lizard that he also named, Lorenzo.

Henry's growing concern over the project after clearly seeing the number two in the stone left his mind continually thinking about time travel and the "what ifs." After everyone settled down for the night, he rolled over to see Megan was in her cot but not yet asleep. In a low voice, Henry spoke, "Megan?"

"Yes?" Megan responded back.

"This may be the raving of an old man, but what if we, the Army, have a man out there, somewhere, trapped in the past?" Pausing for a moment to see the look on her face, "And what if the Army sent him there?" Henry asked.

"Hmm. What would be the point of sending him three thousand years into the past? I can see twenty, fifty, or even a hundred, but thousands?" Megan responded back.

Frustrated, Henry rolled on his back as he responded back, "I know, it doesn't make sense. But what if?" pausing to collect his thoughts. "What if it wasn't planned? What if it was an accident?"

"Like I said, long on questions, short on answers. But with the progress we made today I suspect we might have a few answers tomorrow," Megan remarked as she closed her tired eyes.

Megan was too much like her mother and Henry knew that meant the conversation had just come to an end. He lay there looking at the tent ceiling for an hour before dozing off to the sound of crickets and a gentle wind making its way through the canyon.

Henry heard a noise that sounded like a crash. It caused him to jump forward into the sand and rocks near his feet. Henry rolled onto his side with the hot sun blinding his face. He suddenly grew very concerned and got up yelling, "Where are you!"

"Over here." Came the voice.

Henry turned his head to see Johnny standing near the rock wall next to the U.S. Army logo.

"Hurry up, Grandpa, hurry!" Johnny exclaimed.

Johnny's hand was in the center of the logo as he pushed off from the rock wall, running. Henry rushed to keep up with him. "Hurry up, Grandpa, hurry!"

A strange noise filled Henry with fear. Turning his head as he ran, he could clearly see a flock of birds coming down from the canyon walls. They looked like liquid silver, shining bright in the afternoon light. Terror overwhelmed him at the sight of them. He ran harder with his grandson past the bodies of many dead American Indian people.

He could see by the looks on their faces that they were full of fear when they died. They were not dressed in modern clothes, but the tribal clothing of the past. Henry only gave it a fleeting thought as he and Johnny ran past them, hoping to not become one of them.

As they reached the crest of the little hill. There were no canyons or deserts before them, but the burnt-out remains of a major city. He could see the silver birds destroying everything. Their beaks had teeth and with them, they would rip the top of skyscrapers or bite a person in two. Some birds stood on the ground with heaps of dead soldiers at their feet.

Fading Starlight

The site of this stopped Henry in his tracks as he felt he knew the dead men.

Johnny pulled on Henry's pant leg. "Grandpa, come, we can't stop now." As soon as Johnny yelled it, the closest bird slowly turned his head. And Henry could see his eyes. The eyes were aflame with fire and they were growing brighter. It was a sight that made him feel as if he was about to die.

"SANDSTORM!" yelled a voice. And with that, Henry woke up from his dream covered in a cold sweat and feeling the effects of fear slowly leaving him. It was Dave who yelled and he slapped Henry on the leg as he ran by him. "Come on, we need to close the tent flaps to keep the sand out."

In the early morning light as the wind increased. Henry groggily struggled to his feet and towards the side of the mess tent. He could hear Dave yelling at Josh and Andrew in the tent next door to button things up. Major Watson's voice from the larger tent could be heard over the wind yelling at Buckings to start closing the flaps. They managed to get the three tents closed down with only a little sand in a few people's eyes.

After a moment or so Megan offered to help Dave with the morning meal. Walking past her father Megan spoke up, "Don't worry. It doesn't last long around here. Not like Iraq."

Henry nodded, "Good to know." He remarked as he started to head toward the coffee when his cell phone rang. Slowing down as he pulled out his phone, Henry's right eyebrow raised as moved away from the coffee pot to the back of the tent for a little privacy. With Dave, Megan, and Henry, along with Johnny, all sleeping in the mess tent, that helped to afford Dave a little assistance this windy morning. But it also meant everyone else in the other tents would not get their coffee until the storm ended.

As people moved around Megan changed what she

was doing and began moving the sleeping cots to make room for everyone to sit at the tables as Dave began cooking the ham.

Talked on his phone, Henry looked over at his grandson, Johnny with a grin, who of course, slept through the morning's excitement as usual.

Dave and Megan almost had breakfast ready when the storm began to die down. Henry's phone call ended, so he walked over to join the others and enjoy his coffee. Dave took a broom and pushed it against the tent walls and roof to make some of the sand slide off. Megan noticed the look on her father's face as she walked over to the door to yell, "Breakfast!" to the camp.

"Wow, what a look. That must have been a real humdinger of a phone call," Megan remarked as she picked up a spatula. Henry barely heard, but finally acknowledged her. "Hmm? Oh. No, that was just Samuels back at the office requesting an update." He remarked as his gaze wandered.

Megan continued working but kept an eye on her dad as Johnny crawled out of bed to sit in grandpa's welcoming lap. Finally, Megan spoke, but in a low concerned voice. "Mom used to tell me that you would have intense dreams. And when you had them, they would take you far away, lost in thought. She told me if it happens again I should give you your space but not let you stew too long because it's not good for you."

"She was a wise woman. I wish she was here," Henry answered back as looked down at his grandson. "But I am not as young as I was then. And I would like to think I can manage myself better now." Taking a drink of his coffee, Henry held it in his hand in front of him while resting his elbow on the table, "I haven't had a dream like that since you were a little girl."

Noticing a few people starting to arrive for breakfast Henry gave Megan a look as the two of them mentally... quietly tabled the subject for later.

Tending to Johnny as Major Watson, Dave, and the General talked business Megan sat at the corner of the table. The crew of servicemen filed in and out with plates of food as Josh took his food outside to sit alone on a rock, enjoying the morning sun on his face.

Some of the men finished eating and began cleaning sand off the equipment. Josh flicked part of his eggs toward a small lizard that was near his feet. "You better eat that and run, little guy, before Johnny finds you," Josh remarked as he gave the lizard a wink when he noticed Megan and the General stepping out for a morning stroll.

Talking in quiet tones as they walked past him. Josh's mind wandered to the dig site, wondering what all this was about. Was it really time travel like he overheard some people saying? Was it something else? He knew they only had about two hours' worth of work before they could roll the boulder out. Josh also knew they needed to get all the sand out of the equipment before they could start. But since he was no longer in the Army, he took joy in knowing some other person would get that job today.

Looking back down at the lizard to see the egg was gone and the lizard waiting for more. He smiled and calmly remarked, "Sorry, that's it for today." With that, Josh got up and wandered back to the mess tent.

Major Watson and Sergeant Buckings came out the door before Josh walked in. Watson greeted him with a head nod, "Mister Williams."

"Major," Josh nodded back without stopping.

"Williams," nodded Buckings.

Watson stood there outside the mess tent, looking over his sand-covered encampment with Buckings waiting at his side.

Buckings spoke up in an effort to cut the silence. "If we stay here very long, we are going to need a bigger mess tent."

24

"Yes, Buckings, but I have no intention of being around that long. The General's stone markings are interesting and I am sure there is going to be a fascinating story to tell someone someday. But this is a job for people with hand shovels and little brooms who like to look at dried bones." Watson sarcastically informed him.

Buckings, feeling a little rebuked, responded back, "Yes, Sir."

The Major then spoke up just after clearing his throat, "Come on. Let's get this show on the road." Turning a little to the side Watson walked up to the dig site and yelled at a man standing near the dozer. "Private, let's roll!" Watson ordered as held his index finger high in the air making a circling motion indicating his desire that they all get moving.

About two hours later, Watson sent word via Private Huckins to the General that they were ready to roll the stone. The General thanked the young man and told him to return saying they would be there directly.

Megan, Dave, Henry, and even Johnny walked up to the site. By this time everyone was standing around waiting for the big moment. Ropes, chains, and hooks were all attached to the far side of the stone next to the canyon wall. And the big hole had been prepared for it to all fall into.

The Major looked at Megan and then at Buckings, "Sergeant, are we clear?"

"Yes, Sir. All personnel are out of the way, Sir." Buckings responded back.

Major Watson turned to the General, "General, it's your show. Will you give the word?"

Henry grinned and responded back, "No Major, it's Megan's show."

Megan smiled, stepped forward, and looked at Watson. "Pull it, Major."

Watson's radio then chirped as he gave the order, "Pull it."

The dozer's engine roared to full power and began to move. With each tug the stone did wiggle some. On the third tug, they heard a "crack" come from underneath the stone as it easily slid from its ancient position to its new resting place. As it dropped into the hole, the air from underneath displaced, kicking up a large volume of dust. Several whooped, hollered, and clapped each other's hands as it hit.

Everyone was impressed with the sight of it, including Johnny, who was soon handed off to Dave. Megan was not willing to wait for the dust to settle and quickly started moving around the outer edge of the hole. Hot on her tail was the Major, Buckings, Andrew, and the General as they all carefully made their way.

It soon became necessary to jump down into the hole on top of the boulder to get to the canyon wall. As the last of dust cleared before them was the same U.S. Army logo but below it, about 24 inches, read the following message: "2.5 clicks North by N.E. Proceed 200 yards in. De Oppresso Liber."

Henry was the first to speak, "Oh my God," leaving his mouth hanging open.

Andrew, stunned, said, "What does De Oppresso Liber mean?"

Watson paused before speaking, "It's Latin, son. It means 'To Liberate the Oppressed. It's the motto of the 19th Special Forces Group of the Utah Army National Guard."

"I didn't know the National Guard had Special Forces?" Andrew remarked.

"They do," Watson responded back as he leaned in to get a closer look.

Buckings then asked, "Now what do we do?"

"It means, Sergeant Buckings, that you better put in that requisition for a bigger mess tent," Watson informed him.

As soon as the reality of everything sank in, Megan was almost running back to the camp. She found her laptop and turned it on. As it powered up, other people began to file into the mess tent. Henry came in asking Megan if she had a plan.

"I do." Megan quickly responded back.

"What is it?" Henry inquired.

"It's called Google Earth. I paid for a full version a few years ago. I want to see where we are going next." Megan responded back.

The Major looked at Buckings and barked his orders with his index finger pointing outside. "I want two Humvees ready to go; water, food, maps, and anything else you can shove into it. Go."

Megan spoke up and motioned to her screen, "Looks like the direct route is no good. We can take the main road over here, then this dirt road, and then from here we're on foot." She informed them as she transferred the information to her handheld GPS, closing her laptop. Megan looked at her dad with a grin. "Let's go."

The next several minutes felt like hours to everyone. They had to drive several miles out and around simply because no other roads were available. The General spent most of his time on his phone talking and sending photos to various people in Washington. Soon they were off the main road. Dust kicked up as they dropped from the main road to dirt. Fighting the urge Megan wanted to take her Humvee beyond that, but the road had ended, blocked by upright slabs of stone just a few feet apart. The sight of it, like most things in these canyon lands, was impressive.

Vertical stone walls, only a few feet apart and a few feet thick. Taller than most houses, they worked in a strange way to guide the breezes that came along in the desert. The breeze in their faces was refreshing with the scent of wild sage as they looked at the walls of stone. It felt like stepping into another world for a moment. After traveling a while on foot between the stones everything around them opened up a bit more to a larger area with a deer trail leading down to the other side.

"Are we here?" Henry asked.

"Nope, but we're close," Megan answered back as she watched her GPS. "I'm thinking it's beyond that point over there." Moving forward, Megan led them into a larger, quite spacious area with a lot of rubble from the crumbling canyon walls. Everyone stopped and looked around at the sight of it all. A large black crow then flew past them as a few lizards scurried out of their way. It looked remote, felt remote . . . it was remote.

The Major looked at Megan. "Okay Megan, it's still your show. What are we looking for?"

Megan kept looking up at the canyon walls. "I really don't know. Something out of place I would assume."

"It's a big place," Henry commented as he turned around and looked at Major Watson. "Major, this place just became the main area of interest. We need to shut down our former camp, secure it and bring everything here."

"Yes, Sir," responded the Major.

"Oh, and Major, we do not have enough men to inspect this place. Find more volunteers for Operation Lorenzo." The General informed him.

"Yes, General," Watson responded back with a head nod.

Within an hour, the first Humvee had arrived with supplies from the old camp. By mid-afternoon, a helicopter was dropping off another load from the local base. The General already had his own tent and a makeshift desk for his laptop. He spent most of his time that evening doing video chats with officers back east.

Megan, Josh, and Andrew spent the remainder of the day hiking up and down the hillsides searching, inspecting, and rolling stones despite the heat. The Army finished erecting lighting in the camp just as evening was coming on. The three of them staggered in to get their first meal since breakfast. Buckings looked up from the table and asked them if they found anything.

"Indian petroglyphs; hundreds of them. The place is full of them but nothing we wouldn't expect to see here," Josh answered back.

"The problem is that what we are looking for may be underground like the last place. We simply don't know," Andrew added.

Megan, who had shoved way too much food in her mouth and was attempting to chew, just nodded a confirming "yes."

Johnny was already fast asleep after such an exciting day of men and big trucks. For that, Megan was thankful because she was ready for bed as well.

Sergeant Buckings walked up to Megan as she was eating, "Ma'am, the Major wanted me to report that we will be ready for a full-scale search in the morning."

Megan nodded at him while waving her hand in a sweeping motion, indicating she wanted him to leave. Normally her mind would be occupied trying to figure out the next day's activities. But not tonight. She had rolled a bazillion rocks today and suffered way too many adrenaline spikes due to the snakes she found underneath them. Her only thoughts now were food and a soft pillow.

The morning came way too soon for Megan and her two helpers. The sun was not quite up as people filed into the mess tent for breakfast. The General and his staff were all sitting at the officer's table with Major Watson discussing the next steps when Megan flopped into a seat across from her father.

The General sat there for a moment looking at his sunburnt daughter. Dave walked by and Megan looked up and calmly asked, "Food and coffee." Dave set a tube of sunscreen down in front of her. "I said food and coffee not a tube of goop."

Henry looked at her and announced, "Megan, you're as red as a stop sign and you're obviously suffering from dehydration. Those bruises and cuts on your arms and legs need to be cleaned and dressed. You have pushed yourself too hard. Therefore, you WILL rest until at least noon, drink plenty of water, AND use sunscreen."

With all the coldness Megan could muster, "I am not in the Army anymore and I am not a little girl. So you can't order me."

"True on both. Your stiff neck is going to kill you yet. However, these men here do follow my orders. Major, you will be personally responsible to make sure my daughter uses sunscreen every day and is well hydrated." The General informed him.

The Major, who up to this point was finding this all very entertaining, almost choked on his coffee. He turned his head, looking at the General with a "why me" look.

If Megan was getting mad it was well hidden under her sun-burnt face. As the General stood up to leave, Henry looked over at Watson one last time. "And Major, she will also remain in the shade until after lunch is served and she has eaten it."

After breakfast, Watson gave out the team deployments and eighty men started crawling over the rocks. Some teams carried sensor equipment like metal detectors searching for anything "out of place."

The cool of the morning had long since been replaced by the increasing heat of midday. The local reptiles had retreated beneath the rocks, and most of the men had already refilled their canteens several times. The red stone walls were starting to look more and more like the ruins of some forgotten and nameless ancient city, as all of this fueled the speculation and rumors that were traveling around the camp.

Some wondered if the military had a secret division of time travelers who ran around altering time. Others heard that we'd stolen the technology from Russia and were fighting a secret time war. And that's why it took us so long to win the Revolutionary War because England was backed by Russian agents. Major Watson overheard some of the rumors. At first, he laughed but then he realized his men were serious. He called a few of his men together and ordered a stop to it, calling it, "a stupid collection of children's stories invented by people who had spent too much time in the sun."

"Maybe you old women can find Elvis and Hitler while you're out there and see if they can get you an ice cream cone. Now get back to work," Watson barked as he pointed to the world behind him.

During lunch, Megan sat on the far side of the mess tent away from her father. She had eaten very little and never made eye contact with him. Johnny tried to get his mother to move so that they could all sit together but failed. Most of the men finished eating and headed back out. Megan's table was long since empty and she knew she could no longer avoid what she was ordered to do.

So Megan got up and passed by a soldier standing in line. She did it in such a way that no one from the officer's table could see her scrape her remaining food onto his plate. He looked up, puzzled, and was about to speak when she put her finger to her lips to indicate silence. Then she walked over to Major Watson, who was sitting next to her father.

"All clean, Sir. MAY I go outside and play now?" Megan asked with a snarky attitude.

Major Watson looked at her plate and then at her face. With a sigh, Watson asked, "Where's your sunscreen?"

She tossed her plate onto the table making a loud noise and pulled the dreaded tube of goop out of her pocket. Without breaking eye contact with the Major she spread it on her face, arms, and legs and put it back in her pocket. "Happy now, Major Pain?"

That comment took Watson back a little as he opened his eyes a little wider. Everyone at the table and a few in the room got acquired an "oh no" look on their faces.

Henry looked at his daughter and spoke up. "Megan!"

"Shut up," Megan responded back with a snap.

Turning in his seat, Henry spoke up. "Megan, Megan, why do you do this? You have put yourself up on a dangerous ledge. How can I hope to talk you down when you won't let me in?"

Megan turned on her heels toward Henry. "Like you talked Dan down?" With that, she stormed out.

Henry's face was saddened realizing all the progress he thought they had made in the last few days had just evaporated like water in the desert. For Henry, it felt like everything just went numb around him. Sounds became dull, colors muted. When Watson finally spoke, he realized the tent was empty except for Watson and Dave, who were now sitting directly across from him.

They just sat there, not saying anything. Henry looked down at his cup, "I suppose you're wondering why Megan is the way she is and what all that was about? When I got married, a long time ago, I didn't know anything about being a father. So as a young second lieutenant, I defaulted to the only system I knew that worked, the U.S. Army. I ran our household with a strong hand." Turning his cup slowly in his hands, "In time we had two children. Dan, who you just heard about, and then our daughter, Megan. We were strong. We had respect in the house. It was clean and spotless. But we did not have love in the house and a house without love is meaningless, as I learned too late in life... after Dan died."

Henry continued to turn his cup as he explained. "I suppose Megan blames me for that and she rightfully should. I was grooming Dan for a life in the service but I couldn't see that it wasn't the life for him. The more I pushed, the more he got in trouble. The more trouble he got into, the tougher I got. Until one day he just wasn't there. That's when Megan really started acting up towards me."

"About a year later there was a train wreck. It slid off the tracks near Seattle. A big mess; a lot of people died. The police figured Dan was one of the homeless people involved. They never found a body, just his wallet. My wife grew cold and that was the day Megan started calling me General."

Henry stopped playing with his cup, took the last drink out of it and set it down. "Later, in an effort to show she could do everything better than me, she joined the Army. It was fine at first but then she met Tom. Lieutenant Thomas Becker, the love of her life. Both of them were second lieutenants and served in Iraq. They got married as soon as they got back, and she got pregnant, almost the next day. Megan softened and even started calling me Dad again. She left the Army to give birth to little Johnny and they moved into our house when the Army sent Tom back to Iraq."

Dave looked at Henry's cup, "Want a refill?"

"Please," Henry responded back.

Dave refilled his cup and Henry continued talking. "We got word that Tom's Humvee was destroyed along with another that was a part of a convoy. That left Megan as the only parent to a one-and-a-half-year-old boy. Josh and Andrew brought Tom's body back to the States. After the funeral, I was sitting at my desk looking over old paperwork when I found a copy of Tom's orders for Iraq. I realized that they were part of a large group of men whom I signed the orders for. Megan found out and on that day she started calling me General again."

"Wow. And what did your wife do?" Dave asked with amazement.

"Jeanette died from cancer a year after Dan," Watson responded as he looked at his old friend who simply nodded his head.

The camp was fairly quiet for the rest of the day. Most avoided Megan, so she worked alone except for Josh and Andrew. They both knew how to deal with her silence as they had experienced it before. Nothing significant was found so everyone retired to the evening meal and then their bunks. Henry did not get to sit in his depression for long. Washington had questions and was pushing for a deadline on the project.

Night had come and brought with it a cloudless sky. The stars were on full parade with a thin crescent moon overhead. The guard change took place and the replacement took his position near the General's tent. He looked over and noted the General lying on his cot with a small black book in his hands, reading under a dim light. Turning around, the guard manned his post.

Fading Starlight
Chapter Two
Professor Holten

Henry could hear screaming behind him as he ran. In front of him, Johnny was yelling for him, "Hurry up, they are almost here, Grandpa!" As the sounds of a great battle could be heard all around. Running over ridges, and sliding down rocky slopes, the two had to continually duck for cover from the silver birds. Then in a moment's pause, Henry could see in the distance, over the ridge, giant silver buildings appearing over the canyon walls as if they were watching him. As he looked closer at them, it quickly became obvious as they turned in place, leaning forward, watching him.

Finally, they came to a ledge and Johnny screamed. In the valley below them was a great, towering, silver obelisk-like Washington's Monument coming up out of the ground. Fear shook Henry to the core as he watched it unfurl its giant wings. The many feathers on the wings were not unlike the silver birds that pursued them. Shaking in fear, He turned with his grandson and ran once more. Looking behind himself to see the terrifying sight, he heard Johnny yell in front of him. "In here, Grandpa, get in here!" He went to turn his head back and...

"Pardon me, Sir. The Major asked that I notify you that breakfast is ready." Henry jerked to see Private Huckins above him, gently shaking his arm to wake him.

Groggily feeling the lingering effects of the dream Henry responded back, "Um, yes, thank you, son. I will be there directly."

Breakfast was a quiet, uneventful affair. No one wished

for a repeat of yesterday. Megan presented her plate, with sunscreen on. The Major nodded and the day began. Lunch and dinner came and went and so did the next day. Johnny was not feeling well, so Megan took her son to the town doctor with Josh and Andrew, who were seeking food that the Army did not make.

Henry's reluctance to give a date forced Washington to announce that he had two weeks. After that, all the personnel would be redeployed to other assignments. Henry then made another attempt to have a conversation with his daughter, and even tried to get Dave involved, but nothing worked.

So Henry decided to ask about her plans for kindergarten for Johnny. Waiting until everyone but Dave and the Army cook had left the mess tent.

"That's my call," emotionless, Megan snapped back.

"I know, Honey, I have been just temp...." Henry never got a chance did to finish his sentence. He saw something silver flash next to him at high speed. In a sudden flashback to his dreams, he ducked to avoid a silver bird. As he did so he felt the wind of it brush his hair. He looked up to find an irate, screaming Megan with a silver saucepan in her hand. Shaking it in his face,

"You will not take my son away from me!" She then turned and threw the saucepan it against the tent wall in a fit of rage as she stormed out.

Startled by the event, Henry was helped to his feet by Dave. As the day progressed, word of it was starting to spread around the camp when Major Watson came running down the hill toward Henry.

He started talking the moment his feet stopped. "Sir, they found something." Megan was within earshot of the news and quickly changed her course. Henry, a little excited, glanced at her, turned, and followed Watson.

If Megan could have found a way to compete with her father in this fast-paced walk, she would have. As it even irritated her now to walk behind him. When they reached their destination, they all stood next to a flat stone canyon wall, semi-smooth stone. It had a large crack that was wider at the bottom but extended nearly a hundred feet above them to a closed point.

Everyone looked at it, and then Megan spoke up, "What? I searched this spot nearly ten times already. There's nothing here."

Sergeant Buckings then spoke up, "That's what we thought too, ma'am, but Private Huckins got desperate. Personally, I think he was looking for shade and slid into the crack a few feet."

"What did you find, Huckins?" Henry asked.

Huckins, a little unsure about the comment regarding him hiding in the shade, spoke up, "Not totally sure, Sir. I could not see it, but I could feel a round circle in the stone with markings in the middle. I'm just not skinny enough to make it that far."

Megan, without hesitation and still feeling angry at her father, ripped the flashlight out of Huckins's hand and declared, "I am."

Before anyone could say anything she was already sliding into the crack. She kept feeling around with her hands and searching with the flashlight, desperate to have some victory. After a moment or so of feeling highly confined, her fingers felt something.

Everyone on the outside waited. Finally, they heard her yell, "It's another one. It's another Army logo."

Watson yelled back, "Is there any message with it?"

"No, but it looks to me like this stone slab was once farther away than it is now," Megan responded back.

Henry, who could not take it anymore, spoke up, "Uh, why do you say that?"

Megan paused long enough to gather her sarcasm, "Because, my dear General, my flashlight is reflecting off something up ahead. And unless our Army guy was as wide as a rabbit, this entrance was once a lot bigger."

After pulling rank on the phone and threatening to

"Come down to someone's office." The Army Corp of Engineers was finally released to the site to add their assistance. Captain Jackson of the engineers quickly devised a plan to use stone saws to cut chunks out, widening the path to a full three feet. This was a wet saw with a blade like a chainsaw and a substantial engine. It was flown in via helicopter with a large tank of water to cool the saw.

Lunch was later brought up to Megan and the men because no one was willing to leave the site. By 13:30 hours the last block was almost cut and Megan was running on emotional fumes.

Captain Jackson then ordered the saw to be withdrawn. Turning to General Mullins with a salute, "The place is yours, Sir."

Henry, Megan, and Major Watson grabbed flashlights and eagerly walked in. The narrow crack was now wide enough to accommodate a full-grown man. Saw marks scarred the walls, but they could all see that the Corp of Engineers had expertly preserved the Army logo on the wall. With flashlights on, they all stepped into a small room. Over the millennia windstorms had brought a lot of sand in through the cracks, covering parts of the room, but leaving other parts undisturbed, with the exception of a thick layer of cobwebs.

On one side there were small nooks carved in the stone. In the center of the room, partly covered by sand, you could make out a crude stone table. Then on the far side was a rock shelf protruding from the wall. As Watson's flashlight scanned the area, he saw something reflective and walked over and picked it up.

With a sad look on his face, he turned around and remarked, "Well guys, I know this. Our missing soldier was a captain." Megan and Henry looked at him. "I found some half-tracks," Watson informed that as he held a well-worn, bent captain's pin. They all stood there looking over what was in his hand. Amazed and stunned, Megan's thoughts were doing somersaults trying to process it all.

As they looked around, they found the remnants of a few stone tools and some candles. Henry looked up with his flashlight at the walls that were covered in cobwebs. Watson then picked up a stick and drug it along the wall, pulling a lot of the webs down.

Henry's eyes looked once more at the bent captain's pin feeling a little sad as he spoke up, "This feels like a sad place."

"Look at this," Watson remarked.

Megan saw it first. "Formulas, math formulas."

The General grabbed another stick and started doing the same. "The walls are covered with them . . . every square inch." pausing for a moment to contemplate what he was seeing Henry remarked, "Whomever this captain was, he was smart. I have a fairly good understanding of math but this is… beyond me."

Megan began removing cobwebs as she was now starting to feel strangely numb. All the anger and frustration were taking its toll on her system.

Megan then uncovered something made of wood. "Guys, I think I found something." She pulled on the edge of it and it easily slid out of its resting spot. But it was heavy, extremely heavy. Almost dropping it, Watson quickly helped Megan move it from its resting spot. They almost dropped it when Henry joined them in an effort to get it onto the stone table. Laying it down and looking it over, it was obvious it was a book about eight inches thick, and three feet square in size.

The book was covered in wood with crude leather bindings tied like a rope. As they shined the light on the side of it they discovered the pages reflected back a golden, yellow light.

"Oh my God, the pages are gold," remarked Henry.

"Smart man. Most likely the only thing he could write on that would survive long term," Watson remarked.

Megan was saying nothing and tired of everything. Every comment her father spoke made her want to argue but she couldn't get the words out. She wanted to make a comment on the gold, but couldn't do that either.

"Generally, books all open in the same direction. I think we need to flip it over." Watson commented.

"You're right, give me a hand," Henry responded back.

As they flipped it over, Henry's hand could feel the rough texture of the old leather on the other side. "Megan, I think something's carved into the wood face of the book."

Megan snapped a little at the mention of her name and in an effort to appear normal, leaned forward to read it. All three flashlights were now pointed at the surface of the book.

"Can you read it?" the Major inquired.

With very little room, for there was only enough room for Megan and her Father to be at the table.

Henry and Megan read carefully to themselves. Slowly, a look of horror and shock came over their faces. Megan raised her hands to her face dropping her flashlight. She started to collapse into her father's arms as a silent scream formed in her throat. Henry dropped his light as well to catch her. Both carried such a profound look on their faces that Major Watson was not sure he wanted to know the answer to his question.

The Major called for help, but two men had already arrived at the entrance as soon as he spoke the words. Megan was wailing, "No!" repetitively as they moved her and Henry off to the side. Major Watson stood back up and pointed his flashlight at the cover of the book to read the cover for himself.

"Herein lies the last will and testament of Captain John K. Becker of the U.S. Army 19th Special Forces Group of the Utah Army National Guard, as well as the story of how I got here, the attack on Earth by alien forces in the year 2041 and Project Wingate . . . in the hopes that a future generation may survive."

Lieutenant Cook entered the room, puzzled. "Major, what just happened in here?"

"Lieutenant Cook, our world just changed. And this cave just became a matter of national security. Secure this room. No one enters without the express permission of myself or General Mullins," Watson ordered as he pondered the words before him.

All work stopped at the camp. Henry carefully escorted his daughter to her tent where she spent the next two hours hanging on to Johnny. Henry stayed in the tent with her, staring at the wall or at Johnny, not really wanting to move. Johnny grew restless and finally squirmed out of his mother's arms to play on the floor.

Megan began to speak but realized the need to be careful of what she said with Johnny nearby. The cold, hard shell was shattered and all she wanted at that moment was her family. "Dad, what do I do?" She whispered, "He's here, but he's there? My... Oh God, how do I do this? He is no more."

Johnny who was clueless about his mother's emotional state had found his Lego helicopter and pretended he was bombing cities. The sounds of his playing soon became loud enough to cover Megan and Henry's conversation.

Henry saw the look on Megan's face and could not help himself. He moved closer to give her a hug and to his surprise, she did not reject it. After sitting there in silence for a while, Megan carefully whispered, "How can I be a good mother when I hate my father?"

The question stunned Henry and left him with nothing to say.

Closing her eyes for a moment, Megan barely spoke above a whisper, "When did this scar become a tattoo?"

Hearing nothing from her father, she moved away just enough to turn and look him in the eyes. "I have learned to hate you and have done it for so long that the pain has become like a tattoo. Something I could proudly wear; an accomplishment." Her wet eyes drifted to the floor of her playing son for a moment and then back up, "And I don't know how to get free."

Henry had to shift his weight on the bench because the little black book in his back pocket was becoming uncomfortable. He reached back without thinking, pulled it out, and sat it on the table next to them. As his eyes fell on it, he knew he was being given a chance and that prayer was all he needed. Henry was a little scared but he knew he needed to say it even if she rejected his message. "Honey, do you remember what your mother used to say when you and Danny would get in a fight?"

Megan's glossy eyes opened a little wider as the truth of what was being said was coming to rest in her heart. "Yes."

"Mom used to say, 'Repentance is only a door to freedom. But, it's for you to walk through it,'" Henry remarked, waiting.

Megan closed her eyes, fighting fear, fighting hate, fighting the what-ifs that were running a race in her head. The truth of her mother's words was sitting in her heart like a long-neglected flowerbed, covered in weeds but crying out to be reborn. Time passed and Henry was wondering if he'd just lost her again. In fact, he was convinced he certainly had by the look that was forming on his daughter's face.

With her eyes still closed, she said in a low voice, "All right, I will do it." Megan opened her eyes and looked straight into his. "I will do this. Not for you, not for the past, but for my son, for our future. He needs a normal family for as long as he's got us. He needs as much love as we can give and demonstrate. I am doing this to be free. My heart has been burning for so long. I'm tired of it."

Henry's heart jumped and for the first time, in a long time, he felt his heart was about to leave the prison she had put it in. Megan kept looking straight into her father's eyes. As her face was more wet than dry. "Father... Daddy, can you forgive me?"

Everything within him jumped. He grabbed his

daughter and crushed her into his chest. Freedom came to both through the utterance of a blubbering, "yes."

They kept hugging for a while and then got up as they heard a tap on the tent door. It was Major Watson looking like this was the last thing on earth he wanted to do.

"Major?" Henry quietly inquired.

"I'm sorry, Sir, it was not my desire to interrupt, but due to the growing situation we have here and the fact that Washington is calling...."

Henry raised his hand, interrupting the Major, "I understand. This is my responsibility. Consider it taken care of."

"Thank you, Sir. What are your orders regarding the soldier's artifacts in the cave?"

It was the generic use of the word "soldier" that brought Megan out of her seat and directly into Major Watson's face. With a calm, authoritative voice as if she, herself, was now the General, she informed him, "Major, THAT soldier's artifacts up there belong to my son. It is his last message to his people, his family, to me. I will read them and find out what happened to him and everyone else on this planet. And then, if possible, I will find his bones, if they still exist, and give my son a proper burial. IS THAT UNDERSTOOD, MAJOR?"

The Major had taken a step back realizing he was about to tangle with a bobcat that looked like a woman. Watson turned to the General who also looked surprised but had a bit of a smile on his face. "You heard the woman, Major, and it sounds good to me as well."

Leaving Watson, both Megan and Henry got up and walked out to the mess tent. Megan put her arm inside her father's as they walked. Henry noticed Dave and motioned for him to keep an eye on Johnny so that the two could talk privately before he called Washington.

After a while, Henry called his staff in to have them set up for a video conference with Washington and informed them that Megan would be remaining in the room. The staff set up the equipment as Megan moved her chair off to the side so that she wouldn't be in the video picture. Before she could even get the chair partway, a young lieutenant stepped up and out of courtesy, took over for her. With a smile, Megan politely responded with a "thank you" as he offered to get her something to drink.

Megan smiled, asked for water, and got a puzzled look on her face as he walked away. Sitting down, she realized the fire in her heart causing her to compete was no longer there. Resting on her chair, she smiled with a little joy, watching her father, knowing for the first time in years that she was free.

Time passed as Megan listened to the conversation between the officers. The cave discovery, the book, and the preliminary investigation were all mentioned. They discussed how often the future reports would be sent and the fact that this issue was now a matter of national security. Megan soon realized that she was retaining very little of what was being said. She was just glad to be free and very proud of her father and of her son. Her desire to read his book in the cave was growing within her. However, she felt she needed to wait for Henry because Johnny was his grandson and she would never again rob him of such things again.

After the meeting both father and daughter walked outside the tent to find Watson standing at attention, waiting for orders. Henry looked at Megan who was trying to keep a chuckle from being heard as they walked by. With a grin of his own, Henry spoke up, "Major, stand down. The lioness has retracted her claws."

Megan, looking a little red in the face with her hand

over her mouth said, "I'm sorry.... uh, Sir." Watson's right eyebrow raised as he listened to them giggle as they wandered by him.

Father and Daughter leisurely strolled across the campground before making their way up the trail to the cave.

"Megan, I noticed on the cover it mentioned Project Wingate. Where have I heard that term before?" Henry inquired.

"Well, I don't know what the book is referring to, but if I had to guess I would say they are talking about this place," Megan responded back.

Raising his right eyebrow Henry gave her an odd look. "Explain."

"Well, Dad, all this stone around you, the giant vertical red rock that towers to the sky, it's called the Wingate Formation. It's the type of sandstone around you. They figure it's the hardened remains of an ancient sand dune that may have blown in from the east."

Henry slowly nodded. "How old?"

"Some say millions. I'm not so sure," Megan replied.

"Why's that?" Her father asked.

"Well Dad, when you're out here long enough, digging in the dirt and rocks, you find things, strange things, that don't make sense. In archaeology, they are called Ooparts. It stands for an out-of-place artifact. These out-of-place artifacts are all over the world and we've got them here in the southwest as well. Basically, they don't fit with the contemporary archeological timelines or the current understanding of our world. It would be comparable to taking a modern tank and dropping it into WWI or the Civil War. Out of place, out of time." Megan answered back.

Thinking her comment over, Henry responded, "So my grandson is an Oopart. Out of place, out of time."

The statement caused Megan to take a little deeper breath. "Uh, I never thought of it that way. But you're right."

Deep in thought, they passed a sentry on duty as he saluted. "Did I tell you I had another dream?" Henry said.

"No Dad, you didn't," Megan answered back as she looked up from the trail to the cave ahead.

"It was odd and quite frightening. It felt like a continuation of the previous one. We were running and I knew there was a war going on all around us. There was screaming behind us and smoke. Johnny was yelling at me to hurry up. We ran all over the place; hills, ridges, valleys and it was all very confusing. I kept seeing those silver birds. They were attacking us. Then, in the distance over the ridges, I could see giant silver buildings appearing over the canyon walls. It was horrifying. I felt like they were watching us. Some of the buildings even turned in place as if to get a better look at us."

"All of a sudden Johnny screamed at the edge of a ledge. In the valley below us there was a great, towering, silver obelisk just like the Washington Monument coming out of the ground. It had wings just like those silver birds. We got out of there as fast as we could." Henry remarked as his eyes wandered off to the side for a moment.

Looking back down again for a moment Megan squired a concerned look in her eyes. "And you think it has something to do with this?"

Henry nodded, "Yes, Megan, I do. It started up as soon as I got involved in this project. I think they are all clues."

Silently they continued walking until they reached the mouth of the cave. Henry looked at Megan with a little concern. "Are you ready for this?"

The corner of Megan's mouth came up some, "Are you?"

A guard stood at the entrance as they made their way in. Everything about the cave looked and felt very old except for the fact the Major had some simple lighting installed, but nothing else was disturbed. The lights left very little hidden. There were several niche holes carved into the walls like the one the book was found in. Henry took a closer look at them and discovered more books like the one they'd already found. Pointing with his finger at them Henry drew his daughter's attention to them, "Megan, look."

Megan did a quick look around the room. "It looks like they're the only ones. Everything else is just stuff like tools, bits of leather, and candles. Hmm. Just everyday stuff for a 3,000-year-old man, out of place, out of time."

Henry slowly ran his hand over the stone wall. "It must have been hard for him?"

"I would think so," Megan remarked. "No family, no friends. Everything he knew was blown away like leaves in the wind."

"I haven't heard you talk like that in a while," Henry answered back with a slight smile.

Megan stopped and looked up at the math scribbles on the wall as she ran her hand along them. "I suppose I haven't. I guess my winter is over, Dad, and I'm heading for spring."

Megan walked over and stared at the cover of the first book that they'd left on the stone table. Her father stopped what he was doing and came over to stand near her. Her eyes were totally fixed on the first few words: "Last will and testament."

"I... feel sad just reading the first words," Megan remarked.

With a whisper of a voice, her father responded back, "I know."

Taking a deep breath, Megan spoke up, "Tomorrow I will get Josh and Andrew up here with sifters and buckets to clean out the sand." Megan looked at her father's face for a moment. "But, I think we should have a moment or two alone with Johnny."

A quiet "yes" came out of her father as she carefully opened the cover of the book to the first page. It was a hammered sheet of gold, rough around the edges. You could clearly make out the tool marks that were made in the process of shaping it. Scratched into the surface of the gold, it read:

"Although it is my desire that my family in the future be

the first to find this, I realize that may not be possible. If I am successful, I will have altered the timeline for the better. I understand that any number of years may pass from my day to yours, so on that note: To whoever may find this book, please forward it to the nearest government authority on Earth. The contents within these pages contain vital tactical information for the future of humanity."

"I, John Kenny Becker, Captain in the United States Army, son of Thomas T. and Megan V. Becker, grandson of Henry Mullins and Floyd Becker, would like to convey to you this story that started in the early part of the twenty-first century. The following information is based on the events that preceded my departure to the past."

"On December 7th, 2041, on the European continent, the first wave of alien spacecraft attacked the earth. A total of ten ships descended on Spain and France. The engagement lasted a total of two hours and eight minutes. All alien craft, except one, were destroyed. The tenth retreated back to space. The French Air Force was the first to respond followed by other local nations. One hundred and eight jet fighters were destroyed and the city of Madrid was leveled by something resembling a nuclear bomb. Total known dead: 5.1 million."

"This was not an isolated event. Waves of spacecraft came approximately every three months to different regions of the earth. Each attack was larger and more forceful than the last and more difficult to defeat. Most nations began mass-producing fighter craft and missile systems and for a time, it seemed we were winning the invasion."

"Please note that at the time of the early twenty-first century, atomic weapons left lingering radiation at the blast sites that would last generations. However, the unknown weapon used against Earth's cities would only leave a radiation trace that lasted around fifty-nine days."

Megan stopped reading and stepped back to take in the reality of the moment. Henry was silent, trying to

48

process the information that his daughter was reading out loud to him. He gently rubbed her arm and gave her a nod to continue. Megan looked back down at the gold sheets that her son scratched his last thoughts on knowing his powerful words would change the future.

With a deep breath, Megan continued, "It was not until the third wave against the eastern half of North America that we were able to retrieve valuable technology from an alien craft. Although the items were small, they demonstrated a level of technology far more advanced than what we humans possessed. Therefore, after several other successive waves, it became necessary to assemble the best scientific minds possible. Most teams worked around the clock to understand the most basic functions of this technology. By 2043, the rate of attacks was increasing all over the world."

"In the early days, the alien crafts were small in size. Eventually, they sent larger ones supported by the smaller crafts. Then in the winter of 2043, two events took place that forced us to take more drastic actions. The first event was a government study called the Tollman Report that concluded that at the current rate of increase in warfare, Earth would not survive much beyond 2046. The second event was the arrival of the city-building ships."

"The city builders were very large crafts, over two miles in length. They would set up over the site of a destroyed cities and begin construction. It would take about four weeks to grow the city like a crystal, complete with a glass-like dome so hard that no known weapon could penetrate it. It was after these events that project Wingate was transferred to me. I relocated it to this location and it became the most closely guarded project in human history."

"On a personal note, almost everyone on Earth had a personal memorial day when someone they knew was killed by the aliens. Mine was June 12th, 2042, some years before this date, the last of my close family passed away, leaving me with only a few relatives in Boston. They died in the third wave when the city was nuked,

49

killing everyone."

Megan looked up, puzzled. "Dad?"

"I don't know what he's talking about. We don't have any relatives in Boston or any other place. I was an only child and so was your mother."

"I know. There's none from Thomas' side either," Megan remarked, shaking her head.

"Well turn the page, Honey," Henry remarked.

Megan carefully flipped the golden page, reading on. "Dad, wow!"

Henry moved his eyes towards the gold book, "What?"

"All he says is, 'Oh, how I miss Christmas with my cousins,'" Megan remarked.

Stunned, they both stared at each other. Henry spoke first, "They never found a body in the train crash. They never found a lot of the bodies." The reality of the moment was starting to settle on their faces as they suddenly spoke together.

"Danny's alive," they said together in one revelation. Megan grabbed her father's arm in nervous excitement.

Henry spoke once again, "Come on, Honey. Let's go make some phone calls."

The afternoon shade from the canyon walls was starting to cover the whole camp, slowly bringing down the daytime temperatures. Henry and Megan were clocking in their second hour of phone calls and internet searches. Finally, they gave up looking for a Dan Mullins and found a Daniel Mullins, the right age, newly married, in Philadelphia. He worked for an architectural firm. Megan reasoned out that he just had not moved to Boston yet.

Henry tried calling twice but as soon as he identified himself, the phone went silent. With some disappointment, he handed the phone over. Megan tried and discovered it was, indeed, her brother. With a little time Megan, got her brother to relax about the idea of talking to their father.

Dave brought them both supper as they told stories over the phone throughout the night. When Henry wasn't talking on the phone, he was praying or writing. It had been a big day and no one in this family was likely to get much sleep.

Henry and Megan decided to split up and do separate jobs. Saying goodbye to Johnny after breakfast, Megan headed up to the cave with her team to begin work.

Henry would spend most of the morning on the phone with Washington, updating them, and making arrangements with Major Watson for the large increase of personnel that was to be arriving. He would also order the former dig site to be documented, the stone face to be removed for storage, and the area buried.

Megan would spend the day with Josh and Andrew, examining and documenting the cave. She wanted everything cleaned, cobwebs removed, and photos taken of all the math formulas on the walls. Reading, taking notes, and pictures were also on the agenda.

Far into the Future
2043 AD.

Captain John Becker walked down the hallway toward the meeting in full uniform, all the while wishing he could scratch the bug bites he'd acquired yesterday in the swamp. His entire right hip felt like it was on fire and throbbing. He rounded the corner to a shorter hallway and stopped at a set of closed, wooden doors guarded by two soldiers standing at attention.
The man on his left raised his hand, palm upward, to

reveal a small, round metal bar. John spoke first, according to protocol, "Captain John Becker, U.S. Army."

In the man's hand, the metal bar produced a hologram about four inches high with the words, "Voice Print Confirmed."

The guard lowered his hand to the door handle, opening it. "Have a good day, Captain." John nodded a thank you as he walked in.

General Tanaka was the first to see John. Smiling he motioned for him to come forward and take a seat. The table was simple, made of dark wood with about twenty men seated around it. All were top brass from the four branches of the military, with their aides, along with representatives from different government departments sat ready for him. Due to shortages from the war, the room was a mix of old and new. Old coal oil lanterns were placed in various locations around the room with one modern electric light illuminating General Tanaka's area. Everyone else on the other had to make do with flashlights.

Shaking a few hands from those with familiar faces as he entered John took his seat as General Tanaka spoke up. "Very good, we can get started then. Captain Becker, as some of you know, has been overseeing our information divisions since Lieutenant Colonel Romero was killed in action. I asked him to be present today to brief us on our current projects and answer any questions the Joint Chiefs may have." Tanaka paused for a moment to accept some paperwork from his secretary. "The floor is yours, Becker."

Just as John was about to open his mouth, General Nichole Luhansk of the Air Force spoke up. "One moment, General Tanaka. I wish to express my concern over having someone with the lesser rank of captain oversee such a large division. Does this man have enough experience?"

A man two seats down from her released a stack of paperwork onto the table. The air from it pushed up under the coal oil lamp causing the light to flicker on everyone's faces. John noticed the flicker of light the most in General Luhansk's face. Because of how the light in her eyes reacted, flickering, what seemed to him a little slower and with more red. Even though it seemed odd, he put it out of his mind as Tanaka responded.

"General Luhansk, first of all, I have every confidence in Captain Becker and his ability to do the job required of him. And second, after last month's attack that killed Romero, the Army is now very short on 0-3 to 0-6's. Captain Becker was within six months of jumping up in pay grade so we simply promoted him early." Tanaka informed her.

"So we have a lieutenant doing a colonel's job," Luhansk remarked as she turned to look back at Becker. "You came in empty-handed, son. Are you ready for this?"

John, at this point, did not know which was worse, having a stare-down from the General in front of him or the powerful need to scratch his bug bites. Hearing Tanaka gave him permission to continue, John was thinking about how miserable it would be to sit for very long.

A bit nervous, John acknowledged that Tanaka had once again given him the floor. "Members of the Joint Chiefs and respected department members, I came... seemingly empty-handed for two reasons. One being the need for information security. Basically, no one can steal it if it's in your head. The second is because I wish to highlight this." John reached inside his chest pocket and pulled out what looked like a long, thick pen with a red tip.

Luhansk's eyes opened slightly with a little concern as he proceeded to set one end on the table. John touched both sides of it just under the red-tipped end. The red-tipped end started to get brighter. Within a few short seconds, a holographic image came bursting into view just above the device. About eight feet in size, it looked like blueprints.

Admiral Read from the Navy spoke up, "What are we

looking at, Becker?"

Becker stood up, partly to get closer to the hologram but mostly in an effort to keep his pants from irritating his bug bites.

"Well, Admiral, we took this from a dead alien who had sunk to the bottom of a swamp." John then put his hands into the center of the hologram. "And for lack of better words, we are calling it the Rosetta Stone."

John flung his hands outward enlarging the hologram to the size of the room. This new sizing gave them a much clearer understanding of what they were looking at. For it was the internal diagram of an alien attack ship.

Luhansk lowered her eyes to look at the device in front of her as John continued, "Like everyone, we have had a very hard time making sense of the alien's technology, understanding their simplest systems or even their language. This device gives us the opportunity to begin breaking down the mysteries."

A department guy in a fancy suit spoke up, "How?"

John smiled and waved his hand from left to right like turning a page. As he did, images, pictures, and text began scrolling by like a slideshow.

"Unlike our data imaging systems that are comparable in size, theirs seem to contain much more information. It's a virtual goldmine of useful data at our fingertips. This system comes complete with a translation program built within it. So if you add this data to what we have already acquired from DNA, autopsies, and tests on equipment found at crash sites, our picture of them is becoming complete at an incredible rate."

The admiral asked, "Does that mean we finally have a name for them?"

John smiled. "No, we don't, but not because we can't find it. We've discovered that it's simply not part of their culture. They seem to have no need to name some things. For them, it's us or them or you and I. They do however have a command ranking system similar to ours."

John moved a few more pages along. "Here, as you can see, we have internal diagrams of the city ships." He remarked as he advanced to the next image. "Energy, water, and waste systems as well as internal mission briefs for the division this alien was assigned to."

At this point, the room grew silent as he paused awaiting any comments. Hearing nothing John continued, "This information is still fairly new to us, but within it, we have learned of a small hidden mining base near Bonners Ferry, Idaho."

Several generals stood up to get a closer look, so John adjusted the image for them. "The base is located in some deep brush and timber with a false cover just west of town. According to the information provided, they have two of the larger air assault ships at this location. As well as a device for changing the structure of solids."

General Tanaka felt pride and relief knowing that he'd chosen well in naming Becker as head of this team.

John, who had paused for people to look at the information, resumed speaking. "I have a unit preparing as we speak. The plan is to quietly hit this base on the morning of the 15th. We'll take them alive if possible, and confiscate every piece of alien hardware we find and bring it back for assessment."

Tanaka spoke up, "Good. We may not have a name to call them, but we can at least find out how many different alien races we are dealing with."

"Well, actually, I may be able to answer that now. I ran across a file designated Sar1.89. I have not read it yet, but it says it contains a complete list of all DNA acquired. Let's see if I can find it." John answered back.

A few moments passed while everyone intently watched John move the pages back and forth. A strange smell, like ozone, became evident in the room, and then suddenly, a large pop, a flash of light, and the hologram ended in a puff of smoke.

Everyone was stunned, especially John. Nichole lowered her hands from in front of her, as she was the closest to the fireworks. Her eyes slowly came into focus as she looked at Tanaka's face. "Well I don't know about the rest of the brass in this room but I'm thinking I could really use a drink. Congratulations, son. I think you're the first person I know of to blow something up in the middle of a Joint Chiefs of Staff meeting. At least we are all still alive," she sarcastically announced.

About an hour later in another room, John and the Joint Chiefs were all standing around talking with each other in groups of three and four. General Tanaka and the head of the NSA, Milson Grant, were talking with John about the upcoming mission. Not far away was Nichole Luhansk looking over a small plate of finger food on a nearby table.

"So the next step is to attack the Idaho base on the 15th?" Milson asked.

"Just as the sun comes up," John remarked as he lowered his glass of water.

Luhansk turned and looked at John from several feet away. "You're only drinking water? You're like, the only one in the room."

John glanced at her briefly, "Water's fine for me, Ma'am." Grant and Tanaka ignored Luhansk, as they were eager for John to continue. "We will arrive in Sandpoint, Idaho the night before and meet up with a few other soldiers that are coming from the southern part of the state. There is a small army division near the airport. They will have the trucks and gear we need. It's about an hour and a half to Bonners Ferry, so we will leave while it's still dark. Then it's just a matter of getting in place before the sun comes up."

"Sounds good," remarked Tanaka.

Grant spoke up, "Why on the 15th, and not the 16th?"

John was playing with the bottom of his glass in an effort to forget his need to scratch. "Well, Sir, that device that changes the nature of solids, they send a shipment of whatever it produces out to their fleet every thirty days. I would like to be there before another goes out. They should be totally focused on getting it ready. Hopefully, they will never see us coming."

Luhansk stepped forward somewhat confidently. "The records make no mention of what they are mining?"

"No, they don't. But whatever it is, there are a few hundred places around the world doing the same thing," John commented back to Luhansk as Grant gave him a look like he wanted him to say more. "Unfortunately we lost the records of those locations in that little mishap in the meeting room a few moments ago."

Luhansk had that sparkle in her eyes once more under the candle and lantern light in the room. For a moment, John thought he could see the corner of her mouth start to turn upward. "I see. So we lost vital Intel from an unstable alien device that Mr. Becker should have had in a lab, not in his coat pocket trying to impress the brass with? If you will excuse me, gentlemen, I have another meeting to attend too." With that, she handed her drink to John, turned, and left the room.

Milson Grant smiled as she left. "Well, Becker, I'm glad you're here even if the Ice Queen is not."

John, who was looking a little confused asked, "What's her issue?"

"Romero was her hand-picked man. When he died, the President gave it to General Tanaka and he put you in charge of her pet project. So don't worry about it, she will never like you." Grant informed him.

Present Day

Sitting at a table typing one-handed on her laptop while holding Johnny on her leg with the other. Megan's empty lunch plate was steadily becoming a place for Johnny to put the green beans he did not want as he was far more concerned with the taste of his sandwich. "How is it going, Honey?" Henry spoke from behind her as he approached with his own lunch plate.

Megan turned from the computer screen to greet her father. "Oh, hi Dad... good. I'm trying to write down my thoughts on..." pausing for a second as her eyes looked at Johnny, "...Captain John's report."

Henry looked at his grandson as he sat down. "Ah, I see. And how is old Captain John?"

"Fine." Megan remarked as she continued, "He was writing about some of the more technical stuff that the bad guys were doing."

Johnny looked up at his mother and then at his grandfather. "Mommy, can I get down now?"

"I think that would be a great idea," Megan responded back in response to Johnny who was already trying to get off her knee.

They both watched as Johnny ran outside and right into Dave who almost dropped what he was carrying as he was walking back from across the camp.

"What else did he write?" Henry inquired as he grinned at the sight of Dave.

Megan stopped and looked at her father for a moment, "Well, the gold for the books came from trading with local tribes or digging it out of the ground himself. He talks about various stars in slightly different positions then they are now and based on that, he figures his date to be around 1000 BC."

Henry had a look like someone sucked some of the air out of his lungs, "So it's true? 3000 years ago? Oh my."

"Yep, he records a bright star in the sky that he recalled from a college..." eyeing her father, "...class that detonated around 3000 years ago."

Henry smiled, "Nice, I wonder if it was a military college."

Megan smiled and rolled her eyes at her father. "Dad." Ignoring his daughter's comment,

Henry asked. "Anything else about the aliens?"

"Only that they seem to have no central leader and they have no name for themselves. I guess the concept of names is unknown to them." Megan responded back as she slid her laptop off to the side.

"Hmm," Henry responded.

Megan then slid their dirty lunch plates to the side as she swung her leg over the bench to look directly at her father. "And what about Washington?"

Henry looked at the table for a moment and then spoke up." It has been decided that due to the unusual nature and national importance of Project Lorenzo, only military personnel will be allowed access to it. To comply with this order, Dave Shaver, Josh Williams, Andrew Hansen, and Megan Verity Becker will have their military commissions reinstated, effective immediately. This was ordered by the Joint Chiefs and confirmed by the President." Henry held up his hands in a surrendering motion. "It wasn't my call."

Megan sat there dumbfounded for a moment with her mouth wide open. Henry began to wonder if the old Megan and her anger were about to return. She snapped her mouth closed and jerked her head to the side.

"Wow! Well, I suppose we shouldn't be surprised." She paused for another moment. "I wonder what the rest of the team is going to say? I know Dave's not going to like it."

Relieved, Henry responded, "I don't know, but Master Sergeant Shaver will get used to it."

Megan looked away from the tabletop to her computer. "The things we do for our kids and country. A master sergeant and three lieutenants."

Henry smiled and looked directly at Megan so that her eyes could see his. "Two lieutenants and one captain, Megan."

Megan had a strange look on her face, "Captain?"

"You were up for promotion when you left. And due to your importance in this project, the Joint Chiefs felt we had too many lieutenants in camp already" Henry announced.

Megan was a bit shocked, somewhat excited, but also unsure. She closed the cover of her laptop and looked back at her father. "Two questions: Only Army personnel are allowed in camp. What about Johnny? And, how do you want me to address you while we are in camp?"

"General. And as far as Johnny goes, he is officially listed as an advisor to project Lorenzo."

"Advisor. That's funny. And are the rest of the guys still my team?" Megan asked as Henry motioned for them to get up.

"Yes, they are. Major Watson will oversee the camp and you will oversee the cave. Come on, we should tell everyone else." Henry informed her.

Megan picked up her closed computer and put it under her arm. Henry moved towards the door allowing her daughter to go first. "We don't have any extra uniforms in camp so I'm having them flown in tomorrow."

"Master Sergeant Shaver reporting for duty," Dave harshly remarked, as he saluted the General while slamming the point of his chef's knife hard into the table in front of Henry. Dave looked square into Henry's eyes with as much sarcasm as he could muster. "Sir." Dave quickly snapped as lowered his hand while keeping his other firmly attached to the blade handle protruding from the table.

The mess tent was silent for a moment as Dave then took his hand off the knife and walked out. Josh and Andrew walked up to where Dave had been standing. Andrew gave the knife a tug and realized it wasn't coming out without considerable effort.

Josh spoke up first. "Well, I think you really pissed him off good this time."

"This doesn't bother you?" Megan inquired.

"Nope," Andrew responded back.

"Why is that, Lieutenant?" the General inquired.

Josh raised the corner of his mouth in a smile as he watched Andrew working the knife out of the table. "Andrew and I have been talking about it since yesterday and we could see it coming. Really, Sir, we both agreed that it's time for us to return to active status."

Megan gave them a strange look, "Time? What does

that mean?"

Josh realized what he had said. His body language was telling the whole room that he was unsure as to what to say next, so Andrew spoke up as he got the knife out. "Well, ma'am, after the other day, you don't seem to need us anymore."

Henry and Megan's expressions were part curiosity and part confusion as Andrews's words settled on them.

"Megan, your husband knew what kind of person he married. He made us promise that if anything ever happened to him that we would watch out for his family. You have always been hotheaded and angry. So he knew you needed someone to keep you from going over the edge and doing something really bad. But lately, after the big fight you and your father had, you have changed. We see you leaning a lot more on him so frankly, we feel like our job is done. If the Army is opening the door for us, then we would like to go back."

Megan was feeling the impact of what was being said. "Are you saying you traded in your careers for me?"

They both nodded affirmatively as they watched a tear start to form in the corner of Megan's eye.

"For a promise," Josh added.

Megan's voice cracked, "Thank you," as her father put his arm around her.

Andrew laid the knife down and knelt down in next to her. "When Thomas was dying, he had but seconds to live. His thoughts were on you and Johnny because he knew you would only fight your father. We promised him we'd watch after you for however long it took. I don't know what happened between you and your dad in the past. I don't need to know. But I can see what's happening now. Megan, you can trust your father. He's got your back."

If Megan had been wearing makeup, it would have washed down her face by then. "I wish Thomas was here. I would love to tell him that I forgave my dad, that I am better now, I am whole for the first time in years."

Andrew gave Megan a hug, partly because she needed it but also in an effort to stop looking at her teary eyes.

He knew that if this continued, he was going to cry too. "Meg, it's like you're a whole different person now, and I'm thinking that's a good thing."

As he let go of her, he heard her faintly say, "ya...It was God."

Andrew had somewhat of a puzzled look as he responded, "Well, I don't know what that's about, but you are better."

Henry was feeling the need to explain when Major Watson came in. "General, the supply chopper will be here in under a minute. Looks like they have your guest on board. Also, the Pentagon is requesting more information and your cook is making a big ruckus on the south end of the camp."

Henry, Megan, and the boys all smiled at each other at the mention of Dave. "Andrew and I can handle Dave, General. It won't be the first time." Josh commented.

Henry nodded to Josh and Andrew. "Just get him settled down and out of sight before the chopper gets here."

Josh and Andy walked out of the tent in the general direction that Major Watson pointed them. They passed the crates of Army supplies to the south that were resting next to the canyon walls. Noises could soon be heard as they drew closer, a commotion like metal hitting metal. The suddenly voices were heard yelling, "Give that back!"

Rounding the corner the first thing they saw was Dave, mad as a bear, with a bottle of Scotch in one hand and an M16 rifle in the other. Nearby were four men in uniform trying to talk him into laying down the rifle.

Dave was yelling. The men were yelling and Josh and Andrew looked at each other. Then Josh noticed one of them slowly reaching for a pistol. He looked right into the eyes of that scared private, raised his hand toward him, and said, "Son, stand down. That's not how we're going to handle this."

Andrew cautiously moved forward with his hands out speaking to everyone. "Okay, listen up. I need everyone to just walk away right now. We got this. There's nothing to see here."

"Oh yes there is!" Dave yelled back.

"No. No, Dave, there's not." Andrew responded back.

Dave was looking kind of wild-eyed, so Andy just kept slowly moving closer as Josh began encouraging people to back away.

"I'm going to drink this bottle, shoot out his tires, and hit somebody, " Dave said, very passionately.

"And you think this behavior will keep you out of the Army? Dave, Henry needs us." Andrew calmly spoke back to him.

"I couldn't care less about him," Dave answered while shaking his bottle.

"How about Meg? Johnny? They need you, Dave… more than ever." Andy calmly spoke.

"I'm going to drink this," Dave angrily remarked, shaking the bottle at Andrew.

Andy smiled as he drew closer, "Sure you are, take a drink now."

Dave was somewhat confused by the statement but he took the opportunity and put the bottle to his lips. As he closed his eyes and tossed his head back, Andrew stepped in and grabbed the bottle and tried to pull the M16 away. Dave then pulled it back achieving what Andrew actually wanted. Andy reversed his pull to a push and the gun that Dave was holding in front of him slammed into his head.

Josh could hear the chopper getting close as he turned his head to look over his shoulder just in time to see Dave crumple to the ground, unconscious, with Andy holding the bottle in one hand and the M16 in the other.

About a half hour later Henry, Megan, and Watson were stepping outside the officer's tent with Professor Holton, an elderly man closing in on his eighties. He walked slower than the rest and his beat-up dress shoes and sweater vest gave away the fact that he was not prepared for desert life. Around his neck were two sets of glasses one for far away and the other for close-up reading. The distance glasses were held by an older gold chain. The reading pair however was held by a length of cotton twine with several knots in it from being mended.

Megan held the door open for Professor Holton and smiled at him as he stepped outside. She offered her arm to him as she remarked, "Professor, this is one of our cooler days but it's still 88 degrees. Are you sure you'll be comfortable with a sweater on?"

The professor stepped out. "Perhaps, young lady, perhaps. But first, you must understand that I live in Northern Michigan, a terribly cold place. Have you ever been there?"

"No," Megan responded.

"Houghton, a very cold place. It's where I was forced to retire, cold to cold." Holton responded as he almost shook his head at the thought of the place.

"So you're saying that you're enjoying the weather?" Megan inquired.

"You know, I think I just might get warm for the first time in years," Holton confidently responded.

"Well, I think you will have a few days to get as warm as you like while you figure out the math written on the cave wall," Megan said smiling.

Holton smiled for a moment. "I don't think so. I may have impressed your father at that lecture, years ago, talking about time travel. But I can assure you, no such thing exists. I fully believe this will be a very short trip. I was a younger man then with a college to impress with wild theories and budgets to acquire. Now my biggest issue in life is getting up during the night to pee."

The professor shrugged a little as he thought about his own words. "Although that's not a bad thing. At least I know that I did not die during the night."

Megan was beginning to realize she had quite the character on her arm. A little arrogant, a little full of himself and confident in his opinions, but full of quick wit, and she could appreciate that.

The group rounded the corner to see Josh, Andrew, and Dave, who saluted and came to attention. Megan looked at both the Major and the General as they each noticed the black eye Dave was now sporting.

Henry addressed his guest, "Professor Holton, I would like to officially introduce my daughter, Captain Becker whom I see you have already met, and her team. Lieutenants William and Hansen and Master Sergeant Shaver. The Master Sergeant will escort you to the cave as soon as you are ready."

The professor closely eyed Dave's face as he lifted his glasses to look at him. "Ah... No thanks, General. This arm I am holding onto now is connected to a beautiful woman. One of the few pleasures of life when you're as old as I am. Besides, your Sergeant seems to have already had a hard day today."

Josh and Andrew had a slight smirk as they watched the scene unfold in front of them.

"As you wish, Professor, I am sure Captain Becker will not mind," Henry remarked.

"Now where is that cave?" Professor Holton confidently asked.

Henry turned and pointed, "Up there, Professor, next to the man you see standing guard."

The professor turned to see what he was pointing at. Putting his distance glasses on, "Oh... Oh my." The expression on his face changed as he noticed how far it was.

A little less confident, the professor raised his right eyebrow as he asked, "General, I don't suppose the helicopter could be called back to get me a little closer?"

The corner of Henry's mouth turned upward as he responded. "Sorry, no. Too dangerous. The blades would likely hit the canyon walls."

"I see..." Holten remarked as he turned to Megan. "You know, my dear, I am thinking I should sit for a little bit before we go further."

"I think that would be a good idea, Professor Holton. Perhaps a glass of cold water?" Megan asked as she tapped his arm.

"Yes, and I am thinking you're right. Perhaps I don't need to wear this sweater anymore today," Holton responded.

Megan turned her head and motioned with her free hand to Dave to walk with her and the professor.

As they grew further away some of the men had gathered into a small group, all curious to hear details about the earlier commotion. Watson looked at the lieutenants and asked what happened. Andrew spoke up first, "The Sargent seemed to have the idea that if he got drunk and shot out the tires of the General's Jeep that it might just keep him out of the Army."

Watson's eyes narrowed as he slowly shook his head, pointing a finger at them. "Lieutenant Hansen . . . keep him sober. And out from under my feet."

The Future

Captain John Becker, Ben Hollister, and the sergeants sat in the back of a hover-helo as it prepared for a low-level landing at the Sandpoint, Idaho airport. Much of the city could be easily seen in the dark because the area had suffered very little damage from the war. It was well lit and the holographic runway markers were still in operation, directing them to the landing site.

As they descended, John could see a man in uniform standing near the holographic circle waiting for them. As the hover-helo came to a stop, a guard approached from outside and opened the door.

The man saluted John as he stepped off the craft. "Captain Becker, Sir."

John returned the salute," Lieutenant Yoder."

"Captain, the equipment you asked for is ready as well as any men that you may need." Lieutenant Yoder responded back.

John looked back behind himself to see a larger hover-helo approaching. "Thank you, Lieutenant, but I have changed my mind. Your men will not be needed." John handed Lieutenant Yoder some paperwork. "All you need to know is that myself and my men are going to take your equipment for a little moonlight drive. The less you know, the better. Understood?"

"Yes, Sir." The Lieutenant responded back.

The Present

Lieutenant Williams had formed a work detail at the order of Major Watson "to clear and even out the path to the cave for the professor." This quickly became very helpful, even though it still took Captain Becker and Professor Holton a long time to reach the cave.

Once inside the cave, Professor Holton enjoyed the cool air and the chair that had been provided for him as well as some ice water. It only took a moment of viewing the complex equations on the wall for him to start commenting. First, it was just a quiet "hmm." Then the next minute they heard him remark, "Well, I'll be." Soon after that came the words, "Well, I never thought of that."

Finally, Megan and her father could wait no longer. Henry asked, "Well, Professor, what are you thinking now?"

Raising his hand slightly as if the General was his student Holten responded back, "Be quiet, I am still reading."

Megan and Henry looked at each other as if "dad" had just rebuked them. Megan gave it one more moment and briefly considered raising her voice at him. But after thinking it over, she reconsidered. "Mr. Holton... Jimmy," she politely spoke, "We would really love to hear your valuable thoughts."

The soft suddenness of her voice interrupted his thinking. The corner of his mouth turned up a little as he turned to look at her. "A little honey in the tea is a good thing, my dear. And since you have asked so nicely, I will tell you that this has caught my interest, but please give me just a little more time. I wish to see it all before I render an opinion on this intriguing work." Professor Holten informed her.

Henry gave his daughter a wink and a grateful look as they continued to wait.

After a few moments, the professor continued, "Oh, and could you please set up a small table with some paper and pencils?"

"No calculator?" remarked Henry.

"No calculator. That's for the younger crowd, my son. I prefer to keep my mind sharp," Holton softly spoke as he drifted back into his work.

Taking in a deep breath Megan walked outside the cave to where Lieutenant Williams was talking on the radio. Josh watched her approach and ended the conversation. "Yes ma'am?"

"Lieutenant, bring us a small table, pencils, paper, and some more water. Oh, and construct a tent halfway along this path with a bench for the professor to rest on. Also, send someone an hour before each meal to help escort him back to the mess tent."

"Yes, Captain," Lieutenant Williams answered. "You should know that the next supply shipment is due to arrive at 18:00 hours."

"Thank you, Lieutenant," Megan responded back

Josh Williams started down the hill and was almost to the supply tent when he heard the voice of young Johnny yelling, "Lorenzo! Lorenzo, where are you?"

Opening the door Josh asked, "Johnny, did you lose the little guy?"

"Yeah, can you help me find him?" a frustrated Johnny responded back.

As Josh came to a stop inside he asked, "I can look for a moment. Where did you see him last?"

"I saw him as he ran outside, this way, from the igloo I built him," Johnny said.

Josh was caught off guard by the word, "igloo." He started looking but could not help but ask, "So Johnny, you built him another rock house?"

"No, I built him an igloo, not a rock house," Johnny responded.

This comment made Josh ask another question. "Johnny, could you show me your igloo?"

Aggravated, Johnny responded back, "Why? He ran this way."

Josh calmly asked Johnny, "I would just like to see it. Could you please show me?"

With a little aggravation in his voice and rounded shoulders of aggravation, Johnny shrugged, "Okay."

He opened the door to the next room of the supply tent to reveal one of the largest piles of crumpled paper Josh had seen in a long time.

Josh's eyes widened as he asked, "Johnny, what did you do?"

"I built an igloo, Uncle Josh. There are boxes inside so that he can travel from floor to floor. And I covered it in snowballs," Johnny asked with a proud grin. Turning his head Johnny looked up at Josh's face. "Are you okay?"

"Johnny... uh, you're going to have to find Lorenzo by yourself. I've got some work to do," Josh informed him a less than confortable tone.

A little while later, Josh and two soldiers were setting up a table in the cave. Josh gave a small stack of flattened paper to Megan. She looked down at the wrinkled paper with a look that made it clear that she required an explanation. Josh looked her in the eye and quietly told her, "Johnny built Lorenzo a new house."

Megan's eyes rolled as if to say, "Not now."

Megan then looked down at the paper, "Lieutenant, please make sure a new supply of paper is on the next shipment at 18:00."

Fading Starlight
Chapter Three
**Bonner's Ferry and
Sgt. Peters.**

The Future

John was a little surprised that after all these years Highway 95 north of Sandpoint had not changed. At least the moon was up and the sky was clear. It was enjoyable to see the Selkirk Mountains covered in soft moonlight during the drive. The traces of Alpine snow along its peaks added a bit of a glow to the hills. The scenery and quiet travel were a welcome vacation from the war—a small piece of normal.

At least that's what was on everyone's mind a split second before Sergeant Peters yelled, "Oh no!" and slammed on the brakes. Suddenly everyone's hearts stopped and a few items were flung to the front as the truck as it came to a sliding stop. This forced the truck behind them to stop, as they slid into the lead truck. The last two truck drivers stood on their brakes as they barely missed being added to the mess. John was closest to the door covered in broken glass from the windshield.

His first thought, honed by battle experience, was to find his rifle, thinking they were under attack. He grabbed it as his blurred vision came into focus, cycling the action, ready to fight.

The reality of the situation set in as he saw what appeared to be thick brown hair where the windshield once was. The head of a dead moose was pushed up against Sergeant Peters' chest leaving him gasping for air.

John's eyes came into focus a bit more as he yelled to the men in the truck, "Everyone who's not hurt get up here and help Peters." He picked up the radio and called the truck behind them, "Hollister, get your men

70

up here and get this moose off my truck."

It only took a few minutes for the men to get the moose off the truck as Peters was getting his rib cage taped to support the two broken ribs they found.

Sergeant Hess an older, white-haired man was just pulling himself from under the truck as John, who was growing concerned as Hollister walked up to him.

"How bad is it?" Becker asked.

"Well, we need to change the right front tire. It's slowly losing air. You've got some cracked lines that I can fix with sealant spray and the block is leaking. I can use the core link putty on that, but it will need twenty minutes to harden." Hollister responded back.

"Can we leave this truck behind?" Hess inquired.

"No, we need it. All of it," John replied back.

Growing a little irritated, John knew that they could lose this chance to gain valuable technology. Moving his tense neck around John looked at the moon as he responded back. "Okay, get everyone on this. And roll that moose off into the ditch. We are losing our window of opportunity."

Hess got the core link putty mixed up as Hollister and his men took care of the tire. Peters sat on the back bumper of the truck trying to get his shirt back on as John walked around the corner to see him struggling.

"Let me give you a hand with that, soldier," John spoke as he walked towards Peters.

"Oh, thank you, Sir," Peters responded.

"Well, how many men in this war will be able to say they got wounded kissing a moose?" John remarked with a grin in an effort to lighten the mood.

Peters smiled but then got a serious look on his face as John helped him. Noticing the look on Peters's silent face, John grew a little concerned by Peters's lack of conversation. "Peters, are you all right?"

Peters looked like he was having a problem forming the words in his mind. "Sir, I have been shot at several times and faced death more than once. But this . . . I don't know. It did something. I never thought about dying before."

John slowed, looking at his sergeant as he realized just how shaken he was. He sat down on the bumper next to him. Taking a moment to breathe in the cool Idaho air, John quietly spoke to him, "Tell me what you're thinking."

"Sir, I don't know. I have always been tough; you grow up that way when you have no parents and no family. I fought my way through anything or anyone for what was right. Every few months the system moved me from one place to another, so I never established any roots. I wasn't a part of anything until the Army and I never needed anything else, especially religion."

John looked at him. "Sounds like you've got an issue with religion? What's up with that?"

"I don't have an issue with it, Sir, but I've never been in a church. Have you ever been in one?" Peters responded back.

"Yep, several times. It was a very important part of my grandfather's and my mother's lives." John responded back.

"The idea of a god seems a little crazy, don't you think? Especially after seeing all this stuff with aliens." Peters remarked.

John smiled, "Really? You should know that everything that Christians do and believe, is based on a book that God gave mankind, and in it, He writes about other races, not just ours."

"What?" Peters responded back.

"Ever since this crazy thing started I began to look real close at what's been written. I count four different races so far, besides us. That makes me think God likely knew what He was talking about." John responded back.

John looked at the stunned face of his sergeant, thinking over what he was going to do next. He pulled up the flap on one of his coat pockets and produced a small book. "Son, you're a little beat up so I am going to have you stay back with the trucks while the rest of the men go in. I want you to hold onto this for me. It belonged to my grandfather and I would not want to lose it during any altercations we might encounter."

"Is this the book?" Peters asked as he looked closely at it. John stood up to give Peters a little time alone to himself.

"Yep, it is," John responded back.

"I will give it back to you as soon as we are done here, Sir," Peters remarked.

"No, I'll let you know when I need it back, and Peters..." John informed him.

"Yes, Sir?" Peters responded back.

Changing his tone, John spoke. "It'll be okay. Do a little reading when you get a chance. I will be around to answer any questions."

"Thank you, Sir," Peters answered back.

John smiled and started walking back to the front of the truck. It was not his desire to push Peters too far, too fast. He knew the wisdom of his grandfather's words, "It's better to leave them a little hungry. Feed them too much at once and they might throw up."

Hollister turned to see John walking up to him. "Report," John asked.

"We should be running within a few minutes. We're just waiting for the putty to harden."

"Good. Peters will be out for the rest of the mission. I want him to stay with the trucks while we go in. I'll take his place behind the wheel."

"Yes, Sir. We got most of the glass out of the cab. Sergeant Hess says it will pull a little to the right as you drive." Hollister informed him.

Present Day

Grandpa Henry sat for a while in the supply tent as Johnny cleaned up his mess. Henry took the opportunity to talk about the importance of keeping out of the supply tent. Then he just spent some time listening to his grandson talk. He was beginning to have a hard time with the idea that all this around him was the result of what Johnny was about to do.

In his mind, he played out discussions that he should have had with him, but he had so many questions himself. "How do I prepare my grandson for the greatest fight of his life? How can I help him? What can I give him? My God, is he really going to be a time traveler?" He knew he could not shield him from life; that would be wrong. But he needed to do something.

Henry remembered raising Megan and Danny. Could he do better? He had to. Everything was riding on it now. The officer in Henry was slowly surrendering to the father and grandfather in him, allowing his emotions to surface. Lost in thought, he never heard Major Watson walk through the door.

Watson stood there for a moment looking at the General's face. "Sir?" Watson asked.

Henry shifted back to reality and turned his face towards the Major revealing a little wetness in the corner of his eye. "Yes, Major?"

"Professor Holton is being escorted down from the cave now. He should be at the camp in about ten minutes or so. I believe he has an early report for you, Sir."

Henry nodded that he understood. Watson looked at Johnny playing and calmly asked his old friend, "Henry, if there is any way I can help you during these times, please let me know."

"Compassion, Major?" Henry smiled, returning to his old self. "Terrance, the future of our world most likely rests in the hands of this very child. He is the single greatest national security treasure I know of. He is whom we need to protect."

Watson nodded his head.

"Call Lieutenant Hansen in to watch my grandson. I don't want him getting into anything else he shouldn't," Henry ordered.

"Yes, Sir," Watson responded back as Henry got up to exit the tent.

The Future

John was getting very tired of pulling the steering wheel to the left. Without the windshield, he'd had his fill of the wonderful cold air as it was now freezing him out. His unprotected ears had already gone numb from the cold and his fingers were not far behind. The highway finally leveled out at the bottom of the steep hill as they closed in on the town. In the last of the fading moonlight, it was wonderful to behold the wide open view of the valley near Bonners Ferry.

The sight overlooking the valley with the sharp rise of the Selkirk Mountains was spectacular. He only had a moment too mentally enjoy it as he realized hints of sunlight were starting to overtake the moon. He hoped that this whole effort was not in vain because he knew he should already be in place, ready to strike.

"Captain, look up in the sky." One of the men leaned over him to point upwards at the sky.

The morning sunlight was now reflecting off the bottom of three silver alien craft descending into the valley. They were coming in fast at a sharp angle. "We're too late, Captain." The man from behind him exclaimed.

As soon as the crafts got close they stopped in the sky. With a shocking flash, they opened fire on the mountainside, pummeling it in multiple barrages of weapon fire. John and the convoy stopped in the road to get out and watch the cloud of dust rise as the hillside above it slid down, destroying the site below it.

Shocked at what they were seeing, they could only watch as the craft zipped off to the north after doing their job. John and his team walked further away from the trucks to watch a small red glow rise up under the rock face. The glow suddenly became very bright and then stopped as the shock wave from the explosion swept over the valley with a roar. They knew there would be nothing left to find.

The valley became silent once more as they watched the alien craft move away, turn and then disappear in the sky toward Canada.

Hess and Hollister stepped up to John. "Now what? What are your orders?" Hess inquired.

John stared at the mountainside, his face becoming grim as an understanding of what just happened formed in his mind. "They knew we were coming. They knew our plans. The only people I shared this with were the Joint Chiefs."

John turned around to look at the two men. "We go dark, hidden. Somehow they (pointing an angry finger at the sky) know what's going on. Had we not hit that moose when we did, that rock would be on top of us. Let's get out of here."

Present Day

The professor lowered the small glass from his lips. "Ah, cold apple juice. There is nothing finer," he exclaimed from the comfort of his chair in the General's tent.

Megan put the pitcher back into the fridge as the General crossed his arms and leaned on his desk facing the professor. "What is your preliminary evaluation?"

"Well, I can't speak to the age of the writing. I will have to accept your lovely daughter's word on that. However, I can tell you that whoever scratched all that on the walls was working out a complicated math problem far above my understanding. In fact, I think he was dancing around the edges of quantum physics. His wall was his chalkboard. It looks like he was scribbling it out at a furious pace. Some things were written but then scratched out." Professor Holten remarked.

Megan asked, "How can you tell?"

"My dear, I have forty-plus years of teaching math, much of it before the age of calculators. I can tell the scribbling of a desperate student," Holton confidently announced. Megan stared at the floor, with concern dancing around the edge of her heart, wondering why her son did what he did.

"General, with your permission, I would like to continue my examination tomorrow," the professor asked.

"Actually, professor, I need you to analyze it in every way you can think of. And I can authorize anything you need to accomplish that task," Henry remarked in his official tone.

"In that case, might I have some new paper, not some refugee from the waste receptacle?" Holton asked.

With a slight grin, Henry started feeling a little less official as he thought of the irony that the same person who crumpled the paper the professor was complaining about was the same person who wrote the math he was working to decode.

Henry was thinking of something to say when Lieutenant Williams came into the tent to announce that Master Sargent Shaver had the evening meal ready. "Should I have it brought in?"

Henry nodded a yes, affirming that he should.

Lieutenant Williams turned to leave when the professor spoke up. "Son, excuse me...uh, Lieutenant Williams, might I trouble you?"

"Yes, how may I help you?" Josh responded.

The professor smiled and tipped his glasses down to look over the top at Josh. "What's for dinner?"

"Fried chicken, green beans, and mashed potatoes," Josh answered.

"Hmm. My teeth, I'm afraid, have not aged as well as the rest of me. Could I have just the drumstick and some mashed potatoes?" The professor asked in a simple tone.

The corner of Josh's mouth came up as he responded back, "I will gladly make it happen, Professor."

77

The Future

John was riding in the lead hover-helo from Sandpoint. In the seat next to him were his grandfather and an old family friend named Andrew. The world below them was on fire. The aliens attacked and killed everything that moved below the Helo. Some of the aliens were as big as the trees.

John looked at the concerned eyes of his grandfather who said nothing. He could feel the panic of the moment settling in as he watched the world below. Finally, in an eruption of anger, he yelled at his grandfather, "What was I supposed to do? I tried everything! There is nothing left, they are destroying it all!"

"There is always an answer" Andrew spoke, as the hover-helo was getting rocked from side to side by the ground fire directed at them.

"What?" a panicked John inquired.

Andrew looked directly at John with obvious confidence. "Son, plans fail for lack of counsel...."

John's grandfather then continued the sentence, looking at him with eyes that felt like they were looking right through him, "but with many advisors, they will succeed."

Sergeant Hess jarred Captain Becker awake. "Captain, we are closing in on Helena Air Force Base."

John sat there, reality coming back to him. "Helena? Why not Maelstrom in Great Falls?"

"Leveled. Last month, Sir. Everything was relocated to Helena." Hess responded back.

John sat there for a moment thinking about his dream. Then John leaned forward toward the pilot, tapped him on the shoulder, and gave him a hand signal. They each reached up to their helmets to switch to another frequency that no one else could hear.

"Pilot, how are you fixed on fuel?" John inquired.

"Good, Sir, I can fly for... 124 minutes before I need to refuel," the pilot responded back.

"Very good. Turn due south," John ordered.

"Sir?" The pilot asked.

"That's an order. Notify the other helos to follow and maintain radio silence," John ordered once more.

Everyone else looked at each other but said nothing as the airships turned south in the mid-morning light.

John's team stayed behind to hide the hover-helos in the mountain terrain while he left on a small electro-bike that partly hovered to improve its gas mileage. Soon he was driving down Fish Creek Falls Road in Steamboat Springs, Colorado, on his way to find an old family friend on Pine Street.

John pulled up onto the lawn of a simple one-story house with wood siding. An elderly man sitting on the porch with a copy of *Fir, Fish, and Game* magazine looked up to see him lean his bike against the tree in the yard. The man's nearly gray straight hair was almost past his ears, but his beard was far longer. It was white, with two ribbons of black coming from his chin. It was in stark contrast next to his red flannel shirt and suspenders.

The man looked over his glasses to see John. "Well, I'll be. I see they haven't killed you yet," He remarked as he stood up to meet John on the porch with a handshake that quickly turned into a hug.

"John," Andrew remarked.

"Andrew," John affectionally responded back.

"Sit down. Sit down. What brings you around here? No, wait, where are my manners? Let me get us something to drink."

John was about to interrupt, but he realized it would be pointless, so he just sat on a porch swing, partly enjoying the moment while considering what he was going to tell him.

A small meadowlark landed on the handlebars of his bike, watching him as he watched it. The bird seemed to have no interest in moving when Andrew came outside with drinks in his hands.

"Oh, I see you've met my little friend," Andrew commented.

John smiled and took the glass from Andrew as he sat down. Andrew then looked into John's eyes and knew something was up. He did not need to wait long to find out before Andrew first sip from his glass was interupted.

"I need your help," John asked.

Andrew paused and then continued his drink. As he did, he had thoughts of just saying no right up front. After all, he had been retired from the army for a while now. But he thought about who was asking him, and in his eyes, he could still see his old friend Thomas Becker. He looked over at the meadowlark and then back to John.

"All right, talk to me, Johnny," Andrew asked as he put his glass down.

"We ran an operation at a hidden alien base in north Idaho. It didn't go so well. They knew we were coming," John spoke.

Andrew's face showed concern as he heard the news. "Lose many people?"

John nodded. "Never got a chance. They blew it up before we got there. We would have had a mountainside come down on top of us if our lead truck hadn't hit a moose on the way there."

Andrew played with the condensation drops on the side of his glass as he thought about it. "Someone in your team?"

"Nope, I was the only one with details until an hour prior. It had to be one of the Joint Chiefs of Staff," John responded back.

"Hmm," Andrew responded as he returned his gaze to the meadowlark.

"We went dark, and I came here. It seems obvious to me that a government insider is leaking key information to our enemies. There was no reason for them to destroy their own secret base unless they knew it was compromised. Therefore, we will need to stay dark and keep all the information in-house for our own security," John informed him.

"Any chance this was a coincidence?" Andrew inquired.

"This is not the only issue. There have been other situations over the last year that did not make sense, such as aircraft and missile deployment changed from cities just before being hit. I was aware of it even though it was not under my command," John answered back.

"Why would a person betray us to these destroyers?" Andrew inquired once more.

John nodded. "I don't know, but it's the only plausible explanation at this point."

Andrew put his glass on the little table next to him as he watched the meadowlark fly off. "John, one of the first rules of warfare is to know your enemy."

"That was one of the points of this raid. We were going to collect as much information as we could before destroying it," John commented.

Andrew got up and opened the screen door. "Johnny, you better follow me."

John followed Andrew into the house. Most likely built at the beginning of the century, it was starting to show some signs of wear, cracks in the drywall in the corners of the room, and such. Judging by the clutter throughout, it was obvious that Andrew's priorities did not include housekeeping. The kitchen table was a repair station for fishing rods, and the coffee table held a collection of hunting and fishing magazines.

They walked into his bedroom, and Andrew moved his 12-gauge shotgun off the bed, motioning for John to sit. John complied as Andrew reached for something in his closet.

"Your mother was an archaeologist at heart. Do you remember her talking about ooparts?" Andrew inquired.

John got a funny look on his face and responded, "Don't you mean odd parts?"

Andrew turned around, holding an old shoe box in his hands. "No, that's ooparts, not odd parts. And I guess by your answer to the question is no, you don't remember."

John sat there with a slightly dumb look on his face as

Andrew continued. "Oopart means 'out-of-place artifact.' The term has been around since way before you. Your mother and I used to find artifacts from time to time that did not make sense. Like most archaeologists in the early years, we cataloged and reported them: bag and tag, and then move on.

"But as time went on, we never heard of them again. That seemed strange because some of them were quite profound, and they should have, at the very least, made the news somewhere.

"We visited one of the universities where we sent our findings. After a few meetings and some arguments with them, they claimed to have lost everything. We later ran into an elderly man who was retiring from the university. He was dying of cancer and wanted to come clean and get a few things off his chest. Artifacts from us and many others were given to government agents in the Dakotas, and the university was paid to look the other way. After that, we started keeping our own collection."

Andrew opened the lid and pulled out a terra-cotta object and handed it to John. "We found this in Norte Chico in South America." John looked at it closely. It was a crude figurine of an alien ship with writing on the bottom of it. The bewildered look on John's face continued as he looked up at Andrew.

The tone of Andrew's voice became serious. "Rough guess, 3,000 BC, I suppose. John this was part of a larger collection that we once had. That thing never really made sense until the attacks, when I got to see the first pictures of the alien ships." He paused for a moment, looking at John. "Well, the first thing you need to know is that they have been here before."

John sat there looking it over. He had seen several alien ships like this from a distance and one up close at the bottom of a swamp. He ran his thumb over some of the crude markings on the bottom. Thinking it was writing, he asked, "What does the writing say?"

"We were not totally sure. It doesn't match anything from South America. It's more like something from the

Middle East. We think possibly Sumerian."

John handed it back. "And did you try and translate it?"

Andrew turned the bottom up toward John so that the writing was clearly seen. "Your mother and I think it says, 'We are prey before the hunters.'"

The Present

The General and his daughter stood near their bags as they watched the approaching helicopter. Megan had said her goodbyes to her son who was now in the able care of Dave and Andrew. The Pentagon had ordered them to give a report, in person, to the high-level brass so the base was now falling under the Major's care.

As the helicopter flew in closer, Megan noticed she could see a mule deer in the far distance watching the whole thing happen. It was a nice little mental distraction from what she knew was soon to come.

Major Watson had been tasked with building a tent for the professor and a latrine next door. This was a blessing to the rest of the troops because of how long Professor Holton took in the mornings. The Professor however was watching from the comfort of his chair in his tent. He knew this was a bigger deal than he was letting on, but it had been so long since he had been a part of something so exciting. He was torn between doing a good job and milking it out as long as he could so he did not have to return to the cold and ice. His thumb fiddled with the secret stash of KitKat candy bars he had in his coat pocket as he quietly observed the camp.

As Henry and Megan crossed the Utah/Colorado border heading east towards Pagosa Springs, Henry was once again lost in thought over the importance of doing everything he could to help raise Johnny correctly. He began to replay in his mind all the times he'd failed with his own son; pushing when he should have waited, lecturing when he should have laughed. The thought of the future was almost paralyzing.

Henry was a military man and he could see the danger in what the world was about to face. After hearing Megan read excerpts of his grandson's report, he knew the future would be a costly place.

Megan's elbow nudged him. "Dad, did I tell you I spoke with Danny?"

The dullness in Henry's eyes turned to light at the mention of his son. "No, dear, you did not."

"I told him we were going to be in Washington and I got him to agree to meet us there," Megan explained in an effort to break the silence.

Henry was glad for the news. It was a pleasant distraction from his current thoughts. "Honey, you never had to deal with the top brass at the Pentagon before. You should know that we cannot guarantee any time away from the meeting for something social."

Megan smiled, "And you should know, dear Father, that your family figured that out years ago. Danny and I are prepared to wait."

Henry smiled, half out of appreciation and half out of embarrassment. "Okay, but I am not going in alone this time. You're going with me."

"Why me?" Megan asked.

"You're the one who started all this and you're the archaeologist. A lot hangs on that degree right now," Henry responded.

"Ah, you do remember… it's just a Bachelor's degree?" Megan responded back.

"Four years, it got you here," Henry remarked with a grin.

Ignoring his comment Megan inquired, "What do we tell them? Do we explain about Johnny?"

"They already know," Henry answered.

Megan stopped talking. It made sense, it made perfect sense. But that did not change the fact that the mother in her did not like it. "How much time will we have on the ground before we have to be at the Pentagon?"

"Not sure. Once we get dropped off at Pagosa Springs they will have a jet waiting for us." Henry answered as he shrugged his shoulders. "I have had it many times that I've had to walk straight into a meeting and other times I've sat in a hotel room for days."

Megan turned her head quietly and watched the scenery pass by. After a bit, she turned to her father, "Well then, after we lift off from Pagosa Springs, I will get to work on my presentation and notes."

Henry pulled out a water bottle and handed it to her. "Sounds good. Hopefully, we can meet with Danny after that."

January 3rd, 2044

It had been a month and a half since John had contacted Andrew. They needed a plan and a goal. John had an idea that he had mentioned once to some people who thought he was crazy. Andrew listened and refined it and contacted an old friend for some special "spare parts."

For now, Becker had spent the day working on tunneling equipment, in the mud, on his back. He was cold, hungry, and quickly getting beyond grumpy when he heard a sergeant say to another man that it was getting light outside. John stopped to ponder that thought, "Morning."

He poked his hand out from underneath the mammoth machine he was under. "Hey, could someone pull me out?" John asked. From his cramped vantage point, he could see a pair of mud-soaked boots step near, and then two hands grabbed him and pulled. Soon he was out with mud falling off while leaning against the tunnel wall.

Another mud-covered man, shorter than Captain Becker, walked up to him and spoke. "What do you think, Cap?"

Captain Becker, gladly accepted a canteen from Private

Baker. Turning his head, John looked in the direction that the tunnel was going. Pointing to the end, Capitan Becker remarked "Well, if the old maps are correct, Madrid's subway tunnel should be about 75 feet in front of us. Has everything else arrived, Private?"

"Almost, Sir. They say it will be around twelve hours before the bomb is ready to go." Baker responded back.

Becker wiped some mud from his forehead. "Hmm, well then, let's get some sleep. What time is it?"

Private Baker poured a little water over an old wind-up pocket watch he had with him to get the mud off. "It's 05:25, sir."

"Then lets tentatively schedule the operation for around 18:00," John ordered as he handed the canteen back and started slogging his way out of the tunnel.

Captain Becker and his small team of six men made their way to the surface on a small, old electric transport. The sun had only been up for a few minutes casting its earliest light on a landscape that was like some burnt, alien world where nothing lived. No color remained and the sound of birds was gone as well. Once there were green fields, but now the land hosted muted grays and browns with a few sun-bleached animal bones serving as highlights. The blast from a few years ago had been so hot that the ground was literally cooked and turned to ash, several feet deep. The depressing sight was the same in all directions, as far as the eye could see.

The men found a semi-stagnant pool in a shallow depression in the ground. Everyone waded in to clean some of the mud off. Jerking his hand from the water Becker realized he had another cut. Looking it over, John realized that the mud had made an effective bandage for all the scrapes and cuts from working on the machine but now he could see them all.

After a little while, the soggy soldiers made their way to the remains of a burnt-out warehouse. Inside were two men working on a device with flashlights. An elderly, gray-haired man looked up to see the captain and his men approaching. He smiled and spoke up as

86

he pointed with a screwdriver, "John, I made some soup."

Becker nodded his thanks as he and the men walked past. Dropping their equipment and weapons near the warehouse wall, most of them sat on the floor. The elderly Andrew looked up at his younger coworker and told him, "I've got this. Give them a hand."

The man moved over to a small campfire and opened the lid of a large pot. "Well guys, today we're having the finest re-hydrated mystery food that I could swipe from the British Navy."

Sergeant Hess looked up, watching him ladle it off into bowls. "Does it at least smell good?"

"It smells better than you do," he responded back.

"That's not saying much," Becker replied, "but I'll eat it anyway." With a little food and the stillness of the world around them, all six men were soon asleep on the floor.

The day was growing brighter as Andrew and his crew continued working. John Becker opened his eyes to see a spider, only a few inches from his nose and closing fast. Jerking his head backward, it collided with someone's boot. Sitting up, holding his head, John started searching for something to smash the spider with. After a moment he found his bowl and crushed it.

Then Andrew heard the noise, turned from the makeshift desk he was hunched over, and smiled. "You never did like bugs."

John pulled himself up against the wall to finish waking up. "It's a family thing, I guess." As his eyes came more into focus, he noticed that most of the men were still asleep. Looking beyond that, through a gaping, charred hole in the side of the warehouse, he could see the sun moving toward the horizon. "What time is it?"

Andrew looked at his pocket watch on the table, "16:35."

"How are we doing on the bomb?" John asked.

"Close, but don't get in a hurry," Andrew responded back.

87

"Got it," John responded back as he wiped the bottom of his bowl on the wall to get the dead spider off. "Any more soup?"

"Only if you heat it up yourself," Andrew responded.

Sometime later, John had the campfire rebuilt and the soup just starting to steam again. The rest of the camp was waking up and Sergeant Peters was resting against his pack reading a small black book.

Becker noticed him and the book as he walked passed. "Sergeant, keep an eye on the soup."

"Yes, Sir," Peters responded back.

"Mind if I join you, John?" Andrew asked as he looked up. John waved his hand in affirmation as he headed for the hole in the wall. Stepping over some burnt debris, they strolled outside and then up a small ash-white hill.

From the crest of the hill, you could see in the distance the outline of a semi-transparent dome sitting on top of what once was Madrid, Spain. Standing out in stark contrast to the dullness of the landscape. The dome was bright, not only from the light inside it but also from the evening sun reflecting off it to the west. Four miles wide and a mile and a half tall, this dome city was the first the aliens had built. Standing in defiance against all manmade attempts to destroy it, its hardened outer shell either absorbed or reflected all conventional or nuclear weapons used against it. Now it was a home; a base for alien ships to enter and exit from to parts unknown across the earth.

John stood on the small hill, staring. "There it stands like some cancerous growth atop the graves of five million dead. Hopefully, we will mess them up a bit by this time tomorrow."

Andrew gave a confirming nod, "It should. A nuclear bomb inside a confined space should work like a shaped charge. Who knows how that will play out?"

John smiled. "When I was a kid, I loved putting firecrackers under tin cans and watching them launch up into the air. I wonder if the same thing will happen. I would love to see the look on their faces if we send their dome back up to space."

Andrew grinned in response, "Well... if for some reason it still stays attached, then I would assume the energy will travel downwards and make a really big hole."

John was about to respond with some quirky answer when they noticed two ships exit from the side of the dome and fly off to the northeast, not far from their location. Andrew grinned through his grizzly beard and remarked, "I'm so glad they consider us of such low value."

"It's their arrogance. We are just ants crawling in the dirt to them," John responded. Looking away from the sky for a moment towards the tunnel. "This underground tunnel, which was part of a planned rapid-transit system from Valladolid to Madrid, was never completed. When the blast came, the ground shifted and crushed the tunnel to the north. Because the lake runs just over the tunnel, it was flooded all the way to Valladolid." John remarked as he paused to take a breath.

"This section, however, never flooded, and it was only eighteen days from being finished. Once we detonate the bomb inside the dome, the tunnel will most likely finish collapsing. Hopefully, everyone will be able to get out in time." John remarked as he folded his arms.

"Hopefully," Andrew added with a raised eyebrow, "if my friend's forty-year-old nuke parts work the way they're supposed to."

"Are you thinking they may not?" John questioned with obvious concern.

"Nope, the exact opposite. I'm hoping it goes the way I planned it when you set the timer. Not whenever these old parts feel like it." Andrew responded back with a slightly concerned look.

John turned his head and looked at Andrew with a slightly sick look. "Hmm, gee I can hardly wait."

Present Day

Megan and Henry climbed on board their next flight. As they were getting seated, Henry asked Megan who the text message was from just before they walked to the plane.

"Well, it was actually two texts. The first was from Danny saying that he is running a little late so if the Pentagon makes us wait it will work out for him. The other was Andrew. He just wanted to let me know everything was fine with Johnny," Megan remarked as a stewardess walked up to them with a smile and delivered a drink for Henry.

Megan watched her walk away, a little puzzled by her action she spoke with her father. "You never ordered that drink. What's up with that?"

Henry smiled and leaned in closer to Megan. "It's a message."

Megan's eyes narrowed as she wondered what her father was up to.

"It's a message from an inside friend within the Pentagon. We've been doing this for years. If I get a drink from her, it's a message that the top brass will be expecting us the moment we get off the plane." Henry reported.

Megan looked impressed. "How very James Bond of you."

Henry smiled, "Don't knock it. It works. The funny part of it is that her last name actually is Bond."

Megan watched her smug father take a drink as she buckled her seatbelt and began to put some thought into what all she needed to do for her presentation.

The Future

John and his team were standing next to a very impressive, loud machine with ear protection on as Andrew was running the equipment, boring a tunnel.

John kept checking the computer display on the side of the tumbler. After a moment or so it was now showing that they were within a foot or so of a small shaft to the underground part of Madrid. According to the information, it was part of an abandoned section of the subway.

John raised his hand to let Andrew know that he needed to stop. Andrew then put the grinder into reverse and soon he had backed up a good fifteen feet. The roar of the engine sound in the cavern started to lessen, signaling to everyone that the next phase was about to start. Sergeant Peters was the first to gladly take his hearing protection off. Eventually, everyone else's hearing protection came off as John announced that they would finish with hand tools.

Handing out the tools, the team proceeded with picks and shovels as Andrew descended from the tunneler to speak with John.

"John, once you get on the transport, it's fourteen minutes to the surface. Keep that in mind when you set the timer. Stuart Maxwell is going to stay at the camp, as agreed, to monitor alien traffic. If something odd happens, he will alert me and I will send you a message." Andrew informed him.

John nodded, "Don't worry. I only want to grab as much alien technology as we can carry out. We'll then set the bomb and run."

"Make sure that's all you do, son. I've looked after you too long for it to end here," Andrew remarked.

John put his dirt-covered hand on Andrew's shoulder. "Don't worry."

Andrew's eyes took on a look of concern. "You have your mother's fire. It keeps you alive but it can also get you into trouble."

John smiled, walked away from Andrew, and over to the bomb. He picked it up by the handle and walked to where his men were working as Andrew turned to climb into the cab of the machine to wait.

They dug a little longer than he had hoped for. Nevertheless, the dirt and rock finally gave way to the crumbling wall of an underground sewer. It still smelled foul even though it was totally dry. Stepping out into the tunnel they noticed even the rats and bugs were long since dead. Nothing remained alive in there as it had its own eerie sense of death about it. The team stopped near a section of steel reinforcements that were melted from some unknown intense heat. John pulled out a small handheld geiger counter, looking for signs of radiation. To his surprise, the sensor only registered the normal background readings.

Peters looked at it, a little puzzled as Captain Becker reassured him, "Just wondering. It seems to be totally clean."

Walking a few more feet, they came to a broken manhole cover in the ceiling above. A diffuse, white light was barely visible through the holes in it. John stopped next to the steel ladder and stowed his geiger counter. Pulling out his .45 pistol, he announced, "This is it. Let's go."

After seeing the melted steel John expected the manhole cover to be the same. But it easily lifted, slowly and quietly to the side. The team slowly stepped up to what was once a Madrid street but was now the dead-end hallway between two walls of a room.

Stealthily they moved into the room. It was semi-dark with very plain walls. No seats, chairs, or tables, only a window at one end. John motioned for one of his men to guard the doorway that they had just walked through. The rest of the men followed him to the window.

The view from the window was impressive and very

expansive. The aliens had tunneled downward hundreds of feet, if not a mile or two, making Madrid several times larger than it originally was. Crystal lattice-like structures came out from the sidewalls to support other round structures in the center of the city. It was like a maze of glass spiderwebs that worked both as support and roadways for aliens to travel on.

The hole was deep but the alien structures were also massive in both size and complexity. Hundreds, if not thousands, of aliens of every assorted size and shape were traveling back and forth, in and out of every part of the city. It was an overwhelming feeling to the team as they knew how outnumbered they were.

From ground level, towering toward the dome, stood five, four-sided pillars, like the Washington Monument. They seemed to be radiating energy from the sides of the pillar, like wings made of a crystal lattice towards the roof dome.

Sergeant Benton was the first to quietly speak, "Wow. I could never have imagined this."

Then his eyes spotted something along the side about a half-mile away. "Look, Captain ships." Thousands of ships were near a building that looked like a cross between a warehouse and a black beach ball floating in the air. "Captain, do you suppose that's their idea of an aircraft carrier?" John swallowed hard as he responded, "We have never seen that design before so your guess is as good as mine. But I think you're right."

Peters took out an image recorder and began documenting everything they were seeing when suddenly, John ordered everyone to get down, fast. They all hit the floor with near-lightning speed, motivated by fear. Unknown to them, there was a small walking platform right in front of their viewing window. And there was a small group of aliens passing right in front of it.

Private York glanced at Hollister and Becker with a look of total shock. He fought back the urge to indulge a "colorful adjective," but out of respect for his Captain, who did not approve of the use of them, he decided not

93

to. Becker leaned forward toward him, almost eye to eye. "Don't worry, son. I think that before this is over, you're going to get a lot closer to them than that."

Hess, who was pressed against the corner of the room watching the window, out of sight, gave the "all clear."

Carefully, everyone stood up to look around. Private Baker commented, "I've never seen one so tall and skinny. He was like a walking pencil."

Becker had a confused look on his face as he spoke, "If all these aliens represent other worlds then I think it's safe to say the galaxy has invaded our backyard."

"I would also think that if they are all on the same side, then that means we most likely don't have any allies out there," Hollister remarked.

"Not a pleasant thought," Baker responded.

"What do we do, Cap?" responded York as Becker took another look at the size of the crystal city.

"We continue with the mission as planned. Peters, take charge of the collection and documentation part of this mission. Keep York and Baker with you and fill your pockets with anything that will fit. Hollister, Hess, and Benton, we need to find the best place for this bomb. Although, for the life of me, I am not sure how to move around this city without being seen. Any thoughts?" Captain Becker asked.

Hess, who was standing still near the corner of the room, spoke up, "I do. Look at this." Ben moved his hand close to the wall. As he did, his hand slowly disappeared into it. "When everybody got down and I jumped back I found that the wall was not solid."

Becker walked up to it and put his hand in the same place. "I think it's a hologram but it's somewhat tactile; feels solid, in a way. Strange."

"I wonder what's on the other side," Hollister asked, knowing everyone else was thinking the same thing.

"Let's find out. Guns ready." Becker and his team drew their weapons and cautiously stepped into the next room. To their surprise, it was just like the last and so was the next after it. It really played havoc with their minds. Their training kept them on high alert.

Otherwise, they might be tempted to relax.

As they stepped into the fourth room, Becker and Hollister suddenly came face to face with an alien who was a head and a half taller than the men. The creature was built like a pro weightlifter. And the shock on everyone's faces, including the alien's, was a look of terror. Both men dove towards him only to find it was like jumping a wall with little effect. The alien tossed them backward like toy dolls. This brought a little joy to the face of the alien who just stood there with large, solid-black eyes from his dis-proportionately small head. He cracked a hideous little grin revealing his short, dirty, silver-colored teeth as he forward to attack again.

Hollister, who was lying on his back between both rooms, looked up at the rest of the men who had not entered yet and quickly remarked, "Need help guys." The men, thou puzzled, immediately pulled him back into the other room.

Becker soon found himself in the oversized hands of this monster, crushing the air out of him. Then, to the alien's surprise, the remaining men from Becker's team burst in. Hess had a suppressor on his gun and tried to open fire but couldn't for fear of hitting his Captain.

York took to stabbing the alien's legs all the while trying to avoid the misshapen feet that were quickly moving around. Hollister jumped at him only to be quickly snatched out of the air and then suddenly be used as a club against his own men.

Releasing Becker, he tossed at Hess, and with an intense look of rage, the alien picked up York and brought him up close so they were eye to eye. York feared he was about to have his face bitten off as the monster opened his mouth.

But Baker, the smallest on the team climbed up the Alien and attempted to break the alien's neck. The alien found his efforts to be highly annoying and started using York to knock Baker off. Hess used the opportunity to jump on the alien's back taking Baker's place after he fell and pressed the tip of the gun

Fading Starlight

suppressor to the top of the monster's head. The alien's body went rigid for a moment as the bullet entered his brain. Then slowly, his body relaxed and slumped to the floor like a damp dishcloth.

Everyone lay on the floor, except Hess, gasping for air and holding whatever part of their body was now in pain.

York slowly rolled over, wiping the blood from under his nose. Looking at his Captain he spoke up, "No offense, Sir, but could you please not prophesy how I am going to meet the next alien? I really did not like this one."

Becker could barely suck in air but still found his comment to be funny as he held his head and ribs.

Hess reached out and began helping everyone up and checking for injuries.

Becker finally managed to stand on his own feet to look the big alien over. Light gray skin, massive feet and hands, a small head, a little mouth, and big misshapen eyes only added to the smell that no one could ever describe. It had seven fingers on each hand but the pinky was so small it looked to be of little use. Each foot had two toes without toenails. There was no real form of clothing but it wore a silver-gray work belt with multiple compartments.

"Peters, bag the work belt and take some pictures. How is everyone?" Becker ordered in-between sucking air.

Everyone gave a nod of being okay. Benton, who had been kicked by the monster and was holding his ribs spoke up, "Hope that's the last of those we meet."

Another affirmative nod from everyone as Becker responded, "Let's take it a little slower entering the rooms from now on. This could have been very costly."

Peters and Baker found a few small items near a side wall that this creature was most likely using before everything happened. They looked like tools so they added them to the collection.

Leaving the room to find the hallway, they walked with care to the end of the hall to see the crystal bridge they had seen at a distance. However, it was not open like the others but more like a tunnel.

"What do you want to do, Cap?" Hollister inquired.

John looked around and then at his team. "Benton's in a lot of pain from his ribs. Baker, stay right here with him and alert us if anything enters this tunnel. The rest of us will proceed. I'm thinking that I would really like to get this bomb more in the center of the city if we possibly can. Also, we haven't found much to take back with us so keep your eyes open for any technology you can carry. Hopefully, we will find more in the center."

The men had walked for some time in the strange tunnel. The milky crystal tunnel was not hard to the touch, but semi-soft and would flex and bend as you made contact with it. York made an attempt to get a sample of it but discovered that his knife wouldn't work.

"What is this stuff?" York asked.

"I don't know. It looks similar to some of the stuff inside the alien ship that I swam to at the bottom of that swamp," Becker cautiously commented.

Hess was running point as they walked down the tunnel. He turned and put his index finger to his lips to signal the men to stop talking. Everyone saw him and responded accordingly. Within another twenty paces, Hess stopped and crouched down. As he did so, he put his hand behind him using it to indicate that everyone should do the same.

Becker moved forward to join him and see what he was seeing. Up ahead, he could see that the tunnel reached a small hub where other tunnels and walkways joined each other.

In a slow sway, the tunnel flexed back and forth, corresponding to the weight of those walking on it. As a result, their view of the hub at the end of the tunnel shifted to reveal a small room with equipment and three small aliens. They had the same color of skin as the big guy they killed earlier but were only around three and a half feet tall. Their small arms, legs, hands, and black eyes were way too big for their skulls, but something about them made them no less intimidating than any other alien in this place.

Fading Starlight
Chapter Four
Joint Chiefs

Megan was on the verge of falling asleep in the airplane seat when her father nudged her. "Honey, wake up. We're about to land."

As Megan slowly roused in response, her laptop, which had long since turned itself off, slipped off her lap and fell to the floor. Half awake, she instinctively tried to grab it before it hit. To her, it seemed like the whole thing was happening in slow motion.

Something about it jarred a memory within her. Megan just stared at the laptop before she finally bent down and picked it up. "Dad, I'm not really sure but I think I may have just had one of your crazy dreams?"

Henry's face changed a little as her comment got his attention. "Go on."

Megan struggled at first to articulate the dream but once she began, her memory of it got more focused and the words came easier. "I was somewhere high, maybe on a hill, I'm not sure. It was like some old 1950s, B-rated, science fiction movie. Below I could see hundreds of aliens marching in rows, overtaking the world. Women screamed and fainted like in the old movies."

"But for some reason, I didn't care so much about all of that. In my hand, I had a ball, or maybe it was an egg, but it looked like the world, almost like a child's toy. It slowly fell out of my hands. I was horrified to watch it fall. It hit the ground and kept rolling away and I went running after it." Megan looked at her father with concern, almost on the verge of tears. "What does it mean?"

"I'm not sure. Could it mean we are losing the world?" Henry responded back as the jet jerked as the wheels touched the tarmac. Megan realized then why her father would get so lost in thought after his dreams as the world around her felt somehow 'odd.'

The corner of Henry's mouth came up in a comforting smile as he laid his hand on her arm, "I know what you're feeling. You need to let it settle with you for a while."

Within an hour, Henry and Megan were in the backseat of a government car en route to the Pentagon. The car passed the front gate and came to a stop at the main entrance. With the familiarity of years, Henrys ability to be impressed by the Pentagon had long since faded but not his respect for what was within. But he knew that to Megan, it was all new.

Exiting the car, the driver opened the door for them both as Megan fell in just behind her father with an attaché case containing a laptop in her right hand.

Returning a salute to the guard at the door they entered the building and were soon joined by a first lieutenant who saluted and then asked them to follow. Silently, except for the sound of hard shoes on a harder floor, they made their way down the hallway and then past another guard. Finally, they rounded a corner to a shorter hallway and stopped before a set of closed wooden doors guarded by two soldiers, standing at attention.

One of the guards turned and stopped just in front of them raising his left hand. Henry spoke first, according to protocol, "Lt. General Henry Mullins and Captain Megan Becker to see the Joint Chiefs."

The other soldier checked a small handheld computer and nodded, "Confirmed."

The door was opened for them and the General stepped forward as the Captain followed him in. "Have a good day General...Captain." The guard remarked as they walked by.

Megan nodded a thank you as she followed her father in.

An older woman, a brunette with a single star on the shoulders of her uniform spotted them first. She had a folder in her hand as she passed out paperwork to everyone at the table.

Twelve men and three women were seated around it. All were top brass from the four branches of the service and each had a personal aide with them. Vice President Colter was already sitting at the head of the table as everyone else was getting seated. He looked up to see who was coming into the room next. "Oh, well... you're here," he remarked while motioning toward some empty chairs. "We can get this show on the road now. General, I believe you know everyone here. Captain, we will have to get you caught up at a later time." Colter informed them.

Megan moved to take her seat as the brunette general handed her a paper. Megan noticed the brass name pin that said, "Bond." Megan's right eyebrow raised as she looked over at her father who calmly sat down as if he never saw her.

Colter spoke up. "Okay everyone, the purpose of this meeting is to determine if there is anything here to waste the President's time with. This will be a very short meeting because in twenty minutes I've got some babies to kiss and hands to shake. After all, it is an election year."

Colter then turned and looked over his glasses toward Henry. "And for the sake of time, I'll be blunt, General. I don't honestly believe in your 'little green men are coming to invade theory. But go ahead. The floor is yours General"

Megan was a little taken back by his attitude but it never phased the General. "I perfectly understand, Vice President Colter. I believe this room has all the photos we have sent to date. I will make my presentation short. Currently, we have in our possession over 180 pounds of thinly hammered gold pages, bound into books with ancient wood and leather. We have been analyzing them and according to Captain Becker, who holds a Ph.D. in archaeology and will testify if required, are easily 3000 years old."

Megan's right eyebrow lifted a little at the mention of the degree she did not possess as her father continued.

"These books were hidden behind a large sandstone boulder that has rested in that place for at least 1800 years, possibly longer. The walls of the cave that housed the books were covered in highly advanced mathematic equations as verified by Professor of Mathematics, James Holton. In this signed report he claims that the author was working on formulas related to quantum concepts of time travel. He also states that this person's mathematics skill is Ph.D. level."

"Vice President, fellow officers, in my opinion, for a person to fake all this information is extremely unlikely. Therefore, I fully believe this information to be credible and a course of action should be determined." General Mullins remarked as he ended his presentation and calmly folded his hands together in his lap, never breaking eye contact with the Vice President.

Megan kept her feelings hidden but inside she was rather impressed with what her father just did.

Colter looked at Henry and then moved his eyes toward the rest of the table. "Any questions?"

Admiral James Goodrick was the first to speak up, "Your evidence is impressive, however, I find it highly suspect that the individual that all this information hangs on is a relative of yours. You claim he not only wrote it but also now lives in ancient America. A little self-serving, don't you think?"

Megan felt the need to defend her son but knew better than to speak up harshly in this room. "Sir, all our records are on file. If you feel it necessary, you may produce your own experts to verify our findings." Megan calmly remarked.

Goodrick did not like being addressed in such a way, by a Captain, in front of the other officers. But before he could respond, General Isaacson, the oldest officer in the room, raised his hand to stop him. "Captain, we will make arrangements for your evidence to be further reviewed, as you suggested. Vice President Colter, I would recommend that we adjourn for today as you have other obligations to attend to. A continuation of this meeting will be scheduled as soon as possible."

Colter looked down at his watch and then up at General Bond, who was standing near the door. "Very well. General Bond, please reschedule this ASAP." With that, the Vice President gave a fake smile to everyone in the room and then got up and headed for the door, followed by about half the room.

Megan and Henry stood up as General Bond approached and put out her hand. "Captain Becker, so nice to finally meet you. I am Brigadier General Victoria Bond, assistant to the General of the Army, Collins."

Megan politely shook her hand. "Nice to meet you as well, ma'am."

Victoria Bond turned and shook Henry's hand as well. "Nice presentation, as always Henry. I assume you're going to bring the Captain up to speed on proper protocol when speaking to the Joint Chiefs?"

"You assume correctly," Henry responded with a smile.

"Very good. Officially, Captain, due to your low rank, I need to tell you not to volunteer information unless one of the generals requests it. Unofficially, Captain, I like what you did. This board will remember you. As for Goodrick, you should know he is an over-inflated airbag; a real doubting Thomas. Watch your step around him." General Bond informed her.

Henry smiled at Megan as Victoria continued, "Don't expect any more meetings tonight. I will send word when the next one is scheduled."

The Future

"Okay, listen up. This is it. We are going to kill all the bad guys around us, silently if we can, grab what we can, set the bomb, and get out fast. Got it?" The whole team gave the Captain a thumbs up. John was about to give the signal to go when a small, round device, about the size of a quarter, came zipping up the tunnel.

Stopping in front of the men as if looking them over, it

appeared harmless like a simple, round, brass-colored ball.

The object jerked forward a few feet to look at them from a different angle. After a few seconds, it then took off up the tunnel toward where the men came from. Hollister looked at John with a serious "oh no" look.

Johns's eyes became just as wide as they could get. "We have been made, GO, GO!"

In a blur of controlled panic, the men crashed like a storm into the hub. Hess and Becker were the first to open fire on the little aliens with their sound-suppressed rifles. York was the last to enter the hub and found the aliens all dead. He looked up towards Captain Becker and could see behind him a larger alien coming down another tunnel that Becker had his back to.

"Cap, get down!" he yelled as he brought his rifle up and started shooting. A larger alien, about half the size of the big guy from before, now rolled the rest of the way down the tunnel, dead. Everyone stood still for a moment, feeling the rush of adrenaline through their veins.

Becker rose to his feet and looked around at the three tunnels and two walkways that joined the hub. Walking over to one of the walkways to look outside. He noticed it descended a few hundred feet below ground. John would have loved to have the time to just study it but a feeling of impending doom was now growing all around him.

"Hollister, Hess, guard the room. Kill anything that enters. York, Peters, fill your packs and pockets with anything you find. I will set the bomb." Becker went to the center of the hub and accidentally put his hand on a blue-colored post that was about four feet high. Suddenly, he stopped. Everyone saw it as a holographic projection was activated that filled the whole room. Becker was unsure what his next move should be as he realized it was talking to him. Not in words, but in his mind.

"What do you require?" the Hub asked in his mind.

Becker had no clue how to respond. It was obvious that the alien hub was analyzing his thoughts. "Do you require more information on all Proto Homo Propensive life forms and their histories?" It asked his mind.

Without a pause, John unconsciously thought, "Yes." Unsure as to what he just agreed to.

"One moment," the hub responded back.

John looked down to see the blue post producing a small silver stick with a red tip just like the one that he'd brought into the Joint Chiefs' office.

"Your request has been completed," the post spoke to his mind as John took his hand off the post and picked up the silver stick. Giving only a second to ponder things John spoke up to everyone. "Hurry men!"

The hub was not an empty room like many of the places in the city. It had workstations, round platforms, and what looked like crystal storage lockers. York and Peters raided all the spots they could while Becker set up the bomb. John finalized the programming of the bomb by setting the timer for thirty-five minutes. He paused and shook his head as he discovered he could feel the 'after-effects' of the mind link he had with the alien computer.

Hess noticed that John was struggling to orient himself. "Cap, are you okay?"

Hess's question made John refocus. "Yep, I'm fine. Just pushing the button now. We've got thirty-five minutes. Everyone GO! Run," He ordered.

In a mad scramble, everyone launched back up the tunnel. After a few moments of running, Peters, who was in the rear, heard a noise behind them. Turning to look, he could see two aliens coming up fast.

"Cap! We got company!" Peters yelled.

Becker turned to see what Peters saw and yelled. "Use a grenade!"

Peters was already on it when Becker yelled. Pulling the pin, Peters tossed it behind him.

When Becker turned his head forward once more he saw a large alien like the first one they found coming down the tunnel. "Not another one," John exclaimed.

John cut loose in full auto with his rifle, filling the alien's chest with holes. His massive body collapsed and started sliding down the tunnel as the grenade went off behind the team.

The explosion caused the tunnel to react violently. Everyone struggled to stay on their feet as they kept moving upward. The grenade explosion opened a hole in the side of the tunnel, effectively expelling the aliens that were behind them. Falling to the levels below they bounced off other tunnels and walkways below as they slipped into the darkness of the city. Everyone however was trying hard to dodge the dead alien that was quickly picking up speed as he slid toward them. Hess had the hardest time. Being older, he could not flex or react as fast as the younger men. His leg made contact with the sliding alien, knocking him off his feet to slide on his back. York reached out and grabbed him by his arm, saving him from being totally swept away by the giant.

Due to his speed and massive weight, the alien shot out the end of the tunnel as if being launched from a catapult, bouncing off the central core of the city. John Becker watched with relief. "So much for stealth. It's likely we've woken the whole city now." John exclaimed.

At the top of the tunnel, the men entered back into the room only to find that the alien had killed Benton, and Baker was almost dead. Peters handed off the pack he was carrying to Hess and threw Baker over his shoulder.

Hollister grabbed Benton's body and carried him, as they moved quickly through the rooms. Soon they jumped over the dead alien they had fought before. Shortly after that, they entered the viewing room where they'd gotten their first sight of the dome city.

Captain Becker took one more glance as he waited for York and Hollister to get ahead of him. Finally, he turned to join them as he checked his watch. From behind him, he heard a deep voice that seemed to echo within the city, "Captain John Becker." The sound of it made everyone freeze in place as all eyes turned to look at the window.

Becker turned around to look at the city and saw a very large holographic projection suspended in the center of the city, facing him. It was his own image and it was talking to him. The voice was deeper with a crackling in the background that echoed off the city walls. "You are clever, but your plans will not succeed."

Hollister looked over at John. "How?"

" Two way transfer, It must have happened in the hub when I touched the post. They got in my head," John remarked in amazement.

Hollister, who was carrying his dead comrade, grabbed John's arm. "Stop looking at it. Let's take what we've got and get out of here." Hollister exclaimed. Jerking his Captain hard enough that John's eyes broke away from the image that had him mesmerized. John turned and followed his men out.

The Present

"I got a text message from Danny. I mean Daniel. He is still running late but he wants to know about our schedule?" Megan asked.

Henry was straightening up after a drink from a water fountain. "Find out how late. We can either meet in a hotel room or have dinner at a restaurant. There is a great little place on Hayes Street, just on the other side of the highway."

Megan began texting back as her father stepped to the side to talk with General Bond who was passing by.

Megan overheard them talking about the next meeting and what would happen next as she texted back and forth with her brother. Out of the corner of her eye, Megan noticed Admiral Goodrick standing in the distance, observing them.

Fading Starlight

He was motionless like a statue, just watching. She found it a little unnerving but she turned back to her father and put it out of her mind. "Daniel can meet us at the restaurant in forty-five minutes," Megan remarked.

General Bond looked at Henry with a smile. "Let me guess, Fyve's restaurant?"

Henry smiled back. "At least you'll know where to find us if you need to."

"You're a creature of habit, Henry," Victoria responded.

The Future

The team came bursting into the underground tunnel right in front of Andrew who had occupied his time playing games on an old cell phone. Becker was yelling out updates and orders. "They made us, the bomb has been compromised, Benton is dead and Baker is down. Let's get out of here as fast as we can."

Scrambling, the team pushed as hard as they could in the mud with their electric carts. Baker was slowly waking up and began moaning from the pain. It eventually turned to scream with each bump they hit in the tunnel. Hess took out an electric syringe and shot him with some painkillers through his shirt. Soon their eyes could just start to see the end of the tunnel in the far distance. Andrew looked at John and asked what happened.

"I think they found the bomb," Becker responded.

"When is it supposed to go off?" Andrew asked.

John looked down at his watch, "In about two minutes."

Back in the hub, one of the larger aliens who was built, as Private Baker remarked earlier, "like a pencil,"

stepped behind a workstation to find a pile of the smaller aliens, dead. With his long, skinny fingers he pushed them to the side revealing the device that Captain Becker had buried with the bodies. Bending down to examine it, he moved to the side and then picked it up to examine it. His long fingers almost covered two entire sides of the device. With curiosity he turned it around, slowly, to get a better look at it. A little frustrated, he gave it a good shake to see if it did anything.

A great roar and rumble overtook the tunnel rolling over the top of John and the team as they were attempting to evacuate. Dirt and rock began falling everywhere as the end of the tunnel outside turned violently red. A fireball of intense power quickly rolled by the opening as everyone clung to rocks or each other to shield themselves. One larger rock fell and firmly planted itself in the tunnel, blocking the carts from driving any further.

After a few moments, the roar started fading and the dust began to settle but they still couldn't see more than a foot or two around them. The only real visibility came from a few handheld lights the men had. Protecting their heads, the rocks eventually stopped falling and leaving only the sound of the men coughing.

Andrew, who rolled over on his back, coughed and spoke up, "Did I forget to mention that I built that bomb out of old unstable parts?"

The comment brought some laughter but it wasn't enough to overcome the stress and anxiety felt by the whole team as they gagged for better air.

Struggling, they left the carts and made their way around the rocks as men spit and coughed. Reaching the end of the tunnel they found Stuart Maxwell in a radiation suit pinned between two large rocks. The glass visor of his suit was cracked and he had one eye partly swollen shut. He used his one good eye to watch the men approach and oddly, they looked worse than he felt.

Two of the men worked to get Maxwell out of the rocks as the captain went to see how Baker was doing.

Like dirty moles, Becker's team finally left the tunnel and made it to the surface. Pausing for a second in better air they all stood, looking at the "renovations" their bomb had just created. Wisps of smoke and fire reached height into the night sky. Hollister nudged John's arm, "Becker, look over there at Madrid."

The great dome was gone. From their position, they could see green and blue flames burning deep in the massive crater. The sight of it brought extreme relief to the men as they started to whoop and holler with excitement. After a little while, the light within grew brighter as flames reached high into the sky. Then a smaller "pop" from some internal explosions and finally the light died down to a dim glow.

The darkness of that moonless night slowly overtook the burning glow of the city. As it did, the men looked around at the countryside. "Wow. Captain, look," Hess remarked as he pointed.

There on the mountainside, just above what used to be the small city of Mataelpino, rested a large chunk of that once impenetrable dome. The fading blue and green firelight of the city was reflecting off this massive shard that was now shoved deep into the mountain like the edge of a knife.

"The Russians bombed that thing like crazy and even used a nuke on it. I guess you need to get it from underneath." Everyone half-heartedly laughed at Andrew's comment.

Feeling every bit of the emotion of the moment, Becker opened his mouth to give some orders. "Listen up. I want everyone to double up on their Zeolite pills to flush the radiation out of their systems. We need to bury Baker and get going. We have a long hike back to Valladolid and then we need to get a transport to Ireland to catch our ride back home."

The Present

The day had turned out rather nice. The rain had threatened the Arlington area earlier but now the sun had fully emerged. It would make for a wonderful sunset later in the day.

Henry took his daughter to Fyve's restaurant, located inside the Ritz Carlton. The sophisticated yet simple decor was impressive to Megan. Not unexpected considering how close it was to the Pentagon. She was grateful that the seating hostess escorted them to one of the more intimate, out-of-the-way corners where conversations did not need to be controlled as much.

Megan and Henry waited for some time before Daniel came in. Wondering what he looked like, after all these years, they soon found out. The seating hostess escorted to their table a well-dressed man in a dark coat, dress shirt, and blue jeans toward them. As he walked, Megan took note of his thin frame and slight limp. Megan's growing nervousness mixed with excitement was a giveaway to her father that he had arrived.

Henry turned around just as he neared the table. He stood to offer his hand. "Daniel."

Daniel shook his hand with reserved emotion, "Father."

Megan stood up and Daniel turned to offer his hand to her. She took his hand as she fought back tears of joy. After a quick moment of handshaking, she pulled him closer by the hand into a tight hug. Henry stood there feeling a little awkward and unsure. The hug lasted for several seconds, and both realized how much they needed it. Finally, she let him loose and Daniel sat down next to her.

Megan almost exploded in a flurry of questions and totally dominated the table as she had to know everything. At that moment, she was not a single

111

mother in her thirties with a Captain's pin attached. To Henry, she was fourteen again, giddy and alive and unable to complete her sentences. It was fun to watch and to see his son try to interrupt her with answers.

Looking over his son, Henry felt a sense of loss as he noted a few scars on his sons left hand as well as a small, faded one on his chin. It must have been a few hours since he last shaved and Henry could see some white stubble under his sideburns. Oh, how much he had missed. Finally, Henry decided to interrupt.

"Megan . . . Megan," he added as put his hand on her arm. "Don't you think you should come up for air and let your brother answer your questions?"

Daniel was secretly thankful for what his father did even though he was not going to let him see it. Taking a moment to collect his thoughts, "Well, Wendy's back home. We both felt it would be best if I came alone this time to see how everything goes. Wow, it's good to see you, Meg."

The waiter came up to offer menus. Henry saw him approaching and put up a hand toward him. "Paul, give us a few minutes."

"As I said on the phone, Wendy and I have been married for almost two years now. We are getting ready to move out of our apartment and into a townhome. However, the firm I am working for is talking about offering us a job in Boston," Daniel remarked.

At the mention of Boston, Megan and Henry looked at each other for a moment, reality striking both of them.

Daniel continued, "But I'm not sure if I should take that job and...."

Megan, who was leaning on her elbow on the table interrupted, "Oh, Boston . . . I'm sure they will give you plenty of time to make that decision. Why rush?" Realizing what was about to come out of her mouth Megan slowly moved her hand strategically toward her mouth.

January 14th, 2044
Old Schoolhouse Bed and Breakfast in Ballinskelligs, Ireland.

The air was clean and crisp as John found himself standing on the shore of a river with a cascading waterfall in the distance. John felt he was soaking in the vibrant colors of the red canyons and the flickering light on the water. Things seemed incredibly alive with sound and color. Overwhelming feelings like the very world around him was trying to talk to him. As John looked at the water, it seemed like he knew its history and its desire to live. He could feel the age of the canyon as if it wanted him to know everything. Turning he stared at a boulder in the river and the water rushing by it and he felt like it was lamenting its own past; its former glory on the high canyon wall before it fell.

Looking all around. Everything seemed to have a voice. He knew this place; the smells, the sound, the lizards, and the birds. He began to feel like a kid again in the land he knew so long ago. It was like everything was calling him home and he desperately desired to go there. He looked down from the canyon walls and saw a mule deer near the shore. The buck turned his strong, stately head toward John, fixing his gaze directly on him.

"No, this will not be your home. You shall grow old and rest your head far from here before you return." The Buck informed him.

Stunned by this remark, John just stared at the buck, speechless.

Suddenly, John's dream came to an end as a small group of men came bursting into the darkness of his room. Their entrance was so violent that John's combat training kicked into full gear. A push, a shove, and then John threw a punch into empty air as the attacker moved out

of the way. John suddenly felt pain in his chest as
something hit him. He bent partly over, in pain, but
then used his head as a battering ram and charged
whoever was in front of him. The two crashed into a
lamp and then the wall.

One of them yelled, "You scum, you scum!" As John
fell backward onto his pack laying on the floor. Two of
the attackers jumped on top of him, pounding him with
something in their hands. John felt the handle of his
knife sticking out of his pack and quickly reached for it.
One of them screamed in pain as John slashed the knife
across him in an attempt to make them stop.

"You scum, you scum! You will pay for what you did!"
someone yelled in the dark.

John rolled and pulled himself up to the wall, trying to
get back on his feet. He could see three men, one
doubled over and two others pulling something with a
green glow out of their pockets.

"You die now! You die now for what you did, human,"
one of them yelled as they began to move forward.
Slowly pointing their green objects at him, John
managed to get his right foot underneath himself. His
mind had no time to think about anything other than
this moment and yet, he quietly heard a voice in his
mind say, "your pack." He then realized that's what
was entangled around his leg. And his pack held his .45
pistol.

John's hand shot down to his pack and for some
reason, he managed to find the compartment in the
dark that held his pistol already open. In an adrenaline-
filled moment, he stepped out of his entangled pack and
raised his entire pack-pack up with his arm, and fired
his .45 directly through the canvas pack.

The man on the right jerked from the impact of the
bullet as another man on the left hissed something as
John watched him fall to the floor. The third man
watched the other fall, turning his head in the dark he
looked back at John and jumped toward him. John
however securely placed two slugs in the man's chest.

Moments later, John's team came storming into the

dark room in their underwear with guns drawn. Hess found the light switch and everyone discovered John was seated on the edge of his bed, holding his gun in one hand and clutching his chest with the other. On the floor lay three men, one near death, the others were already gone. Andrew looked at the men, then at John. He just shook his head, "What?"

Trying to shake off the strange effects of whatever they used on him, John nodded that he didn't know either.

The man whom John slashed with the knife rolled over on his back revealing a deep cut from his stomach to his right ear. Andrew placed the barrel of his gun between the man's eyes and yelled for him to start talking. He almost smiled as he coughed up blood and said with his last breath, "You murderous scum, all you humans, die."

Andrew pulled his pistol back as everyone looked at each other. Could it be? "They look so human. How do we tell the difference?" Andrew asked.

A crowd started to form outside the door; men and women were half awake in the early morning. Young Moyá from the front counter, who had been flirting with Peters earlier in the day, carefully made her way past the crowd. Half listening to John's explanation to his men and half in shock at all the blood on the floor.

Something caught her eye about one of the dead men who was lying face down. She bent down to the body, feeling the tension and fear rising within her. She rolled the man over and her eyes grew large. The men were suddenly aware she was in the room when she let out a small scream. They turned to see her crouched down on the floor with her hands over her face. She looked up at them and then at Peters. Moyá said something in Gaelic that they did not understand and tore out of the room as fast as her feet could move.

Andrew's right eyebrow came up as he bent down to roll the body back over that Moyá had dropped onto its face. As he did, you could feel the air being sucked out of the room by the whole team.

Andrew looked up at John. "Well, I think we have

115

another problem." Their on the floor lay a man whose face was an exact copy of Sergeant Peters.

A couple of the men took a step back from Peters with their guns ready. John looked at his team and remarked, "Don't worry guys. I'm pretty sure the one standing here in his flame-red underwear is the real one."

As the team got dressed and bagged all the alien paraphernalia they could find. John ordered that samples of the Peters' imposter be taken as well. By then, the first evidence of sunlight was coming up over the eastern horizon. Moyá was nowhere to be found as she had left so fast, even her purse rested near a lukewarm cup of tea. Most of the other guests had closed and locked their doors, signaling that they wanted no part of what was going on.

Andrew walked outside to the parking lot. He checked his watch and looked back at Peters, who was following him. The sky was clear and you could smell the cold sea air of the Atlantic moving towards them. "Peters, it will be morning soon, and our ride should be landing. I want everything loaded and in the air as soon as we can." Andrew informed him

Peters nodded back as he put his coat on.

"Where is the Captain?" Andrew inquired.

"Captain Becker just went back in to take one last look at the room. He seemed to be in a lot of pain, Sir." Peters responded back.

"Watch the skies, I will be right back." Andrew ordered as he handed him a pair of binoculars and walked back to the building. He found John emerging from under the bed. "Find something?"

"I'm not sure, but I think it's whatever they hit my chest with." John held up something to Andrew that resembling a black stick, about as big around as a half dollar and as long as his hand.

Andrew took it from him and held it closer to the one working light in the room. "It's light, not many features on it, but it does look like you can turn it on from the bottom," Andrew responded back as he did just that. The device produced a few small needle-like points on

116

one end. Seconds after the points came out, they developed a faint light blue glow. Then a small "crackle" of energy moved between the points.

"Wow," Andrew remarked.

"Tell me about it. That alien stun gun burned a bunch of small holes in my chest," John sarcasticlly informed him. Andrew turned to look at John, whose unbuttoned shirt revealed the red and swollen battle scar.

"Does it sting?" Andrew asked.

"Some but it's getting better," John remarked.

Turning the device off and offering his hand to help John off the floor, "I'll toss it in the bag with the rest of the alien toys we don't understand." Andrew remarked.

The team stood outside in the cool Atlantic air waiting for a hover-helo to arrive. John went back inside to try and pay for the damages but Moyá was still missing. So he ended up leaving some money under the computer keyboard with a note of apology.

Walking back out, daylight was just starting to illuminate the yellows and greens of the B&B as the hover-helo could be seen in the distance. As they grew closer, the team noticed it was not a hover- helo but a larger transport.

"I guess Stuart decided we needed something bigger," remarked Andrew.

"Hmm, well, radio and tell him there's no place to land near the B&B. His transport's too big. Have him use the field just to the northeast of us near the intersection. We will pack everything up there." John ordered.

Soon the hover-transport, which looked more like a cross between a jet and helicopter, was coming to a landing in the green field. Most of the men were in place with their gear. A small truck from one of the farmers had also reached the intersection. An older, white-haired man stopped his weathered light blue truck to take in the sight of it all.

Hess and Hollister looked at the driver with a smile on their faces. "I bet they don't see this everyday around here," commented Hollister.

Lunar Orbit—Alien Command Ship

Down the dark halls of the vast ship on the far side of the moon walked a smaller alien holding a crystal. He walked through the holographic wall to the control room of the vessel. A taller alien, who looked almost totally human except for his elongated head, was standing in the center of the room.

The little alien bowed in respect and handed him the crystal. Holding it in his bony hand, he looked it over for a moment then he gently tossed it into the air. It stopped at about head height and dissolved into light.

The holographic image around him changed into a collection of moving images from the explosion in Madrid. He spotted what he wanted and enlarged it, stopping on a single frame. With a growing look of disgust, the alien examined a picture of Captain Becker.

A good hour passed, filled with conversation, and then the better part of another. Most of the time Megan and her father just listened to Daniel tell stories about getting mugged and thrown off the train that crashed two days later, falling off the roof of a house to break his leg from doing construction, as well as being trapped in a shed by a drunk housewife's dog for a day until she came to.

Daniel talked about repairing an old gentleman's house, Mr. Kepler, who figured out he had an eye for design. Mr. Kepler turned out to be the senior partner in an architectural firm and he was willing to mentor Daniel. He figured it was a mutually supportive opportunity since he had a bad leg from falling off the roof and the Keplers had no children.

"So Megan, on the phone you said you had a son but that you are a single mother now. If you don't mind me asking, what happened? Do you still see each other?" Daniel asked.

Henry looked down at his drink, sad for his daughter, but at the same time wondering how she would respond.

Megan softly responded back, "Well, Thomas was killed in Iraq."

Daniel's face changed as he responded, "Oh, I'm sorry, Sis. I didn't mean to...."

"No, that's all right Daniel. It's okay. We met in the Army during a tour in Iraq. When our units returned to the States, we got married. It was a wonderful time. We had Johnny and then one day the Army sent Thomas back for his second tour. Four months into it, his convoy got pinned down. Half the men died, Thomas included. After that, I got a degree in archaeology and Johnny and I as well as the rest of my team have been kicking around the desert ever since."

"I am sorry to hear it but I'm just a little confused. You're still wearing a uniform?" Daniel asked.

Megan suddenly realized what she had just said. At this moment she was wondering how she should proceed. Project Lorenzo is classified, but at the same time, what they are finding out is a matter so incredibly central to the family.

"Sis, for the first time tonight, you're silent. What's up?" Daniel asked.

Henry decided to speak up. "I'm sorry, Daniel, there have been some recent events that made the Army feel it would be wise to recall Megan back to active service. Your Sister has some, shall we say, unique skills, specific to this assignment. It's all classified so she can't speak about it."

Daniel gave his father a slightly resentful look and then turned to Megan who was looking at the table. "So you got in, the Army killed your husband, you got out, and then they pulled you back in. Right?"

Megan did not respond. She felt a little trapped with what she knew.

"Like father, like daughter," Daniel coldly remarked.

Megan's face shot up, "That's not fair."

"Really? For years, Dad kept secrets. He put up walls and kept us out. Now it looks like you're doing the same." Daniel remarked.

Megan started to open her mouth but stopped. She looked at Daniel and then Henry, and then looked off in the distance to the fireplace across the room. Henry looked straight at Daniel. "My God, son, you're not a kid anymore. How long are you going to keep beating that dead horse? Don't blame your sister; she had enough happen in her life. If you want to blame somebody, then blame me, or the Army, or fried green tomatoes. I really don't care, but leave your sister out of this. I'm sure, once she is no longer needed, the Army will cut her loose. In fact, I will make sure of it."

Henry was starting to get the same look on his face that his son had. "She has been doing a fine job raising her son and she's a brilliant archaeologist. In fact, it's this skill that the Army needs her for right now. I am proud of her skills, her team, and what she has done with her life. Henry calmed down a little but they never broke eye contact with the son.

With a cold look, Daniel responded. "When I was growing up it seemed that all you really wanted was an Army family that walked, talked, and looked like you—clones."

Henry reflected on those words. "Yeah, well, I'll be honest. That's what I thought I wanted. Recent events," looking at Megan, "have changed my mind."

That comment caught Daniel a little off guard. "Recent events?"

With a bit of frustration, knowing how it would sound to Daniel, Henry responded, "Well, it's all related to the classified assignment that Megan's involved in."

"Oh, how convenient," Daniel sarcastically responded back.

Henry looked at the growing hardness in his son's

eyes. "No, it's not like that. All you really need to know is that I have come to the realization in the last few weeks that I have been the south end of northbound water buffalo to my family."

"Dan, when I got married, you could have fit everything I knew about raising a family into a shot glass and it wouldn't have even made it to the halfway mark. I used the only system I knew, the Army. I know now that it was a terrible mistake to replace love with structure."

The fire in Daniel's heart was slowly being replaced with confusion and traces of compassion. Megan turned away from the fireplace, her green eyes were wet from the emotion of the moment. Henry caught sight of it and the toughness in his eyes began to melt.

Daniel felt a little uncomfortable with this new image of his father. The "old man" sitting in front of him somehow seemed a little less like barbed wire fencing and more like someone with a broken heart. The dark hair and mustache he knew as a kid were more salt and pepper now. And the lines on his face indicated more road miles than he could imagine. The awkward silence after Henry spoke left Daniel feeling strangely numb, yet a little painful.

"Dan..... Daniel, I need to tell you and Megan something. Even if I never see you again." Henry remarked he as lowered his face toward the table. "I am sorry that I'm your father."

Megan moved her hand across the table to rest it on her father's hand that was holding his half-empty drink. Megan's napkin had a few tear spots on it that had dripped off her chin. Silently she sat, just resting her hand on his.

The heaviness of the moment was starting to rest on everyone's jumbled emotions as Daniel was not sure about his own feelings at this point.

The waiter who was bringing the check rounded the corner, noticed what was going on, and turned around, thinking it best to 'give them more time.'

"I'm... not sure what to say," Daniel replied, as his

voice grew a little shaky.

Henry looked up with watery eyes. "Can you forgive me?" Henry blinked to focus and then looked at Megan as well. "Can both of you forgive me?"

The mention of those words only made Megan's fingers squeeze her father's hand a little stronger. Daniel took a deep breath as he looked at his sister to see what she would do. "Sis?" Daniel asked Megan.

"I already have Dan," Megan responded without turning her eyes away from her Father.

Daniel looked around the room and then up to the white-painted ceiling. "Yeah. It's time I guess." lowered his head Daniel looked at Henry, "I forgive you too, Dad."

The Future

The hover transport landed just outside of Saint Johns's New Brunswick alowing the team could transfer to another craft. As they unloaded and then reloaded their equipment for the next phase of their trip, Hess saw Becker hand Andrew a paper envelope. Andrew shook John's hand and walked off.

"What's up?" Hess inquired.

"I have a job for him. He will meet up with us a little later," John remarked without further information.

Hess asked, "Do we have a secure location to go to yet?"

Becker pushed the last bag into the craft. "We do, but we will only be there for a little while before we move again."

"Sounds fun. I'm hoping we end up somewhere that we can get a decent burger," Hess sarcastically commented.

Becker climbed in and offered a hand to Hess. "Only if you cook it."

Looking a little aggravated Hess responded back,

"Like I said, fun."

Present Day

Henry, who was paying the bill at the restaurant, reached inside his uniform to pull out his phone which just made a noise. "Hmm."

Megan and Daniel looked at him as Megan asked, "News?"

"The main event is at 07:00 tomorrow," Henry responded back.

Fading Starlight
Chapter Five
**The Traveler in
Eternity.**

The team spent several days outside Green Bay at a secure facility while a small group of scientists examined the Madrid collection. Walking past them Hollister picked up a cup of coffee from a small desk as he looked at some guys in white coats. He blew on his coffee in an effort to cool it as he turned a doorknob into a small warehouse office.

Peters and Becker looked up from what they were reading to see who was coming in.

"Anything new?" John asked.

"Yeah, one of the scientists will be in shortly," Hollister responded back.

Hollister sat down in a hard-backed chair, spilling a small amount of hot coffee on his hand. Trading his hands, he shook off the coffee as John smiled and looked back down. Peters, lightly grinned at Hollister as he noticed one of the scientists walking up to the room through the glass window.

"Heads up, here he comes," Peters announced.

Dr. Harper, a young British scientist, walked in. "Captain Becker, I have the report on the skin samples you gave me." Everyone looked up, especially Peters.

"All the samples initially appeared to be normal. However, we finally determined that although this 'being' is predominately human, it's also something else." Harper remarked.

John's eyebrows lifted. "You mean he was a clone?"

"Please know that he was genetically engineered to look exactly like your man but there's no genetic material in common between him and Peters. He was more like a synthetic copy of a human, made to look like someone you know." Dr. Harper responded.

"Synthetic copy," muttered Hollister.

John stood up and walked across the room, looking for a moment at the map on the wall. "So they are able to make copies of people. People we know."

"How do we trust anyone?" Hollister added.

Dr. Harper interjected, "Also, Captain, the other scientists wanted me to let you know that they will have their reports ready shortly."

John, who had turned to look at Dr. Harper, looked back at the map and remarked, "Hollister, get the rest of the team together. Let's all hear the reports together."

"Got it." Hollister tried to take another sip of his coffee before he stood up but only managed to spill it again. He gave up and set it down on the table and excused himself as he passed the doctor.

Present Day

Master Sergeant Dave Shaver was just finishing up cleaning duties from dinner when he heard a chopper quickly approaching. He put down the kettle he was carrying and walked outside to see Major Watson watching it approach.

"Were we expecting anyone, Major?" Dave asked.

"Nope, but it's got Navy markings," Watson added as the wind from the rotors started to move the dust around them.

The chopper only landed long enough to drop off three men in dark suits with sunglasses. Major Watson's eyes narrowed as walked up to the lead man who was about the same size as himself. He noted the extremely clean-cut look the man had and challenged him as he approached. "Since a Navy bird just dropped you off, I'm assuming that you have the proper clearance to enter a restricted zone?"

Fading Starlight

The man did not smile or show any emotion as he stepped forward to answer the Major. "I'm Johnson, this is Davis and Lopez. We are here at the request of the Joint Chiefs of Staff to monitor the situation." Major Watson looked over the men. "That's it? Just Johnson, Davis, and Lopez, are here to monitor. Nothing else?"

"Yes that's it," Johnson responded back.

"I'm thinking you guys are CIA and this whole thing just ruffled some feathers in that five-sided foxhole in Washington," Watson answered back.

Lopez, who was a little shorter and looked more Asian than Hispanic, cracked a fake smile as Johnson reached into his coat and handed Watson some paperwork. "No comment."

Watson looked over the paperwork as Johnson continued in a mono-tone voice, "These are our authorization papers. We would like to see the cave now."

The Future

Hollister got everyone together in the lab, which was nothing more than just a large, empty area in the warehouse. Becker then ordered Dr. Harper to repeat his findings for everyone.

Dr. Rodriguez was next, talking about the returned alien hardware and some of their discoveries. Unfortunately, as he reported, they could actually only report on what it did; they couldn't yet however explain how it worked. The equipment was so far advanced, technologically, that they could only guess at this point. One thing they did know was that the aliens did not use holograms to create or control images, they used particle synthesis.

Next, it was Dr. Healey's turn to talk about physics. Everyone listened, but after a while, John interrupted, "Okay, Doc. I've got a fairly good understanding of physics and mathematics, in general. But what you're describing is like some new level of quantum physics," Becker remarked.

"Sorry to correct you once more, Captain, but what I have been trying to say is this is not quantum physics. At least not how we understand quantum physics. It's something way beyond that. Let me try to explain part of it and maybe you will understand. Tow-kef is the closest the aliens come to assigning a name to the unseen energy that pulls all things through time."

"What do you mean, 'pull through time?'" Captain Becker inquired.

"Well, you see, that's the thing really. Time is not what we thought it was. According to what I'm finding, time is actually a byproduct, not the main product itself." Dr. Healey answered back.

"Doctor Healey, you're talking in riddles," Becker remarked as he raised his right eyebrow.

Healey walked closer, "I know, I know. Please bear with me on this one. The second law of thermodynamics states that all things are moving towards decay, right?"

"Right," Becker responded.

"To the aliens, that's Tow-kef, what we call death. It pulls all things along the timeline. If you can turn off the effect for a moment, then for that moment, time has no power over you. You will be temporarily outside of time." Dr. Healey answered.

John sat there, taking it in. "But Doctor, for that moment, when you are outside of time, where are you?"

The doctor leaned in as his eyes grew wider, "That's the really exciting bit. The aliens don't have a word for it but based on current descriptions, I'm calling it eternity."

John Becker did not know what to say as Dr. Healey had the look of a little kid who'd just got to tell his biggest secret. "You see, this is more complicated than anything we have ever thought of. And at the same time, it's very, very simple. Time and eternity are like oil and water, totally separate, and yet, at the same time, they can co-exist and have an effect on each other. Cool, right?"

John, whose mind was still a little stuck at the word "eternity," as he echoed the word "cool" out loud as if he was following the doctor's exciting tale.

"All things in this world are subject to the Tow-kef effect but not all things have eternity within them. Even though all things are subject to eternity. As a result, time pulls on all things but it cannot pull on eternity because it has no decay within it. It is, in effect, eternal. The aliens know this and they have had the technology for time travel all this time."

Sergeant Peters, who was tracking it in his head a little faster than the Captain was, spoke up. "So why haven't they used it?"

Healey stepped up to him and put his hands on his shoulders. "That's the even cooler part. They can't. They're scared of it. Terrified."

"Why?" John spoke up.

"Because apparently there is no trace of eternity within them. They are in complete decay. That's why they look the way they do. I am thinking that many of them have a very short lifespan." At this point, Healey started to suspect he had lost his audience. "Okay, let me back up. Time and eternity exist in all things, including us. The degree or amount of each affects lifespan. Eternity is life and time is death. Eternity has always existed. It's not so much unchanging, rather it's ever-changing. It moves, and breaths, it is the very definition of life itself. Time, however, seems to have had a starting point and is just as alien to eternity as the aliens are in this world. So the reason that the aliens are scared of eternity is—"

"—because eternity does not exist within them so they are devoid of true life," Peters remarked.

"Yes, you're starting to get this. How exciting!" Exclaimed the doctor.

Peters had an odd look on his face. "Not long ago I had to fight one of them, face to face. All I could think of, when I looked into his face, was how evil he was."

"All they ever say in the documents is that it is

painfully changing. And I might know why that is." The doctor remarked.

The words, "painfully" struck a cord within Captain Becker. Hoping this might lead to something to use against his enemies, he looked straight into the eyes of Doctor Healey. "Tell me what you know."

Doctor Healey smiled. "It's all about DNA, the base of who the aliens really are. We see different kinds of aliens: tall, short, long necks, short necks, and even changes in skin color. But they are all the same; they are not different races. These aliens are unnaturally born; they are created by the manipulation of DNA in a laboratory. If they want a tall one, they make a tall one. It's as simple as that. So they are artificial which is why there is no eternity in them. My guess is that they can only exist as long as Tow-kef has a limited effect on them. Eternity would most likely undo much of the DNA manipulation within them if they suddenly encountered it."

"Why do you think that, Doctor?" John asked.

"Because oil does not mix with water. Once you release the Tow-kef on an object that does not have true life within it, eternity and Tow-kef collide, distort, and rip. Time would then distort within the object or person. I would think that would be very painful." Healey responded back.

Peters looked at the doctor. "So they can manipulate the basic code of life but they cannot create life?"

"Correct," responded the Doctor.

"Doctor Healey, can we use this to travel through time? And if so, how would that work?" John asked in an official manner as he folded his arms.

The doctor got a look on his face, pondering it for a moment, and then looked at Peters. "Mr. Peters, can I borrow your hand for a moment?"

"Sure, Doc." Sergeant Peters answered as he offered his hand. The doctors then had him make a fist with his thumb and index finger extended.

"So let's pretend for a moment that Sargent Peter's

129

hand is going to time travel and this rubber band represents the reality that holds his hand in place. I am now going to put a rubber band across his fingers." Healey remarked as he smiled at Peters.

"So let's say my right-hand takes hold of the band on the right side and it represents eternity and my left, of course, represents Tow-kef. Tow-kef, or death, pulls slightly harder than the eternity side, pulling the object along the timeline. If I pull even harder, stretching the band even more, then this would give the perception that time has increased and death is closer. But what if I suddenly let go of the Tow-kef side? What happens?"

"Snap!" Went to the rubber band as the doctor released it.

After a second the doctor commented on what everyone just witnessed. "One side snapped back against the other causing the Sergeant's hand to respond by moving slightly in the opposite direction. "This effectively demonstrated that for a brief moment, time had no effect on the object and it resided for a moment in eternity by its move forward.

John questioned, "Okay, I get that. But how does that help? The object would only come back to the time they left. That would be a mighty short trip."

The doctor pulled the rubber band off Peters' fingers as he responded back. "That's because we carry a measure of Tow-kef relative to the time we are now in. Theoretically, if you entered eternity and then exited with a different Tow-kef/time measure, then you would appear in that time. Eternity is everywhere so in my mind contains doors through which you can exit to any point in time."

John raised his hand to his chin, rubbing it as he thought it out. "How do we do it, Doc?"

"Well, there are a lot of very complex calculations to figure out, but I think it can be done," Healey responded back.

John turned around to look over the warehouse. "Doctor Healey, pack your bags and equipment. Pull together whatever support staff you need. You're going to be leaving tonight for a new location that's more secure."

Doctor Healey's excitement abruptly ended with that

comment.

For the first time in this meeting, he had no words. John turned his head to speak to Ben. "Hollister, you will oversee the transfer of personnel and equipment. Acquire whatever resources you need to make this happen. Hess, make arrangements for transport. We will be flying to the southwest to meet up with Andrew." Captain Becker then reached down to the table and collected his paperwork, turned, and left the room.

Doctor Healey turned and looked at Sergeant Peters with a look of "What the—?"

The Present

The moon was a sliver of white silver resting high in the night sky over the canyon. The faint aromatic memories of Dave's cooking had carried most of the camp off to sleep. Leaving only the men on guard duty to watch the night calmly march through the hours. In the faint light of the moon, Agent Lopez moved quietly around the rocks just upwind from the camp. His outline if it could be seen showed he was carrying something in his hands.

There was a faint "hiss" of escaping air as he placed his object in the rocks. A few feet away, the gas mixed with the canyon air, forming a light fog, and slowly drifted into the camp as it made its way through the canyon. One of the guards on duty looked over and noticed the strange sight.

From behind him, agent Johnson put on a strange-looking glove. He tapped the guard on the shoulder and as he turned, he put his gloved hand over the man's face. Feeling paralyzed, the man was slowly lowered as Johnson moved the guard and then sat him down on a rock. Agent Johnson then leaned in close and whispered in his ear, "It was a calm night and I did not see anything unusual."

At 05:00 in the morning, Henry's alarm went off. Sitting up in bed, Henry rubbed his tired eyes as his ears could hear a sound next door. In the next room, he could hear Megan's alarm going off as well. Then he heard her hand banging on something to make it stop. Henry smiled and looked over at his briefcase.

He got up and walked to the window. Night still controlled the city skyline as the sun had not yet come up. Reflecting on yesterday's meeting with Daniel. He said more than he'd planned; things he never thought he would voice to his children. But in the end, he felt better about it. In some ways, he was on unsure ground with his family. But on the flip side, it felt stronger than anything he had known in the past.

Henry then heard his cell phone vibrate on the nightstand. It was Megan and it made him smile a little reading the message. "What time do they pour the coffee around here?"

Josh, who loved to sleep with his face buried in his pillow, was protected from the fog as it traveled through the camp. He woke up to what sounded like a helicopter. With only his pants on he walked outside to see what was going on. He noticed that no one else was awake and the strange CIA men were loading boxes into the chopper. Everything within him knew something was wrong. He quickly approached the men.

"Hey! Hey you, hold on there," Josh commanded.

Johnson turned, revealing that he was wearing something that looked like a gas mask. His eyes looked a little strange, full of anger. Moving swiftly Johnson kicked Josh in the chest, tossing him backward. Josh landed on his back and was halfway back onto his feet when Johnson landed on him. He held Josh's head down with his gloved hand and motioned for help from another. Davis ran over with a syringe and drove it deep into Josh's chest.

Johnson leaned forward and spoke into Josh's ear. "Life will get progressively more hopeless."

The Future

The hover-helo was flying low over the desert floor to avoid being picked up. Behind it, there were three other helos flying in formation. Hess and Hollister gave Becker a look but said nothing.

Becker smiled, a little puzzled John asked. "The two Ben's are silent?"

Hollister, who was getting tired of sitting in the same spot, decided to speak up. "Sorry Sir, just thinking. We have been in the air for hours and there is nothing out here but sand, rocks, and snakes."

John responded, "A very long time ago when I was a teenager, Andrew and I hiked into a small area that was secluded and very private. That's where we are going, gentlemen. Andrew has been there for days getting things ready with a few old friends."

The rough and rocky desert floor was zipping past them at high speed as John looked at his watch and then at the desert beyond. "We should be there shortly."

Eventually, they began to decelerate and turn towards a very narrow opening in the sandstone world below.

Soon Becker was stepping off the craft to see Andrew walking down from what looked like a small cave in the canyon wall. They shook hands as Andrew pointed up toward the other helos, "Not enough room."

Becker gave him a thumbs up and turned to Hollister who was just getting off the craft. "Ben, they will need to land, one at a time, in this little valley. After that, park them over there where you can conceal them under netting."

"Got it, Cap," Hollister answered.

John slipped his pack over his shoulder and walked up toward the cave with Andrew. "John, we just finished boring out and enlarging the old cave with the Cameron drills. Good thing because I don't think we can recharge the batteries on them anymore."

"Okay. Well, that's one good thing," John remarked.

John and Andrew ducked down a little to enter the cave, walking past a set of tools heaped up on what looked like a stone table. The wall next to it had been carved out by the Cameron drills that melt their way through the stone. The opening shaft was like a hexagon with crude rounded corners and extended only a few short feet inside the rock. The lighting inside revealed a decent-sized cavern of about 80 to 90 feet across.

Four older men with gray hair, old jeans, and suspenders got up to greet Becker. John was shaking hands with all of them as Hollister entered, a little amazed at the whole sight.

"Becker, Andrew, who are these men?" Hollister inquired as he entered in. Andrew turned around with a big smile on his face. "Ben Hollister, let me introduce you to my jar-head friends, the Colorado Steamboat Springs hunting club. A bunch of smelly ex-Marines who just rolled out of the backwoods."

An older man with a long white beard stepped forward, and in a jolly, friendly way announced that this could have never happened without the Marines. This led Andrew to respond in kind as another Marine was about to comment when Becker interrupted. "All right, all right, this could go on all night. Andrew, you want to introduce your buddies?"

Andrew cleared his throat and pointed to the man with the white beard. "Colonel Silas Wilson." Silas looked at Hollister and gave him a friendly finger salute off his eyebrow.

Andrew then pointed to a significant rounder

gentleman with a bad comb-over. "Warrant Officer Jack Peabody and the walking stick of a man behind him is Staff Sergeant Lee Han. To the right, with the coffee cup, is Staff Sergeant Keven Yerkhov. Some of the best duck hunters, trappers, and fishermen you will ever find in Steamboat Springs."

The Present

Henry and Megan, who were fully dressed and ready to leave, were saying goodbye to Daniel in the hotel lobby.

"How long do you guys think you will be in Arlington?" Daniel asked.

Henry put his cell phone in his chest pocket. "Hard telling. These things can take a while. We're at the mercy of their schedule."

Daniel nodded, "Sounds intense. Well, I think I will hang out for the next day or so. Maybe go see some of the monuments and take some pictures to give me design ideas for the future."

Megan happened to look outside to see a car drive up. "Uh, sounds good. Our ride is here. I will text you if we get an open window."

Dan smiled and gave each a hug. After embracing Henry, he looked him in the eye. "I think I would like Wendy to get to know both of you."

"Sounds good, son. I look forward to it," remarked his father.

Daniel watched them walk to the car where a driver was waiting. He couldn't help but wonder where they were going. And why would the Army require Megan's archaeology skills? With a deep sigh of wonder, he turned to walk back to his room.

The Future

Baker helped to bring the last bunk of gear into the cave but he was doing so, carefully, due to his wounds. He sat down on one of the boxes as Hess brought him some water and a few pain pills.

"I see you're still in pain," Hess said.

A tired Baker responded, "Yeah, it's gotten a little better each day. Now it's mostly my leg. The throbbing starts and all the pain just tires me out. If we get into another fight any time soon, I think I'm going to be fairly useless."

Hess slowly nodded his head in agreement as he looked at him with his fatherly eyes. "Just rest, for now, son. We are a long way from any battle line out here in the middle of nowhere."

Baker took the pills and drank his water as he looked around at the cave. "I heard everything the doctor said about time. Is the Captain really thinking we are going to time jump?"

Hess who had sat down not far from him turned from Baker and took a drink of his own water. "No choice. We've got to try something."

As those words sunk in, Baker asked, "What do you mean, no choice?"

Hess took a breath and then exhaled slowly. "Ever heard of the Tollman report?"

"No," Baker responded back.

"Last year a lot of the top people analyzed what the aliens were doing. They basically concluded that they are going to win and we are going to lose. We're fighting a lost cause. The human race will not exist beyond 2046, or at least that's what it says. Only officers and above know about it." Hess remarked.

"That's grim," responded Baker.

"Yes, it is. So personally, if I am going to die, I would rather die trying to do something with the doctor's time contraption than be killed by one of those big-eyed, gray monsters we saw," Hess announced.

136

On the other side of the cave, John was moving some of the gear to make more room when Dr. Healey walked by. "Healey, what do think of this location?"

Healey pulled out an electronic pad and turned it on. "I think it will work fine. Really, I need very little room. It will take more space to build the device than to operate it."

John had a confused look on his face. Seeing the confused look, Doctor Healey commented. "Captain Becker, like I said before, this is one of the most simple yet complex things we have ever encountered. If you were thinking of some old monstrous time machine, like in the movies from a hundred years ago, please stop. It will be an easy thing to stop the Tow-kef effect for a moment. The real trick is to keep the person from coming back to this time."

The doctor stroked his chin as he thought about it. "We are going to need to calculate another time and somehow embody that in the person. In reality, it would be simple if we just had someone on the other end of this journey holding the door open. Then there would be no need for some of this. But we don't, so we are going to have to figure out a time to jump or step into."

Becker was partly lost after he said it was going to be simple. He looked at the doctor for a moment and handed him a bottle of water. "I have every confidence in your ability to complete the task, Doc."

Healey smiled and accepted the water. He turned to walk away when Becker had one last thought. "Doctor Healey."

"Yes," Healey answered.

"Do you have any idea when this will happen?" John inquired.

"I think I can confidently say within one to two weeks," Healey responded back as most of Becker's team overheard his words. Slowly they all turned their heads to look at each other.

Fading Starlight

The Present

General Mullins and Captain Becker were in the process of being escorted down a hall to a much larger room than their last meeting was in.

As the door opened for them Henry was surprised to see the circular arrangement of the room with so many people inside not wearing uniforms. Leaning into Megan's ear he quietly commented, "They brought in some congressmen, watch what you say. This could get real nasty."

That comment made Megan slightly more nervous as a junior officer escorted both of them to their seats. Reaching the chairs in the center of the room Henry looked up to see Bond giving him a serious look that seemed to say, "I'm sorry. I had no idea."

Taking their seats, encircled by the "board. All eyes slowly shifted to the side as the Vice President came in and sat down. Smiling at a few of the congressmen, Colten accepted a drink as he quickly glanced at a note before he raised his voice. "Ladies and gentlemen, officers of the military, the President has asked me to bring into this meeting various congressmen so that we may explain what is going on to them, and why the Army is currently excavating land that belongs to the National Park Service. This will be considered a closed meeting. To get started, General Mead would you like to start?"

General Mead of the Air Force was the first to speak up. "Thank you Vice President. General Mullins, could you condense the chain of events for us?"

"Certainly, General Mead. I was contacted by my daughter, Megan Becker, who was working on an archaeology dig with her team in the southwest region of the state of Utah. I was asked for my help after the original stone carving was found."

Admiral Goodrick pointed up towards a large TV screen that showed a picture of the Army logo. "Is this the carving you are referring to?"

"Yes, Admiral, it is," Henry responded. "Based on the

138

information provided by my daughter as to its age and the fact that we could see there was more information below, it became necessary to bring in additional resources."

"Let the records show he is referring to Major Watson," General Mead added.

Henry continued, "Yes, Sir. Additional digging uncovered more details and eventually, we found ourselves at an impassable entrance to a cave."

Sam Arris of the CIA put his glasses on as he leaned forward. "According to your report, it was found by Private Cameron Huckins, is this correct?"

"Yes," Henry responded. "The situation after that point required the Corp of Engineers to enlarge the pathway to the cave opening. A good-sized stone had fallen in front of it, some time in the past, and largely blocked the entrance. After that, we discovered a captain's rank pin and the gold books."

The Future

Four days had passed since Becker's team arrived at the new site. Becker had spent plenty of time with the doctor learning what he knew and helping him as much as he could. But honestly, all the talk from the "Colorado Steamboat Springs hunting club" from Andrew was starting to appeal to him. He seriously started to fantasize about sneaking out with them to scout out the countryside and see if they could find someplace to do a little fishing or hunting. Being stuck inside this cave was getting to him.

John had been letting his stubble grow into the beginnings of a beard. Ever since Madrid, he had gotten a little lax with some of the rules. After all, it was war and there was the old tradition in the Army to allow men in combat to grow beards, so why shave now?

Walking outside to enjoy a moment of fresh air. To his

surprise, John noticed the sun was going down. Folding his arms, John leaned against the stone wall just to take it in the amber sunset, when Andrew walked up to him.

"What'cha thinkin'?" Andrew inquired.

"Honestly, very little. I'm tired, but there is so much to do. And my back hurts." John commented

Andrew snickered a little, "Wait till you get older. Your back will talk to you every day just to remind you it's still there."

John smiled, "And what are you thinking?"

"Tanaka needs to know. It's been a while since you filed a report." Andrew responded.

John's smiling face grew a little grim as he looked at Andrew. "I will have it ready in the morning."

The Present

Goodrick and Arris bounced questions back and forth off Henry and Megan. They called into question even Megan's grades and her record of service in Iraq. In the end, their questions kept coming back to how convenient it was that the "person" who was talking to them through time was her own son.

The board soon took a break at midday and Megan stood up feeling like screaming at the stupidity of everything. Henry could see it on her face and so could General Bond. The two Generals walked her out into the hallway to find sandwiches being offered. Megan simply stared at the food tray as Victoria spoke up. "You better eat something. You'll want to keep your blood sugar up for the next round. I suggest the roast beef."

Accepting her advice Megan took a bite out of her sandwich and stared down the hallway. "I don't get this. We are bringing them information of a profound nature and they want to talk about how much dirt we moved. And whether or not I followed protocol in

Iraq."

General Bond was selecting his own sandwich as he spoke up. "It's just how things are done around here. Sometimes they have to go down a rabbit trail or two before the big event." Henry remarked as gave his daughter an affirming nod as he turned to pick up a cup of coffee from another passing tray.

Victoria continued, "Don't worry. I will make sure the right questions get asked before the end." Victoria's eyes wandered to the side to see General Ahrens of the Marines walking by. "And speaking of that, if you will excuse me."

Henry looked at his daughter, who was doing her best to hide her frustration. Megan had almost all of her sandwich eaten when a smaller, friendlier-looking man in a dark blue suit walked up to them. His short, dark hair had slight traces of red in his sideburns. He looked somewhat out of place in this high-powered meeting.

He offered his hand, "Hi. I was wondering if I might introduce myself. My name is MacCallister MacWilliam. My friends call me Mac."

Henry gained a slightly friendly look as he shook the man's hand. Megan however looked him straight in the eye. "Nice to meet you MacCallister. And who is MacCallister MacWilliam?"

With a slight trace of a grin, Mac partly ignored her question as he looked at both of them to continue his introduction. "Hello, General Mullins. I've heard a lot about you and your daughter. I represent the Office of Management and Acquisitions. We are a small government agency."

Raising his chin a little Henry responded back with a slight grin he was trying to hide. "I've heard of the Office of Acquisition Management, but not Management AND Acquisitions. Son, are you sure you said that right?" Henry responded back.

"Yes, Sir, I said it correctly. The OAM deals with the acquisition and management of unusual objects and gadgets. I was wondering if I could have a moment of your time later to talk about your operations in the

141

deserts of Utah?" Mac responded back as he pulled a business card out of his chest pocket and gave one to Megan but not one to Henry. "If we don't meet up later, please call me." As the door to the meeting room opened.

With an announcement from a female Lieutenant, everyone was soon summoned back into the meeting room. Henry took another bite of his sandwich and gave the Mac a nod of good by as they departed from each others company.

"Strange little man. Unusual objects and gadgets?" Megan quietly spoke to her father as they walked away.

The Future

In a semi-lit room on an upper floor within a battered military complex, an older gentleman, General Tanaka sat down in an office chair. He had a blue folder in his hand stamped "Wingate." He studied the cover as his hand slowly waved over the right side of his desk. A holographic image came into focus just above the place his hand passed. He moved his index finger over the graphic image of a door, touched and slid it to the right. Below, in red letters, "Area sealed" appeared.

General James Tanaka took a drink from a glass of water that he sat back down to open the sealed folder.

Project Wingate—Final report:

"The following is a brief summary of the United States Army project entitled "Project Wingate."

"This Project was transferred to Captain John K. Becker of the 19th Special Forces Unit, Army Reserve on May 15th, 2042. The purpose and scope of the project are to acquire and assimilate alien technology from each invasion wave on our planet and determine its possible uses in developing a

142

deterrent against our given common foe. This project, as you know, General, has been moved to an underground, hidden compound. It is made up of select scientists and guarded by Captain Becker and his hand-selected team known only by selected members of the Joint Chiefs of Staff, Captain Becker, and members of Project Wingate.

This report is based on recent known events:
A. The Tollman report-2043, stated that the earth would not be able to effectively withstand the continued attack much beyond 2046.
B. The effective planting of alien dome cities in two locations.
C. The information gathered from the Madrid raid.

This report is meant to update General Tanaka. After reviewing three possible courses of action, based on alien technology, it has been determined by Captain Becker to pursue the project code-named, "Wind Tunnel." For the sake of project security, further details can only be discussed face-to-face.
We believe that this project may become viable within the next few weeks.

Signed,
Second Lieutenant Ben Hollister, assistant to Captain Becker."

General Tanaka set the report down and picked up his glass once more. He held it in both hands tapping the glass slowly with one finger as he thought over the report. The General then turned to stare out the window.

Highway 395 was close to his office but no one had driven on it for over a year. The highway was rubble and most of the buildings around were running emergency lighting if they had lighting at all.

He got up slowly, painfully due to his bad hip that was still healing from last year's attack on Washington looked out the window. He reflected on all that had happened. Once a bright city of military and historical life, now dark and smoky, with little fires for the homeless mixed with horrible smells.

143

Unconsciously he whispered to himself, "It's all over."

A female computer voice then interrupted, "I'm sorry. I did not understand the last command. Do you wish to override the security for this room?"

James Tanaka closed his eyes with frustration. "No, retain room security," Tanaka ordered as he walked back to his desk and picked up the folder. "Computer, open shredder."

"I am sorry. Did you want me to open a voice interface with Doctor Mannher?"

Tanaka sighed heavily and responded back, "No, computer. Open the shredder."

"I am sorry. Opening a voice interface with Doctor Mannher would break the security of the room. Do you wish me to override the room security?" The computer asked once more.

Tanaka walked over to a small panel on the wall. Pushing a button and the panel lifted. "Never mind, computer, I will do it myself." He placed the document inside the wall, touched the same button, and watched the document get brighter until it was gone.

As he did, he heard the computer, "Security lifted."

Tanaka scowled in a low, aggravated voice and asked the computer, "Computer, open maintenance schedule. When is the repair crew coming to overhaul your mainframe?"

The computer voice paused for a moment and then spoke, "Maintenance requests were placed by General James Tanaka on February 20th, March 3rd, 8th, 12th, and 20th. All requests were filed and responded to by Staff Sergeant Kevin M...."

Interrupting the computer with aggravation, "STOP. I am not asking for a history of requests. I simply want to know when you're going to get fixed?"

"I am sorry, General. The historical database you are requesting is vast and will take some time to access. Do you wish me to proceed?" The computer voice responded back.

The General never responded. He picked up a small computer pad as he headed for the door. Leaving his room behind, he could hear the computer voice in the background still asking the same redundant questions over and over. Rounding a short corner, he passed by his lower-ranking coworkers, including Jean Abdula, his secretary, who sat just outside his office. Some people were lighting their desks with a flashlight; a few even had candles. Most were learning to use paper and pens to hand-write reports.

With energy being rationed in every form, only the highest-ranking officers and a few key personnel were using computers. The world had become so comfortable with advanced technology that the attacks had now crippled two-thirds of the population. The mid-twenty-first century had come crashing right into the nineteenth century as used computer parts and generators were being shipped around town by horse and cart.

Militaries around the world were reduced to looking for antique ham radios in museums and flea markets just so that they could talk to each other. The situation seemed to bring out either profound selfishness and cruelty or immense kindness and generosity in people.

Most larger cities became a living hell on earth soon after the power fell. In time, the military and local community groups brought back much of the peace that had left. However, away from the cities, the people who had stocked up food and supplies were either overrun or became highly valued teachers, protected by their students.

General James Tanaka came from such a background. As a young boy, he grew up on his family farm. His grandparents were Japanese Americans in Oregon during WWII. Right now, every part of him loved the idea to turn back the clock and just sit next to the grape arbor he remembered from his youth.

Tanaka however became instrumental after Boston. When Dallas fell, much of Midwest farmlands and communities lost their protection when the hungry rioters came. To some, it seemed cruel, but his actions most likely saved much of the nation by preserving agriculture in the United States providing the stability that the nation so badly needed.

It was hard for him to think that everything he had fought for would soon be over. He was so lost in his thoughts that he never noticed the look on Jean Abdula's face as he passed by. It was a look of surprise, not expecting him to exit his office so quickly.

Jean relaxed and watched him walk away, Tanaka was leaving her alone. She picked up what looked like an older laptop. It was plugged into a very small outlet that was hidden just behind her desk. She passed a gold ring that was on her middle finger over the right side of it. It grew very bright all around it. From the side of the laptop came an exact copy of the report that Tanaka had just placed in the shredder.

The Present

Captain Megan Becker had just answered her fourth redundant question from Goodrick when General Ahrens slid up closer to the microphone. "Admiral, if I may, I would like to change the direction of the current questions."

Admiral Goodrick did not like it but politely nodded for him to proceed.

General Ahrens paused for a moment before speaking, "Captain, what year did you say the alien attacks started on Earth, according to the information you found in the cave?"

"2041, Sir," Megan responded.

"I see. Can you please read for us the main text that was written down concerning this attack?" Ahrens requested.

"Yes, Sir." Megan almost didn't need to read it. The words from her son had become etched in her mind like indelible ink.

"On December 7th, 2041, the European continent. The first wave of alien spacecraft attacked Earth. A total of ten ships descended on Spain and France. The engagement lasted a total of two hours and eight minutes."

"All alien craft, except one, were destroyed. The tenth retreated back to space. The French Air Force was the first to respond followed by other local nations. One hundred and eight jet fighters were destroyed and the city of Madrid was leveled by something resembling a nuclear bomb. Total known dead, 5.1 million."

Megan then stopped and looked up from her laptop at General Ahrens.

"Captain Becker, did these writings give any additional information as to why the Spanish and French Air Force had suffered such high losses?" Ahrens continued to request.

"Yes Sir. Captain John K. Becker made journal notes in various other places of his writing as to the alien craft." Megan responded back.

"Please continue, Captain." Ahrens requested.

"Yes, Sir. Reading from his gold journal, I quote, 'The effectiveness of even the smallest alien raider craft seemed to be due to a combined collection of highly advanced technologies. One was an energy shield under the craft that defended it by absorbing energy. The lower, outer hull seemed to be a mixture of palladium, germanium, and a few trace minerals. The aliens within seemed to supercharge this area as if it was a battery. It is our belief that this supercharging has an effect on its anti-gravity properties.'

"The second issue is the craft itself. The outer hull is composed of an unknown aluminum alloy that provides one-way viewing for everyone inside. It is self-regenerating if damaged, and also seems to be photo reactive against bursts of intense light and high energy particles." Megan then stopped once more and looked up from her reading to notice some curious looks on some of the generals' faces. In fact, that would include most of the people in the room.

Fading Starlight

Mac sat far in the back and he was slowly nodding his head as if he had not thought of that idea before.

General Bond spoke up, "General Mullins, you have heard some of this testimony and have personally read many of these writings. Is this correct?"

"Yes, it is," Henry responded.

Ahrens inquired, "In your opinion, how trustworthy is this information?"

"At present, General Ahrens, I have complete confidence in it." Henry responded back.

"And why is that?" General Bond asked.

"My confidence is based on the authenticity of the evidence and how the facts played out during the operation." General Mullins responded back.

The Future
Lunar orbit-Alien ship.

An alien turned his elongated head to examine the holographic images moving around him. He watched the images of Madrid being destroyed not only from the ground but from orbit as well. Just above it, various images of John Becker were displayed. A very small light flashed off to his right. Turning, he placed his index finger in the center of that light.

The light expanded into a small, three-dimensional box. He took hold of the box and brought it up in front of him. It opened into the image of a paper letter. It was the letter that General Tanaka thought he had destroyed.

Anger slowly moved across his dark face as he spoke in a human, Middle Eastern accent to the unseen, smaller aliens behind him, "Release the hunters. Find the target."

Doctors Rodriguez, Harper, and Healey, with the two guys they brought, were working on some odd-looking, round equipment when Andrew walked back in from the outside.

"So what are these things for?" Andrew inquired.

Healey smiled and motioned for Andrew to hand him some tools. "To protect us."

Andrew just gave him a look. "Doc, I often don't understand a lot of what you have said. So for once, could you expand on that just a little for me?"

"Sure. When we open the door to step through, it will open for everyone and everything in this room. We really only want the main team to travel and not the rest of us. I am creating a dampening field so that only the people and things we want take the big step." Healey responded back.

Andrew looked around the small area of hollowed-out rock. "But that is like the whole room. You got those things everywhere, protecting the entire space."

"True, true. But not the tunnel we walked in from the outside."

Andrew turned to look at where he just walked. Turning back, "Well, warn a guy before you turn that thing on. I would hate to come back in and find myself dancing with the dinosaurs or something."

Healey and Harper laughed. "No worries, Mr. Andrew, we have only made calculations for just a few years back. You and your team will be safe. Besides, it will be at least twelve hours before it's operational."

Andrew slowly nodded his head as he thought about it. "Question, why aren't the rest of you joining us? You know when this happens this timeline and everything with it will be gone, including you?"

Doctor Harper smiled for a second and then reached out and placed his hand on Andrews's shoulder. "Were you ever married?"

"No," Andrew responded back.

"We were, and we would like to see our families again," Doctor Harper answered back as Healey nodded in confirmation.

The Present

Mac was texting as he listened to Megan read another excerpt from the cave journals. What caught his attention were the descriptions of the inside of the dome city and the face-to-face encounter with the aliens. As he looked up, he couldn't help noticing the body language of various people around the room as he sent another text.

For some people, it left them unsettled, others nervous. One or two were showing signs of being a little angry at the concept of how many people were killed in Madrid alone.

General Ahrens moved his coffee cup off to the side as Megan finished. "One last question, Captain, before we go to break. Did these cave writings include a list of the destroyed cities?"

"General Ahrens, I have assembled a list based on the various cities that Captain Becker mentioned at different points in his writings. They are Madrid, Boston, Jakarta, Dallas, Osaka, Lima, Moscow, Quanzhou, and London, England. Most likely, Sir, I believe this is not a complete list." Captain Becker responded back.

The Vice President looked over at the congressmen who were checking their watches. "Very good everyone. Uh... let's break for the next hour and a half."

The Future

Hess and Yerkhov were hitting it off as new friends. Yerkhov was the youngest of the hunting club so his age was only about sixteen years from Hess. They had wandered a little distance from the cave to look for signs of a mule deer to hunt. All this was being done under the ruse of "guard duty."

It was still mid-morning so it was not uncomfortably hot yet. The thought of something to eat, other than the rations they brought, was just too tempting. In the distance, they could still see Peters and Baker standing near the cave who knew they were using guard duty as an excuse to hunt.

Yerkhov was the first to "feel" something strange in the air. He did not know what it was but Hess had become way too familiar with it. He looked up just in time to see an alien craft, moving from right to left across the sky, about a mile away from them. Yerkhov happened to look up at Hess and then followed his gaze to the craft.

Peters and Baker were oblivious. If they had been paying attention, they would have seen two old men moving as fast as they could through the small desert valley below to get back.

Baker finally heard something and turned around just in time to see two large aliens exiting a landed craft near Hess and Yerkhov. "Peters, look!" Baker exclaimed.

In the distance, Peters could see the aliens were on them way too fast. Hess raised his gun to fire but never got a chance. The alien fired his own weapon that emitted a bright light. Hess fell to the ground just as Yerkhov pulled the trigger on his old hunting rifle. It hit the second alien square in the chest, killing him. He didn't get a chance to fire another round before the same bright light killed him.

The shocking sight of it stunned the battle-hardened guys. Looking up, Peters could see more alien craft coming in for a landing behind the first.

Peters barked at Baker, "Hold this position. I will alert Captain Becker."

Everyone was just getting ready to take a rest when Peters came rushing in yelling, "They're here! The aliens are landing, Hess and Yerkhov are dead!"

The Present

Bond took Henry and Megan back to the restaurant to relax a bit. This time, they were seated a little more in the center of the room. Victoria ordered a drink for herself. Megan and Henry however decided to wait.

General Bond looked at Henry's daughter, "Megan, you are doing much better during this session. Thank you."

Megan looked at Bond, "Well, I hope you don't mind, but I would really rather not talk shop right now."

Victoria gave a quick glance toward Henry and saw the agreement in his eyes. "Uh, sure."

Henry, looking for a new topic, So he asked Megan a question. "Have you heard from Daniel or Dave today?"

Rubbing her head with her fingertips, she gladly accepted the new direction for their conversation. "Uh... nothing from Dave so I sent a text, but I haven't heard anything back yet. However, it is mid-morning so he is most likely cleaning up from breakfast and getting prepped for lunch. As for Daniel, we texted twice. I told him that it looks like we'll be in meetings for most of the day but maybe we could meet tonight. He responded back that he was going to try to get into the Smithsonian."

Henry smiled. "Good luck with that. I have been in and out around here for years. The line to the Smithsonian has always been a long wait. I've only made it inside a few times."

Victoria, trying to be socially polite, "So who is Daniel? Do you have a new man in your life?"

Megan's back straightened up as she responded to Victoria's comment. "No."

It then dawned on Henry that Victoria did not know. The last she knew, Danny had died years ago. "Actually, Daniel is her brother, my son, Danny."

Victoria, who had known Henry for many years, knew the story of Danny and was shocked by this new information. "What? I thought Danny died in the train wreck after he ran away?" Victoria responded back.

Megan cracked a smile, "Yep, that's what we thought too."

"How did you find him?" Victoria asked.

Henry smiled like a proud grandfather as he leaned forward to speak. "My grandson, Captain John Becker, told us about him."

Megan leaned back to watch her father tell the story. "When we first began reading John's journal, he mentioned that Boston had been destroyed and that he was now alone. He wrote that he missed Christmas with his cousins." Henry explained as he looked at Victoria's eyes, which were wide open. "It took a little time of hunting, but we found him. And because the events John wrote about are yet to come, we cannot tell him the truth about how we found him. In John's writings, Daniel was an architect, and we now know that he just became one."

Megan spoke up to interject, "This is one of the many reasons we believe the cave writing to be authentic."

Victoria was beginning to understand. Unknown to them, Mac sat against a wall in the back, watching and listening.

The Furture

Suddenly, the quiet, little canyon valley was full of gunfire and yelling. Some of the rocks that were hit by alien weapon fire exploded. One did so near Peabody, who was the first to make it outside. A chunk, about the size of a man's fist, hit him squarely in the head, knocking him backward. He was dead before he stopped rolling.

Lee Han, who saw it all happen, was filled with emotion and rage at the death of his dear friend. He scrambled to get to his feet and charge the gray, alien warriors who were advancing on them. Quickly all the men who had run outside had taken cover from the heavy weapons fire.

York grabbed hold of Lee Han to keep him from getting killed but it was of little use. Before he had even made it halfway up, he collapsed and fell to the ground. York looked up and saw that he was only holding onto part of his coat. The other part was charred and burnt as Lee Han fell.

Hollister brought out of the cave an M-28 pulsed-energy rifle. It was heavy and took a moment to set up on its short-legged tripod.

Ben pulled the trigger as soon as it was ready. It made a whirling sound as a rotating light within the main housing started to spin. The energy fire bursting forth from it was so continuous that it looked almost like a solid stream. Ben moved it back and forth over the alien's advancing position ripping open all that it touched. The M-28 was effectively reducing their number. One of the energy bolts even made it into the open door of one of the down-range attack craft. The small explosion inside the craft cascaded and pushed it into another. The two aliens that were left took cover as Becker let out a "YES," in celebration.

He was standing about five feet back toward the cave entrance with York and Silas Wilson. Becker looked over to see Andrew standing near Hollister who got a slap on his back congratulating him.

Then, to everyone's surprise, the M-28 was suddenly hit by an enemy ship they did not see overhead. The weapon exploded, blowing Becker, York, and Silas backward into the cave. Peters, who was already inside grabbing more weapons, watched it take place. As the dust cleared and a few rocks fell, he could clearly see there was nothing left of anyone outside beyond the entrance of the cave, except a burning shoe.

The Present

Laughter had replaced the serious mood within the restaurant as the plates were being cleared from the table. Mac, who sat in the back, watching looked at his watch and then pulled out his cell phone. He typed out the word "go" and hit send.

He sat there, patiently waiting. Soon, Victoria Bond's cell phone went off.

Henry stopped talking about the old days as she put the phone to her ear. Victoria's right eyebrow came up, as she pretended to listen. Nodding her head once or twice, Victoria then spoke up, "Yes, I will be right there."

"Sorry, it looks like I need to get going. Apparently, there's a water leak in my office just above my desk." Victoria informed them.

Henry and Megan, who had been laughing, found it funny. "Yep Vic, I think you better run. Or maybe it would be a good spot to put a plant. You know you always wanted to see new things sprout up around you," Henry remarked a little sarcastically, poking one last comment at her.

"Funny, old man," Victoria sarcastically remarked as she got up. She looked over at Megan as she pulled her share of the tip from her purse. "Did this old guy ever tell you about the time when you were a child and he tried to plant a garden in the backyard?"

Megan, still smiling, "No."

"Well, I need to go, but let's just say it involved a backhoe and a flood as he hit the city water main," Victoria remarked.

Megan gave her father gave a look at Victoria as she walked away with a grin. Henry smiled, shook his head, and checked his watch wondering if they should get up as well or just enjoy another moment of peace. With a deep sigh, Henry got up as his daughter moved

155

to join him. As they did, Mac "accidentally" bumped into them. "Oh, General, Captain, glad to meet you here. I wonder if you might have a moment to talk."

The Future

The situation was growing more grim by the second as everyone realized that the aliens had found them. It would only be a matter of time before they were completely overrun. The team took a very brief second to grieve for their dead as they prepared for the next wave.

Becker, Wilson, and Peters took up defensive positions to prepare for the attack that was about to come into the cave. The scared scientists continued as best they could, working as no one spoke. No one needed to because the situation was fully understood.

Suddenly, a small round device that looked like the one in the crystal city but larger came zipping into the cave. Everyone saw it and gasped. Silas grabbed a board and stood up, smacking it like a baseball. It bounced off the side wall of the cave and came to rest several feet beyond the entrance at the feet of a large alien entering in.

The alien was not like the others they'd been fighting. He was tall and even thinner, like a human. His skin tone was different too —a darker gray. He picked up the device and looked it over as he turned to address the few remaining troops with a single word to them. "Attack."

Shots of light suddenly entered the cave from behind the alien as lead bullets soon exited back out towards the aliens. After a few seconds, Peters looked behind him to see Harper and Healey dead. As he turned his head back forward once more, Peters saw two of the giant aliens charging the entrance as another round device entered in, only to cloak itself.

The alien rushing in front took the full force of the bullets being fired at him. He was dead but the momentum of his massive body caused him to crash forward and fall to the ground, rolling like a bowling ball. He crushed several crates between himself and Silas Wilson before he finally stopped, pinning Silas to the wall.

John Becker was fully involved with the second giant. He got one last shot at the monster. The bullet traveled through the left side of his gray neck but not before the giant knocked John's rifle out of his hands and sent it flying across the room. When it hit the far wall, it fired one more round that skipped off the cave wall and punctured a canister of some sort of compressed gas, triggering a light fog to form in the room as the battle waged.

The giant's second swing then sent John flying as well, but it opened up a clear shot for Peters. He placed a short burst of three rounds cleanly into the face of the monster. The alien jerked and then slumped to the ground as Peters bent down to Becker with his rifle pointing toward the cave entrance.

"Cap... are you okay?" Peters asked.

John, whose mind and body were running on adrenaline, did not notice the blood coming from his nose and leg. Something in the explosion had hit him, hard. John got to his feet saying nothing in response as he picked up another rifle.

To Peters's surprise, he looked over to notice Rodriguez bleeding from a head wound, but still working among his dead comrades.

"Cap? Peters asked.

"Yes?" John responded back.

"I'm not sure, but I think the old guy, Silas, is dead. There are only the three of us left." Peters informed him.

Fading Starlight

Lunar Orbit.

The alien who looked almost human stood in the center of his holographic database. Watching the battle from the lens of one of those hovering orbs. It was enjoyable for him to watch the destruction below from the image being sent to him from inside the cave by the capsule that accompanied his trained hunters.

He watched the horror on Captain Becker's face and could clearly see Peters and the device that Rodriguez was working on. He took joy in seeing that they had arrived in time to prevent its use. Soon, they would all be dead and the cave destroyed.

The alien watched Peters try to come to his Captain's aid but only get flung across the room. He turned his viewing capsule around just in time to see Rodriguez connect something to the device. Curious, he moved it forward and grew concerned as he watched a look of satisfaction come over Rodriguez's face.

Rodriguez flipped a switch and the image being transmitted from the cave to the alien ship cut out.

The Alien stood looking at the blank screen in disbelief. His eyes grew very large and he took a deep breath in as a new horror started to wash over him.

Inside the cave, the battle raged on. The alien was bleeding heavily from the knife wound Peters gave it. John's second rifle had been knocked out of his hand once more. This time it landed near the entrance to the cave.

Peters was getting his feet back under him for the third or fourth time when he faintly heard the doctor behind him. He turned to see Rodriguez, who was dying, say to him, "It's done, it's on. Look." Rodriquez painfully pointed toward the cave entrance and through the fog, just beyond the Captain's fight, a pale blue light was forming.

Neither Becker nor the alien was aware of it. Only Peters and Rodriguez could see it. Mixing with the gas fog, they could not tell what was truly unfolding, but it almost seemed like "wisps" of something were coming and going from a light barrier. One even came out and passed by John's head. It paused for a moment during the fight and moved across the room toward Peters. To Rodriguez, it almost seemed like it was communicating with Peters as he stood there looking at the formless mist.

Peters then looked down at the floor and among all the rubble he saw the device that the Captain had acquired from the crystal city. As quickly as he could, he picked it up and grabbed one of the backpacks in the room. He shoved it inside but then stopped as if listening to something. Reaching into his chest pocket, he pulled out the little black book that the Captain had given him to hold onto in Bonners Ferry. Into the backpack, it went, and then he took hold of the straps and swung it as hard as he could. Letting it go and it crashed hard into the Captain's back. The momentum of it pushed Becker forward into the alien. The impact of which pushed both of them as Peters watched them go into the glowing light barrier.

Suddenly everything changed around John. The pain and shock of the fight left him. It felt like he was floating away. John's mind started clearing even though he was unsure where he was, as nothing looked familiar. Colors suddenly became more alive and real. The sound was almost solid and reacted to his thoughts. If it was possible, everything around him was alive. As he was aware that he was moving very quickly, but at the same time, slowly. The sheer beauty around him captivated his senses until he caught sight of the alien.

It was becoming beyond hideous. The alien was in obvious pain, as everything within him seemed to be ripping apart. Such a beautiful place made the alien painfully uncomfortable. Reacting like a raw nerve whenever color or sound touched him. The very same thing that was bringing Becker joy brought nothing but agony to the creature. And in that place, John began to fully realize the demonic horror twisting in front of him.

As he turned a little more around to see that the sights and the sounds around him seemed to be giving way to a presence that was drawing closer. He couldn't tell if it had the shape of a person or not. As it drew nearer, the horror and fear he was feeling from the alien's presence left and he knew only greater joy than ever before.

It was close now and seemed to form a mouth. It then blew like a person would blow a bubble. With that, John and the alien were blown from that place to the desert floor outside the cave.

John lay there with his back against a large rock, turning his head as he watched the alien take its last gasps of air. He had no desire to finish killing it. Once it died, John rolled over to get up.

Looking at the hideous mess in front of him, John removed everything the alien had been carrying, and then in disgust of the creature, he pushed the carcass off the small ledge with his foot so he wouldn't have to look at it anymore.

John came back and sat down near the rock, reflecting on everything that had happened in the fight, the friends who died, and his strange trip.

In the distance, the wind was slowly moving closer by the evidence of the tufts of grass that popped up along the landscape. Raising his head he noticed the old, original, smaller cave before his team expanded it.

Knowing that everything worked, John looked up at the small clouds dotting the horizon against the deep blue sky. The contrast of the pure white against the deep blue sitting on top of the warmth of the brilliant red canyons was soothing to him as he felt the after-effects of adrenaline leaving his system.

In pain, John raised his leg to a rock, only to notice droplets of blood now setting on top of the rock. With a deep breath, John worked to calm himself while using the place to rest and bandage his injured leg. The leg was hurting and twinges of pain were coming from the wound that looked more like a burn. But that event was all in the past, now John could rest. The battle was over and he was in a safer place. Project Wind Tunnel had succeeded.

All that was left was the cave as it existed before. Tomorrow he would hike out and find the road up the canyon. For tonight, he would make a campfire, have a meal, and enjoy the starlit evening that was to come, resting in the knowledge that maybe, with the information he now carried, he could save a few million lives and humanity would not die.

In the well of fading emotion, John barely noticed that the canyon looked a little different than what he remembered. Pushing those random thoughts to the back of his mind as well as the thoughts of what he'd just been through. He had been in battles before but this one cost him his team; people that he cared for, traveled with and planned on taking with him through the time jump to 2025. He wondered how the enemy had found their base. Did they intercept a message? They had been so careful, limiting the details of their location to just his team and a few select others.

All those questions echoed in his mind as he limped along the hillside gathering a few sticks for firewood. He heard a noise other than the wind in the canyon and looked up to see a brightly plumed bird sitting on a dead tree branch nearby. He smiled and thought, "I have never seen a bird like that before. Someone's exotic pet must have escaped its cage." John shook his head and went back to gathering firewood.

With his arms loaded, he limped back up the hill to the cave. It would be his home for the night. John then noticed the outline of a lizard near his backpack as he drew closer. It scattered, flicking sand up with its feet as it left. John thought that the lizard was a little bigger than what he had seen in the area before.

After a few minutes, John was resting with his head on his pack near a small campfire. He looked at his selection of ready-to-eat meals—Meatballs in Marinara

161

or Chicken Tetrazzini.

"Hmm, chicken it is," he said to himself.

John sat the packet down next to where the lizard was. Sitting up, he opened the packet and poured hot water from his canteen that had been near the fire. His mind was still on the battle earlier in the day, thinking about Peters and the others and how they died.

While his food absorbed the hot water, John got up and leaned on the cave wall, looking outside as he stirred his food with a spoon. The shadows of the canyon had grown long, covering the desert floor below him. The evening was coming and he could just barely see the first star of the night. He had taken astronomy in college so he naturally took an interest in the night sky. It was one of the few constant joys while growing up and even during the war. It never changed, always bright and friendly like these old desert canyons.

He tried to take a bite of his food only to get burnt. He moved back to where he had been resting and set his food down on a rock. As he did, he noticed the lizard tracks from before. The lizard tracks were peculiar, so he bent down to get a better look at them.

Shaking his head, John remarked out loud, "Strange. I thought I knew the tracks of every kind of lizard that lives in these parts."

Captain Becker then heard a noise coming from outside. His battle-hardened instincts took over and before another second passed, he had his weapon and was up against the cave wall. Carefully looking around the corner, he could see the faint outline of an animal in the distance. He lowered his weapon and began to relax. Strange tracks and time jump aside, he was wondering how much sleep he was going to get.

Somewhere in his pack were some binoculars. Pulling them out he turned the night enhancement on and looked around. The low-light setting not only increased the light level, but it also gave body heat information. Whatever that animal was, it had already stepped behind a boulder and was moving on. John increased the magnification to see that the subject had left a large heat signature but it was walking on four feet so it had to be an animal, not a human or alien.

John had to talk himself down a little. He had just traveled back in time. If anything bad was out there, it had to be an animal, not an alien. But he still decided against putting the fire out.

He pulled himself up near the rock face so that the fire would reflect heat onto him. With his pack and his rifle nearby, he reached over to grab his food..

Like an old black-and-white movie from the 1950s, Megan stood near the top of a small hill. Wearing her old military combat-issue uniform, she felt like she was somehow back in Iraq. The hair on her head had wrapped a bit around her face in the wind as she looked downward to her right, she could see a small American town from the past in the valley below her.

Feeling a bit of curiosity, she looked closer. Aliens right out of the old 50's movie, "The Day the Earth Stood Still," marched through the streets, destroying every person and building in sight. As they marched, they carried a banner high in the sky that read, "Terrors of the Earth and Mind."

As they continued to march, Megan's eyes looked upward, the stars above her now growing dimmer...fading. Everything was so odd she wondered if it was even real because it all looked so fake. Then her right pocket, without her help, opened up. To her horror, in this colorless world, a small blue ball about the size of a ping pong ball rolled out, fell, and then bounced off the stony ground below her.

Like in slow motion, the gray landscape around her started to acquire color as her body slowly turned to watch the ball. Megan followed it as it bounced and rolled around her and then down the hill. Megan dropped her Army rifle in shock as she started after it.

The ball grew to about the size of a man's fist as it steadily rolled farther and farther away from her. As it grew, it took on the look of the earth, with its extreme blue, green, and white colors. In the distance beyond the ball, Megan's eyes soon saw a Python moving fast up the hill toward it. The sight of its eyes caused her to stop suddenly in her tracks as a cold feeling of fear started to grip her.

Her hair, for some reason, was now becoming very long and curly, and rushed past her as the wind from behind her moved it. Her combat clothing was gone, replaced by a simple, long white and blue dress that moved with her. It had thin silver detailing, almost like armor, which hung off her shoulders and hips.

With a pointing finger and the sound of anger in her voice, she declared, "It's you."

The Ball of the World stopped just under the chin of the snake that almost seemed to be smiling. Gathering itself, the Python stood up, all dark green with scales, fangs, and large dark eyes. That form now started to fade as a more human image replaced the former. Standing there, with dark eyes and even darker hair the man held the world ball in his right hand as the last of his scales slowly changed to perfect human skin in a dark business suit.

Megan's feelings of fear were soon replaced with the confidence of a warrior, as she now noticed a long, thin-bladed, silver sword in her hand. "Thief! Return what you have stolen," she ordered as she partly pointed it at him.

The serpent man laughed and tossed the ball up playfully in the air, only to catch it.

With a slight hiss in his voice, he looked Megan in the eye. "How about I just eat it?" he announced with a grin. He then placed it up to his mouth to take a bite out of it, as if it were an apple. Megan's confidence was suddenly stripped away in a flash as she lifted her white-gloved hands to her mouth to scream in horror.

The shock of the dream was so intense it jolted Megan backward in her bed. Nearly knocking the air out of her lungs as she collided with a thud to the floor next to her hotel bed. Four in the morning, and in the distance, the sounds of the early morning city life slowly settled in as she started to realize it was just a dream.

A few hours later, Henry exited his hotel room only to be met by a blurry-eyed daughter with a slight red mark on her forehead, Megan, who looked at her father's face; silently communicating to him that she seriously needed coffee.

"Bad night?" Henry asked as they walked.

Megan chose not to answer as she walked along the

hallway with a slight limp.

The General noticed the limp as he tucked his hat under his arm. "Based on the noise from your room this morning, I am assuming you fell out of bed?" Henry remarked as he looked to his left where she was walking. Megan looked up with an unfriendly look "it's too early in the morning for this."

"I'll take that look as a yes. Must have been quite the dream?" Henry asked.

"It was," Megan responded with a low voice.

"The mark on your forehead?" Henry asked.

"Nightstand" was Megan's only comment.

They turned towards the hallway elevator when Henry pulled out his phone to check his messages. "Just got a text from Daniel. We are going to meet him for breakfast in about ten minutes. Apparently, we are ordering eggs and ham for him."

Megan closed her eyes for a moment as they continued walking before responding, "sounds good to me, but I think I'll have coffee to go with mine," Megan announced rather bluntly.

Stopping in front of the elevator as Henry pushed the button. "I kinda expected that," Henry remarked with a slight grin.

A New World

The early faint light of morning added a bit of brightness and life to the desert world. John Becker, who had gained very little sleep, was slowly waking up to the low, deep sound around him. It sounded kind of like the low deep sounds of a cow or bull from a farmer's field. John slowly opened his eyes to see, less than a foot from him, the monstrous head of a buffalo looking right at him. With shock and a jolt of adrenaline, his suddenly wide eyes registered he had now become unwelcomely awake.

But the old cow never flinched as she looked at him. Chewing her cud near a tuft of desert grass that grew out from between the rocks. John's sudden jolt and scramble had pressed him very close to the rock wall as his unfocused eyes gained bits of clarity, and his mind raced in disbelief at the sight of this old giant.

John lay there; his brain had no way of processing this. Having never seen a buffalo up close before, let alone one standing here, in this desert. As he stared at her, John started noticing in the corner of his eyes two more in the canyon valley below. Unsure of what to do next, he just watched and waited as the light, dry morning air was slowly bringing her scent toward him.

After a few minutes, the sun was starting to crest, adding more viewing light to his eyes as the buffalo's below started to migrate, moving out of the valley, the old cow in front of John belched a truly obnoxious belch as she decided to turn and join her herd. The raunchy smell made it up to John, whose eyes started to water.

That bit of putrid reality shook off any doubt that this was a dream as he instinctively pulled his t-shirt up over his nose, muttering the words, "Oh God, what died inside of you?"

Shifting his position to pull himself up a little higher against the rocks, John watched them in disbelief as the small herd wandered out of the valley. His leg had become a little stiff during the night. Looking downward he noticed the wound he had been laying on did not look good to him.

Looking around for a moment at the small valley before him, a few small birds flew past him to flutter down and sit on the backs of the migrating buffalo. As they wandered out of sight, John then became aware of another smell that was wafting up from below. It was like a combination of bad potatoes, vinegar, and something he could not describe, even if he wanted to.

Looking over the small ledge, it was the dead alien, who was rotting at a fast rate. The smell was not sitting well on John's stomach, so he grabbed his gear bag and started to hobble out of the area. Since the alien was starting to smell now, John had no desire to be around when it became midday in the hot sun.

As he moved, his leg muscles started to loosen up making his leg feel a little better as he moved around between the sagebrush and rocks. Then he wandered past a few dead, tall pine trees John stopped, a bit puzzled he look at one of the large stones, "I don't remember this being here." He quietly remarked.

After a moment or so, John found a large flat rock to sit and rest on. Slipping his pack off, he laid it with his rifle on the rock next to him. Within moments of digging in it, he found a small medical kit. Pulling out a small white stick like a Q-tip, he put the end of it in some of the blood on his leg. Then he put his Q-tip sample on the rock and pulled out a handheld device a little larger than his hand. Flipping the protective rubber cover off from around a port at one end, he placed the Q-tip sample inside.

A small red light was on, and after about five or seven seconds, it turned green. He pressed the green light and a screen came on with the words, "Sample confirmed positive for infection. Recommend transport to the nearest medical unit."

The corner of John's mouth came up in a small grimace as he looked at it. "Well, we will see what we can do about that."

Cutting his pants around his leg open a bit wider. He then took out a small can and sprayed the wound with a spray-on bandage. It would prevent any other infection from entering his system and even numb the pain for a time. Putting his MED kit back, he located some food in a foil pouch and put it on the rock, along with his Army issue communicator, which he turned on. Figuring he would not pick up anything on his communicator, because the canyon had always been a dead spot for any communication device. He then hooked the radio on the right side strap of his backpack after putting his pack back on.

The cool morning air was pleasant and the scenery around him became welcoming as he slowly traveled.

Even with the buffalo and weird lizards, he decided he was going to enjoy this hike to the road and then into town.

With his pack on, rifle in his left hand, and some food now in his belly. John departed towards a vertical rock formation that stood like a wall at the edge of the valley. The communicator volume was turned down on low and left on scan mode. Only a random background pop of static came from the small speaker from time to time.

As he walked, eating his food, he replayed the events of the last day in his mind.

Jack Peabody was playing a very old song on his guitar. He never sang it; he just loved the sound of this classic song.

Doctor Healy asked him what it was called.

"Well, Doctor Healy, it's called, 'All Quiet Along the Potomac Tonight.' It was a poem that was written just after the Battle of Bull Run in 1861."

"Do you know the words as well?" inquired Healy.

"No, not really, the only part I remember is the ending," remarked Jack.

"Well, how does it go then?" Healy asked.

"All quiet along the Potomac tonight, No sound save the rush of the river; While soft falls the dew on the face of the dead, The picket's off duty forever."

The memory of the song with Jack's words seemed to echo around within John's mind as he walked. Compartmentalizing the loss and pain of the last several days as he was trained to do, John decided to shove it down deep and not deal with it right now. It was not the right time; he still had the mission in front of him. Besides, the memories of everyone who died were too fresh for him—too close.

He finished the rest of his food and placed the wrapper in his pocket just in time to steady himself by putting his hand on the side of the increasingly narrow stone walls. He always enjoyed running back and forth along this path as a kid, although it seemed there were more rocks and dead sticks in the path than he remembered.

Oh well, maybe it was just a child's mind that painted a different picture.

Walking about a hundred feet or so, John's foot rolled off a rock, which caused him to slip and slam his wounded leg into the stone wall. The sharpness of pain quickly reminded him of his wound as he leaned against the wall for a moment waiting for the pain to leave.

As it subsided, he took a step forward and noticed he had torn open his spray-on bandage. Shifting his weight to the other side, he leaned for a moment on the opposite wall to slip his pack off. The narrow walls did not provide any convenient place for him to conduct first aid. So after a moment or two of the awkwardness of leaning, John tore off the old bandage and reapplied a new bandage in order to resume hiking.

Stepping over a very old rotten log that was on the path, he was finally clear of the narrow pathway that quickly opened up in front of him to a few scrub pine trees and rocks. Dumbfounded for the second time that day, John just stood there, surprised at what he was seeing.

"What?" he exclaimed aloud. "Where's the road?" Unsure what to say or do next.

Just to his left, he heard the faint sound of a lizard's tail as it flicked off to go under a rock. He moved his head to look at the sound and noticed the small boulder the lizard was on, about the size of a car.

The scrub pines were just thick enough so that he could not see any real distance. Making the decision, John climbed the rock to get a better look around. The morning sun quickly greeted John's face as he stood above the tops of scrub pines. Raising his hand to shade his eyes from the glare, he took a deep breath. As far as his eyes could see, it was desert, scrub trees, rock, and sandstone formations. All the roads that he remembered were gone. The hollowness of the light desert wind that was now moving the finer hairs of his body brought an aloneness. The sagebrush and the random chirps of his radio were the only sounds he heard now, not the distant traffic of highway 191.

A growing, unsettled feeling was slowly coming to rest in his heart as he looked at the silent desert. The thought occurred within him that he did not land at the time Doctor Healy programmed. The road that was here when he was a child was now gone. As far as he knew, it was here for at least fifty-some years before he was born. "Could I have traveled further, maybe to the 1930s or '40s?" John whispered to himself.

In desperation, John pulled his binoculars from his pack to his eyes to scan the world before him. Some five or six miles out, he could make out what looked like three coyotes or dogs. They were chasing down something small, likely a jackrabbit.

John turned and looked towards the La Sal mountain range to the east. Somehow they looked a little different, and then he realized the radio towers on the top seemed to be missing. "Pre 1930's" he whispered once more.

John could now feel a low level of adrenaline moving through his body bringing tension to his heart as he started to feel alone. This whole plan was based on the idea of only jumping back a few decades. His team would arrive and walk out within a day. Finding a ride, they would report to the nearest military base. Now his team was gone and so were his plans. He only had enough food for three or four days, and water for less. Civilization could be several days or weeks away if this time jump was really off.

Crazy thoughts were now jumping into his mind, playing games with his emotions as he climbed down from the rock. Adrenaline was pushing him to the point of intense fear and confusion. Closing his eyes as he squatted next to the rock, trying to hold onto his military combat training. He was not prepared for this; he had never been trained for anything like this. As his combat training slowly took over, he thought about what he would say if one of his men had just asked him what to do. Opening his eyes, he quietly said to himself, "Food and shelter. Look for water."

Climbing back up the rock John put his binoculars

back up to his eyes, he scanned the land once more to see a patch of green in the distance. "That way, Captain," John spoke to himself.

The Present

"Really, so Wendy has worked as a professional cook? That's really cool, son. Does that mean that someday you're going to design a restaurant for her?" Henry asked.

Daniel smiled and even laughed a little, "I would love to, but not right now. Not only do we need money for that, but she would really like to try her hand at just being a housewife right now."

"I get that," Megan responded.

"How about what you want, Daniel?" Henry asked.

"Well, I love to design things—places and buildings that look good. It's what I love. I think someday Wendy will take up cooking again. But her last boss was really a nut job, so I can understand her to need to take a break." Daniel looked down at his breakfast plate that was being taken away.

Turning his head towards Megan, Daniel asked, "What about you?"

"What about me?" Megan replied.

"What about you? I mean after the Army no longer needs you. What will you be doing?" Daniel inquired.

"Well, don't worry about your little sister," Megan remarked with a smile." I have been thinking about it. And I think, after everything is done, I plan on kicking around the desert a little less. Johnny's almost ready for school. Besides, Dad here is looking to retire." Giving her father a quick glance as her right eyebrow raised in the hope he would understand her message, "So, I was hoping I could talk to my dear old father…and maybe… we could move away from Virginia and join Johnny and I out west. Maybe in a smaller town, where his grandson can enjoy the outdoors."

Henry's back straightened up a little as he quickly started to think over what Megan was saying and offering. He realized that she was starting to cook up a plan on how to raise Johnny that included him.

"Really?" Daniel remarked.

"Really, I have been thinking about it. Every young boy should get a chance to learn to camp, build forts, and fight off imaginary bad guys. You know, like giants and aliens and crazy boy stuff like that." Megan quickly pulled up her water glass, pretending to take a drink from it, hoping her father would catch her hidden meaning.

Henry was a little stunned at her comment, but very quickly caught on. Thinking it over fairly quickly, Henry responded before Daniel said anything.

"You know, Meg, it's funny you should say that. I've been thinking about things as well. That old house hardly ever gets used, and I am almost never home anymore. And it's way too big for an old guy like me to take care of. You're right, you're absolutely right," Henry exclaimed. "I think I should downscale what I have, and sell it." Henry paused for a moment, looking at Daniel as Megan's face was starting to show signs of relief. "And come to think of it, Daniel, you and Wendy should drop by. You should have some of the stuff I've got. You know, for whatever new place you might decide to live in."

Daniel sat there for a moment, thinking it over as Henry was surprised at what came out of his own mouth. As Daniel thought over his dad's offer, Henry's mind was racing as he thought about Megan's offer and what he just agreed to do. Megan was also a little taken back over by the speed of everything that just happened in front of her.

Daniel rolled his tongue around in his mouth as he thought about it, "Ok, I will talk with Wendy and see what we can do. Maybe if you manage to get Megan some free time, we could get the whole family together with Johnny?"

Fading Starlight

Henry raised his chin and smiled, "I would like that, son."

Daniel turned his head towards his sister, "Sounds good, I'm in."

Smiling Daniel looked around at everyone's faces and smiled as he started to stand. "Well, it's been a fairly wild and over-the-top family gathering. I need to get going so I don't miss my flight. Do you think maybe we could do this in four to six weeks?"

Four to six weeks left an unsure feeling in Henry and Megan's hearts because of project Lorenzo. Neither one had the slightest idea where they would be at that time. Daniel picked up on the awkward silence, "It's your Army assignment?" Daniel asked.

"Ah yes son, it is," Henry responded.

Daniel half smiled as he buttoned his coat. "No problem, I get it. Call me in a week or so to keep me updated."

"We will get together, big brother, I can guarantee that," Megan responded with a smile.

Henry stood up to hug him. "Well, we need to get going as well. We need to get in early to prep for our meeting.

The Past

John was making good time for his next stop, even though he had to pause twice to re-bandage his leg. The extra voices in his mind were trying to play havoc with him, but he had managed to turn most of them off. He canceled each one with either a logical answer or told himself, "We will just need to wait and see."

But then a new thought marched its way in. It was a "what if "question and it caught him off guard. "What if I did not go backward, but forward? The aliens won, killed everyone, and I am the last person left on this earth." That thought did more to dislodge the confidence he had gained in the last hour than anything else

All these thoughts and the growing pain in his leg were working to develop a kind of tunnel vision. Leaving him unaware of everything else around him.

In the far distance, the pack John had seen finished eating their jackrabbit meal. They were not dogs or coyotes, but a small pack of desert wolves, scavengers of whatever they could find when they could find it.

It had been over a month since they had taken anything of real size for food. The few jackrabbits and lizards they found had left them mostly hungry. Past his prime the older alpha male and his pack had been forced to relocate from their prime hunting area in the La Sal Mountains. They had successfully taken down an old buffalo when they suffered a surprise attack by several younger males.

Overpowered, they withdrew from the area, hungry once more as they had lost two of the younger females who stayed with the new pack.

That was almost two weeks ago, and now the older male picked up a new scent, far in the distance. Eager for more food, his pack followed him toward a tall rock formation in the distance.

To John's surprise, he started up an old habit from his youth—he started talking out loud to himself. "Well, I'm thinking because it's still relatively cool it must be early spring or late winter."

John smiled as he pulled out his canteen to get a drink. "Well, that's good. At least I can travel farther during the day then."

He screwed the lid back on and stopped for a moment, looking at it. Laughing a little, "Wow, not even one full day out here and I have started to talk to myself... Hmm."

The old male and his pack made it to John's cave and found the traces of blood John left. One of the females soon found the decaying alien. After sniffing it, she backed away, shaking her head back and forth, blowing her nose to get the foul scent out.

The pain in John's leg was slowly getting worse. The infection was advancing, and he could feel his leg getting warm and cold at the same time. As much as he hated the idea, he was going to need to perform a deeper inspection of his wound. He was hoping to make it to the green area about a half-mile in front of him. But it was becoming obvious that was not going to happen.

Following John's trail, the wolf pack stopped for a moment in the narrows and sniffed the ground to discover the discarded spray-on bandage John left. Inspecting everything, the old male took his pack and continued on along the trail.

Sitting on an almost flat rock, John was dealing with sharp stabs of pain as he probed around in the wound with a pair of tweezers. Finally, he felt and heard at the same time a "tink" sound as the tweezers made contact with something metallic.

John had never been a person who used alcohol, but at that moment with the pain, he was feeling, he felt the need for its numbing qualities. John raised his head in pain as he extracted the object from his leg.

Soon after the extraction, John was looking at a thin, two-and-a-half-inch long piece of silver-looking metal. It looked kind of like a thin, flat wire, smooth with a broken end that displayed evidence of some kind of microcircuitry.

Dropping it on the large rock near him, slowly his eyes came into focus to look at it. In pain, as he held his leg John exclaimed, "Great, a parting gift from the gray space goons."

As soon as he said it, he heard a noise from behind. John turned around on the rock to see several wolves closing in on him. The sight of them startled him as he rolled to his side. Unfortunately, John rolled in the opposite direction of his rifle.

The Present

Tapping the side of her cell phone, Megan was growing concerned as the day passed on. No one from project Lorenzo was returning her texts—not Dave, Josh, Andrew, or even Major Watson. Megan had hoped for some word by the early morning recess. Turning her head, Megan noticed her father was talking with General Bond. After a moment or so her father's eyes looked over at her. Their eyes met as she slipped her cell phone back into her purse. She had a disappointed look on her face, as she nodded a "no" toward him.

With a sigh, Megan turned her head toward the window, wondering what might be happening out west at the camp. Standing there for a moment, watching the dark rain clouds in the distance slowly move in towards the city. Megan could sense the presence of someone standing near her. Megan turned to her right to see Mac, with his arms folded watching the same sky patiently next to her. Mac smiled with a reassuring look on his face that was strangely comforting too Megan. "According to the weather report, the storm should produce quite a bit of rain this evening." Mac calmly remarked as he looked out the window.

The corner of Megan's mouth turned upward a little as she was a little taken aback by the pleasantness of this conversation in this 'official place'. Megan slowly nodded her head in affirmation of his statement as Mac continued.

"I noticed it seems you're a little concerned. Is someone not responding to your text?" Mac asked.

Megan's hand slowly, unconsciously moved towards her purse. "Oh, just checking on my son out west."

Mac, who was a little shorter than Megan, looked upward toward her with a thoughtful, compassionate look. "Johnny, your son...must be hard. Is this the first time you two have been apart for this long?"

Megan nodded a "yes" as she started to relax into the conversation. "He is what I hang on to."

Mac paused for a moment, unsure how much he wanted to talk about. "It's good that you have him," Mac remarked as he turned back to the window. "When my wife died, I did not have the advantage you have of a child to hang on to. If we had a child, I'm sure I would be less of a workaholic now."

Speaking softly, Megan responded, "How long?" With a bit of care in her voice.

"Four years this June," Mac calmly responded back.

Megan's tight shoulders relaxed a little as she turned her head to look out the window, pondering his words.

In an effort to be comforting, Mac spoke up, "I understand, we have had a lot of sunspot activity messing with cell phones. I'm sure things are fine out west. Dave and Andrew are most likely taking good care of your son."

The look on Megan's face slowly changed to a look of curiosity as he turned to look at him. "Mr. MacWilliams, are we on your radar?"

A smile slowly started up on Mac's face as they both turned away from the window. "Captain Becker, OAM makes it its business to become acquainted with everyone who has ever had contact with aliens," Mac responded back

Megan was a little unsure about the direction the conversation just took. Narrowing her eyes as she looked directly at him, " We are not the first, are we?" She inquired.

Sidestepping her question Mac smiled, "The three of us really should get together and talk."

"I not sure how. Each day is very packed," Megan responded.

Mac kept smiling with a look that said he knew something. "I am sure Captain, that a window can be arranged. Perhaps lunch tomorrow?"

Megan's right eyebrow rose, "That would be a miracle, Mr. MacWilliams."

Mac nodded his head a little to the side as he stepped away, "Tomorrow then."

Puzzled by the smile on his face, Megan folded her arms as she watched Mac walk away.

Henry watched everything transpire from a distance, wondering what was going on. Excusing himself from General Bond who was also watching, to walk over too Megan.

"What was that?" Henry inquired.

Megan, who was unconsciously rubbing her thumb against her index finger, watched Mac walk down the hallway with a puzzled look. "I'm not sure. I think we just got an invitation to lunch tomorrow."

Henry turned his head to look at the man who was leaving, then back to Megan. "Tomorrow? Hmm...I don't think so."

"He said that a window could be arranged," Megan responded.

179

Henry's right eyebrow raised as he watched Mac walk down the corridor, out of sight. "Ahh... I see. "Henry responded back as if he also knew something. "Meg, I will join you in a little while inside. General Bond tells me there is a message coming in for me and that this next session will just rehash as the Admiral is bringing in scientists to testify."

"Ok, don't be too long. I will need someone to keep me awake," Megan responded back as she half smiled.

Henry returned the smile as he walked up, handing his daughter a sandwich he had picked up from a passing service tray. "Keep your protein up," he remarked as walked away.

Henry walked down the hallway, away from the crowd. Taking the elevator to the next level. He carried his hat under his arm as he exited the elevator to walk down to the next hallway. Several doors down, a dark-haired woman in a Navy uniform turned and walked away from a service window. Henry walked up to the same window and caught the eye of the woman working on the other side of the window.

Henry looked the woman in the eye, "Mail for General Henry Mullins."

The blonde-haired woman in uniform responded back "Yes sir," as she turned to check a stack of mail. After digging in it she produced a sealed mailer and placed it in front of the General.

"Sign here on the clipboard, Sir." She informed him.

Henry signed for the mailer and then opened it to find a typed phone message.

GENERAL MULLINS,

ALL PHONE SERVICE IS OUT. THREE MEN FROM THE CIA ARRIVED LAST NIGHT. ALL CONTENTS OF THE CAVE WERE FOUND MISSING IN THE MORNING. NO ONE HAS SEEN ANYTHING. MEN FROM THE CIA ARE GONE AS WELL. GOLD BOOKS CAN NOT BE FOUND.

PLEASE ADVISE.

MAJOR T.A. WATSON, COMMANDING.

A cold chill ran down Henry's back as he read it. Stunned, he stepped out into the main hallway. Something was going on and it felt like it was attacking the very core of his family.

Slowly, as he walked down the hallway, Henry looked up to see the slightly thinner frame and dark brown hair of Sam Arris, CIA Director, walking into the washroom. The cold chill Henry felt was soon replaced by the fire of injustice as he calmly walked towards the washroom himself.

Henry paid very little attention to Sam as he walked in behind him to see if anyone else was in the washroom. Finding that he and Sam were the only ones and he turned his head back and forth for confirmation. Henry's right foot hit the back of Sam's legs, causing his legs to buckle in a violent manner. This was quickly followed by Henry's hands grabbing Sam's jacket and tossing his face into the wall.

Sam's face hit the wall first as his body followed. Sliding to the ground, Henry grabbed Sam once more, giving him no time to respond. Henry flipped Sam around like a rag doll, pushing his face under the faucet of a sink that was too small to fit his head. Henry turned on the water as Sam gasped for air and his arms flailed around.

"I want answers, Sam none of your games this time," Henry commanded. After a moment, Henry pulled Sam up with his left hand, only to let him drop to the floor.

"You better start talking Arris," Henry ordered.

Sam started spitting water and blood out of his mouth. "About what?" Sam passionately responded.

Henry's eyes grew more intense with fire as he raised his right fist. "I want them back, Sam."

Sam Arris quickly raised the palms of his hands up near his face. Henry's sheer adrenaline-filled strength was becoming obvious as he slowly lifted Sam off the floor once more.

181

"Wait. Stop, Henry, I don't know what you're talking about," Sam pleaded.

As soon as Sam spoke, Henry's fist crashed into his face. Henry let go of his shirt, letting him crash to the floor.

Sam crumpled to the floor, laying on the cold floor for a moment, coughing. Henry's left hand grabbed the back of Sam's coat while his right hand grabbed Sam's belt.

"Wrong answer Sam," Henry informed him as he carried him to the toilet.

Sam's mind slowly started clearing as he saw the water in the toilet that was inches in front of his face. Henry held him there for a moment so that Sam could reflect on what was about to happen.

"I just got word from my people that you sent a team of your people to the camp. You stole all our stuff Sam; you cleaned us out. What's this all about?" Henry barked at him.

In sheer desperation, Sam started to blubber some words at a speed that could not be understood. Henry responded, "Say it once more, a little slower."

Sam spit once more into the toilet, and in a desperate voice of emphatic words, "It wasn't me."

Henry seriously considered holding his head underwater but chose another option. Henry spun Sam around once more, letting him fall with his head hitting the toilet. With all the coldness of a winter wind, Henry looked him straight in the eye. "Start speaking Sam, if you're lying, we're going to see if you can grow gills and breathe underwater. Should fit nicely with your yellow spine."

Sam was holding the back of his head as blood was coming out of his nose. His heart and breathing were racing from the adrenaline and fear in his system. Because this was not his first run-in with Henry Mullins, he knew Henry would back up any threat he made.

"Henry, listen to me. I seriously have no idea what you're talking about." Sam responded back.

Henry's body made a slight jerk toward Sam, causing him to involuntarily twitch for a moment on the floor next to the toilet. "I AM NOT LYING, don't hit me. I don't know what happened to your stuff. Listen to me, it wasn't me." Sam emphatically responded back.

Sam's hands were now jerking from one spot to another in front of his blurry eyes trying to protect himself from anything Henry might do. Henry stood there watching Sam's reaction like a scared child. General Mullins' body relaxed a little, as he realized Sam knew nothing. After a moment or so, he looked around and found a hand towel on a wall ring. He grabbed it, tossing back at Sam.

"Here, clean yourself up," Henry ordered.

Henry stood there for a moment wondering who took it. As he watched, Sam pulled himself up to sit on the toilet seat.

"Can you at least tell me what I got beat for?" Sam inquired as he held the towel on his face.

Henry's very old disgust of Sam overruled his common sense as he turned away towards the door. He stopped at the door taking a breath to pause and rethink his actions. Henry turned and marched back towards Sam. Sam was growing a little concerned when Henry reached into an inside jacket pocket.

His fears subsided as the General produced a small typed message. Henry held the message in front of Sam to read, not letting him touch it. "Read it," he ordered.

Sam's eyes slowly focused on the note as his brain processed what he was reading. Henry slowly pulled it back as Sam thought about it for a moment.

"Understandable," Sam quietly muttered.

"What? Speak up." Henry asked.

Sam lightly chuckled through the pain for a moment as he coughed and wiped the blood from his nose. "I said, understandable." Sam responded in a louder tone. Looking up at Henry's face, "and predictable Henry. You got played you old turd. Someone out there knows our history and you got played."

The Past

John's pack was unfortunately open as the contents were now flung in all directions, away from where he rolled. The old gray wolf landed on all four where John was, to look John over. Then another wolf quickly joined in, stopping a few feet short of the first, to stare at their prey who was now lying on his side. John looked around and could clearly see his rifle behind his attacker. The knife he was using for surgery had flung out of his hand to parts unknown. Now, a low growl was starting to come out of the old male as he slowly moved his left paw forward.

John slid a little farther backward as his right elbow came in contact with a metal can. Picking it up to toss at the wolf, John paused for a moment as he realized what he was holding. The old wolf lifted his right paw forward as he decided to start closing in on John.

Gaining an idea, John held the can in his hand and rubbed his thumb over the setting selection on the spray can. As he passed his thumb over it, he changed the texture sets from tight weave, to open weave, to finally a full open spray.

The old wolf was getting ready to jump as John raised the wound spray can up toward the wolf. Pressing the button, John covered the face of the old wolf with a self-sealing bandage.

The old male let out a strange yipping noise and backed away quickly shaking his head. This left his pack confused and unsure of what to do, giving time for John to get on his feet. The pack then turned to gather closer, around the male who was pawing at his face. This gave John a little time to evaluate everything around him.

Not far from him, he saw his three-dimensional image recorder next to a rock. The sight of it gave him an idea of something he had not done since he was in boot

184

camp. John carefully moved towards his recorder as the wolves dealt with their new problem. Picking it up while keeping his eyes on the old wolf that was not enjoying the antiseptic bandage stinging his eyes.

John picked up his military-issue green rubber-coated recorder to access the side compartment. Pulling out a small card about the size of a quarter, he flipped it over and put it back in.

John could see the old wolf had about half the bandage off. Hurrying, he took the front lens off and snapped it on the back of the unit. Pushing the power button, he was happy to see the main display come alive. This was just in time because the pack had regrouped, toward him.

John rapidly tapped the power and setting buttons with his thumb and index finger as he placed the front of the device towards his face. Recovered, the old wolf and his pack launched toward John causing him to take his fingers off the buttons and let out a roar from deep down in his lungs.

Suddenly, a ten-foot wide, highly distorted holographic image of John's face projected just in front of the advancing pack. The hungry, bloodthirsty pack suddenly found themselves spinning from the shock, in any available direction they could find to get out of there. Yips, squeals, and high-toned barks came out of them in rapid-fire succession as they dug their paws deep into the ground to leave.

A mischievous smile now crossed John's face as he stepped up on a small rock to watch them drift away in a cloud of dust. Enjoying the sight of it, John stood there watching them run, the pack slowed after a while to a trot about a mile out, at the same time John found himself squinting a little just to see them. The growing infection in his leg was causing him to sweat a little as the pack was starting to look a little blurry that far out. In his mind, the knowledge of his growing medical condition was starting to eclipse his fun.

Sitting back down on the rock to finish bandaging his leg. The fight with the pack caused him to lose blood and now his pant leg was soaked. Carefully, John collected the contents of his pack that was tossed all around him. Reaching down next to a rock, he noticed something small and black. John picked up the small, black Bible that he thought he had handed to Sargent Peters.

Holding it up, the corner of his mouth curved slightly as he realized what had happened.

"Good man Mr. Peters," he quietly spoke as he gave it a small kiss and put it in his pack.

Putting his pack back on and picking up his rifle, John looked toward the distant green area he had seen earlier. "Half a mile, I sure hope it has water." He quietly spoke to himself.

The heat of the desert grew hotter and hotter as the sun ascended the sky. Or at least it seemed that way to John's fevered mind as he dragged his feet along. Soon it was not just his feet that were feeling heavy but his pack as well as a feeling of sickness started to wash over him.

As John grew closer, he realized that the "green area" he had seen in the distance was only the tips of brush or trees sticking out of a small canyon ahead of him. Pausing for a moment he noticed the canyon had a gentle slope downward along a deer trail of small red stones in the sand. Starting down the path, the side of his boot hit one of the stones. Grasping at a small tree to steady himself, John almost hugged it as he repositioned himself to walk again.

After a few more steps, something came close to his eyes, instinctively he grabbed a tree limb that almost hit him in the face, forcing himself to stop. John just stood there for a moment, looking around and then down at a lizard that was on the trail. He tried hard to focus on it. In front of him were two lizards that looked exactly the same. The sight of it was confusing. They both stuck their tongues out at the same time as well as blinking in unison.

John was already breathing hard out of his open mouth as he finally noticed that his twin lizards had both turned at the same time, departing together. John laid his

186

left hand over his eyes to stop the confusion for a moment.

"Ahh... Great, this is the last thing I need now." John remarked as he wiped his forehead. Re-starting his moving down the hill, within two or three yards, John's right foot stepped on a rock that seemed to disappear out from under his foot.

He desperately grasped around for anything to hold on to, but it was too late. John had nothing around him but uprising air as he was falling downward. He spun like a ball as he hit something like wood and bounced off it. Another terror-filled second or two in the air and John landed on some loose rock. However, he did not stop; the loose rock and he was now in the air together once more.

Suddenly everything came to a stop as he hit the flat ground. Barely aware of things around him, something sounded like crunching and then a woman screaming. The rocks he had hit followed unmercifully behind him. The impact of them quickly caused everything around John to go black and then silent.

Stings of pain—was it his leg he felt? Or does everything hurt? He screamed, but it seemed he could not move. He opened his eyes to a blurry thin man in front of him. "Oh God, it's an alien," he thought, or maybe it was his mother? He could not tell. Everything was blurry and filled with pain. These things, these images around him made no sense when they spoke, something big and hairy held his arms. Why was everything so dark? "Oh, God. FIRE, FIRE," John yelled at the top of his lungs as things passed in watery form in front of him.

Finally, John's body relaxed as the pain overwhelmed him and he fell unconscious. The hands that held him down as his leg was being set slowly moved away from him. In the flickering firelight of the fading afternoon, an elderly man with sun-touched wrinkles and white hair stood up, looking down at John as he lay on a mat.

It was the Native American face of Kaviu, respected elder and father of Lonan who had held John down.

Fading Starlight

Kaviu had a concerned look on his face as he looked at this strange man who fell from the mountain into their camp. Lonan and his sister Kasa both turned their faces of concern from John to look at their father.

The Present

Megan had just finished answering the most recent round of questions when she noticed her father had arrived to sit near her. Megan glanced at his eyes and then the corner of her eye drifted down to his folded hands on the table.

Her eyes quickly moved back forward to Goodrick who motioned with his hand that he had no further questions. Megan's eyes then drifted off to General Bond who was looking over her paperwork, getting ready to ask Megan questions. But something about her father's hands caused her to look back at them and notice the bandages that barely covered his scuffed-up knuckles. Henry feeling her gaze slipped his hands under the table.

Raising her eyes slowly, she started to look upward at her father's face as General Victoria Bond's questions snapped her back forward. "Captain Becker, after the fight in the cave with the alien that you spoke of, and after their time device was activated, how many personnel made the trip backward in time?"

"Just one Ma'am. Captain John Becker," Megan responded.

"Thank you. Do the books end at this point or do they continue?" Bond inquired.

"They continue. So far, we have found four volumes. The bulk of the writing is after this point as he describes everyday life." Megan responded back.

"And have you read everything written?" General Bond asked.

Megan calmly responded, "Ah, no I have not."

"Why is that?" General Bond inquired.

"Because, General Bond, I have been cataloging the events as they happened, keeping detailed notes in an effort to make sure everything is recorded in the first book." Captain Becker responded back.

"Why the first one?" Bond asked.

Responding, Megan remarked, "Book one seems to contain the bulk of the information regarding the future events. Both the battles, discoveries, and enemy tactics."

General Bond paused for a moment, then asked, "And there is none of that in the next books?"

"From what I have seen, there is not. Book one ends with just a few pages into his new life in the ancient past," Megan calmly responded.

General Bond lightly nodded her head as looked down for a moment and wrote something. "Captain Becker, in that case, could you summarize the ending events of book one after he arrived in the past?"

Megan's shoulders relaxed some as she was a little taken back. She only expected that she would need to reconstruct information related to the future and alien technology. "Ah. Yes, just prior to the time jump, the aliens attacked their hidden base. In the fight, Captain John Becker and one alien somehow slipped into the device, sending both backward in time. Captain Becker found himself alone with an infected leg wound after killing the alien. After traveling several hours in the desert, the infection made him delirious. Apparently, he fell off a rock face, sustaining a broken leg, ribs, and a dislocated arm. He then received medical attention from a local tribe, and according to the end of book one, it seems he became a member of that tribe."

Megan sat there looking at General Bond with an emotionless look as she tried not to think about what she had just said. Somehow, Victoria Bond could see it and for a moment, she considered what would be going on in her mind if that were her son.

General Bond's eyes looked up to see Sam Arris, who had just entered to sit in the back of the room. He had obviously changed his clothing from early that morning and his face looked a little puffy. In fact, his right eye looked slightly swollen as he was carefully trying to look normal. It did not take much imagination on her part to know that Henry, who sat next to his daughter, had an odd look on his face—the desire not to be noticed.

Turning her head, she looked at the clock. "If no one has any objections, I would like to suggest we break for an early lunch." Just as Victoria finished saying that, she was handed a note from another officer who approached her. Reading it, she looked up, "Let me change that. Due to some recent events overseas, I think the rest of my day will be occupied."

General Bond looked around the room noticing who else was now receiving notes. Admiral Goodrich quickly finished reading his note and looked up; "Ah, General Bond, I move that we table this conversation, and reconvene this meeting tomorrow so that we may take the rest of the day for other issues we need to get up to speed on."

With a quick agreement on everyone's part, everyone started standing up to leave. General Bond stood up and waited for a moment to watch the people make their way out. Walking up to Megan to congratulate her on making it through this round of questions, they saluted and shook hands with a slight grin.

As they did Megan's eyes wandered over to look once more at her father's hands. This, of course, caused Victoria to do the same. Henry calmly picked up a folder and placed it in his right hand turning it away from their sight. Victoria turned her head to look with her now emotionless eyes, straight at Henry. Quickly giving him the look of an unhappy older sister, Victoria nodded her head towards Sam, "Anything I need to know, General Mullins?"

"Not on that issue, but I will need to talk with you later," Henry responded.

Victoria Bond's eyebrow raised a little as she pondered his words for a moment. "Very well. If you will excuse me, I have other matters that I need to look into right now."

Megan caught all the little signals of body language that way yelling 'something' had happened, even though she had no clue what. "Are you going to tell me what happened?" Megan asked her father after General Bond exited the room.

"Nope, I'm not. We have bigger problems to talk about. But, not here." Henry gave her a head nod to follow him as he moved to leave the Pentagon.

Walking outside into the damp air as the rainstorm was almost in the city. The dark black rain clouds creeping across the sky stood in stark contrast to the blue sky it was now covering. Standing in uniform, Megan's mind started to wander a little. Looking at the approaching dark sky, she was gently reminded of her dream. Finally, the car came around Henry nudged Megan's arm, as he noticed how lost in thought she was, "Meg." At the mention of her name, Megan's mind came drifting back.

Henry had quietly handed the driver a note just before a marine opened the door for him and his daughter. Megan and her father climbed into the back of the car as the same marine in dress uniform closed the door. Slowly they drove away as Megan noticed something and spoke up. "This is not the way to the Ritz. Where are we going?"

"Oh, sorry honey, I promised General Bond that we would drop by her house and pick up some files she forgot," Henry responded.

Megan turned her head towards her father, General Mullins, "Is it far?"

"Not far, but when we get there totally depends on traffic," Henry remarked.

Nodding her head slowly in confirmation, Megan responded back, "Ok, do you want to use this time to talk about other stuff ?"

Henry glanced up to look at the driver's rearview mirror. "Ah... yeah, you mentioned the other day about getting a house and raising Johnny together. I was wondering if you had any more

191

thoughts on that?"

The question seemed totally off-subject and caught Megan off guard as her eyebrows came together in a curious look. Megan's mouth opened for a moment with nothing coming out as she looked at him. Then she opened her mouth once more, speaking slowly at first. "I was thinking maybe we could try finding a place in Santa Fe, Albuquerque, or even Flagstaff. Why, what were you thinking?"

"Well, I'm not sure, but I wasn't thinking anything that southern. Maybe Denver or Steamboat Springs," Henry answered back.

Playing along with the conversation, Megan responded, "Denver is way too large of a city for me, and I think I would have to research Steamboat Springs."

Henry looked for a moment out the window. "Oh, good. The traffic seems light today. So what kind of research would you need to do in the area?"

Megan slowly pushed her back into the corner of her seat as her right eyebrow raised a bit contemplating what her father was up to. "Well, you know, the average things like schools, crime rate, and weather. Maybe even restaurants, museums, jobs, and stuff like that."

Megan started to shrug her shoulders toward her father, wondering why they were talking about this. Henry slowly raised his hand a few inches off his lap. With his index finger, he made a circular motion indicating that they should keep talking. Megan's eyes looked down at his finger and then up to his eyes. She followed his eyes as they moved in the direction of the driver.

Slowly she nodded her head as she resumed talking. "I think... I would have a serious problem moving to a place like Steamboat if it did not have a good Mexican restaurant. I mean seriously, I like almost live off this stuff. And Johnny seems to really like to build shapes of mountains and things out of the rice and beans."

Henry did not smile, but asked, "Does he ever eat his creations?"

"Sometimes he does, mostly he just likes the tacos. He digs the lettuce out when he thinks I'm not looking," Megan answered back.

"Typical, so he's really just a meat and potatoes type of kid?" Henry remarked. Giving her a big smile, his mustache moved upwards into that grin she has known all her years. "At least, he came by it honestly."

"I guess I will never get him to eat much at a Chinese place. Hopefully, some future girlfriend will get him to improve his diet," Megan remarked.

Henry continued smiling as he turned his head to look out the window, noticing they had arrived. With a serious look in his eyes and a fake smile on his face, he spoke to the driver, "Driver, wait here. Hopefully, we will be just a moment."

"Yes, sir," responded the young man.

Henry and Megan walked quietly up to the door. They stopped in front of the deep red cherry wood door of the brick home. Henry punched in the access number on the pad near the door. After he heard a click, he turned the door handle to walk in.

Inside, Megan turned to look at her father whose smile was now gone, replaced by a look of concern she had only seen a few times in her life. Each time it was connected to a major loss. She knew the look and it was starting to shake her.

"Dad, what is it? Why did we come here?"

"...Victoria and I sometimes use this place as a secure place to talk," Henry reached into the inside pocket of his uniform and handed her the note.

A cold numbness started within Megan as she read Major Watson's note out loud.

GENERAL MULLINS,

ALL PHONE SERVICE IS OUT. THREE MEN FROM THE CIA ARRIVED LAST NIGHT. ALL CONTENTS OF THE CAVE WERE FOUND MISSING IN THE MORNING. NO ONE HAS SEEN ANYTHING. MEN FROM THE CIA ARE GONE AS WELL. GOLD BOOKS CAN NOT BE FOUND.

PLEASE ADVISE.
MAJOR T.A. WATSON, COMMANDING.

Megan just stared at the note when she finished reading it. Henry reached up and slowly tugged it from between her fingers, causing her to look up at him.

"Why?" was Megan's only word.

"I don't know, but it totally guts everything we are doing if we don't have the physical evidence to back it up," Henry responded.

"Why the CIA?" Megan emphatically asked.

"It wasn't the CIA," Henry responded back.

"Are you sure?" Megan asked.

Henry opened his eyes a little wider as the finger on his right hand touched his left cheek slowly moving downward. "Pretty sure."

"How can you be sure, do you know some...?" Megan stopped for a moment, her thinking drawn once again to the bandage on her father's knuckles. Pausing for a moment to reflect on what she was seeing, "Can I assume that," pointing to his hand, "the bandage on your hand has anything to do with you being sure?"

Henry briefly looked at the back of his hand. Wishing to avoid that discussion, he just looked at his daughter. "Ahh, no comment."

Megan gave her father "a look" that told him she was willing to table the question for now.

"As long as you're sure. Do you have any idea who took them?" Megan asked.

With a slight amount of depression in his voice, Henry responded, "None." Pausing for a moment, he spoke up once more. "Megan, I would like to say, you seem a lot calmer about this than I was."

Megan's eyebrow raised in a very matter-of-fact look, as he glanced once more at his hand, "Apparently," Megan remarked as she pulled out her cell phone and held it at eye level. Turning she sat down in one of the chairs in Victoria's living room, pausing for a moment she looked up at her father as she put her cell phone back in her pocket. "Well, that explains why I've got nothing this morning from them. Watson's message said nothing about Johnny so I can assume everything is ok with him." Looking up at her father's face, Megan asked, "What's the plan now, Dad?"

Henry pulled up a chair and sat down in front of his daughter. "Not sure, at this point, we don't know who took it or why. So, be friendly to everyone, and don't let anyone in on what's happening. We can trust Victoria, she is one of a few people in this town I would trust."

Megan slowly nodded her head to confirm what he was saying.

"As of right now, we just need to wait it out until these meetings are over," Henry added as he sat for a moment. Pausing, Henry took in a deep breath and then got up, and walked over to an old antique desk. Opening the left drawer, he pulled out a manila-colored folder. "Let's get back."

The power of the cold rain was becoming stronger as it was now starting to blow in sideways across the land. Henry's driver was driving a little slower with the sudden gusts of wind jerking the car from time to time on the road under the darkening sky. Megan and Henry made a bit of light chitchat about the rain as they moved along toward the Ritz Hotel. But after a while, even the chitchat came to an end, as the storm seemed to help emphasize that their world was changing.

The driver turned into the parking lot of the hotel, finally stopping under the covered parking near the front door that did little for the rain coming in sideways. Henry thanked the driver as they stepped out into the strong winds. Without much comment from either one, they entered the main lobby and turned towards Fyve restaurant.

Soon, the seating hostess was walking them to a booth in the back of the room. As they walked, Henry noticed several officers sitting with General Bond at a table. Henry calmly, without a word, set the manila folder down in front of Victoria as he passed.

His actions caught her a little off guard; Victoria paused as she saw it sitting in front of her. The other officers at the table stopped talking and looked at her. Calmly and professionally, she moved her hand in front of her to indicate that it was nothing special.

"He was just returning it," Victoria remarked to them.

Megan and Henry sat quietly at the table, half looking at their menu, and a half reflecting on the day's events. Soon, the waiter came up to ask for their selection.

Henry put on a fake smile and handed him the menu back. "Just the Angus beef burger, no mustard, extra cheese, sweet tea."

The waiter, who was maybe twenty years old with the beginnings of his own mustache, smiled, nodded his head responding, "Thank you, and your selection ma'am?"

Not really wanting to eat, Megan ordered anyway. "Ah, yeah... I will take the Quinoa and Kale Salad with the Turkey Club."

"Very good, and anything to drink?" The waiter asked.

"Just water please," Megan responded as she returned the menu.

The waiter then nodded his head with a smile and left.

Time passed as they sat there in reflective silence until the food came. Megan smiled when it arrived, picked a fork, and looked up at her father. "Well, at least we have been taking pictures of everything."

Henry nodded his head slowly in response, "True." Henry took a bite of his burger, "That will be good for us, but almost useless to the chiefs because photos can be faked."

Megan stopped and looked at her fork, "Thought of that, but at least we have several years before the aliens come. We may not be able to convince the brass today. But maybe we can somehow get people and things ready for the future."

Megan flipped her fork around and lightly stabbed her

salad. Pulling it up, Megan took a bite of the salad as her mind continued thinking about the situation she now found herself in. "I hate this. I would rather be back at the camp." She quietly whispered.

Henry nodded a yes as he slowly kept eating.

"Dad, any idea how these people pulled it off? We have an armed camp of almost forty people. The only thing I can think of is some Special Forces team. And in that case, if it wasn't ours, could it have been another government?" Megan asked as she stopped eating.

Henry calmly responded, "Could be."

"And is this part of something we can change, or is it inevitable?" Megan asked.

Henry's head slowly moved back and forth, "I don't know." He responded between bites.

"And how can you just keep eating with everything that has happened?" Megan asked in protest with a growing layer of frustration in her voice.

Henry looked his daughter in the eye and asked, "Can you think of anything else that should be done right now?"

Megan inhaled a large breath of air, held it for a moment then exhaled. "No, I guess I am just frustrated."

"Well, we have the rest of the day and you have read more about little Johnny's story than I have. Tell me what happened after the tribe found him." Henry asked as he picked up a napkin.

Megan tried a bite of her sandwich, thinking about where to start the story. "Well, my guess is that after he passed out, he most likely had no idea of how long he was unconscious. When he woke up, he found himself bandaged up and was being helped by several people, including what he thought may have been the chief of the tribe and his family. They could not speak to him; all they could do was point and smile. After a few days, they helped him hobble out of the hunting camp."

"Sounds painful, I would think the primitive level of medicine could not have been good for him," Henry remarked as he responded to his daughter.

"I would think so. They did give him something for the pain. And they kept treating his leg with something that he learned came from a Yucca plant. Plus, it sounds like they did a good job setting his broken leg. After three days, they made it back to the main camp." Megan remarked as she lifted her sandwich to take another bite. Pausing for a second with her food near her lips, Megan added, "Sounds like they had about thirty to forty people in the camp. Everyone was shocked to see him."

"Wow, and what happened after that?" Her father asked.

"Not sure, haven't read that far yet. I did however take a lot of pictures also with my phone, so I'll let you know as I read them." Megan remarked with half a smile as she pulled out her phone.

Fading Starlight
Chapter Seven
Kasa.

John limped into camp along the Colorado River with the help of Lonan. Slowly, several people came out of their adobe earthen homes to see the strange man. John had not shaved for several days, so his black beard with red highlights was starting to grow in. It was maybe a little over half an inch long as everyone gathered around to look at him.

They had never seen anyone like him. Hair grew on his face...was he part animal? His clothes and skin were different. Where did he come from? The elder of the tribe, Kaviu, told everyone the story of how he fell down from the sky into the camp. And how they had taken care of him.

Everyone agreed this had to be a sign, but a sign of what no one knew. The camp then conferred together several paces away from John. From a distance away Kasa could see the pain on John's face as he tried to keep standing on his bad leg away from them.

With a smile on her delicate face, she came over and helped him to a rock so that he could sit under the shade of a bush. As the tribe talked, Kasa wandered back with water for him to drink. John smiled and tried, unsuccessfully, to figure out how to say thank you. Kasa smiled, then walked away to talk to Malia, her half-sister.

John slipped his pack and rifle off as he watched the meeting in front of him. An old Indian woman started talking to everyone, making hand motions that made John think she was talking about an animal. To his surprise, she turned and pointed at him. At this point, John realized that she thought he was an animal. Kasa heard her say this and spoke up from the other side of the group. Everyone looked at her as she spoke, and rebuked the old Indian woman. She pointed at her groin area and then at John, making a fist with a strong look on her face as if to tell everyone that he was not an animal but a man. The look on everyone's face became a look of relief as she spoke.

John got a slightly shocked look on his face as he looked down at his groin for a moment. "Oh, ok."

One of the other women, Chochmingwu, spoke in Kaviu's ear while pointing at John. Kaviu got a strange look on his face, but slowly nodded his head in an affirming manner. The tribal discussion went on for some time until it seemed to John that they had reached a natural ending. Kaviu then ordered his son to help his sister prepare a place for John to rest and sleep for the night.

John had chosen to say very little, but instead watched and learned. He was a man out of time and he was feeling it. He reasoned that it would just be best to try and fit into their world. Thankfully, no one had figured out how to open his pack. The Velcro, zippers, and micro-magnetic latches were unknown to them. He was a little concerned that if he showed them what some of his things could do, they might try to kill him.

Watching the tribe, he decided to evaluate what he was seeing. Nomadic tribes living off fish, deer, and a few buffalo. The few words of Navajo he learned as a child seemed useless here.

John looked at Kaviu. He was not the oldest of the tribe but seemed highly respected as if he was the leader. His face was weathered, there was almost no color left in his hair, he had many scars on his left arm, and he was missing his left pinky.

Logan, taller than his father, had the same nose. He had no scars, but it seemed like the other young men would not dare challenge him. He had black hair, two short braids, sported a wide leather armband, and he was slender in overall body type.

Kasa was the shortest person in her family. She had a delicate face and pleasant eyes that could move very quickly. She seemed to have many friends in the camp.

At this point, John realized something as he continued to watch. The young girl and her family seemed to have the most slender body type and face compared to the rest of the tribe. Also, most of the people, including the women, dressed in either deer or some other big animal skin. The chief's daughter, however, seemed to prefer coyotes or fox furs. He noted it as an interesting fact as he kept looking over the tribe.

Their housing was nothing more than depressions hollowed out in the earth, reinforced with rock walls, and capped with wood and brush. Some of the young men grew tired of the talk and wandered off to the river to check the fish traps, while some of the women returned to their fires to work. John noticed a few children, but the overall lack of them seemed odd, considering the number of adults.

Kasa started to walk over to him with a small container she carried from the river. Bending her knees, she came down to his level and offered it to him. John pointed at it and smiled.

"Kuuyi," Kasa responded back.

John was unsure if she was talking about the water or the container it came in. He had started to notice some words were getting used over and over again for various objects. So it seemed to him and her that it was time for his language classes. He pointed to the container and said, "Kuyi?" Then he stuck his finger in the water, "Or Kuyi?"

Kasa smiled and stuck her finger in his water as well. "Kuuyi." She then nodded her head left to right and spoke once more, "Kuyi" indicating with her hands that he should expand the word, "Kuuyi."

John smiled and tried harder, "Kuuyi." She smiled in return at his proper speaking of the word "water."

The young lady Kasa then stood up and walked away as John thought about it. "One word at a time, he thought." John looked around at the overall camp. In his mind, he talked to himself about what he was seeing. "This must be before the Spanish came—no

201

horses. The few petroglyphs I have seen, not even a hint of them. Five to eight hundred years ago, maybe? In that case, could I find my way to Europe? Maybe I could influence science in Europe and make the earth advance faster?"

John looked over to his left to see the women working on a few baskets. Their style of baskets looked familiar, then he remembered his mother's team digging up baskets similar to them. "I think Mom called it the basket maker period. I wonder when that was?" He whispered to himself.

Time passed as he watched Kasa and Lonan work on a small structure near one of the other buildings. The bright blue sky was now shifting to darker hues in the east, indicating the coming of night. Soon both of them came and helped John to his feet. Lonan picked up John's pack and a strange metal stick as the three of them moved toward the small structure.
Both of them smiled and pointed to it. John returned the smile as he realized they had made it for him.

As John lay there in his little hut resting his broken body, he found himself relaxing to the sound of the tribe working on their daily activities. The sheer exhaustion of the past several days had caught up to him. The pain of forcing his body to walk every day to reach this place had brought him to the point of burnout.

The voices of the women soon intermixed with the sounds of the river as the light wind brought him the smell of something cooking over the fire. With this and more, John continued to relax as he slipped off, peaceful sleep had found him as he offered no resistance.

During the night, John rolled in the wrong direction onto his sore ribs, causing him to wake up from the jolt of pain. Rolling over on his back, his eyes could clearly see through the dark gaps in his roof covering. The glory of the night sky was spectacular. Lit up in a spectacular display the intense beauty of the stars, with no light pollution contaminating the sky. The Milky Way overhead displayed its bold band of alabaster and porcelain-colored stars to satisfy John's mind as his eyes enjoyed the sight.

In college, he took several astronomy classes. So, in the childlike part of himself that John rarely allowed himself to enjoy. John admired the night sky as he allowed himself to think once again about what those worlds looked like. After a couple more moments John painfully pulled himself by his elbows a little further out of the hut to see the full sky. The thin crescent of the moon with Mars, Jupiter, and Saturn could clearly be seen. In his mind, he gladly recalled several of the stars overhead.

An hour or more passed as he slowly became aware that there was a difference in the sky from what he remembered. Concern passed over his face as he stared at a few of the stars. Finally, he just stared at one star in the black sky. Lying there, just looking at it, a tear slowly formed in the corner of his eye as he realized the idea of traveling to Europe was not going to happen.

England had not even been formed yet, as most of the earth was still very primitive. He thought about what did exist at this time in history and realized that the only world power he knew of was far away in Egypt.

The Present

Henry had long since finished his burger as Megan talked. He welcomed the stories as he also welcomed the fact that they kept her mind off of what just happened. With her sandwich gone, along with half of her salad, Megan slowed down as she decided she was done eating.

Pushing her plate forward, Megan stopped talking when Henry got a text message.

"Who is it?" Megan inquired.

"Victoria. Apparently, the morning meetings have been canceled. I will need to attend situations meeting in the morning concerning events overseas."

"Hmm, lucky you. I guess that means I get to sleep in," Megan responded as she picked up one of her father's uneaten French fries off of his plate.

"Well, I was hoping Major Watson would reconnect with us so that we can acquire more information," Henry calmly responded as he put his cell phone in his shirt pocket.

"Sounds good to me," Megan remarked.

"And if he does, then I would like you to question him and find out as much as you can about what happened at the camp," Henry remarked to his daughter.

Megan nodded a yes as she took a drink. Henry slowly gained a look on his face, wondering what he would have done in his grandson's position. Looking at Megan, he asked, "What did our Johnny do next?"

"Well, he realized roughly the period of time he was in. He resolved to learn the language and start teaching the tribe how to improve and build better things. Kinda also sounds like he was hoping to start a school."

"A school?" Henry's eyebrow rose.

"Yep, he figured if he could not get to any place advanced, then he was going to advance the people in the area as far as he could. Build a culture, build a civilization." Megan remarked.

"Wow, " Henry responded." And personally? Did he ever get close to anyone?" Henry asked.

"Hmm... he talks a lot about his teacher, Kasa. I wouldn't be surprised if they built a relationship," Megan responded as she glanced at the next picture.

Henry smiled, and nodded his head slowly, "Good for him."

Megan smiled as she looked around the room. "We should let the people here clean up for the dinner crowd."

With a nod of his head, Henry and Megan got up and made their way to their rooms as they chatted about living in the past. Reaching the rooms, Megan looked over at her father, "Ya know Dad, in a way, I am jealous of my son," Megan remarked.

"Jealous, why is that?" as he pulled his electronic room

key out of his pocket.

"He describes the simplicity of the past, and by the tone of his writing, well, I can tell he is really enjoying it," Megan responded.

Henry stopped for a moment, looking at the electronic key in his hand, thinking over the contrast between his key and Johnny's simpler life. As he did, he remembered a camping trip when he was young where he stayed in a cabin. Something deep within pulled at him, a long-lost longing for that life. Henry looked up and spoke in a low voice, "I get it. You know with everything he had been through, alien wars, the death of his friends and family, I'm glad his last years will be pleasant ones. He deserves something nice after all that." Henry paused in his speaking for a moment, reflecting on it all. "I guess I'm a little jealous too."

Henry then looked back down at his room key; he ran it through the scanner and walked in without saying another word. Megan stood there, watching him disappear behind the door. For the first time that she could remember, she could see in her father's face that he looked like a tired old man.

Someone who just longed for a quiet place to stop for a while. She stared at his closed door, pondering for a little while. Lowering her own eyes Megan turned and entered her own room.

Megan was hard asleep that next morning when her room phone started ringing. With her eyes still closed, her right hand fumbled around until she found the phone. Rolling over, her red hair wrapped around her face like a mask as she pulled the handset to her face. Megan made a grunt of a sound to indicate she was awake.

Henry's voice started speaking, "Sorry about waking you. Victoria would like to speak with us this morning. Please meet us for breakfast ASAP." With that, Henry hung up the phone as Megan's arm phone arm went limp in defeat, letting the phone fall to the floor.

Henry watched as Megan rounded the corner of the restaurant, dressed in her uniform, with her hat under her arm. Her uniform and hair were "almost" perfect, showing off her skill to be ready at a moment's notice. Sitting down at the table, everyone was aware she was doing an excellent job of faking being ready in the morning. Henry slid a cup of coffee directly in front of her as her right hand came into place to receive it.

With a semi-glazed look in her eyes, she looked at Victoria's face as if to say she was reporting in for duty, just... having problems articulating the needed words. Victoria resisted the urge to laugh at the sight of her, as the corner of her mouth barely lifted upward.

Victoria sat her own cup down as she started to speak. "I wanted to give you both a report on what is going on. Both here and all things related to project Lorenzo. First of all, your father, General Mullins, notified me of the events that happened at your camp. This is a serious breach in Project Lorenzo and I have talked quietly with several people here, including CIA Director Arris. And it seems no one knows what happened."

"We had a pilot from Hill Air Force base conduct a flyover of the region to discover that two of the local cell towers in the area suffered some sort of damage. We talked with the local cell provider and according to them, it looks like storm damage knocked them out, maybe lightning, they're not sure."

"But according to the National Weather Service, it was a normal night with no recorded storms. Partial cell coverage should be available shortly." Victoria's face gave a look of 'I'm sorry,' as she continued, "Because of this, the midday meeting will be short and most likely very unfriendly. If they believe that you are lying to them, you could all be disciplined."

At this point Megan found her words, interrupting,

"So they are calling us liars? They can call Major Watson as well as some of the others in the camp to testify," Megan announced.

Victoria was about to respond when Henry spoke up. "Nope, most of the people in that room know that the Major and I have worked together for years. To them, he would only back up what I would have to say. As for the other officers, most of them were once part of your personal archeological team. If we get disciplined, I can guarantee that Watson and the other officers will have a hard time reaching their next pay grade."

Megan's mind was now stirring awake as she looked at Victoria, "Well, how bad can it get? What's the worst it could be?"

"The discipline will be at their discretion. But you could watch your son grow up while you sit in a jail cell," Victoria replied with a stern look.

Stunned at that statement, Megan sat there quietly as she started to remember a dream she did not like. Henry's hand slowly moved over on top of hers as he tried to quietly comfort her. "To continue, you will need to be refreshed, awake, and ready for them today," General Bond inserted as she looked at Megan.

"Your father, however, will already be present because of the growing situation in East Africa. It has not made the press yet. All the press knows is that an earthquake in the Indian Ocean caused a tsunami. What they don't know is that one of China's most advanced spy ships just got pushed up on the Somalian coast. An Islamic group has taken it, but China will not allow it. So they have sent their Navy to take it back. The British and the United States have a chance to beat them to the vessel two hours before they get there. Your father is required in the situation room for this."

Henry looked at Megan to gain her attention, "And I am sorry, Meg, but I have to leave now. I have put off attending the meeting as long as I could because of what Victoria was going to say. But I need to leave now."

A bit stunned, Megan watched as her father stand up

to say goodbye. Her world was not right and she could feel it slipping away.

Victoria took a deep breath and spoke up, "Captain Becker, you should know that a small group of us are trying to do all we can. We would really like to know who took the golden books."

In desperation, Megan's mind tried to think of anyone who could have done it. "General Bond?"

"Yes?" Victoria responded back.

"In the last few days, there has been one person that has seemed different. Have you checked out MacCallister MacWilliams?" Victoria smiled as Megan continued talking. "He is in charge of the Office of Management and Acquisitions and I was...."

General Bond slowly raised her right hand in an effort to let her know to stop talking. "I'm sorry, Mr. MacWilliams, Mac, is one of the few people you can trust around here on this subject. I know he's a little odd, but he's safe. Mac is one of the most tech-savvy people around, but at the same time, he is very old-fashioned. You should see the man's office in his home. He's got a lot of homemade gadgets that I have no idea what they do. I would call it the mad scientist look. Today's youth would call it Steampunk. Trust me, he's about as loyal as a puppy dog," Victoria exclaimed.

Megan sat there for a moment and then asked, "Then who could it have been?"

"I really don't know. Right now it feels like the world is about to explode. The people who took the books were good; they thought of everything. It may not have been anyone from our government." Victoria remarked.

Megan finally took a drink of coffee. "What do you mean, they were good?"

Victoria got a funny look on her face, "Did you notice your father's hands?"

Megan's eyebrow raised, "Yes."

"They knew to blame the CIA. They played off Sam and your father's history."

"They have a history? What kind of history?" Megan inquired.

Victoria leaned back a little further into her seat. "Normally I would not tell you this. But in view of what they may put you through today in the meeting, you should at least know what happened. Sam and your father have a history because of your mother."

Megan's head lowered a little and turned to the side in puzzlement, looking at General Bond.

"After Danny was born and before you, there was a junior officers' party. Sam had way too much to drink, and let's just say, he got way too close to your mother. Henry saw it and it took four men to pull him off, Sam. That's why Sam has that scar on his nose. Henry broke it, as well as Sam's right hand that touched your mother, and maybe a rib or two." Victoria remarked with a slight grin.

Megan leaned backwards and rested her head against the wall behind her as she took it in. Her mouth slowly opened partway in shock at the report. Then her head straightened up as she thought of something. "Wait, so my father's hands... did he just beat up Sam Arris again?"

Victoria had a mischievous look in her eyes as she raised her coffee cup to drink. "Neither Sam nor your father is talking about it. But Sam's aide said that he did request a clean shirt and jacket just before entering the room. And, I would say, his face yesterday, was evidence that something happened."

Megan's face changed to a curious look mixed with a little pride as she raised her cup to her mouth. "Well, that certainly puts a new light on things."

Chatting for a moment about her father a text message arrived on Megan's phone. She pulled it out as Victoria asked if it was from the camp.

"Yes, it is. It's Major Watson," Megan responded.

"What does he say?" Victoria inquired.

Megan quoted from the text, "I assume you got the report we sent. Your son is doing fine. Captain Williams is not feeling well. Captain Hansen is taking him into town. Cannot contact the General's phone. What does the General advise?" Megan looked up at General Bond.

Fading Starlight

Victoria thought about it for a moment. "Tell him to continue to hold the camp, document everything, and that you will call him in one hour," Victoria ordered.

"Got it," Megan responded back as she started to send the message.

The Past

John walked out to the edge of a red rock overlook. His body was growing a little older. He had long since started to adopt some of the local clothing. His once broken leg now showed the evidence of a scar, as did the side of his chest. His black and red beard had become longer as was his hair. Tied in a ponytail behind him, it now contained a few traces of white, like his sideburns. He thought very little of his injuries as he was only reminded of them now by his limp and each year's return of winter.

The camp, only a few hundred yards away, was now feeling like home. The fading welcoming warmth of the afternoon sun on his face and canyon walls were hints of the approach of fall. Pulling his rifle up closer he flipped it over his shoulder to hang by its strap. Over the last year, John had pulled a few things out of his pack that he thought the tribe could handle, even though the people viewed them as strange.

Everyone left his strange metal stick alone out of respect. They knew it made a big sound and that it could kill a buffalo. So John was becoming known as the great hunter who walked the land with a limp. To the tribe, he was the strange man they had saved, who fell from the sky. The hair on his face matched the reddish-black hair on his chest. He was kind, giving to the tribe, but protective of the things he had brought with him from the future.

John had mastered the tribe's language, or at least enough to cover everything he needed as well as the words needed to speak to Kasa. He knew he would never be leaving this world, these people, or this life. So why shouldn't he be planning his future now? She was lovely and kind, and her father had been pushing him at her. Here, he could teach, build, and equip the young for the future.

It had become a wonderful thing to think of a future with her, so he made it a reality. A new family, a father-in-law, two brothers-in-law, and her half-sister Malia, who had apparently married before they met. Her husband was Ahote, who from John's perspective was a better hunter than a builder, at least from the looks of his pit house. In time, John taught him some simple stone skills—teaching him how to make the walls stronger so that they could go higher.

It was a start, a simple start at improving civilization. John knew, with a little effort and encouragement, he could jump them about a thousand years down the road from the basket maker period to the Pueblo period. And his brother-in-law was a good start on that project. He reflected on what he was going to need. A good source of clay to teach pottery, maybe a source of copper and tin to make bronze. They had already met a small tribe from the north, who gladly traded the small amount of gold they had to acquire John's improved bow design he had made.

The warmth of the day settled in as John let his eyes wander the horizon. Entertaining thoughts of the future were soon interrupted as his brother-in-law at the edge of camp waved his arms and yelled his name. John noted that Lonan was standing near John's pit house when he called. A little concerned, he stepped off the small rock he was on to descend down the slight hillside towards the camp.

As he grew closer, Lonan spoke up, "John, I need to tell you. The old woman said Kasa will come early. She is in pain with your child now."

The sound of that announcement shocked John as he thought about it. A strange mix of adrenaline, fear, and numbness slowly overtook him, as he was not sure what to do next. His father-in-law, who was standing close by, slowly walked up near John. He had seen the look before and was not surprised.

"She will be fine... our family has strong women," Kaviu remarked as he spoke in a strong calming voice.

"I need to see her," John said.

His father-in-law slowly took hold of John's arm, causing him to stop. John turned his head and looked into his reassuring eyes.

"No," Kaviu remarked. "You would only get in the way. If I do not hold you now, the old woman would only throw you out." Kaviu smiled and nodded for John to follow him.

The afternoon soon grew into the evening as John sat there listening to everyone talk. His mind was full of thoughts as he contemplated things. Finally, he leaned over to his father-in-law and asked, "Why are there so few older children in the camp?"

Kaviu's face seemed to grow a little dark, as he did not want to answer this question. John, however, soon forgot he asked the question, as he heard Kasa cry out. John's body tensed just as Kaviu's gentle hand raised up to meet his chest.

"Be still, you can do nothing right now," Kaviu reassured him.

John's mind went over everything he had in his pack. He thought about anything that could help. After a moment or so, he fought his mind as he thought to himself, "Calm down you idiot, women around here have been doing this for a long time, it will be fine."

Time passed into the evening as the first stars of the night started to twinkle against the black of night. The nearly full moon was now a thin crest, peeking over the canyon lands in the distance as the tribe waited.

To fill the time, John and Kaviu and Lonan discussed that this fall; the tribe would travel west to another land to hunt, fish, and trade with other tribes. By their description, John figured they were heading for what he knew as Zion National Park. It sounded exciting to him, as it would be another chance to acquire more gold so that he could work on his book, and maybe a little copper. But, this subject was just meant to fill in the void of time as they waited.

Nampeyo, a gray-haired old woman whose face was delicately covered in the sun-inspired wrinkles of age, got up from a small cooking fire in the center of the camp. She brought a simple broth made from a turkey for John, Kaviu, and Lonan to drink.

With the arrival of the full darkness of night, Ahote walked over to the birthing hut in an effort to talk to his wife, Malia. Malia however was far too busy attending to her sister Kasa. John could not hear what she said to him, but from the reaction, it was obviously not the best decision Ahote had made today.

John knew that Kaviu's first wife had died long ago after giving birth to the twins, Lonan and Malia. So Kaviu married Chochmingwu, Kasa's mother, who spoke very little. All the women seemed to respect her position in the tribe, even though there were many women older than her. She seemed to have a good internal understanding of times and seasons. As a result, she somehow knew when things should or should not be done.

John found out later that Chochmingwu had foreknown that John was coming. She had seen in a vision two winters before that John was to be Kasa's husband. As a result, Kaviu stopped a marriage that was about to happen at that time for Kasa. For some reason, John started to remember all those things as he listened to the sounds taking place next door.

In the stillness of the dead of night, the conversations of the adults had died off as heads around the fire started to bob. The sound of children of the camp asleep was now enticing the remaining adults to join them. Soon, however, John heard the sound of a child crying, jolting the men awake in the pit house to excitement. With a hoop and holler, the men shouted for joy.

John moved forward as his eyes focused closely on the birthing hut to see Chochmingwu who soon brought out the child for John and the rest of the tribe to see.

Getting up, John quickly walked over to look into Chochmingwu's arms, "It's a boy," John exclaimed.

Chochmingwu looked up at him and asked, "and what shall we call him?"

John thought about it for a moment, realizing that if his mother were here, she would roll her eyes to hear him say it. "There is a name I have always liked, I will call him Lorenzo."

John reached out to take his son, but he quickly found several of the women getting in his way. Kaviu put his hand on John's arm and whispered into his ear. "Wait one moment, it is a custom that we as a tribe must welcome him into the tribe before we can hand him to you."

Before John could open his mouth, Chochmingwu stepped back from the other women and raised her hands, and spoke up in front of everyone. "My people, stop we must not do this." Her words caused everyone to stop, looking at her in confusion.

"I had a dream last night before Kasa had her pains. I was told that we should not do this. A tall man with a kind face and hair like John's came to me to say that this child is to be a sign that things have changed in our tribe. He said many are the trees of our tribe, but he has made this little tree to live when all others have fallen. He said that we would live on in his children."

Her words stunned the tribe and it left them uneasy as she handed the child to John.

"Here, take him, John. Kasa tells me that you speak to her late in the night with stories of what she calls a black book. Take your son and honor him according to the traditions of your people, for his eyes are like yours and not ours."

John looked down at Lorenzo's eyes as he accepted him from Chochmingwu. John smiled as he realized his son looked a lot like his old baby pictures.

Several people, including Kaviu, approached Chochmingwu to ask her more. As they talked, John slipped away from them into the pit house to visit Kasa with Lorenzo in his arms. Malia smiled as he came in,

214

kissed her sister on her forehead, and departed.

"John, is he beautiful?" Kasa remarked.

"Yes, yes he is," John answered back.

"I will think about Chochmingwu's words another day. But today, I would just like to hold him," a tired Kasa remarked.

John started to pass off Lorenzo to her as Kasa started to speak once more. "I have thought this over. I know that you have said that your past is dead. And that the life you had is gone."

A little puzzled by her topic of discussion, John answered. "Yes, that was the only place I have ever known. Now this place, this future has me. Here I live with you," John calmly spoke.

Kasa smiled and slowly moved her head back and forth. "You must not forget who you were. You have told some stories, but then you stopped."

"I stopped because I realize I have woken up. I have chosen to let go of that world," John stated.

"No, I want you to tell me the stories once more, husband. And I want our son to know these stories. You must hold your tongue no more," Kasa strongly stated. Kasa turned her head and kissed her son. Then turning him around so that John could see his face, "He has your face—let him know who he is. Otherwise, he will always feel alone, even with his family around him."

John smiled at her even though he did not fully understand everything she was telling him.

With a relaxing sigh, Kasa moved Lorenzo close to her. "John speak to me from your black book as I rest with our child. For your stories remind me of the words my mother told me from her old village, far to the east before coming here."

John relaxed into the moment as he laid his back against the wall. John's emotions traveled back and forth through his mind as he moved in closer, next to Kasa, who had already closed her eyes to listen. Opening up his backpack that was in the corner of the room, he pulled out his grandfather's old pocket Bible. Finding the place he left off so many months ago, he

215

started reading once more from Genesis. Unknown to John and Kasa, Malia and her younger two-year-old daughter Tablita, sat quietly on the other side of the wall listening in on John's stories.

The Present

Megan finished up her phone conversation with Major Watson as she walked back into the Pentagon. It was good to hear about everything that happened and that Johnny never noticed anything happening at all.

There was much to be concerned about—the strangeness of the three men, obviously the main thieves, as well as the strange report from Watson about Josh. She had never known him to sleepwalk. So the idea of him taking a midnight walk for the first time on the same night as the theft was odd.

But for now, Megan needed to put this out of her head, as she took off her hat and put it under her arm upon entering the building. Crossing the threshold of the doorway, Megan could clearly see Mac standing alone some distance away near a display case.

The corner of Megan's mouth turned upward a little as she slowly changed her direction toward him. Drawing closer, Mac turned a little in her direction as he acquired a calmer look, more pleasant, softer as the corners of his mouth came up a little.

Megan stopped in front of Mac, looking inquisitively down at him with her green eyes. "So, General Bond says you're a safe person to talk to around here."

Responding with an unchanging face, "I would like to think so." Mac remarked.

Megan paused for a moment, studying his face. "Any ideas on who took my books or where they are, little man?"

Mac's head tilted a little to the side as he responded. "No information has come forth as yet. But we are looking into every source we have. And good things come in small packages."

Mac's response stunned Megan a little, as her back and neck stiffened up very quickly in surprise. Both her eyebrows narrowed a little as she responded back. "My, you're a little sure of yourself, Mr. MacWilliams."

Mac's face changed ever so slightly to an embarrassed look as he responded back. "In my line of work, you need to be sure of everything. You find yourself learning to make decisions very fast on whom to trust and who not to trust. Who you should like and whom to stay away from."

Mac's body language was a little confusing to Megan. His confident look had the shades of something else as they talked. Was it what Victoria called his "loyal puppy dog side?" Or was he acting a little bit like he was attracted to her? And what was up with his comment? Deciding to change the subject because of the impending meeting that was in front of her. Megan nodded her head announcing, "Well, that's good to know. Now if you will excuse me, I have a meeting to attend."

Megan turned and got two steps away when she heard Mac speak up behind her. "That meeting has been canceled."

His message caused Megan to stop in her tracks. Then, turning her head behind her to look over her shoulder at him. "What?"

Mac stepped up too Megan as she turned around. "It was apparently a sudden thing." Shrugging his shoulders as he continued to speak, "It seems several of the Generals, including Admiral Goodrick, are not feeling well. I think it was something they had for breakfast."

Megan walked up to Mac, standing face to face. "Did you do something?"

Ignoring her question, "With the rest of the brass occupied with events in Africa, they felt they needed to postpone the midday meeting. So it looks like we will be able to have that lunch meeting after all." Mac remarked, just standing there, somewhat emotionless, waiting to see what Megan's reaction would be.

Megan in turn watched his face carefully and silently. Due to her unwillingness to speak, Mac added to the conversation. "I checked. Your father, the General, is busy. So he said we should go to lunch without him."

Megan's eyes narrowed as she carefully looked at him, "You are very sure of yourself!"

Mac smiled in response, "As I said, I try."

Megan's eyes softened a little as Mac continued speaking, "I know of a nice little cafe. It's not as nice as the Fyve at the Ritz, but we can talk without anyone listening in."

Henry stood behind a control board with another General as the paperwork was being handed to them. The situation control room was dark and large as they watched the satellite feed from Africa. The tension in the room almost created a numbness as they watched the events unfold. The British had just decided to pull out, fearing a bloodbath as China's Navy closed in. Someone on the other side of the room spoke up saying that the Chinese government just hung up on a phone call with the President and that the Chinese government was determined to get their stuff back at all costs.

They watched the satellite video feed as the Islamic militants hooted and hollered at the killing of the Chinese seamen. Henry, in his heart, knew this was only going to end one way as he slowly took a deep breath in.

General Morgan of the Marines, a bald man in his 60's, asked about his team that was deployed. A blond-haired female Lieutenant, who was standing near a computer screen, looked up and shook her head left to right, "No, sir, they are currently still pinned down about a mile away."

Henry turned his head and looked at the same Lieutenant and asked, "And the Chinese?"

"18 minutes from landing, sir." The Lieutenant responded back.

"And what's the situation with the militants?" Morgan asked.

Looking back at the computer screen for a moment. She gained a concerned look as she responded back. "They have about two hundred on the ground, with at least one to two thousand arriving from local villages. The Somali government is sending its troops as well."

General Morgan nodded his head as he looked at the rest of the brass in the room. "Bloodbath."

General Bond's right eyebrow raised up as she spoke, "General Morgan, pull your people. That's a rock and a hard place out there, and our people don't need to be in the middle."

General Morgan nodded his head and gave the order.

A young Air Force Lieutenant by the name badge of Alanis walked up as she spoke to General Mullins. Henry noticed how the light in the room reflected strangely off her eyes. "Sir, this just came in," the Lieutenant informed him.

Henry nodded his head to acknowledge and accepted the paper. He did not think twice about what he just saw, as the unfolding events were his highest priority. He quickly read it over as he moved closer to General Bond.

Raising his voice Henry announced, "Generals, we have another problem. Apparently, the Royal family of the United Arab Emirates has family in that area. They contacted China advising them of this and told them not to attack, fearing their death. The Chinese Admiral in charge of the fleet refused to respond. So the Saudis are scrambling their Air Force and a few ships to stop the approaching fleet."

General Morgan put down the paper he was reading to face Henry, "My God, it's going to be an all-out war."

Victoria Bond swallowed hard, "I need to call the President."

The corner of Lieutenant Alanis' mouth came up a little as she watched from a distance. Turning her head away, she stood at attention on the other side of the room as her

219

eyes slowly surveyed the room. Her eyes stopped on another Air Force Lieutenant who was sitting at his station. Their eyes locked for a moment and then he looked away as if he had received a message. Sitting at his desk, he turned to his computer screen and started typing as he picked up a phone.

Mac and Megan walked up the white steps to the porch of an old colonial house. The red Cafe Del Ray sign was one of the few indications that this was not someone's house, but a cafe.

This simple two-story house, with its dark trim, delivered an enjoyable mixture of cooking smells into the atmosphere as they approached. After the last few days in the hustle and bustle of the Pentagon, Megan found this small cafe with its narrow streets a pleasant, far-reaching change to her mind. The creaky porch with its outdoor screened-in dining was going to be a nice distraction. The sights and sounds were already whispering to her soul to relax.

As they walked in, a blond-haired woman who obviously worked there, looked up at them.

"Mac, nice to see you." She remarked as she looked at Megan for a moment. "And I see you are not alone... for once."

Mac, who was looking a little embarrassed by her comment, responded, "Ah, nice to see you too, Ms. Margaret. Just two for lunch today."

The lady smiled, raised an eyebrow, and gave him a look that said, "You can't fool me." Ms. Margaret walked them over to the covered porch and turned around. "Will this be fine for you today?"

Mac had a simple smile on his face as he responded, "Yes, thank you."

Walking to the outside porch, Ms. Margaret directed them to a table. Megan smiled at her and placed her hat on the seat next to her as they sat down. "Seems like a nice place," Megan commented.

Mac was repositioning his chair as he spoke up. "It is, I enjoy it here. The food is organic." Pausing for a moment to think, "And it's out of the way, so most people won't look for me here. So it's a good place to think."

With a mischievous look on her face, Megan responded, "And take girls?"

Mac stopped in mid-motion and gave her a look.

Megan smiled, "Sorry, couldn't help it after Ms. Margaret's actions. I get the same look from people I know if they see me around any man who I am not related to. They're so hopeful to see any whisper of hope for you."

Mac resumed moving his chair and smiled, "They mean well, don't they?"

Lunar Orbit

A small alien walked his way along the hallway past a window. Outside, the blackness of space was only interrupted by the image of the cold gray lunar surface below. Locked in geosynchronous orbit, the vast Vos ship sat in the cold darkness of space behind the Moon. Being the only command vessel for Master Vos in this section of space. It commanded the highest level of fear in even the smallest gray alien over many solar systems.

As he walked, his thoughts were not his own. His thoughts were the result of centuries of higher genetic programming, which was designed to serve in fear the command structure above him. In his mind, he had prepared for his meeting with the new Vos who had just recently emerged from the lower chambers of the lab.

The genetically designed race of Vos was re-created for commanding sectors of space. Each possessed a lifespan of a few hundred years to guarantee continuity of leadership. Vos 158 would, today, replace Vos 157 in a simple effective way. All sub-leaders around this section of space would observe the transition via the projected images in the command hall.

This small Barda class alien led a group of two other Bardas, who escorted a large box that floated behind them. The Bardas entered the great hall through the holographic wall. They entered just in time to see both the older and the younger Vos standing in the center of the room. Encircled by the thirteen images of the Pasha commanders, as well as the five Vos masters from other parts of the Galaxy.

As they entered, one of the Pasha commanders was speaking to the older and younger Vos. "...as of the last battle. We have critically injured our enemies on the outer rim. Their fleet is broken with only six vessels left and we will overrun their worlds and acquire their slaves. Therefore I can now pledge my forces to you after we hunt the remaining Draygon ships and their worlds down."

157, who was having problems standing, spoke up, "And we thank you, But today is the day of transition." Carefully, he reached up and took a very Egyptian-inspired-looking hat off his elongated head and held it in front of him. "Does the Vos and the Pasha agree with the transition?"

Slowly the eighteen images bowed their heads in agreement.

Vos 158 turned towards 157 with pure demonic glee on his face. His left hand reached out and took the hat from 157. As his right hand moved to surround 157's neck, suddenly, a crack was heard as the older 157 slumped to the ground like a wet sack of grain.

Vos 158 put both hands on the hat and placed it confidently on his head. After it came to rest on his head, he looked around him. "I will divide 157 and send him to the Pasha. As you consume him, remember that I, 158, am the new Master of the foundation sector."

All the images around Vos nodded as their images faded away. The cold stark walls of the command hall, with a few select crystal control knobs, were all that was left in the room. The three Barda were filled with the fear they craved as they watched Vos turn around to look at them.

"157 said you were bringing me something of importance," commented Vos 158.

The Barda moved closer as the leader spoke. "Yes, my Master Vos. Here it is."

Vos pointed to a spot near him. "Leave it there. And take the old Vos away for processing."

The Barda picked up the old Vos and started to drag him from the great hall. Then the lead Barda spoke up, "Master Vos, what part shall we bring back to you?"

Vos turned his elongated head to look over his left shoulder. "The eyes, of course."

With that, the Barda bowed and exited the room. Vos turned and looked down, putting his full attention towards the box. Extending his right hand over the box, he slowly passed it over the cover. The cover turned a light green as it seemed to vanish.

The Vos commander smiled as he looked upon the ancient golden books written by Captain John Becker.

Back on Earth

Time passed with folded hands under his chin as Mac sat in his seat listening to Megan speak about her son's new life in the past. The technical part of this briefing had long since been over. Mac soon found that he was now content just to sit and listen to these "family stories" of the son Megan admired. Mac found that she was totally invested in her son's life as she soberly told him about the death of his teammates. Horrified to find that he almost died after walking off a cliff. Glad to find that she now had a daughter-in-law by the name of Kasa.

But the best part was the semi-contained excitement to find, as of last night's reading, that she now has a grandson. And of all things, John named him Lorenzo.

Mac's eyebrow raised, "The lizard? Didn't you say Johnny gave that name to a lizard back in camp? And that's where the name for the project came from?"

Megan giggled as she took a sip of her water. "One and the same."

Mac lightly laughed as he looked at the table for a moment, pushing the bill for their meal around with his finger in a circle. "Kids, I should look up what Lorenzo means someday." Mac lightly commented

Megan got a serious look for a moment as she put her glass down. "I would love to see him."

"Lorenzo?" Mac asked.

"Yep," Megan answered with a forlorn look in her eye.

Megan and Mac just sat there quietly for a while as time passed. Finally, Mac spoke up in an effort to add a little sound to the room. In an effort not to betray his knowledge, Mac kept his eyes on the bill on the table as he asked, "So I noticed you have a little accent to your voice."

Megan's look changed a little as she responded, "That would be my mom. She and my dad met after he joined the Army. They sent him on a trip to London as an aid for some officer. Dad went for a walk one evening and found my Mom, fresh out of Saint Andrews, Scotland with a flat tire. One thing led to another and here I am."

"So you picked it up from her?" Mac asked.

"Yep, that and the fact that one summer Dad got sent on a long-term mission. So Mom picked up my brother and I and we spent the summer with my grandparents in Scotland." Megan responded back.

Mac smiled and was about to speak when his cell phone beeped. He pulled it out and read the message. "Oh, my."

"What is it?" Megan inquired.

Mac got up and walked from the porch to the other side of the cafe. Megan had a "what happened" look on her face as she got up to follow him.

"Ms. Margaret, can I bother you for a moment?" Mac asked.

Margaret turned around with a slightly concerned look on her face after seeing his. "Sure."

"Do you have a TV I can look at for a moment?" Mac inquired.

Margaret could see the highly concerned look on Mac's face as she responded, "Ah, yes, come this way into our little office."

They passed the serving counter and rounded a corner to a little spot that was little more than an alcove in a hallway. Margaret reached over and turned on the small TV only about ten or twelve inches in size.

Mac spoke up, "I need a news channel."

"Sure," responded Margaret.

All three stood there as they watched. A female voice was speaking on television. "We are learning that yesterday evening's earthquake created a tsunami from an unknown location in the Indian Ocean. The main energy of that wave seemed to have directed itself toward the African coast. Creating a military disaster evolving several countries. The latest update on the disaster is now coming in with startling reports of a highly advanced Chinese ship that has been washed up on the Somalian coast. Various terrorist and government factions are now claiming ownership of the vessel. As a result, a Chinese admiral is but seconds away from landing an army in Africa to reclaim their ship."

All three watched as the images on the screen of the armed conflict continued as a second voice, male spoke up. "Yes, thank you, Jen. Also, I am getting reports of a second conflict related to this between China and Saudi Arabia. Apparently, the Saudis are attempting to stop China and as a result, have... wait, we can confirm this now, fired several air-to-surface missiles at their main Chinese fleet. The President's words of caution on both sides are apparently going unheard as the situation escalates."

Margaret put her hand over her mouth as Mac looked at Megan. "I need to get back."

Fading Starlight

Megan nodded at Mac's face as she responded, "Let's go."

The Past

Over seven winters had passed since John fell off the cliff and into a new family. Lorenzo was getting bigger and finally reached the point in his life where he wanted to do more than just run around the camp. He had raced past the "terrible twos" with a million questions a day of his parents that all started with the word, "why." He almost burnt down their home when he was five. And last year, his cousin, Tablita, gave him a bloody nose for picking on the girls. Lorenzo was getting old enough now that John was starting to consider taking him on his next yearly visit to his hidden cave.

John had traded with several people from other nomadic tribes for bits and pieces of gold. His plan in this world was simple— be a teacher of his people here and now, and to live and grow old with the people of this land. Along the way, build a book and hide it as a message to the future.

On his yearly trip to the old cave, he tapped the gold into flat sheets, reminiscing to himself about future days long past, good and bad times as well as faces of people he would never see again. As a result, a longing started to build in his heart to share some of it with his son. Added to this, the fact that Kasa was now starting to think that she was with a child once more.

But the trip this year with his son would need to wait. John's father-in-law, Kaviu, had informed the tribe that it was now time to travel once more to the lands in the west. Every few years, all the tribes gathered in one place to trade. By the description of it, John knew they were headed back to Zion National Park.

All this moved around in his mind as he was sitting on

a rock some 30 paces away from the camp. Watching the setting sun and feeling the evening heat of the desert give way to a coming night time breeze. They had been hiking for a week and John was keeping his eyes open for any fresh game that might offer itself for an evening meal.

But in the end, he forgot to keep watch for the deer that easily slipped by him as he watched his son from a distance. Lorenzo was playing with his older cousin Tablita. She was only a year and a half older, but they were best friends. John enjoyed watching her whisper something in Lorenzo's ear, only to see him take off running and laughing. She would then hide and he would to find her once more.

As John waited for a deer or some other animal to pass by him, he was whittling with his knife on a present for his son. It was a small wooden sword that he kept hidden in his backpack. He knew Lorenzo's birthday was coming soon and even though that was not a big deal with the tribe, it was to him.

Soon the sky was growing a little too dark to hunt. So John picked up his stuff and walked in for the night. It would be a long day of hiking westward in the morning. If Kasa was pregnant once more, he was going to make sure she had all she needed.

Drifting in and out of sleep during the night, John's eyes opened as his mind became aware of noises in the distance. As a veteran of many battles, he was now fully listening for anything that told him danger might be close. Kasa however was sound asleep near him with their young son, Lorenzo, on the other side of her. John's hand slowly moved out from under the blanket of buffalo robes to touch his rifle.

As he listened, he noted that the sound seemed to be staying far away. Curious, he slowly got up, collected his rifle and a small mono-ocular scope from his pack.

Fading Starlight

Slipping outside, he looked around the camp, and saw nothing noteworthy around. The stars were vibrant as they framed the crest of the new moon in the sky. Lonan walked up to his left side as they both looked in the direction of the strange noise that seemed to be fading in the distance.

"You're awake," John stated.

Lonan nodded his head. "Yes, I felt someone needed to be guarding the camp tonight."

John looked at his brother-in-law and nodded his head towards the noise. "What are we listening to?"

"I have only heard it a few times in my life and saw it once. It is an Átahsaia, a skin-changer. Walkers of deception and evil, a horrible giant who lives in the caves." Logan remarked.

Even in the dark, John could see the look on his brother-in-law's face enough to know he was serious. In the past, he would have blown off this kind of thing as a fairy tale. But after all the things he had seen in his life, anything was possible now. John slowly nodded his head as he thought about it.

"Tell me more, what is an Átahsaia?" John inquired.

"The old men say there were once many of them. Some say they came up from the world below. Others say the gray wolf hunters from above made them. Now, only this one remains, the biggest of all of them." Logan commented.

John was reflecting on Lonan's choice of words, gray wolf hunters, when he asked, "How big is he?"

Lonan raised his chin as he drew a breath in to speak. "Last spring, you saw the old bull elk in the valley. Átahsaia would look down on that elk. He has the hide of a bear and his hair looks like quills. Because of this, he is very hard to kill with the arrow. No one has ever put an arrow in him. They only die in the trying. He is but a demon of the old world."

The disgust, Lonan's face was mixed with memories of loss and pain. John could see this was painful for him, so after a moment, he decided to ask one more question. "Has he ever attacked the tribe?"

The look on his brother-in-law's face only intensified as his eyes narrowed. "Yes," was his single answer.

John looked closely at him, wanting more and Lonan could feel it. Turning his head towards John, Lonan spoke in a low voice, "He is a hunter and the children are his food." Lonan turned abruptly and walked away into the night.

That comment answered the question John had been trying to learn ever since he arrived. It was a shock to his mind and soul. Tonight, he would stay awake with his rifle on guard duty.

In the first light of morning, John could smell the start of the campfires as some of the women arose to prepare the morning meal. Kasa approached John from behind with a little water. "Husband John, were you awake all night?"

Smiling at her in the early morning light as he accepted the water, "No, not all night. Lonan tells me that the noise that woke me up was Átahsaia."

That name caused a sudden change in her face as she looked at him very seriously. The hand that just handed John the water was now lightly starting to shake. John watched her eyes slowly look at the ground and then back at him. Her eyes were becoming watery fast, red and panicked as if she was trapped. He had never seen her eyes like that; they were exploding with emotion and fear. This hit John to the core to see his wife as her hands instinctively reached for his arms. As they did, she quietly released the word, "No."

Legs shaking and buckling, John dropped the water and caught her as she folded over towards the dust of the ground. John was unsure what to do as he held her. Her body was losing the strength to hold on to him as she transitioned from crying to wailing.

The tribe slowly moved together around them,

confused, they looked around at each other.

Noting that Lonan's face seemed to contain the answers they needed. Kaviu, who arrived, looked at his daughter and then at his son. Grabbing Lonan very sternly by the shoulder, he turned him around to face him. "Speak, what is it?

He spoke only one word and that one word changed the very mood of the camp, "Átahsaia."

Soon, many of the women with children were crying. In their hearts, they were already mourning the loss of their sons and daughters.

John could not help it; the sheer magnitude of the moment— the flood of emotion was overwhelming. John quickly acquired a panicked look as he held Kasa. Turning his head upwards towards his father-in-law, he spoke sternly to him, "Move the people away from here now."

Kaviu, whose heart was in pain over this, slowly shook his head back and forth. "It is pointless, Átahsaia knows we are here. He is faster than the deer, we have tried."

That was an unacceptable statement in John's mind. Breathing heavy as if he was in a battle, his old war-hardened instincts marched over his heart leaving only the basic desires in his emotional state. Protect, kill, and hunt the hunter was all that was in his mind now. Letting go of Kasa, John stood up and looked his father-in-law in the eye. "Then I will kill the monster."

Kasa suddenly found the strength to move and grab hold of her husband around the waist. She moved so quickly, it knocked him a little to the side.

"No, I will not lose you as well," exclaimed Kasa.

John's father-in-law shook his head in agreement with his daughter. "You are good, my son, but Átahsaia is fast and cunning. I fear, even with your metal stick, he will only outwit you with his speed and tricks."

"I have fought many monsters in my time, he will fall like them," John announced.

A great sadness overcame Kaviu's face as he looked at John's face. " I can see in your eyes that I cannot change your mind. We will mourn your death."

John shook his head with all the sternness he could muster. "No, he will die. Or we will die together."

After several pain-filled minutes, John tore Kasa away from his side to walk back to get his backpack from his home. His in-laws stepped in and held Kasa from following. As he entered, he looked down at Lorenzo, who was playing with the other children. The young cousin, Tablita, watched over him.

Picking up his son, John looked him in the eyes, gave him a kiss on the forehead and set him back down to be watched by the young girl. Exiting with his pack firmly fastened on his back, with his old Army cap on his head and his rifle in hand. His family watched as he approached, his walking seemed a little different to them. His Army combat training was as much a part of him as his new life. It was his old training that would protect his new family now.

Stopping in front of his father-in-law, "Kaviu, take the tribe and continue on your way to the lands in the west. I will join you after Átahsaia, when he is no more," John announced. Kasa slowly moved her head back and forth as she bit the side of her hand. John chose not to look her in the eye, knowing he would never leave if he did.

An hour or so passed as John carefully climbed the rock outcrop to the south where they heard Átahsaia the night before. He looked behind himself for the first time since marching out. He could see his camp was getting ready to leave. As he watched, he put away his internal desire to join them as he took his pack off.

In his pack, he pulled out several devices that he had kept hidden. He clipped a small device onto his ear. It automatically expanded to cover his whole ear and then it extended a small arm forward to cover his right eye with a lens. The lens was ruby-colored, and form-fitting to the surface of his face. He now had enhanced vision in his shooting eye and his hearing was now three times that of normal.

Pulling out a small vest, he put it on over his bare chest. Activating it, the outer covering changed from the dull Army green to dark brown with denser, thicker places over his vital organs. Pulling out his Army-issued Tactical Armbands from the bottom of his pack, he placed them around both wrists. They were about five inches wide and a small strap was attached to them that rested in the palm of each hand. Squeezing the strap, the dark green turned to brown as it extended up his arm to his elbow.

John then opened a side pocket of his pack and pulled out four small grenades, two reusable sonic grenades and two incendiary types and hooked them to the side panels of his tactical vest. Smiling, John put his pack back on.

John then slipped on what looked like a pair of shorts that came to just above the knees. Pulling out a small rectangular box, he activated it, hooking it onto his belt. In a few moments, his shorts also changed to dark brown and extended to his ankles.

The box counted down from ten with a light beep sound. Then a female voice came from the box with the words, "All systems connected." John then lowered his right hand down and pressed one more button. Slowly, the dark brown of his uniform changed to almost transparent, but not in the normal sense. As John's outfit had now become almost the perfect camouflage, the same female voice came on once more, "adaptive camouflage enabled."

"Ok, Mr. Átahsaia, let's see how you handle twenty-first century light battle armor," John remarked as he picked up his rifle preparing to hunt the hunter.

It was near midday when John became aware that he was hearing something moving up ahead him, among the rocks. The rocks were too large to kneel behind and since he was looking uphill, it forced him to stand on his tiptoes to look over the rock in front of him. Leaning against it, he waited with his rifle in place, ready to shoot if it was Átahsaia.

Soon, a foul, rotten smell started working its way down the hill as the sound and smell grew closer. The first sight of the misshapen hideous body of Átahsaia came into view. He was worse than Lonan had described. He was about eighty yards in front of John and a good six feet taller then the very rocks John had to stand on his tiptoes to look over.

The only resemblance of being human stopped at having two arms and legs. He was more animal in appearance than human, and the sounds he made seemed more like a bear.

The shock of it kept John from pulling the trigger for a moment as he looked him over. The hair was matted and he was partly bald in places. He was every bit of the kind of nightmare that a child would have had. Refocusing his thinking, he placed the crosshairs of his rifle in the beast's chest for a heart shot. Slowly squeezing the trigger, his right foot slipped a bit on the rock he was standing on.

The gun shifted and the bullet skipped off a rock near Átahsaia. John quickly looked back at his prey—Átahsaia was gone.

John waited for a moment, listening. His enhanced hearing told him Átahsaia was moving away, so John carefully started moving to the monster's former position. Reaching the top of the small hill, he scanned around the area. He could not see anything in the distance, nor could his eye unit detect movement.

Watching for a moment, John then looked down at his feet. Átahsaia tracks were huge. One foot had only four toes, while the other seemed to be missing two toes.

"Wow, you're one big dude," John quietly exclaimed.

As John raised his head, his eye unit alerted him to something on the side of one of the boulders. It was blood.

"Not a complete loss. Big feet, blood trail. Your days are numbered," John remarked to himself as he set his rifle down and took his pack off to look closely at the blood. It was bright red and he had never seen blood quite like it. Digging around in his pack, John pulled

233

various things out and setting them on the rock as he looked for what he wanted. Without thinking, he set the alien silver stick on the rock near the blood. Finally, he found his medic kit and put it on the rock. He turned it on as he picked up a small stick and got a sample of the blood. Putting the sample on the sensor of his kit, he waited for the results.

Finally a message came on the screen, "Error, sample contaminated with other non-human sources. Obtain clean sample."

John's eyebrow raised. "Oh really, just what are you, Mr. Átahsaia?"

As John started putting his gear back as quickly as he could, his hand grabbed the alien device. Pulling it towards his pack, the red tip barely touched Átahsaia blood. The device made a small beep sound causing John to stop. Looking at it a little closer, thinking he must have turned it on by accident, he moved the slider to make sure it was off.

The device in turn self-activated and the red tip turned brighter. In a moment, a small holographic image appeared in front of him.

"Oh, maybe you were off," John whispered.

The holographic image in front of him showed that it was processing the blood sample. After a few short seconds, it stopped on an image very similar to Átahsaia.

John bent his head forward in disbelief as he looked at it. "What? Átahsaia, you're in the alien database?"

John took his left hand and enlarged the image to read the words on the right side of the image. Seeing it better, John started reading it out loud: "Species 6464, Genetic warrior improvement over 6463. Foundational Impu DNA acquired during the time of Vos 1. DNA was later spliced from three improved carnivorous animals during the time of Vos 23. 6464 failed to bond with command units, resulting in rogue tendencies with unstable genetic structure shifts."

John's eyes grew wide as his head tipped backward. "So... you're a failed genetic experiment." John's head pulled back as he turned his little stick off.

Putting his pack back together, John realized he had not thought about aliens of the future in a long time. Finally, he picked up his rifle and started following the tracks, as he wondered what else he did not know about his new world.

After a while the blood trail stopped at a point where the monster destroyed some brush, but the tracks continued. Unsure if Átahsaia actions where the result of anger or self administered medical care, John carefully continued. The wind had picked up a little, but this did not concern John much as the trail was still going into the wind. John got a whiff from time to time of Átahsaia's smell, so he knew all was on track.

After a quarter mile, the rocks grew further apart and Átahsaia prints disappeared. This left John a little concerned as he looked around for him. Adjusting his headset, it revealed some of the rocks had been disturbed in front of him.

"Ah, so that's it," John remarked as he figured it out. Átahsaia was jumping from rock to rock, slightly shifting the rocks in their place. Did Átahsaia know he was being tracked? Or did he just assume it? John walked a few more feet to realize that if he was jumping rocks, then he should see him somewhere up ahead.

"Humm, are you resting? Did you die?" John muttered.

Suddenly, John heard something from behind him. He managed to spin around just in time to see Átahsaia face to face. The monster had doubled back behind John. With a large flint like knife Átahsaia slashed the air in front of him, hitting part of Johns armor. Next thing John knew he was flying like a rag doll in the air.

Átahsaia then roared with a noise that sounded like a cross between a bear and a wolf as he watched John land in the sand between two large rocks. As he walked towards John, the hair on his back started to stand up like a bear going in for an attack.

After John hit the ground, he looked at his chest where the knife had cut. His tactical armor showed a large knife cut across the front that was self-repairing, closing up the cut. His gun was gone, and this monster was approaching fast. Looking down at his tactical armbands, he quickly pressed the buttons on them with this index fingers. Just below his wrists, a blue light around them started to grow brighter. John got to his feet and started to run toward Átahsaia as his armbands started to emit a loud hum.

Jumping up on a small rock in front of him, he used it as a launching platform towards his adversary. Átahsaia's hands came together to grab John around his chest as John's hands reached for his enemy's head. Once his hands were in place on either side of Átahsaia head, a loud crack was heard as the tactical armbands released an electrical charge. This caused Átahsaia to scream in agony and spin wildly about to get John off him.

John came to rest suddenly on his back once more in the sand a few feet away from Átahsaia. The monster was still holding his head in pain as John watched. But soon, he started to learn why his brother-in-law called him a skin-changer.

Átahsaia's very form started to shift and change right in front of him. What few human features he had were disappearing. For a moment, his face became more wolflike and then, it shifted once more back to a bear.

Finally Átahsaia's whole form turned into a very large bear. The sight of it was shocking to John, since he recognized what he was looking at. From his days in college, he knew he was not looking at a black bear or even a grizzly. But in front of him, standing on his hind legs and roaring at full volume, was a primitive short-faced bear, extinct for many generations. And John knew he needed his rifle.

John looked around very quickly. His scanner showed that there was something made of metal in the distance, maybe twenty yards. Scrambling over and around the rocks, he heard the bear behind him. In his panic, his mind started to remember he still carried other weapons.

Feeling that Átahsaia was close, he reached to the side panel of his vest and pulled out a sonic grenade. Putting a hand over his one unprotected ear, John pressed the activation button before he tossed it over his shoulder as he ran. The grenade bounced about at the foot of a rock and then exploded in cascading waves of hypersonic sound. The sound concussion caused the sand around the rocks to jump up just in front of the bear. The full force of the sound waves hit Átahsaia under the chin causing him very real pain. He came to a sudden, crashing stop right into a patch of prickly pear cactus.

John looked back and stopped. To his amazement the bear slowly got back up. He had never seen anything get back up, let alone live after a sonic blast. Blood was coming out from the bear's nose and eyes as he worked up a low growl.

Átahsaia's body started to transform once more. He became a little more wolflike only to return back to his bear form.

John watched as he slowly, carefully moved closer to his rifle. Never letting his eyes leave Átahsaia, John picked up his rifle, as he noticed Átahsaia's eyes following his movement. Stealing a moment, John looked down at himself, he could see his tactical camouflage was starting to fail. It apparently had taken a bad hit. With his right hand he grabbed the control box on his hip. It made a slight rattle sound as he shook it.

"Oh great, something is loose," John remarked with an exacerbated tone.

There was no time to fix it; Átahsaia was starting to move. The great monster kicked off with his back feet sending a few small rocks flying. John raised his weapon to his shoulder, clicked it from semi-auto to full, and squeezed the trigger.

At that close range, the volley of bullets ripped into Átahsaia's head, splitting it apart. The sheer momentum of this beast kept him moving forward as his body ground into the earth. The front of his body slid into a small stone, causing his back end to roll over the top of him. In slow motion, he finally stopped as his back came to suddenly rest on the ground. With his head split open like an overripe watermelon, John finally exhaled, knowing this beast was down for the count. Lowering his weapon to look at him, confident his hunt had just come to an end. John took in a very deep breath.

With his rifle lowered, John put his hands on his knees for a moment, just breathing, feeling the stress of the adrenaline in his legs. After a few moments, in between labored breaths of air, came the words, "Thank you," as he raised his head upward to look at the sky.

Picking up his rifle, he straightened his back and started the process of gathering up his stuff that was strewn all over. As he picked up the last of it, he heard something and looked over at the bear. In his position he could clearly see its face, as it was only a few yards away.

To his surprise and horror, the bones of the face were pulling together and the monster's chest was starting to move. John, in a panic, very quickly pulled another device out of his pack and started snapping it onto the bottom of his rifle, as he exclaimed in astonishment, "No way."

Just as the last part of the device was in place, the bear started to roll over onto his chest. As the last of his skin was starting to close over his face, the bear's eyes met John's. John pushed a small button on the side of his rifle as he raised it to his shoulder. The holographic screen projected next to the barrel displayed itself next to the gun sight.

The numbers on the holographic screen rolled by very fast, counting upwards as the bear started to stand. As he did, John was starting to look very small next to this bear as he rose to stand his hind feet. Then, the holographic screen number suddenly reached 100, flashing the number with the words, "MORTER CHARGED."

As soon as it signaled that information, John pulled the

trigger. He was not even thinking about how close he was going to be. The energy mortar tore a hole in the chest of the bear like a hot knife in wax or butter. It was the last thing John saw as it exploded in a massive ball of arcing electricity charged with blue light. The impact of the shockwave flung John backwards as all the major pieces of the bear were sent outwards from the blast zone.

Present Day

Henry walked outside the main control room as Mac and Megan came into view. Megan looked up to see her father. "General!" Mac exclaimed.

Henry's eyebrow raised a little as he received Mac's handshake.

Mac looked Henry in the eye and inquired as to the condition of the situation.

"The Saudi Arabians sank one of their smaller surface craft and heavily damaged a destroyer. China responded with their own aircraft. And as of this moment, China has lost six fighters. The Arabs however lost their entire squadron." Henry informed him.

Megan was about to open her mouth when the door opened to the control room. Everyone stopped talking for a moment as a young officer exited the room. Lieutenant Alanis of the Air Force walked out the door. Seeing the General, she snapped to a quick salute.

"Oh, sorry sir. I did not know you were there, sir." Alanis quickly remarked.

Henry returned the salute, "No problem, carry on Lieutenant."

"Very good, sir, thank you, sir," she responded as took a step back, turned, and exited the area. As she walked a few feet away, she carefully looked back at them from the corner of her eye as she turned her head looking over her shoulder.

"Is Saudi Arabia done? Why did they get in the way?"

Megan asked after they were alone once more.

"Apparently, for some reason, part of the Royal family is down there. And they feel the need to defend them. And no, you would think the Saudi's would know better. China has many times more equipment and people than they do. But they are calling everyone, including us, to come to their aid." Henry responded back.

"What happens next?" Megan inquired as she looked at her father eyes.

"They know they cannot stop China. So they are hoping to buy as much time for their people as possible by giving them a bloody nose. To that end, they have several older Baynunsh class Corvettes that it looks like they have deployed. They are equipped with the older French Exocet ship missiles. This is going to get real ugly fast because it looks like the Chinese Admiral has gone rogue." Henry answered back.

For the first time that day, Mac's voice grew with a strong emotion and concern. "Rogue, what do you mean?"

"Well, as soon as the earthquake happened, he turned his fleet towards Africa. And then he turned his radio off. Bejing has been yelling at him on the radio, but no response. As a result, China has no desire to lose face in front of the world. So they will most likely back him." Henry remarked.

"Even though he is starting a war," Megan exclaimed.

"Oh, yes, and it gets worse. China has sent a message to the Saudis. If they fire one more missile at their fleet, then they will respond in kind to the closet Saudi naval port." Henry informed them.

Megan looked at the floor for a moment, "My God."

Henry nodded his head in an affirming manner at his daughter's statement. "Listen, I only have a moment. I just came out to use the restroom and grab a sandwich from the vendor down the hall."

The look on Megan's face changed to a more concerned look, because of the news she had to deliver. "Dad, one moment."

Henry, who was just starting to walk away, stopped. Turning around, he gave his daughter a look that responded to traces of emotion she was allowed to show on her face. "Yes?"

"I just got a text from our camp. Josh has been admitted to the hospital, It looks like he has developed a very advanced, aggressive form of cancer. And it started in his chest." Megan remarked

Henry face developed a very sad look as his eyes wandered to the floor for a moment. He knew what Megan's team meant to her and what they had done for her. Megan's eyes soon developed a little wetness around the edges as she looked into her father's eyes who rose to meet hers. Henry chose to put protocol aside and reached out, pulling his daughter towards him.

After a moment or so, the embrace ended, and Henry spoke up, "I will press the Brass for a resolution, so that you can fly back." He whispered.

Megan sucked in her upper lip for a moment and nodded a "yes."

Henry looked at Mac's face and noted the concern he had for her. It was a curious thing, but at this moment with everything happening around the world, Henry decided to go with his instinct. "Mr. MacWilliams, could you please take my daughter somewhere for a while?"

Mac nodded and reached out with his hand to Megan's shoulder, "It would be my pleasure, General."

Megan and Mac walked to the elevator as Henry moved towards the restroom. Lieutenant Alanis stood just beyond the hallway around the corner in a storage area. She looked up just above her head height to something in front of her. In the dim light of the storage area, a barely noticeable distortion of light moved in front of her face.

Lieutenant Alanis reached up and tapped it with her index finger. The distortion rolled backward, and there before her, was a small, hovering ball. The front of it, closest to Alanis, grew brighter with a dim green light. As the light reflected in her eyes, she stood motionless

241

Fading Starlight

for three or four seconds. Then it stopped and she retapped the ball as the distortion re-enveloped the ball, only to dash out the door and down the hallway.

Fading Starlight
Chapter Eight
Hidden Things

John stood in a valley and watched a large mule deer buck, who majestically stood at the edge of the river. The warmth of the day was soaking into him, it was relaxing to every part of John as he watched. Stepping forward, John desired to get closer to this buck. The lungs of the buck slowly sucked in the air around him. John paused for a second and then stopped. Slowly the buck started to exhale and then suddenly everything changed around John felt like it was floating away, taking him to someplace he had felt before.

Unsure where he was, as nothing looked quite the same. Colors suddenly became more alive and real. Sound had become almost a solid thing as it reacted to his thoughts, dancing around him as he thought about it. Everything seemed possible in this place, as he now noticed he had a tightly woven tunic of many vibrant colors around him. Raising his hand John touched it, The cloth even seemed to react to his touch.

Everything around him seemed alive. As the sheer beauty of the colors of this place captivated his very senses. Just as he was turning in this space, from behind him, he could feel the presence of the buck and knew it had compassion for him. John turned fully around and found it was not a buck, but a man. He was the same age as himself and the black beard that he wore, framing out a smile on his face.

The man reached out and rested his hand on John's shoulder, captivated by the man's green eyes. Suddenly, John knew he had been here before and he really wanted to ask some questions.

The whiteness of the man's teeth became obvious as he spoke. "Ask," he offered.

Realizing, but not shocked that this man knew his thoughts, John spoke up. "Last time I was here... when I passed through *here. The alien was in pain, but I felt no pain."*

With a warmth that can only be described as comfort, the man responded, "The dark has no place in the Light. Death cannot exist in Eternity."

"What about me?" John asked.

"There is a time to be born and a time to die, a time to plant and a time to uproot. The winds of change are soon to blow on you. And you will be in another place." The kind face of the man exclaimed.

John felt something crawling on his arm. He jerked quickly, and flicked some bug off. Lying there on the ground for a moment as he woke up, was this just a dream? Or was it... perhaps, real. It felt so real. His mind began to transition to the present, becoming aware that several hours had passed since his fight with Átahsaia. The sky was growing dark, as night was now overtaking the day from the east.

He lay there for a moment longer, slowly running his hands over himself. Then rolling over to his right side, he sat up. Everything hurt, but nothing was broken, and he was thankful for that.

John finally got up enough to look around. Various parts of Átahsaia were scattered over the ground just as all of his equipment was.

Pulling himself to his feet, John walked around, picking up his stuff, he found his medical scanner. He turned it on, but it had trouble starting. Over the years his equipment had suffered many accidents. It was slowly getting beat up, with no way to replace it. The nearest repair shop was 3,000 years in the future. He tapped it a few times on the side until it came fully on. Holding it to his chest for a moment, and then turning it around. He could barely read the cracked screen, but he was satisfied with the limited results he got. So he put it back in his backpack along with everything else.

Looking around, the battle site afforded no real protection from the elements, so John decided to hike west in the hopes of finding a place for the night.

Soon it was very dark, as the moon had not risen yet.

So John flicked a switch on his rifle, turning a small light on. It added just enough light for the night vision in his banged-up eyepiece to work. Up ahead, his enhanced vision unit detected an opening in the rocks that could be a cave.

Within a few more minutes, he was standing near the opening of a cave that extended some distance back. John slowly and cautiously began exploring the cave. He soon realized it smelled just like Átahsaia, so he figured it was fair to assume it belonged to him.

Within another step or two, he confirmed it, with a grizzly discovery. Human bones littered the back wall of the cave. It was repulsive to John as he looked around. As a result he decided he would rather sleep outside than be in this place. As he turned to leave, something caught the corner of his eyes. Looking back, he realized what it was.

Reaching down, he picked up the skull of an alien. It was slightly less than twice the size of his. Brown from age and damaged from Átahsaia, John could clearly see the large eye sockets with a very small nose hole. He rolled it around in his hand carefully, looking it over. Then he had a thought.

Pulling out his silver stick to get a reading. The holographic screen came on, "Early Ashuri class during Vos 24. Discontinued by dividing it into various Barda classes. Unstable central cortex with increased vision." The device reported.

With slight disgust, John let the skull roll out of his hand onto the floor. "Well, apparently you didn't care where your food came from." John watched the skull fall and roll until it stopped against a leg bone. John was about to turn once more when his enhanced vision started detecting metal just under the surface of the dirt where the skull rolled.

John kicked the dirt to the side with his foot to see a small metal device about the size of a silver dollar. John picked it up, discovering it was flat with writing he could not read on it. He placed it in his pocket after attempting to look it over, unsuccessfully, in the dark.

Present Day

To honor what General Mullins ordered to "take her away for a while," Mac took Megan across town to a small four-story building. Part of him wanted to get more information, but another part felt himself being drawn closer to Megan.

For the first time in a while, his normally strong mind was a little unsure of what to do. So he decided to take her to his office. Not the official one that all the senators show up at, but the hidden one, this one, where he could really work, think, and bounce a ball off a wall it he needed to.

They drove under the building to an underground parking area and got out near a gray van that was parked near the staircase.

Megan felt like saying something sarcastic strange about taking a girl to a dark place as they got out. But after the last few minutes of thinking over what was happening in the world, she elected to say nothing. The car and driver then pulled away leaving them and headed back to the main street.

Megan turned to walk over to the staircase when Mac motioned with his hand for her to stop. Mac smiled and put his hand on the side of an older gray van next to its door handle. After he did that the sensor in the handle recognized his hand print. A second later you could hear a "click" and the sliding door of the van released.

Megan's eyebrows narrowed, "What's this? Are we just changing vehicles?"

Mac smiled, "Not exactly, step inside," he said as he motioned with his hand.

Megan approached and slid across the bench seat to the far side to make room for Mac. Getting in Mac tapped a button on his watch that made the door close. Megan noticed an old rotary phone on a small, round wooden table just in front of them between the driver and passenger seats. Mac reached over, picked up the handset with his left hand, and dialed eight with his right index finger. After it dialed back to zero, he hung up the handset and sat back in his seat.

Megan looked at him and started to speak, "What..."

Her words were quickly interrupted as the van's bench seat "clunked" with a jerk and then started sliding downward.

Mac turned his head towards Megan as their seat traveled downward below the floor.

"Several years ago, I realized that if I was ever to accomplish anything in this town, I was going to need to build a secret place where I could get away and think," Mac stated as he looked at Megan's face.

Lowering several feet, their ride soon stopped and the door started to open next to Mac as Megan spoke up. "This is very James Bond... just to have a place to think?" Mac smiled and finished pushing the door open as he stepped out. He then offered his right hand to assist her.

Arriving at the bottom, Mac motioned with his left hand for her to look at the rest of the room as they exited the lift. Megan paused for a second and just stood next to the door. Her eye looked deeply into a room that was big enough for a small aircraft if it had one. Well-lit by the Halogen lighting, the rough-cut stone walls spoke to the depth of how far underground they were. Four or five people were spread out around the room working on various projects. Some of the projects seemed to be robotic in nature; others Megan could not tell what they were.

Walking away from the lift, Megan noticed an older black lady, who was working at a computer station, looked up at them and lowered her glasses to the end of her nose to see who just entered. Mac waved at her in response to her wave as he took off his jacket.

Megan was taking it all in, as she heard Mac ask the group, "Where's Mozo?"

Megan moved her head forward from the things she was looking at on her left to see Mac looking around the

247

room, flipping his jacket over his arm he started to whistle and clap his hands together. "Here Mozo, Mozo, come."

From behind a machine, something large with four legs and made of metal came running.

"All right, that's my boy," Mac happily announced.

Megan was very surprised to see a robot, obviously mimicking a dog as it ran towards them. It had no outer skin or anything like that to hide the robotics parts sliding around within it. The electronic pistons and wires were all clearly seen as it ran and jumped in place. With a spinning sensor on top of its mechanical head, it moved it back and forth as an excited dog would.

"Good boy," Mac remarked, handing him his jacket. "Mozo, put this in to be cleaned. And have the mainframe download to my desk the ESR report for the day."

Mozo beeped, turned and ran off with Mac's coat.

Megan stopped for a moment watching him run as she folded her arms. "Well, secret hideout, a van that's not a van, and a robotic dog. General Bond was right, you are a mad scientist."

Mac smiled and turned toward Megan, "Victoria's a good friend, so I will take all of that as a compliment. And this is nothing. Wait till you see my office." Mac remarked with a mischievous look as he turned and suddenly started to walk away without talking anymore.

Megan was taken a little off guard, expecting a little more conversation. She watched him take a step or two, but quickly decided to follow. Mac walked up to a large oval-shaped metal door that looked like it belonged to an old steamship.

Pausing in front of the door, "If you think that was mad scientist, wait until you see this," Mac remarked with a smile as he put both hands on a large iron wheel in the center of the door and started turning it. The door made a clunk sound as he stopped turning the wheel. With his right hand he gave the wheel a tug and pulled it open.

The older black lady watched from the corner of her eye as she shook her head slowly, exclaiming, "Children!"

Both stepped inside to the strange room, every corner filled with a collection of old and new things. Some had been rebuilt and put together; others left in their original condition. To Megan, it felt like a working museum that Albert Einstein or Tesla would have lived in.

Megan had walked about seven steps when Mac asked her what she would like to drink. Not really thinking twice about it, Megan looked around, spoke up, "Lemonade would be fine."

Mac smiled and offered her a chair to sit in that was obviously from the 19th century. As she moved towards the red velvet chair, she was startled to see a brass disk. It was about the size of a dinner plate, as thick as her thumb, and it came hovering towards her with a glass of lemonade on it.

Her eyes grew wide as she watched it stop near her. Snapping her head around to look at Mac's mischievous grin, she looked back at her approaching drink. "How in the world?"

Mac folded his arms and sat on the corner of his desk looking towards her. "You once asked me the question, if we had ever found anything else? The technology that keeps your lemonade from falling to the ground, it came from an exploded wreck we found in Mexico."

Megan just sat there watching it hover. So Mac reached over and picked up the drink, handing it to her. The brass disk was glowing at the bottom then moved away to the other side of the room to slide into a slot under a painting from the Middle Ages.

Megan just sat there for a moment, holding her drink as she thought about how real all this was becoming. Suddenly, past and future were very real. Megan lowered the drink to her lap as she looked up at Mac with wide eyes. "So that's why you never doubted our story."

Mac moved closer and pulled up a chair close to

Megan. Sitting down, he looked at her, "Not for a moment."

Megan's eyes wandered away from Mac's understanding face. Ever so slowly, her eyes panned around the area in front of her, looking at everything near his desk. Odd things here and there rested within her view. Something semi-round and crystal-like held a baseball on his desk. Something gear-like sitting behind the desk held up a calendar. Flat, square stacks of glass of different colors were stacked near the back wall next to some black glossy gears.

Turned her head to look in the direction the flying disk traveled, only to see another disk resting on something strange, almost a liquid like aquarium with no fish within it. Just under its stand was a small glass set of bricks with golden centers. The writing on them looked almost Egyptian.

Bending her neck back towards the door behind her. A very old, Egyptian looking in nature golden pillar of no more than four feet high with a ring around the top stood to function as a plant stand for Mac's Venus fly trap

Megan looked back at Mac, "Is everything in here alien?"

Mac slowly nodded his head. "No, but a lot of it is. The fact is we really don't understand the majority of what we find. We can tweak it, turn it on and off, but some of the basic concepts of how these things fiction...we just no clue."

Looking into her eyes, Mac continued, "That's why we got really excited about your find in the desert. Your son's letter told us a lot. But in reality... it has only created more questions. With the theft of the golden books, we have lost a big opportunity."

Mac paused once more, and then continued, "You testified that John covered the walls with math formulas. I would like to get access to that with a team."

Megan's face changed to disappointment. "Sorry, according to Major Watson, they cleaned the walls with something as well. It just looks like a normal stone wall now. All I have is what's in my camera."

"Do you have it with you?" Mac inquired.

"Yes, I do." Megan responded back.

Megan pulled out her camera, opened it and pulled out the small card within it.

Handing it to Mac, he held it up to look at it. "Thank you, Megan."

Mac then reached over and pressed a button on his desk that looked like a button from an old typewriter. Megan turned her head to hear a mechanical noise like a spring behind her. Mozo, Mac's robotic dog, came into the room via "the dog door" that was built into the wall next to the plant stand.

Mac handed the card to Mozo, who opened his mouth for it. "Mozo, make a copy and send it to the team outside." Mozo bounced his head up and down in response to his command. "Also project the images for us to see."

A small device came out from the side of Mozo's head and turned on. About ten feet in front of them, Mozo started projecting images.

Megan stood up as they came on. After several seconds and a few pictures she responded, "That's not right, where did they go? Every picture is blurry or black."

Mac looked disappointed as he asked, "Did you ever let your camera out of your sight?"

Megan stood there, silently thinking. Finally, she responded, "Yes, Just after we talked with dad. I set it on the counter in the women's bathroom at the Pentagon before I went into a stall. No one else was in the bathroom."

"No one else?" Mac asked.

Pausing for a moment Megan responded back, "Ah... I did see through the space in the stall doorway an Air Force uniform for a moment, but it was only for a moment as the person was just washing their hands."

Mac slowly nodded his head, realizing what happen as he motioned for Mozo to leave. "Whoever they are, they're good. Now I really want to get a team into that cave ASAP."

Fading Starlight

Megan sat back down feeling a little defeated. Mac walked over to the door, opened it, and talked with someone on the other side for a moment. He then walked back to his desk, and without thinking, put his hand on Megan's shoulder as he passed by.

Megan felt the comforting tone of his hand as it rested for a moment on her. She watched him sit down in his chair as he picked up an old phone. And for this brief moment, she allowed herself the freedom to relax and enjoy someone else taking charge.

After a couple of hours of phone calls, Mac finally stopped and hung up the phone. Megan had been texting back and forth with her father and Major Watson. She stopped texting for a moment to look up as she realized Mac was finally done.

"Where do we stand, Mac?" Megan asked in a snappy way with a slight grin.

Mac raised one eyebrow in reference to her childlike humor. "Not too bad. The mess in Africa is keeping all the brass occupied, so they have kinda forgotten about aliens for now." Mac smiled as he put his elbows on the desk with hands together under his chin. "It looks like we have a green light to skip on over to your camp."

Megan's shoulders relaxed as she realized what that meant. "So we can leave?"

"Yes, however, in a quick meeting, they did decide that your father should no longer supervise, due to a conflict of interest. General Bond will oversee the project by-remote," Mac stated. Megan nodded slowly with her head as she acknowledged what he said.

"Is that going to bother you?" Mac inquired.

"Nope, Dad knew it was going to happen. So we talked about it." Megan stopped texting and put her phone in her pocket. "And Dad just texted me that information about 10 minutes ago," Megan remarked with a smile.

Mac lowered his hands and slowly nodded his head in a confirming manner as he smiled at her. "I will activate Team Four and we should be in the air within an hour. Karen will drive you back to the Ritz to get your

252

luggage."

"Team Four, who is that? You've got teams?" Megan inquired.

Mac rose to his feet as he talked, "Maxwell Lewis, we call him Max, Danny Connor, Carol Hess, and Rick Chen. Good people, mostly a scientific team. I would think you would like them. Carol, Rick, and Danny all hold various multiple degrees in science. Rick is good with his hands and feet in a pinch. It all comes in really handy, digging in the dirt looking for alien stuff."

Megan spoke up as Mac opened the door for her, "And Max, what is he?"

Mac smiled, "He's the muscle of the team. That comes in handy as well at times. And a hand full of military guys in various places. Plus we got a few others who don't work in teams like Jenny."

"Mac, who is Jenny?" Megan asked.

"Jenny is General Bond's granddaughter. Many years ago, when she was ten years old, her parents were killed in a horrific event. It shook the General up, but even worse, it messed up Jenny. It was more than her ten-year-old mind could take. Victoria took her in, of course, and everything was all nice for about a month. Then Jenny kept disappearing, getting into trouble. By the time she was twelve, she spent her first night in the county lockup for teens on drug charges. Victoria tried everything she could think of to help her, she even emptied her savings trying."

"Wow, that's bad," Megan responded.

"Yeah, but it got worse. Jenny has a highly gifted mind, very creative. When she was fourteen, she built a fire bomb out of household chemicals in the police personnel bathroom. Because of her small size and beautiful eyes, she made the police think she was the victim. So an older police officer let her use the regular bathroom. About a minute after that, she let loose a fireball that came bursting through the door. By the time they got the fire put out, Jenny was long gone with a police car."

Surprised by the story, Megan responded, "That's bold,

253

how did she end up working for you?"

"A few years ago, she got badly beat up from a drug deal gone bad. Victoria found her in a hospital and spent some time talking to her. Jenny could barely speak because her face was so swollen. She had no choice but to sit there and listen. When she got better, she ran once more. But this time, she decided to kill herself."

Megan's eyes grew a little wider as she listened as Mac continued. "Some homeless man showed up and made her stop. He talked her into joining him at a local soup kitchen. The kind lady who ran it once had a life like hers. So she listened and when she got up to leave, she noticed the homeless man had disappeared. That night, she had a powerful dream that she hardly talks about. All I know is that the homeless man came to her dressed in white, talked to her in her dream, and changed her life."

"She went home, and according to Victoria has never been the same since. In time, she got into some private education to help her out. But Victoria knew she needed something more. The Army was out with her drug history, so she turned to me."

"And you turned her into an agent?" Megan asked.

"Basically, yes, we tested her and found out about her highly creative side. As well as her strong sense of internal justice."

"What else?" Megan asked.

"Passionate lives for the moment, Jenny likes Goth or at least I think so, sings, and dances," Mac remarked.

Puzzled, Megan responded. "That's a strange package, an agent who sings and dances?"

"Well, it's more skills, she does that privately when she thinks no one is looking. She calls it her alone time with her God. It seems to me to be her internal way of processing the day's events, like grief or loss," Mac stated.

Megan's eyebrow rose up at that last comment.

"But, I can't complain. Jenny has become a valuable asset to the organization. Fixed several problems for us.

So, in the end, I really don't care how she processes her stuff as long as she does it in a healthy way. She got a tattoo on her right arm a few years back. It was some sort of an epiphany for her."

"What do you mean?" Megan asked.

"Not really sure about it myself. She just said it was something she felt God told her and was going to be a part of her life forever," Mac responded.

"Hmm, what was the tattoo?" Megan asked.

Mac smiled and responded, " It was just one word. Honor."

The Past

The breaking rays of morning light greeted the distant eastern horizon, warming John's right side as he lay on the ground. Slowly, he became more alert in the morning light, as he listened to a songbird near him. Pulling himself up, he noticed his hands as he leaned against a rock, grimy, covered in scratches and dried blood. As his mind cleared, he realized that most likely he never really knew just how dirty he was.

He pulled his pack close to him to look for a little food as he watched the sunrise. A little deer jerky would be today's breakfast as he watched a hawk traverse the morning sky. Finally, John remembered what he had found in Átahsaia's cave.

Pulling himself all the way up, John was feeling the effects of his sore body as he sat down on a rock for a seat. With a pain-filled sigh from landing on the stone, he just paused for a second, perhaps two as he looked around for a moment. With care, he slowly slid his right hand into his pocket. Digging around he found what he was looking for. The small disk was shiny and about a quarter of an inch thick. Inspecting it, he realized he was never going to read the writing on the face of it.

Within a few moments, he had his answer with his

alien stick. Turning off the holographic image, he raised his eyebrow. "I'll be darned, it's a battery. Powerful little guy, 690 volts." John exclaimed as he slipped it back into his pocket, pondering what device would need that many volts.

The morning songbirds kept singing as John's head slowly turned back to look towards Átahsaia's cave. "I wonder what else is in there," he whispered out loud.

Hiking back up to the cave, he stopped and pulled out his banged-up headset. Putting it back on his ear, he turned it on. It started to unfold like normal, but then stopped, made a buzzing sound, and retracted back. John pulled it off his ear and looked it over. "Hmm, I guess your days have come to an end."

He put it back in his pack as he stood there looking over the cave. After about thirty seconds or so, a new idea came to him. So he pulled the alien stick back out and activated it. "I wonder if..." John did not finish his sentence, as he found an informational screen. Tapping an image, the holographic screen ended and a dull light projected from the red tip like a faint flashlight. Stepping forward into the cave, John moved it around the cave. Quickly it started to create a holographic image before him over the cave floor, displaying the densities of whatever it was pointed at. Holding it in his left hand, John knelt down and dug under the sand with his right hand to find a rock. A little aggravated, he looked at his alien stick once more. Giving it a small "twist" in the middle, he found that if he adjusted it correctly, the holographic images came in greater detail and color. He could clearly see what was a rock and what were bones.

Pausing, John sat on his knees for a moment in awe, as he realized that in one corner of the cave, Átahsaia had been feeding on humans for a very long time. The holographic image displayed hundreds of layers of bones, descending many feet below the surface. The sight of it was disgusting and John realized how glad he was to kill him. Panning around the cave, John spotted other objects near one wall that looked like metal.

Within twenty minutes or so, he had them all out of the cave and set them on a rock to look them over. Some looked complete, and others were obviously broken. Passing his alien scanner over his small horde of strange objects, he discovered he had an assorted collection. Scanners, broken weapons, radios, everything a small scouting party would need. Except most of it did not work.

Looking around at the outside world, John realized he was less than a day's hike to his old cave. He really wanted to head in the opposite direction and reunite with his tribe. But after thinking it over, he realized it would be best to cart his collection back to the Wingate cave. It had become obvious to him that a few thousand years in the past his enemies' level of technology was significantly less and barely above what he knew in his time.

The Present

Mac raised the remote control for the TV in the airplane and turned off the news feed. The background rumble of the engine replaced the sound of the TV as the look of disgust on Mac's face settled in deeply. Folding his arms as he slowly shook his head, Mac spoke up. "Is it me or has the whole world gone insane? It seems any event nowadays is an excuse to riot and steal."

Megan just shrugged her shoulders as Max Lewis from Team Four spoke up. A larger, dark-skinned man, built like a pro weightlifter, the muscle of the team, responded to Mac's question. "No clue, boss," As he sat in his chair.

Rick Chen, a short, black-haired man, just walked in from the front of the jet to sit down. "Mac, the pilot says we are about to land at the camp."

Megan's head jerked slightly to the side as she looked

at Mac. "What landing, we don't have a runway?"

Carol, who was looking out the window, had a slight grin on her face as she spoke up in her German accent. "We do not need one."

Mac smiled at Carol's comment, and gave a look at Danny and the rest of the team, as he responded to Megan, "As I said before, the Office of Management and Acquisitions has been playing with alien stuff for a while."

Megan gave Mac a serious look, partly mixed with confusion and partly with surprise. The plane noticeably slowed down in the air, giving everyone the clue it was time. Mac stood up and grabbed a handhold that projected down from the ceiling. Looking back down at Megan with a smile, Mac spoke up. "Remember the lemonade?"

Major Watson stepped outside because of a noise in the sky. As he walked out, he noticed everyone's faces were looking upward. Moving his right hand in front of the sun so that he could see, he observed what looked like a standard leer jet with a faint glow under it, as it gently descended down to the center of the camp.

Watson, like everyone else in the camp, was speechless as it slowly came to rest on the sandy earth. Between the tent and trucks.

The Major took a few steps closer to the plane after it stopped. Observing the round logo of the Office of Management and Acquisitions, realizing the game was about to change in the camp.

The tension within him that was starting to build relaxed a little as the door opened. Megan stepped out and smiled at the Major.

"Megan," came a burst of surprise out of Watson's mouth as he quickly corrected himself. "Captain Becker... I did not expect this."

Megan stopped in front of the Major, saluted, and reported in. "Major Watson, I would like to introduce MacCallister MacWilliams, Director of the Office of Management and Acquisitions, and his team behind him, Max Lewis, Danny Connor, Carol Hess, and Rick

Chen. They have come to document the events of the last few days as well as take a closer look at the camp."

Mac stepped forward to offer his hand to the Major, "Major."

Watson shook his hand in return, "Mr. MacWilliams."

"Call me Mac," Mac responded back.

Watson turned to look back at Megan. "General Bond notified me that you would be returning with a team. But I must admit, this is a little over the top."

Megan nodded, "It is for me as well, Major."

Watson looked at Megan for a moment, nodding his head. Then turning to his side, he saw Sergeant Buckings in the distance, "Sergeant, find private Huckins and help move any gear they have out of that plane."

Buckings saluted, "Yes, sir," and he left for the mess tent.

"Major is the..." Megan did not get a chance to finish.

Johnny rounded a corner, saw his mother, and came running at full speed yelling one word, "MOM."

The conversation stopped for everyone as mother and son embraced at high speed. True to form, however, the embrace was short as Johnny now made it his mission to tell her everything. The sand, the big trucks, helicopters, why he can no longer eat anything but ice cream and hot dogs. Megan did not really care what he was saying, it was just nice to see and hear him once more.

Mac patiently stood there watching this moment. He swallowed once or twice as he watched. Saying nothing, wondering how someone so small could someday make such an impact. At least that's what he was trying to make his mind think about. In reality, all this moment did was bring up memories of his departed wife and the family they would never have. No birthdays, no diapers, no endless questions, just his job now. He would have rather had the messes to clean and broken toys to fix.

"Mac," Megan interrupted his downward thinking for a moment. Snapping him back to the moment.

Fading Starlight

"Johnny, I would like you to meet Mr. MacWilliams. He will be here helping Mommy," Megan announced.

Mac stepped forward, "Hello Johnny, I've heard a lot about you."

Johnny's eyes narrowed a little to look him over. "Is that your plane?" Johnny cautiously asked.

"Yes, it is, would you like to see it?" Mac inquired.

Megan's head jolted a little backward as her son excitedly snapped in a loud tone, "Yes."

Mac looked at Megan and asked, "May I escort your son to my plane?"

Megan slowly answered as she knew what was about to happen. "Ah... sure."

Mac started to put out his hands as if he was going to take Johnny from Megan's arms. But Johnny already had hands and feet moving as he was tearing out of his mother's arms as fast as he could go.

As soon as he hit the ground, he had one of Mac's hands and was leading Mr. MacWilliams to the plane. Megan folded her arms as she watched it all unfold, with a smile on her face.

Major Watson stepped up next to her. "I wonder if he knows what he just got himself into."

Megan had a little mischievous sparkle in her eyes as she responded. "Nope, I'm pretty sure he is clueless to what he just started." As they both watched Johnny dragging Mac into the plane.

Megan turned around to look at Watson with a concerned look in her eyes, "Sir, how is he?"

Major Watson's face changed as well, turning a little to the side and then back again to respond. "Not good . . . the docs have never seen cancer like this so aggressive. We had to move him out of here. Something happened that night, something very bad. No one remembers anything and Josh was found in the center of the camp.

It's not in my report, but we did find the faint outline of something that landed in the camp. Whoever it was had advanced tech. Probably just as advanced as Mac's plane. And all of that is feeding the rumor mill around here. Frankly, I am starting to wonder if some of it is true."

Megan sucked in a little on her lower lip, "I would like to see him."

"I will make transportation arrangements for you in the morning. Lieutenant Hansen is with him in Salt Lake," Watson announced.

"Salt Lake, hmm. Mac and his team are going to want to talk to Andrew. I have a feeling that they will want to see Josh as well," Megan spoke out loud as she thought about it.

Watson and Becker retired to the mess tent to continue their discussion as the men unloaded the jet. After a little while, Mac came in looking a little overwhelmed. Megan, Watson, and Dave looked up to see him walk in.

Megan smiled as he entered. "So, how was it being a tour guide? That's the most excitement I think I have ever seen on your face."

Mac stood there for a moment, nodding his head up and down as he evaluated it in his mind. "Interesting, overwhelming, generally enjoyable," Mac responded with a smile.

Dave looked at him from where he was sitting with a less-than-thrilled look on his face. "You want a cup of coffee?"

Megan lifted her cup off the table a few inches as she raised one eyebrow at Mac. "Best in the area, better than any you're going to find in Washington."

Mac raised the palm of one hand up. "Ah, no thanks. I think this late in the day that would be a little too much for me."

"Hmm," was Dave's response as Watson turned his head to look at Megan.

"Does he always sound a little bit like a computer?" Watson inquired as he used his thumb to point at him over his shoulder.

"Sometimes," Megan responded with a grin. She put down her coffee cup and motioned with her left hand for him to sit down with them. "So where's my son off to now?"

As Mac sat down, he responded back up, "He ran off

261

to the west, said there was something that he needed to dig up and show his mom."

Megan's eyebrow raised a little as she looked at Watson, who simply shrugged his shoulder as he took a drink of his coffee. After putting it back down, Watson spoke up, "Hard telling what he's got today. That boy's mind runs a mile a minute and could be another dead lizard he played with. The other day, he figured out that baking soda makes things foam with vinegar. Made a big mess in one of the supply tents."

Megan's mouth opened a little as she heard the news. "Well, who taught him that?"

"I think it was the professor," Watson replied.

Megan slowly shook her head and rolled her eyes as she changed the subject. "And where is the professor?" inquired Megan.

"He was done here, so he went back up north," Watson replied.

Looking over at Mac, Megan asked, "How long do you think before Team Four is ready to work?"

"Should be any moment now. Rick will let me know," Mac responded.

"Also, it sounds like the cancer Josh mysteriously came down with on the same night is highly aggressive. They have flown him to Salt Lake," Megan said.

Mac's eyes looked downward for a moment. "Our team will want to see him as well."

Watson looked at Megan. "Becker, we are just holding the fort here right now. Everything is gone and we are highly overstaffed to guard sand and rocks. So I sent a third of our team back to base. If nothing changes, I am going to reduce what I have here by half."

"Have you talked to General Bond about this?" Megan inquired.

"I have, she agrees. But she wanted me to wait and see if OMA dug up anything first," Watson responded. Picking up his coffee cup once more, "My orders are that if nothing is found, I am to shut everything down and return to base."

Everyone continued to talk for a while until Johnny

came bursting in. Rushing up to his mother Megan, he interrupted the conversation, "Mama, look what I dug up, ain't it cool?"

Johnny shoved into his mother's hand a very well-worn, old carved piece of wood. Megan held it up to look at it. Holding it by the small child-sized handle in front of her, was a beat-up, ancient wooden sword.

Megan went silent as she realized what she was holding. Her hand lightly started to tremble as the impact of it settled in her mind. Everyone at the table stopped talking, realizing that something was happening in front of them.

Finally, Mac spoke up. "Meg, what is it?"

Megan's eyes started to water as she slowly turned it in her hand. Slowly, a tear fell to the table as she spoke. "It's my grandson's sword, Lorenzo's sword. I read about it, his father carved it for him as a birthday gift. He hardened the wood in a fire by partly burning it and then treating it with oil." Megan's voice started to break a little, "Because he knew how hard he was on his own toys."

The impact of those words caused everyone to sit back.

Johnny was a little confused at his mother's words. "Does that mean I can't play with it?" Johnny insisted.

Megan did not talk for a while as Mac quietly commented, "It is becoming more and more real every day."

Megan and Mac looked at each other as she responded to her son in a slightly choked tone, "Mommy is going to keep this for a while."

The Past

John made it back to the Wingate cave just before dark. He stopped at the entrance and looked around for a moment. A little surprised, he could easily remember seeing the battle in his mind just outside the cave before everything changed. He happened to glance down at where the alien had died. The blood spots had long since been washed away by each year's spring rains.

Remembered how disgusting it was. Not only the smell but also returning the next year and tossing what has left of the skeleton far away so he did not have to look at it.

Shaking off the emotions that came with memories, he walked inside. He dug around in the sand on the floor that he had packed in. Feeling around with his hands, he found his hidden stash of gold plates he was working on under the sand. Pulling them out, and counting them, he realized nothing had changed. Smiling, he cleaned his hidden floor stash out. Scooping all the sand out with his hands, he located his homemade tools.

Before he would leave in the morning, he would take the opportunity to scratch out more of his story in gold. For now, he would build another campfire in the ring of stone he made outside. He would also take the opportunity to look through the database in the alien stick a little more closely. He was becoming more and more amazed at what this little thing could do.

The Present

Johnny showed everyone where he found the sword. The team looked at the spot intently for more, only to come up empty-handed. Carol Hess ran some tests on the sword and realized that three millennia of dirt had hidden the carved name on the blade. "Lorenzo." Making Megan cry a little more as Carol handed it back to her.

Carol waited for a moment or so after the impact of it subsided some. "Captain Becker... Megan. There is one more thing about your grandson's sword we found."

Megan wiped her eyes with the back of her hand as

she looked up at her. "Yes?"

"Presuming Captain John Becker carved the sword from a freshly cut piece of wood and not something that's been dead for a while, we have dated the sword, plus or minus 10 years, to 1335 BC."

Megan sucked a little air in and held it as she spoke, "Oh."

"Had he not treated the sword with heat and oil, I doubt we would be holding it today," remarked Carol.

Mac turned to Megan who was holding her sword as he turned to Carol to speak, "Did the team find anything else?"

"No, sir, I think we are done here," Carol responded.

Mac nodded his head and then walked over to Rick Chen who was standing a few away. Rick had just finished talking with Danny, who had some equipment in his hand.

"Mr. Chen, if there is nothing else here, I would like to relocate the team up the hillside to the cave," Mac ordered.

"Yes sir, I would think we should be up there in five minutes," Chen responded back.

Mac nodded a thank you and turned to walk back to Megan. Carol's and Rick's eyes followed Mac as he walked away. For a brief moment, they looked at each other across the short distance with a slightly concerned look.

Mac talked with Megan for a moment to let her know they were going to start scanning the cave now as Major Watson walked up at the same time to inquire an update. Soon all three of them, along with Team Four were walking back through the camp on their way to the cave. Max packed the heavy stuff on his back as if it was light, as they passed one of the crates they had shipped.

Max looked over to see Private Huckins sitting on the crate with a can of pop in his hand. Raising his voice towards him, "Son, if I were you I would not want to sit on that," Max informed him as everyone else passed. Both Danny and Mac smiled at they thought about

Max's words.

Soon everyone was inside the cave. Megan was totally amazed to see that everything was erased as if it had never existed. "Wow," was her only comment. Carol started running her hands carefully over the sandstone rock face with her glove. Mac watched her as she looked carefully at it.

Carol then turned to her boss, Mac, "Sir, I think the sandstone face has been prematurely weathered to look old. To know more, I will need our bigger scanner."

Mac nodded his head and looked at Danny. "Sounds good, let's get him in here."

Danny stepped outside the cave and let loose a high-pitched whistle. Private Huckins had placed his drink on top of the crate which suddenly made a "beep" sound. It shook for a moment and the top of the crate flipped off, sending his can of soda flying. The front of the crate also fell to the ground as Mozo stood up. All his lights came on as he became aware of his surroundings.

Danny clapped his hands and yelled, "Hey buddy, we're up here. Come on."

Mozo stepped out of his crate and started prancing up the hill like a happy dog. Megan, who watched it happen, looked over at Mac, "You brought Mozo?"

"Yep," Mac responded.

Major Watson watched the robotic dog prance effortlessly up the hill and into the cave. Shaking his head a little to announce he's seen everything now.

Lieutenant Alanis watched the computer screen as Saudi Arabia engaged China in an air battle. As the situation in the room unfolded, she could overhear the Generals talking. Some felt it would be necessary to jump in, even pushed for it. Others, like General Bond, recommended that they tell the President that they should let the dust settle on this for a while before taking any action.

A light, atmospheric distortion came up from behind the Lieutenant and touched the back of her neck. As it did, her eyes stopped following the events on the screen. Her breathing remained constant as she remained in that position. Then, without warning, the distortion left her and zipped away. Alanis resumed her actions, then she slowly moved her head to look behind her at the senior staff.

Everyone watched as Mozo scanned the walls. Danny had a computer pad in his hands controlling Mozo's scan. Ever so slowly, Mozo started building a holographic image, one or two symbols at a time on the wall. Danny raised his finger to point out the first ones as they came into view.

"Look, there's the math they tried to erase," Danny exclaimed.

Looking closely at it, Major Watson spoke up, "Amazing, how did you do that?"

"Well, they destroyed the outer layer with some sort of energy. And then applied something else to make everything in the room appear normal. Kinda like it's been here for thousands of years. But our scanner looks at the micro pressure that Captain Becker would have put on the wall by engraving it in the first place," Danny explained.

Watson's eyebrow came up, "Micro pressure?"

"Yes, the echoes in the stone, it's like a record." Seeing that his words meant nothing to him, Danny spoke once more. "You know, like when we were kids and someone wrote something on a piece of paper. They would take it with them, but if you rub the next sheet with a pencil and see what they wrote. It's kinda like that."

"They may have taken the paper. But we got a really strong pencil," Mac remarked as he lightly tapped Mozo on the head.

Megan and Watson watched in amazement as the process took place. "How long will the process take, Mac?" Megan inquired.

Mac looked over at Danny, expecting him to answer.

Danny suddenly realized the question was meant for him. "Oh, I'm sorry. Based on the speed Mozo's working on and the surface area of the walls to be covered, I would say just over an hour from now."

Everyone watched for a moment, then Rick turned towards Mac. "Mac, I'm going to take Max outside and look around with hand scanners. See if we find anything out of sorts around here."

Mac nodded his head, "Sounds good, I want everyone to keep me updated. The rest of us are going to walk back. Major Watson, can we use the officers' tent as an office?"

"Yes, you may, Mr. MacWilliams," Watson responded.

Far away in the Indian Ocean, the Chinese naval fleet destroyed the last of the Saudi Arabian task force that was sent against them. Admiral Zheng Zo effectively destroyed them with little damage to his own fleet. In response, he ordered an air strike on the Abu Dhabi military base to teach them a lesson.

His Navy had effectively retaken control of their missing ship, killing everyone present. His own men on the ship were becoming very nervous about his actions. But he remained steadfast and unmoving while standing in the control room. All the while, a small atmospheric distortion that no one could see remained closely connected to the back of his neck.

Team Four, Mac, Megan, and Major Watson all convened in the officers' tent. Mac asked if there was anything else anyone had to report.

"Just this," Rick answered.

Mac and everyone else looked as Rick held up a small white cloth with something "bluish" smudged on it.

Max stood up to speak. "We're not totally sure, sir, we will need to get it back to the lab. But I'm thinking it is the remnants of some sort of chemical compound. We found traces of it all over the area. I'm thinking they used it to put everyone to sleep."

"To sleep?" Watson responded.

Rick lowered the cloth to a zip lock bag. "I'm thinking all they needed to do was get upwind of the camp and release it. So we looked around on the other side of the camp and found footprints up in the rocks."

"And Josh?" Megan inquired.

"Collateral damage," Mac responded. "I would like to talk with him tomorrow in Salt Lake. Find out more."

Megan thought about it and then responded, "Can we call General Bond and keep this operation open?"

Mac slowly nodded his head no. "I don't think that would be a good idea. This is no longer an archeology dig. It's part of a cat-and-mouse game with a group of highly powerful people, whomever they are."

Mac turned and looked at Major Watson. "Major, I would suggest you report that nothing has been found officially and shut down the base here. Unofficially, I will handle the back channel with General Bond. I know her and I'll keep her in the loop. That way, we can keep the evidence we have found so far secret."

"Agreed, I will call ahead to Lieutenant Hansen to tell him you're coming. Then I will start pulling out of here as soon as you leave. Everything should shut down shortly after that," Watson responded back.

Shadows
Chapter Nine
Strike back

John had been hiking for some hours after sunrise, making good time, in an effort to reunite with the tribe. He saw in the far distance some deer and for a short moment considered hunting one of them, but then decided against it. It might be a while before he rejoined the tribe and packing that much-uncooked meat in the sun just seemed like a waste to him. His military-issue boots were still in fair shape, even though he assumed that this would be their last year.

As he walked, he spent his time reflecting on everything he had learned. How these aliens had been here for a long time. Far less advanced in the ancient past than in his future. They fought with each other, caused wars, and attempted to dominate the human race via DNA, only to have that blow up in their faces. Their population had gone up and then crashed at times in the past. They seemed more like a race of spoiled brats who only got along on the surface when someone was watching. With their reduced level of technology, John was becoming convinced that he could fly, fix, or drive anything that they created in this timeline.

He had become so lost in thought on this issue that he forgot the direction he was marching. Then at one point, he stopped and looked around after becoming so distracted that he walked into a dead-end canyon. Shaking his head and laughing at himself, John looked up at the canyon walls. The corners of his mouth came up as he realized what he had just done. In the old days, on the battlefield, he would have never done this. At that point, he remembered a comment he made to Andrew once about getting lost—that it was a sure sign of getting old. He smiled as he thought of him and what he would have said about walking into a dead-end canyon.

As John left the area and rounded the end of the trail to turn west again on his journey, he saw something out of the corner of his eye. He raised his hand up to block the sun. It had been so long since he had seen anything like it. He honestly said in his own mind, "Look at the size of that bird."

Ever so slowly, his thinking changed, as if a long extended vacation just came to an end. His eyes slowly made out the outline of a large aircraft traversing the sky towards the east. Most likely, it was about 15 thousand feet in the sky and was similar in design to the modern aircraft he knew.

He watched it move along the sky as he felt a low level of tension settle into his neck. Something he had not felt in years, at least three thousand. How he hated them, what they did, what they had turned his world into. He remembered the first time they attacked, he remembered the images on TV—the fights in Madrid, Ireland, and his own base. He remembered those men who never made it.

Too much of his mind was flooded with emotion. The winter wind of his combat coldness seemed to be ready to greet him like an old friend. Putting one foot in front of the other, he returned to traveling, hoping to soon rejoin the tribe. From now on he would be keeping an eye on the sky.

After a few hours of walking, he realized his causal walk had become more like a march. He now held his rifle close to him, ready for war. Old habits were coming back as reality slowly broke his dream. Even when he fought Átahsaia, it was no longer normal for him to function like this anymore. John slowly became aware of what his mind was doing. He did not like it but realized he needed it. For himself, there was going to be very little sleep tonight.

The Past

First light was coming to the canyon walls as the camp stirred. Guard change was taking place as the smell of Dave's morning coffee came to the camp. The light dew on the outer walls of the mess tent would only temporarily hold in the morning smells coming from Dave's cooking.

Max was already looking over his plane, checking her out to make sure she would be ready for the flight. Danny had spent most of the night looking over the data he had acquired. And Megan, for some reason, enjoyed Johnny's foot on her back. It was normal, and even though she had to roll around a few times to get comfortable, she would never trade it for her hotel room.

Soon everyone was moving, the day was starting and Megan was still on the edge of her bed, enjoying the smell of the sagebrush as it came up the canyon.

Megan then rolled over and gently shook her son. "Come on honey, it's time to get up."

Outside her tent, Mac walked around outside to look around at this peaceful place. He watched Megan and Johnny from a distance exit their tent and head out for breakfast. It had been a long time since he felt this kind of calmness. It was in the wind, the brush, and the sky. It was enjoyable. But slowly, there was another feeling—it was almost "lurking" on the outside, like the bite of a cold wind. He could not help but feel it—it felt like something terrible was near.

Rick walked by on the way to the mess tent, when Mac stopped him. "Did Max check the plane this morning?"

Rick had a slightly confused look on his face. "Yes, why?"

Mac shrugged his shoulders, "Not sure, I just want to be careful..." Mac thought for a moment and then spoke up once more, "I want everything double checked before we take to the air."

Rick knew that look Mac had on his face, "No problem, I will get the team on it."

The Present

General Mullins spent the night at the Pentagon, being awakened every hour or so with an update. The world had erupted into a nightmare. China now occupied parts of Africa and Saudi Arabia. As a result, oil shipments to China were being restricted by some countries. Three African nations agreed to march troops into Somalia to remove China. The Chinese government sent officials to their fleet to replace to the Admiral in charge, only to find he shot himself in front of his bridge crew just before they entered.

The British then decided to add troops in an effort to contain the growing violence in Africa. America was now looking to the President for action. And of all things, a Chinese General was scheduled to be a guest today at the Pentagon.

General Mullins sat on the side of his bed, wishing he wasn't there.

The Past

After two days on foot, John reached the river to find tracks from his tribe moving westward. Looking it all over, he realized he was only a few hours behind them. He wanted to take off and run, but it was midday and he needed to conserve his energy. The days were getting very hot as summer dried out much of the brush around him. His comfort was in knowing they would stop and seek shelter for a few hours. So if he just traveled slowly, he knew he should catch up with them.

Within a few hours, he could see a woman and a young girl, about a hundred yards in front of him, drawing water from the river. It was his sister-in-law Malia and her daughter, Tablita, who sat in the river playing with the sand. John smiled and thought for a moment about wasting a bullet and firing it into the air above him as a message.

Thinking better of it, he decided to just keep hiking. He did not need to wait long as he passed through the thick brush. He heard the faint sound of a bowstring being drawn back. He could not see who it was, so he stopped and spoke up to whoever was listening. "Wait a moment, I don't think you're going to want to do that," John announced.

A head jerked around the corner in surprise to see who was talking. Ahote's eyes locked on to John's to see his smiling face. Letting out a holler of excitement, Ahote dropped his bow to rush over to John. Ahote's holler was nearly lost because of the sound of the river to the ears of his tribe, but a few of the ones closest to them, at the edge of the camp did get up to investigate.

To the tribe's excitement, the men soon led John out of the brush to the rest of the tribe. Kasa, who had hardly spoken in days, heard the noise and looked up. Her almost dead looking face came to life as she realized who the men were celebrating. She screamed and ran as fast as she could. John looked up and watched it all unfold, adrenaline filling his excited mind as he watched her run. His mind quickly blocked out the sight of anyone else rushing up to him, and his eyes started to water.

On the banks of the Colorado River, the tribe rested for a few days. That night there would be stories to tell, and food to eat, and John would fall asleep with his arm around Kasa feeling their new child kicking within her.

One tent over Ahote eyes opened to the sound of John snoring, "John is definitely back," he quietly commented. His wife Malia who was rolled over on her side quietly responded back, "like a bull moose." To which their daughter Tablita smirked to herself in her bed.

The Present

Max had landed the plane in Salt Lake and stayed behind to guard it per Mac's orders. The rest of the team accompanied Megan and Johnny to the hospital to see Josh. To her surprise, Andrew was waiting for them on the main floor near the elevator.

Andrew had a look of extreme concern on his face as they approached. Johnny wanted to run up to him, but Megan held her son back because of the look on his face.

"Andrew?" Megan tried to calmly speak.

Andrew looked at the team of people approaching with caution. "Megan, who is this?"

"Ah, Lieutenant Hansen. This is MacCallister MacWilliams, Director of the Office of Management and Acquisitions. And this is his team, Danny Connor, Carol Hess, and Rick Chen. These are good people Andrew."

Andrew quickly looked Mac in the eye. He was about to speak when Mac spoke first with concern in his voice, "What's up?"

Swallowing hard the lump in his throat, Andrew gently grabbed Megan's arm and motioned for the others to follow. He moved them to a private spot in a corridor. "I am pretending that I needed to get away in order to find you first. "

The look on everyone's face grew a grimmer as he emphasized the words, "you first."

Andrew took Megan by the shoulders with both hands and looked her straight in the eyes. "Some people showed up about two hours ago, wearing suits and holding documents from the government." Andrew paused for a moment, "This doesn't feel right Megan, they knew you were coming and they're looking for you."

Megan could feel the emotions change within her. A coldness was starting to rest on her back as she did not know how to process that. Why her? The cold chill that Mac felt all day grew a little stronger as he spoke up, "Do you know why?"

Andrew swallowed hard and looked over at Mac. "All they said was that someone has made an accusation against her."

Slowly Megan turned her head, her eyes glanced at Mac for a moment as she felt the warmth in her hands slowly growing a little cold. She turned her head back towards Andrew and asked, "What about Josh?"

The wetness was starting to gather in the corner of Andrew's eye as he responded back, "He slipped into a coma this morning. It won't be long now."

Carol slowly bent her head to the side to whisper to Rick, "I need to get up there."

Rick whispered back, "I know."

Megan held onto Andrew for a moment as she felt the impact of her world crumbling. Mac reached over and put a hand on her shoulder, causing her to turn around. Mac slowly replaced Andrew as he took hold of her shoulders, looking her in the eye.

"We need to get up there, I will help you face whatever is coming," Mac informed her.

The elevator was a quiet ride as Megan's mind slowly turned, realizing that in some strange way, this was all happening just like her dream. She felt helpless, alone, not even daring to speak.

Johnny's restlessness to hug Andrew had become stilled by this strange moment. He decided to just settle with leaning on his mother's leg.

As they rounded the corner to the ICU, the team could clearly see two men and a woman in black suits standing near the ICU door.

This black-haired, European-looking woman, who was a bit taller than Megan, stepped forward. With no smile, coldness, and almost anger in her eyes she looked directly at Megan. Mac and his team took note of her coldness and the men with her—for they all had the same suspicious gun bulges under their coats.

"Ms. Becker?" she announced as she stepped up.

"Ah, that's Captain Becker. And hello, you are?" Megan stuck out her hand to be polite only to find the woman placing a piece of paper in it.

As she stopped in front of Megan, she started the conversation by saying, "Not anymore." Looking her straight in the eye. "Upon review, the Joint Chiefs have come to the conclusion that you and your father, General Henry Mullins, did falsify evidence before the Joint Chiefs for unknown and possible personal purposes. And under these false pretenses, General Mullins did knowingly manipulate the government into bringing you, Andrew Hansen, Joshua Williams, and David Shaver back into the military. Therefore, it has been decided by the Joint Chiefs that everyone involved will be returned to civilian status and that you and General Mullins will be taken into custody to stand trial. These men behind me are to escort you to lock-up and I am here to escort your son, John K. Becker, to the Utah Department of Social Services, where he will undergo evaluation for charges of possible neglect."

Danny slowly took a step back, as Carol and Rick took a step forward.

Megan was totally in shock and speechless as Mac's growing tension within him burst out in a yell. "Possible neglect—what evidence do you have?"

Without turning her head and continuing to look into Megan's eyes, the unnamed woman simply answered, "I'm sorry, it's not our policy to discuss an ongoing investigation."

Johnny pressed himself a little closer to his mother's leg as the woman started to reach down to grab him, only to find Andrew now had him first.

The woman smiled for the first time as she spoke, "Come now, hand him over or I will have my men take him."

Carol and Rick moved in front of Andrew. Rick, however, kept moving and stepped in front of Megan to look the unknown woman directly in the eye. Face to face, they looked at each other as Rick spoke in a very resolute manner, "I would like to see you try."

Quietly, Mac reached down and pressed a button that was built into his cufflink. The two men in suits took a few steps forward to make their presence known. As Andrew took a few steps back with Johnny, Mac reached over and grabbed the paperwork out of Megan's hands as Carol tugged Megan backward.

Looking it over quickly, Mac spoke up, "It was signed by General Kohlenberger." Looking directly at the unknown woman "A paper pusher, whose nickname around town is General two-face. This smells like a setup."

She broke her eye contact to look at Mac for a moment, "Tough break, Mr. MacWilliams."

Mac then stepped forward to get up close and personal in her face. "When I look at the spot where other charges should be listed, it's blank. That means you have nothing, it's all a farce to get the boy."

The woman continued to smile, "I'm sure we can find someone to testify."

Mac's face was turning a very bright red as he spoke. "Unless you want a shootout and a blood bath outside ICU, I suggest you and your men stand down for a moment. You're putting this family through enough trauma. They came here to see a dying friend and I suggest you, at the very least, give them a few minutes alone with Mr. Williams."

Seeing the wisdom of the moment she responded, "Very well, I will give you fifteen."

Mac calmed down a little, "That's all I'll need."

With everyone standing down, Andrew escorted Megan and Johnny inside ICU. To them, it seemed Josh had more tubes than any one person needed coming out of him. His skin was pasty white and dry as he lay there, unaware of the moment.

Mac and his team stepped to one corner of the room, giving them some privacy as the rest stood outside. Rick leaned in close to Mac to speak privately. "Got a plan?"

Rick took a deep breath in as Mac spoke. "Protocol

Epsilon, new faces, and identities."

"Danny can handle the identities," Rick responded.

"Carol can do the faces," Mac calmly spoke.

Rick slipped out of the room as Mac walked up to comfort Megan. At that moment, everyone was unaware that Mac slipped off his cufflink and put it in Johnny's pocket.

After fifteen minutes, the unknown woman announced it was time. Everyone slipped back out of ICU except Carol, who opened a small bag she had with her.

As they stood there, Mac looked the woman straight in the face. "If you take them down the elevator together, you're going to have a very loud obnoxious scene. Do you really want that?"

The woman looked at Megan, who was starting to catch on to what Mac was saying. "I will scream and fight every step of the way," Megan responded.

The unknown woman slowly nodded her head, "Very well, I will escort the child in the elevator and my men will take Ms. Becker, via the stairwell, out the back door."

Megan knelt down and looked Johnny in the eyes, whispering to him. "I love you, just trust me and go with her. I will see you soon."

Mac, Andrew, and Danny watched as they departed in different directions. Soon Carol emerged to quietly announce to Mac that she had gotten her sample. Mac nodded and responded, "We will need to get it to the jet as fast as we can."

Turning towards Andrew, Mac spoke up, "I need to make a call, be careful."

Megan was making her promised fuss as they walked down the stairs. Kicking and attempting to bite the men, who were completely occupied with this wildcat, rounding the next set of stairs past the fourth-floor access door. As they did, they started to see Rick standing at the bottom.

He had his arms folded, smiling. Pulling his right arm out, he waved, saying, "Hi guys, remember me?" Suddenly from behind them, the fourth-floor access door opened with Max stepped into the stairwell. He kidney-punched the first man, sending him down the stairs in pain toward Rick. The second threw a punch at Max, hitting him in the face.

Megan ducked down and landed with her bum on the cement stairs. Soon, she joined in the fight, punching him in the back of the legs.

Rick had his hands full as they traded punches. At one point, he dogged a punch, allowing the attacker's body weight to toss himself down a few more steps. The man caught himself and pulled out his gun. Rick tossed himself downwards in the air towards him. His feet hit the man's hand and chest, knocking the gun off to the side as it discharged.

Max managed to break his opponent's nose and soon a rib as Megan unsuccessfully pounded his backside. Her fighting skills were limited and it showed. It looked more like a Bantam chicken trying to fight a gorilla.

Soon Max got the man's arm behind him and ran his face into the wall, knocking him out. Taking a deep breath, Max and Megan looked around the corner at Rick, who had blood coming out of the corner of his mouth. He was standing over the body of his opponent. Looking up the stairwell, Rick asked, "I'm ready, are you?"

Soon the whole team was exiting the hospital. "What about Johnny?" Megan inquired.

Max looked at her as they entered the roof, "It's being worked on as we speak."

Soon they were all loaded in the jet when Carol asked Mac, "Any luck with General Bond?"

Mac looked at his cell phone and put it back in his pocket "No, she must be in a meeting or something, hmm . . . strange."

As the plane took to the air, Megan spoke up, "Why do they want me and my son? And who are they?" she emphatically asked.

Rick looked at her and spoke, "Cleanup, first they remove all evidence and then they remove key witnesses."

Megan sat there for a moment, "It's kinda like my dream."

Mac looked at her, "Dream?"

"I had a dream that the devil was an alien and he was about to eat my world," Megan responded.

"Sounds accurate," Mac responded back.

"I need to notify my dad that he could be in trouble," Megan remarked as she pulled out her cell phone.

Mac reached over and put his hand over her phone. "Please don't, you're going into hiding now for your own safety, so no electronic devices registered to you are allowed. Besides, I already tried, your Dad is not responding any more than Bond is."

"Ok...What's your plan for Johnny?" Megan asked.

Mac looked over at Danny, "Is it working?"

Danny smiled, "Yep, as long as we stay within eight to ten miles, we can follow them."

Megan's right eyebrow went up as Mac responded to her facial expression. "I planted a bug on your son."

Mac walked over and handed Rick a computer pad saying, "I just talked with Jenny, who happened to be in the area. Everything should be ready just as soon as they make the 185 turnoffs on Highway 80."

The dark-haired European woman calmly drove her Mercedes government-issued car up the Wasatch Mountains on Highway 80. Johnny sat there in the backseat, unsure of what to do. He tried to hit her once from the back of the car, but she only raised up a protective bullet-proof screen in the car between them. There wasn't much traffic as she traveled, so it seemed a little out of place, as a collection of Harley-bikers slowly rode up from behind her.

Thinking very little of the bikers that started to pass her, several of them slowed down in front of her. She could not move over, as the lane next to her was full as well. Looking to her left, she noticed one older gruff-looking gentleman with a long white beard simply pointing with his finger, motioning to her that she needed to take the next exit. With no other option, she took the 185 exit off the main highway.

Soon they all rolled to a stop on the side of a dusty dirt road. The old biker motioned with his finger that she should roll down the window. As she did, he and a few others got off their bikes.

"Yes?" she politely asked.

From just behind her, the barrel of a shotgun was suddenly pressed hard against the back of her head. The woman heard the owner of it cycle the action, as the old biker ordered her to get out.

Standing on the dirt road next to her car with her hands up, one of the men tried the back door only to discover it was locked. The owner of the shotgun, who was a woman then ordered her, "Unlock it."

"No, this child is...." She never got a chance to finish her sentence, for the owner of the gun slammed the gunstock into her kidney, then she grabbed her by the hair, and then slammed her face into the hood of the car.

She slumped to the ground as the biker gal spoke once more. "Open it."

Slowly, the European woman produced a fob from her pocket, pushed the button and unlocked the door. The biker chick then offered her hand to Johnny, who was wide-eyed and enjoying the moment.

"Son, would you like to go for a bike ride with me?" the biker chick offered with a smile.

"Yes Ma'am," Johnny responded with a smile.

"Ok, my name is Sarah. And you will be ok now," the biker chick gladly informed Johnny.

The old biker with the white beard knelt down and spoke to the unnamed woman ear. "Don't mess with children, I don't like that."

Another biker, who was a little younger, took out his shotgun and shot out her back tires, while another found her cell phone in the car and shot it in the seat. Then he popped the hood open and fired several

282

rounds into the engine.

Johnny and the gang left her in a cloud of dust as she lay against her car tire holding her broken bloody nose.

After several minutes, the biker gang drove a few miles up the road to a private area where the jet had landed. Johnny jumped off the bike and ran up to the arms of his mother who stood next to the jet.

Mac smiled as he walked up to the lead biker. "Thank you for responding to Jenny's call. How much do I owe you for your services today?" Mac inquired as he held out his hand.

The man whose name patch said, "Jimmy," shook his hand and responded. "Nothing. For children, we work for free."

Mac raised his right eyebrow a little as he responded back with a "Thank you."

The bikers simply turned to leave as Johnny waved goodbye to Sarah. Sarah smiled and blew him a kiss, disappearing as quickly as they came.

Mac watched them ride away, turned and looked at Max as he walked by him. "They're not much for chitchat, are they?"

"Apparently not," Max responded back as he turned to follow him back to the jet. "It's surprising some times who Jenny knows."

Megan, who was kneeling on the ground, finished hugging her son and looked up at the approaching men. "What's next?"

Mac stopped in front of her with a slightly concerned look. "What electronic devices do you have with you?"

"Only my cell and laptop," a slightly puzzled Megan responded.

Danny stepped to her side, "May I have them please?" he calmly asked.

Megan stood up and handed him her cell phone. "My

laptop is in my bag."

"Thank you," Danny responded back as turned his head and looked at Mac. "This will only take a moment, sir."

In a quick moment, Danny came back out with her laptop hooked up to a box about the size of his fist.

"What are you doing?" Megan inquired.

Danny kept looking at the device as he walked over to a large flat rock. "Well, luckily, your laptop has a thunderbolt connection. So I am almost done backing up all your information." He remarked as he set the laptop down on the rock and within a second or two he heard a small beep.

"Ah, good, we're done." Unplugging the backup, Danny then placed her cell on top of the laptop. He dug around in his pocket and pulled out a small aerosol can and sprayed both the cell and the laptop. Within seconds, both started to dissolve into an ooze that started to run down the side of the rock.

Megan's face looked highly concerned as she turned and looked at Mac.

"Congratulations, Megan, you and your son just dropped off the grid." Mac held out his hand as Danny started to walk past them. Danny, who is a genius with a touch of autism, paid very little attention to the emotion of the moment. He simply reached into his shirt pocket and handed Mac a few small cards.

Mac in turn handed them to Megan, who turned them around to see a Wyoming driver's license. It had a face that looked kinda like hers with the name, Mary B. Johnson. "What? This looks kinda like me, but not really," Megan protested as Mac's hand gently pointed her back towards the inside of the jet.

"We have good makeup people," Mac responded with a smile.

"Ugh, and the name Mary, not good. What does the B stand for?" Megan inquired.

Danny, who was stowing her backup drive, spoke up as he kept working, "Beatrice."

Megan's head turned to look at Mac with a disgusted

look, "Worse."

Megan sat back down in the jet with Johnny next to her, looking at the cards. She raised her head as Mac motioned for Max to get the jet in the air.

"What about Johnny, Dad, and the rest of my team?" Megan inquired.

"We are drawing up new birth records for you and Johnny now. I sent one of our people to be with Andrew, as well as Major Watson. Your father, of course, is in the middle of the beehive right now. I've tried making contact with him, Bond, and a few other people in the Pentagon. But everyone has gone silent. And I don't like that, something is going on and I am starting to get a bad feeling about it," Mac stated.

Megan's eyes narrowed a little as he asked, "Any idea what's going on?"

Mac just sucked his lower lip in a little closer and shook his head to indicate he did not know. The jet started to lift off and move a little from side to side as Carol, who was sitting at a small control panel with an ear bud in her ear, spoke up. "Oh, my God."

Everyone's eyes moved to look at Carol as she pulled her ear bud out. In a slightly shaken look, her eyes lowered to the floor for a moment before she raised them to speak to Mac. "Sir, I may have an explanation. This... is coming across the television news feed right now. "

Carol pointed the remote in her hands toward the jet's TV screen to turn it on. It felt like the air got sucked out of the room with everyone's gasps. A TV helicopter shot from high above the Pentagon, showed one of the five sections of the building leveled and two sections on fire. Fire trucks were pouring water on the building as a ticker ran across the bottom of the screen, letting the world know that a major bomb blast just happened inside.

Everyone continued to watch as the reporter talked about what was taking place. She talked about people reporting two blasts within the building, and seeing a large amount of bodies. The reporter then noted that a high level Chinese General was most likely inside during the explosion.

Megan just sat there, holding her son who was quietly looking out the window. Her eyes watered as she watched as her face slowly became slightly lighter in complexion. The tears silently started to run down her face.

Rick, who sat next to her, happened to see her asked, "Megan?"

Calmly and in an almost detached manner, she responded, "My Father was in there."

The Past

After many days, John and his tribe had entered the area he knew as the future Zion National Park to trade with other tribes. From his father-in-law Kaviu, he learned from times before that all the tribes in the area would gather to trade in this place for, what John would call, "One large flea market."

There was no real organization to this "flea market." Tribes camped all up and down the Virgin River. The only rule seemed to be, "if the trade felt fair to you, then it was fair." In time, many came into John's camp just to hear the story of the "great warrior who killed Átahsaia."

John's brother-in-law, Lonan, seemed to be the main marketer of John's story. And in some way, he felt Lonan was acting more like a used-car salesman and he was the used car. Still, John found he could get a little mileage out of it by telling some of the people. In turn he could get them to trade their stories about any strange visitors from the skies. Most were reluctant, but many soon gave in due to the excitement of the moment within the camp.

As the days and weeks strolled on, Kasa's belly continued to grow, making John realize she was much further along than they thought. John started traveling a little less to the other encampments along Virgin River because of this. Besides, camping in the same area as the waterfall next to the Emerald pools was a relaxing joy.

Somehow, watching Kasa's pregnancy progress seemed to subdue the bad dreams that had resurfaced after seeing the aliens in the skies. As long as they left him alone, and they left him alone he was fine with it. He had no more desire to see fight aliens, or watch his new friends die. It was one thing to tell his son stories about fighting them, it was another to tell him all the facts about the pain it caused him.

Lorenzo was turning eight years old, so he spent increasingly more and more time with his father learning to fish, hunt, and build small things for trade. He started dreaming of the stories his father told him of fighting the gray aliens in faraway places. He wanted, like all little boys, to be like his father—a hunter, fighter, and traveler of strange places.

Lorenzo even tried to sew some hides together to look more like the strange clothing his father had brought with him from his world. By night, as he often drifted asleep, reenacting his own version of his fathers stories. Mimicking as much of his fathers actions, Lorenzo soon started to develop his father's habit of watching the skies.

The next day, jumping from rock to rock along the river shore, Lorenzo had reached a spot where he decided to stop. His father had placed some homemade fish traps along the river. Occasionally, Lorenzo would find fish and bring them into the camp for his dad. Looking down into the water, he found a small catfish, so he sat down on the rock to deal with it. He heard something to his left and looked up to see his dad talking with the latest group from a southern tribe, who came to hear his story.

He watched for a moment as John handed the man one of the improved fish traps that he made. The man looked pleased and handed him more of the yellow rocks his father was collecting. But even at this distance,

Fading Starlight

Lorenzo could see this yellow rock was different than the others.

Lorenzo took hold of his long, jet-black hair and tied it behind his head with the leather strap that he was going to use to string the fish. Jumping up, he wandered over to see what his father was given.

Standing near his father as the men talked, he heard them talk about the location of where this gold was found, and that there were also more strange bits of metal all over the area, with one larger piece, so large that you could walk inside. The men explained that the whole place made them all feel unsettled. Perhaps it was because of the strange sights or the strange bones left in the area. But regardless they did not like it, so they left.

The oldest of the men knelt down on the sandy river shore. Lorenzo watched his dad make the man scratch out a map in the sand with a stick of how to find this place. He then leaned over to Lorenzo and whispered in his ear, "Son, remember this map." Puzzled, Lorenzo turned his head to see his dad wink at him.

That night in the family hut, John brought all his tradable items out and set them near the cooking fire to look at them. Kasa smiled and motioned for Lorenzo to go sit near his father. Half in an effort for him to learn, but mostly to get him out of the way so that she had room to cook.

Word had filtered out about what kind of stuff John was looking for. So, for the most part, bits of gold and a little copper were starting to flow into the camp. Mostly small rocks and a few bits of rough jewelry. Grand total, John figured he had collected nearly three pounds of gold so far. Lorenzo watched him pull out the new strange piece he had traded for. It was round in shape, like a skipping stone. But the sides were flat with even shaped grooves. The top and bottom were very smooth—you could almost see yourself, like your image on water. The top had a hole in it with something flat, green, and hard like a rock in it. The bottom had a small gray and white stick coming out the other side of it.

Lorenzo did not understand what his father meant when he said it was part of something bigger and that the "stick plugged into something and the green stone would have made things go."

Kasa sat down to watch the fish cook. Looking over at John, she asked, "So these things came from your world then?"

Not wishing to confuse the issue with the subject of time travel, John smiled and responded, "Maybe."

"Would they have been enemies or friends?" Kasa inquired.

"Most definitely enemies, I think," John responded as he handed Lorenzo the alien artifact.

"Hmm, are they dangerous now?" Kasa asked, a little concerned.

John slowly shook his head, "No, the man I got this from tells me their bones had turned white in the sun. Any danger has long since passed."

Kasa looked at the fish for a moment and then spoke up, "So are you going to visit this place?"

"Not now, it's too far away and you're too close to giving birth. I talked with your father, and we agreed not to pack up the tribe and head back until after you give birth. Then I am thinking, at one point along the trip home, Lorenzo and I will visit it. We should not be more than three to five days from the tribe," John responded.

Kasa smiled and decided to change the subject. She leaned forward and slowly slid her hand on to John's leg to get his attention. "Husband, have you thought of a name for our child yet?"

John stopped what he was doing and looked up at her in the firelight. With a slightly sarcastic, playful tone in his voice, he responded with, "You know, you are the other half of all this. You can help decide the names as well."

"Nope, Nampeyo, the old woman has had too many dreams, saying that you should decide this kind of thing," Kasa replied.

In a totally sarcastic tone, that he most likely inherited

from his mother, John responded, "How about, old stinky dog?"

Kasa's eyebrows narrowed, one more than the other. "Hmm, be serious, Husband, and careful with your words. I want to hear your thoughts."

"Well, there was an old family friend we had long ago. His name was Andrew," John replied.

Kasa's head slowly moved up and down as she thought about it. "And if the child is a girl?"

"I really don't have anything yet," John responded back.

Kasa's head went back and forth slowly as she did not like that answer. "How about the names of one of the women in your black book?"

John thought about it, and then he thought about how Kasa responded to some stories and not others. "How about Rebecca?"

Kasa smiled and responded, "I liked her story; it was good."

The Present

Andrew sat near Josh's bedside in the ICU slowly moving a half of an oval shaped metal coin connected to a chain around and around between his fingers. The earlier commotion of the day was gone now. It was only the two of them, as the medical staff had left after trying to make Josh feel comfortable. This strange, fast-moving lung cancer ravaged his body quickly like a wolf.

Slowly, Andrew became aware that someone else had entered the room. Andrew turned his head to see a young dark-haired woman in her early to mid twenties. She wore dark pants and a black jacket with leather sleeve's starting at the collar. She smiled at him as he looked at her. Inside, Andrew knew somehow that she was not some random visitor. She was small in size, with a light complexion and a single black and red earring in one ear.

"Who are you?" Andrew quietly asked.

"A friend, but I can wait to talk until a better time," her soft voice replied.

Andrew turned his head back to look at his friend. He paused, as if in reflection, and he then spoke up. "It's ok, we can talk now. He's been dead for some time."

A few moments of silence passed and Andrew felt her small hand slowly make contact with his shoulder. With reddened eyes locked on Josh, Andrew whispered. "We survived Iraq together." Slowly turning his head to look at her hand for a moment to notice a dark ring on her middle finger engraved with a gothic font, the word "Honor."

"I'm sorry for your loss, it's hard to lose someone like that," she responded with care in her voice.

Andrew blinked and slowly turned his head towards the window for a moment, changing his tone. "Does my new friend have a name?"

"My name is Jenny, I work for Mac who is helping Megan. I've been sent to relocate you to a safe place." Jenny quietly remarked.

Slowly nodding his head Andrew responded back, "ok." As he stopped playing with the odd metal necklace. Looking at it for a moment he considered leaving with Josh as he stood up.

Glancing at it Jenny asked in a subdued tone, "that looks like half of one of those squashed pennies?"

Slowly breathing in Andrew responded back, "Ah…ya, when we were kids we would put them on the railroad tracks. We saved this last one because it was the oldest and you can still see date, 1939. Josh had it with him all through the war."

Jenny noticed the look on Andrews face as he looked it over, "I think… you should take it with you. Something to remember."

Andrew eyes lifted away from his hand and looked at Josh's face. Staring at it for several long moments he finally lifted the necklace and put it on.

"Have you notified his family?" Jenny asked.

Fading Starlight

Slowly shaking his head as he turned to pick up his coat, "No...his parents died long ago so all he had left was his sister Julie, who is a doctor and they don't speak."

The Past

After about a month or so, during a cool, starry night near the falls, Kasa was giving birth. Chochmingwu had died two winters back, so Nampeyo took her place overseeing the births in the tribe. Stepping out of John's family hut, Nampeyo announced that a baby girl was born. The tribe was excited, but this time they knew that John must hold her first and name her before they could gather around.

To the tribe, it was not unusual anymore that John would give his child a strange name. A name like Rebecca seemed to almost fit the changes that were taking place in the tribe. Lorenzo looked over at his older cousin, Tablita, who announced with a smile, "I will enjoy playing with her when she gets older."

John heard her, turned his head and responded to her with a smile, "I think by the time she gets as old as you, you will have your own daughter to take care of."

Tablita giggled, "Then I will help teach her."

Lorenzo rolled his eyes at Tablita. It was cool he had a little sister, even if she was a girl.

People talked, laughed, and admired her. Exclaiming all the typical things like what part of her looked like which parent or grandparent. Soon John's ears could hear Kasa inside, gently clearing her throat more than once. It was his reminder that she would like to see her own child now.

John finally got his daughter free and clear from the other mothers and little girls. Entering the hut, John came in to place her near Kasa's side. Smiling, Kasa watched her daughter arrive. "It is so nice to finally meet you, my Rebecca. You are my little rose among the thorns."

Sitting down next to them, John thought about it for a moment and then dug around in his pack. Pulling out his shiny Captain's pin that he once wore on his dress uniform, he attached it to the small blanket around Rebecca. Kasa's eyebrow raised a little as he did this.

"It's my first gift to her. Because I think every little girl needs something shiny and pretty." John remarked with pride.

Mean while Nampeyo took a deep breath and noticed Lorenzo standing with the other boys. Walking over to him she tapped him on the shoulder. Lorenzo looked up as she motioned for him to follow her to the river. Nampeyo had words she needed to share, words that weighed heavy on her heart, and the edge of the river would be a good place to speak

The Present

After learning of the events in Washington, Mac ordered a course correction for the jet. He had growing concern about Megan, who had fallen silent after seeing the TV images that signaled the potential death of her father. But he had some bigger issues to deal with. Megan was not the only person now who might need to go into hiding.

After some time, Mac gave Carol a head nod towards Megan. So Carol left her station and decided to sit down next to Megan. She needed to start explaining to Megan all the new changes she would need to do, so that she could effectively hide in plain sight.

Megan just sat there taking some of it in, trying not to focus on what might have just happened. Carol rolled a large pan on a cart behind Megan's head and made her tilt her head backward. Then to Megan's surprise, Carol started to wash Megan's hair.

"What are you doing?" Megan inquired.

"I am getting your hair wet so that I can treat it with a special shampoo we developed called MCS-85. We will need to let it sit in your hair for five minutes and then rinse with water. After that, I will blow dry it to set the chemical compound," Carol remarked as she worked.

"What does it do?" Megan continued to inquire.

"The shampoo is made from a microcrystalline structure of alien origin. We found it seven years ago in a digging operation in Cameroon. It contains unique light-altering properties similar to a prism. When the structure is induced with certain frequencies, the microstructure alters by bending light, allowing us to isolate only the desired color required.

We are currently using it for covert purposes, to alter at will human hair to one of five color shades. That way, no one needs to wear a wig and it looks more natural," Carol replied.

The conversation was slowly pulling Megan a little out of the growing darkness that she was starting to feel. "You mean I can make my red hair disappear and be a blond or brunette?"

"Blond, dark red, light or dark brown, or platinum blond. Sorry, black is out. If you push it that far it turns blue for some weird reason." Carol commented. Pausing for a second Carol looked around the corner of Megans face to smile. "I'm still working on it."

Megan's eyebrow raised in response, "How fast is it?"

Carol stopped what she was doing and took her gloves off, "I'll show you."

Setting her gloves on the table, she continued as she moved to stand in front of Megan. "You can either choose a ring or a watch. Typically, men take the watches and women the rings, like mine. See, on mine, it has a hidden outer ring. When you turn it on, you will hear a slight click as you progress in a clockwise manner. Your color settings are from light to dark accordingly. Then after that, it's a simple thing, press and hold the center of the ring for five seconds to charge the transmitter like this. And then slowly move it from one side of your head to the other like this. What do you think?" Carol asked Megan as she demonstrated it in front of her.

Megan watched in fascinating disbelief as Carol's shoulder length brown hair grew lighter before her eyes. Turning her into a stunning platinum blond.

"It looks so... natural," Megan exclaimed as stared at it for several seconds and then asked, "How long does it last?"

"The microcrystalline structure is not permanent. The binding system does break down over time. In the case of human hair, the binding system starts breaking down after four to eight shampoos, leaving the subject with some degree of streaking. And in the case of our other project, clothing, it breaks down quickly, within one to two washes," Carol calmly explained.

"Clothing, how many things have you applied it to?" Megan inquired.

"Many things, but sadly only hair and natural clothing works so far. We think the problem has to do with the electron transfer in the underlying substrate of the host material," Carol remarked as she walked back behind Megan to apply the white MCS-85 shampoo.

Carol mentioned that she should close her eyes during the next part as she continued talking. "Also the clothing we have applied it to is activated just as easily. As a woman, you will be issued two dresses and two jackets. If possible, bring them back to headquarters for washing. We have filters in the washing system —we are trying to reclaim the crystals."

"No pants? I would rather wear pants than dresses," Megan asked with her eyes closed.

"Nope, sorry. Most pants are a mixture of manmade and natural fibers. As a result, we are having a hard time finding the right products for our agents," Carol remarked as she massaged the shampoo into her hair. After a moment, she spoke once more. "Cotton, silk, wool, any plant fibers and surprisingly, even leather."

"Hmm," was Megan's only response as she lay there with eyes closed listening to the jet fly.

Fading Starlight

About twenty minutes later, her hair was fully blown dry. Megan really wanted to surprise her sleeping son with it. Being a little bit ornery, surprising her son was a fun mental distraction from reality as she turned her ring to select platinum blond. Looking in the mirror that Carol provided to watch the process, she was totally amazed seeing it happen on her own head.

After admiring it, she picked up a ham sandwich and sat down in front of her son—whose neck was stretched out and face bent backward a little in a strange sleeping position. He had fallen asleep near the window watching everything pass by. Now his face was becoming part of the window as his drool slowly ran down the glass.

She unwrapped part of the sandwich and shook him on the arm. "Hey... hey their, little guy."

"Mmm, what?" Johnny sleepily responded back with his eyes closed.

"Are you are going to help me eat this ham sandwich or not? It's mighty big just for me," Megan informed him.

Slowly, Johnny rolled his head over and reached out to take the sandwich, barely opening his eyes. Not really awake, he took his first bite and started to chew. Everyone on the jet slowed down to watch. Johnny kept chewing as his eyes came into focus. Something was different, and everyone was looking at him. Ever so slowly, he finally stared at the one person who was sitting across from him with a big smile on her face.

"Eww, Mom, yuck. You got old," Johnny loudly remarked after seeing her white hair.

The jet erupted in laughter for a moment as Megan was taken a little back from the comment about getting old. "Sorry honey, it's a new thing. Watch your mother's new magic trick," she responded as she activated her ring giving herself dark brown hair.

Amazed with new ideas, Johnny dropped his sandwich on the table next to him as he now saw the potential for a whole new toy to play with. Showing her son made Megan quickly regret her action as there seemed to be no end to her son's pestering.

The Past

Two days had passed since the tribe started back for home. Lorenzo and John were keeping their eyes open to find the path to where John thought the wrecked ship would be. For an eight-year-old boy, John was becoming amazed and proud of him. Lorenzo, as well as the other kids of the tribe, was unlike the boys he knew back in his world. Living in this primitive environment, fishing and hunting as a way of life. They had more personal stamina than any 21st century boy, who had all the pleasures of life around them.

In fact, he felt they were more like men than some adult men he knew in his past. He was very proud of his son who, two months ago near the Virgin River, killed a coyote by himself. Lorenzo saw that it was trying to get into their food stash when no one was around. So he took the problem on himself and handled the situation.

It was still cool in the early morning light, the tribe had only been walking for an hour or two when Kaviu picked up his pace to walk near John and Kasa. John smiled and acknowledged his father-in- law's presence as he came alongside.

The light desert wind moved Kaviu's salt and pepper hair as they strolled along the sandy desert path. "John, I admire the way my grandson moves and thinks. He gets that from you," Kaviu remarked with a quiet, even-toned voice.

John, who had come to know the ways of his father-in-law, smiled as he answered. "Yes, I would like to think so. The smile, he gets from Kasa." John stopped talking, knowing that if he just waited, Kaviu would get to the point of the conversation at his own speed.

After several long moments of walking, Kaviu, who

was watching Lorenzo in the distance near the head of the tribe, spoke up once more as he lifted his left eyebrow, "You hunt differently than us, and you build differently than us, John. You fight differently than us."

John's right eyebrow slowly raised in quirosity as he continued to walk. Responding back, John simply answered, "Yes I do."

Kaviu's right hand, that carried an old scar, slowly came to rest on John's left arm as they walked, causing John to look at him. Kaviu continued, "Let him learn more from you. He should accompany you on your trips," Kaviu finished saying, as their eyes met.

John smiled in acknowledgement of his father-in-law's request and then spoke up, "I will."
Content in John's answer, Kaviu nodded his head and reduced his walking speed, falling back to where he had been. John thought about the request a little, he knew in his heart it was time. It's not like he hadn't been thinking about it. After all, Lorenzo did accompany him on a few of his hunting trips. Now, it seems he needed to join him for every journey.

Suddenly, John became aware of Tablita's giggling voice growing closer as she was running by them with some of the older girls, John put up his hand to motion her to stop for a moment. Tablita slowed to a walk as her long braided hair whipped around hitting her in the face. For her, it was a mild irritation that she quickly forgot as she looked up at her Uncle John to see what he wanted.

Speaking up, John asked, "Tablita, next time you get near my son, let him know that I would like to speak with him."

Tablita smiled and before John could get another word to say, she was off and running. Closing his mouth, John expected no less from her. She was, after all a girl who always traveled at full speed in life. John watched her run away to find Lorenzo and as she did, John slowly bent his head to the right to ask Kasa a question. "Did you run that much as a child?"

Kasa, who was carrying Rebecca on her back,

responded, "Yes, as much as I could and as fast as I could. I loved the feel of the wind in my face, gliding from rock to rock as I jumped. I only started to slow down just before you came."

With a pleasant sound in his voice, John spoke up, "Hmm, well then, I can assume Rebecca will be the same."

"Most likely, but if she is anything like the rest of the women in our family, she will often get in trouble for doing things her own way," Kasa responded.

"Well, it's nice to know she won't be a doormat," John commented.

Kasa's eyebrows narrowed as she turned her head to look at John. "What's a doormat?" Kasa asked.

Realizing he just made another comment out of time, John calmly answered back, "Well, that's a common thing that people said in my day. They said it of a person who has a strong internal understanding of who they are. Basically, it means no one can walk over the top of them."

Kasa laughed a little, showing off her bright white teeth, "Yes, we are not doormats."

They continued walking for a little while, chatting as Lorenzo got closer. Kasa then changed the subject for a moment. "John, in our tribe, when a father starts including his son in all that he does, he often gives him a gift. Please consider doing that, otherwise the other boys might look down on him."

That thought struck John for a moment, as he realized he had seen it happen before, but did not think of it for his own son. Seeing a flat place near them to sit down for a moment, he motioned to Kasa that they should sit and wait for Lorenzo.

John pulled off his pack and sat down just before Lorenzo arrived. Looking at his son, who was barely winded from the run, John spoke up. "Son, you are getting older and faster. And you are starting to develop the desire to protect the things around you. When you fought the coyote by yourself and killed it, that was a good thing, but you could have been hurt badly.

299

Therefore, I want to give you something."

Kaviu slowed down as he started to reach their position to see John digging around in his pack. Kaviu then stopped and stood back at a distance to watch. John slowly pulled out an old K-bar knife with a sheath and leather belt. Lorenzo's eyes grew very wide and round at the sight of it. He had seen it several times whenever his father skinned out a large animal.

Holding it flat in his hands before his son, "Son, this was given to me by my Grandfather, who owned it as a young boy. It's a tool, not a toy, and should not be used carelessly. Tonight, around the fire, I will teach you how to care for and sharpen it. Now, step closer and I will put it around you."

Lorenzo said nothing as he excitedly stepped forward. John took the old belt, reaching around his son, bringing both parts of the belt forward. The buckle was a simple Ranger buckle, with a little detailing on the frame. John pulled it semi-tight and then slid the prong of the buckle into the appropriate belt hole.

John lifted his head to look up directly into his son's eyes. "Lorenzo, I am very serious when I say this. It will cut you just as easily as a deer. So do not play around with this. DO YOU UNDERSTAND?"

Lorenzo, with pure excitement in his face, nodded his head up and down. John smiled and spoke up once more. "Let me hear you say it. Do you understand?"

"Yes, Father, thank you, Father, I understand," Lorenzo responded back.

"Good, and one more thing. From now on, if I go hunting or exploring, you will go where I go, do you understand?" John calmly spoke.

Lorenzo, who was starting to feel a little light-headed, responded back, "Yes Father."

John smiled, placed his right hand on Lorenzo's head to rub it for a moment. "Good, you can rejoin your friends now if you want."

Lorenzo slowly turned in awe, walking at a much slower speed than when he arrived. With his adolescent confidence, his right hand held on to the knife at his side as if he was guarding a great treasure.

John and Kasa sat there for a moment, watching him walk away. Kasa nudged John with her elbow as if to say, "good job." Both of them caught Kaviu's eyes in the distance as they stood up to resume walking. The pride in his eyes spoke volumes to them.

That night, Lorenzo slept the best in weeks. Under his hand was his new treasure that he had learned to sharpen and care for. Armed with the family history of it, he had heard once more about how his grandfather died in a great war. And how it was his great-grandfather who helped raise his father. In his heart, he knew his family carried a great responsibility as protectors and warriors.

Soon, the first light of morning came to the encampment and Lorenzo started becoming aware that his father was moving around. Not wanting to disappoint his father on some level, he got up to help in getting things ready for travel.

The Present

Mac's jet had been hidden on the ground outside Steamboat Springs for a few hours as his team worked to gather information. The press was not providing any official information as to the list of dead officers from the Pentagon blast. So, Mac's team worked with facial recognition software and a live satellite feed to start building their own database.

Ever so slowly, the list grew into three lists. Presumed dead, alive, and unknown. Megan watched carefully as they continued to work. The "presumed dead" list seemed to be the biggest list, as congressmen were now being added to it. Megan took a little comfort in seeing that her father's name never made it to that list.

Soon, however, the one main shocker that hit everyone hard came into view from the satellite feed. It did not require complex software for every one to identify the broken body of General Victoria Bond in the rubble.

The sight of her in that picture was a shock to everyone on the jet, including Mac who closed his eyes for some time. Silence and a few tears filled the small room on the jet for a moment as they beheld the sight. Mac's only words that came forth when he opened his eyes were, "Oh my God," as his lifted his right hand from his folded arms to his face. Megan moved over near him in silent support.

The continual flow of images, some of them people they knew, kept rolling in, leaving the room with a solemn silence in the wake it created. Finally, after several long minutes of watching the events unfold on the live stream, Max spoke up, "Who or whatever it is we are up against, does not play around and neither should we."

Mac was about to make a comment when Danny looked up from his computer screens, setting his pen down to make his statement, "Aliens... that's who we're fighting. It's the only thing that makes logical sense in all of this."

Everyone's eyes turned and became fixed on him as he continued, "I have been analyzing all the events, patterns, and things that have happened since Megan found the golden books in Utah. Looking all the data over, I can rule out all the other factors, including another government on earth. The only thing that logically fits is a government outside of earth. Therefore, we are fighting aliens and their need to control all information related to Captain John Becker, regardless of his age."

The reality of Danny's words sunk in as the picture became clearer. Mac's eyes wandered above the computer screens for a moment, just to stare at the wall in reflection. Resuming command once more of the situation, he put aside his emotional thinking that was starting to take over. Looking around the room, he started giving orders.

Pointing at Rick, Mac opened his mouth to speak, "Contact all divisions and departments. Notify them, as of this moment, we are on command protocol Starlight. Megan, I am sorry, but I am pressing you into service as a full time agent. Carol will bring you up to speed on all our procedures, you just became our new Communications Officer." Turning his head back toward Danny, he ordered, "Stay on top of all information in cyberspace. Max, your job is this plane and the protection of Johnny. He's our number one priority—they want him and we have him and I want to keep it that way."

Megan was a little shocked and leaned over towards Mac to ask, "What's command protocol Starlight?"

Mac swallowed hard and answered, "It's an old command code dating back to the original founders of OMA, letting everyone know that as of this moment, we are now entering into guerrilla warfare with unknown alien forces."

Rick got up and moved towards the other end of the jet to access a computer panel. As soon as he arrived, Mac yelled more commands to him, "Activate Teams Five and Six and have them pose as first responders at the blast site. If General Mullins is still alive, I want him removed ASAP to a safe location. We don't want to gain our enemies' full intention, so I want to control as many of the variables as possible."

Mac looked over at Megan, whose eyes silently said there was more. "What is it?" Mac inquired.

"My brother, he will think that we are all dead if no one responds to their cell phones. He's going to go looking for Johnny," Megan responded.

"I'll take care of that," Mac responded back.

Mac stepped away from Megan so that Carol could talk with her. As Mac stepped up to Rick, Mr. Chen pulled out a cell phone that had just rung, Looking at the face of it, Rick handed it to Mac with a concerned look. "It's Jenny, you're going to want to take this."

Accepting the cell phone, Mac swallowed hard, knowing this was something he was not going to want to do.

The day was growing into late evening as the first responders carefully searched the blast site. A black woman in her early thirties carefully removed a piece of twisted steel. Underneath was a smashed toilet near a leg that was not moving. She carefully removed more debris to discover the bruised, bloody face of General Mullins.

She looked up towards her coworker, another woman of the same age but of Middle Eastern descent. Giving her a head nod, she came over quickly to look down and see the General on the ground. Bending her knees, she put her finger on his neck, waited a moment, and looked up at her coworker. "It's faint, but he's alive." She quietly informed her.

The black woman looked around to see a male first responder and gave him a head nod as well to come over. He brought a stretcher as the women tried to move him. Henry's body twitched from the pain, causing them to lower him back down.

The black woman looked him over quickly and softly spoke, "I think it's a broken leg."

"Got it," responded the other woman.

The second woman reached into her medical bag side pocket and took the cap off of a pre- measured injection. Giving it to him, Henry's body relaxed once more.

Everyone worked together, carefully slipping him into a body bag to hide his identity. Lifting him onto the stretcher and looking around, they stealthily exited the rubble. Calmly looking around, the man opened his cell phone, pressed a button and spoke, "Package in hand," as they walked out. All around the blast site, a few people carefully departed the area. Teams Five and Six had completed their mission.

On the jet, Megan was being brought up to speed on how to run a covert Communications Command Center, something she had not done since leaving the Army. Reports were now coming in from around the world as she started to learn just how big OMA truly was. Not only was she a little overwhelmed with all this information and the day's events, but she also got to hear about the continually exploding events around the world.

Things had seriously escalated with the Pentagon blast. Most of America's top military had been taken out. The few that were left now seemed to be giving the President strange advice.

Somehow, the Saudi Arabians had been better equipped than anyone thought. As a result, they sank the Chinese aircraft carrier. In an effort to not lose face in front of the world, the Chinese started sending troops to invade Saudi Arabia.

Many western nations led by America promised to protect Saudi Arabia, bringing everyone into what looked like the first days of a new World War.

Megan kept listening, writing, and handing off information to Mac and Rick. Finally, the encoded words came across her information feed, "Package in hand." Megan stopped and stared at the message, not moving. Her professional image soon changed to emotional overload as she started openly, joyfully crying.

Mac and Rick stopped what they were doing for a moment to see what had happened. Rick looked at Mac and then spoke up. "Looks like they found him."

Some of Mac's tension was released as he responded back, "Thank God," as he placed his right hand on

Fading Starlight

Megan's shoulder.

In an effort to avoid as many roadside cameras as possible, Jenny and Andrew had finally found an out of the way, lonely little gas station along highway 93 in central Idaho. Strolling out of the inside of the store into the dry wind with a small bag of over priced groceries in his hand, Andrew noticed Jenny who was on the phone as she put the gas cap to their car back in place.

Opening the drivers side door he was starting to put the bag in when he noticed the 'look' on Jennys face. Pausing for a second, something felt wrong as he started to realize her right hand was lightly starting to tremble.

Almost dropping the bag in the seat, Andrew quickly made his way around the car to stand before Jenny. The trembling was increasing as was the redness around her eyes. Raising her eye almost to Andrews chin as the cell phone slipped out of her hand, tears started to roll.

Then in a quick second as Andrew reached out for her Jenny started to fall. Quickly dropping with her, Andrew caught her just before the pavement.

The Past

The tribe had long since departed the Virgin River and headed east. The trail was fairly easy, nothing really unexpected, as they ascended from the lower canyon area, leaving the river behind.

Soon they made the upper plateau where John and Lorenzo said goodbye to Kasa as they turned from the tribe. They headed off on another trail, towards the crashed alien vessel they heard about. It would be a few days before they would see each other, but for Lorenzo, it would be the adventure of a lifetime.

The tribe agreed to stay a few days in a cave they knew of along the path to wait for them. The tribe had stayed at it many times in their travels. To John, he recognized the cave from his youth.

The men had described the crashed ship as a half-day trip from the main trail. John soon discovered that they were not telling him a fairy tale, as he could see something had impacted the side of the sandstone outcrop in the distance. Even at a mile away, the sight of the crash was obvious.

Realizing that the level of alien technology was considerably less advanced in the past, John had great hope for finding usable equipment to work with. The more he had, the more he figured he could advance the future for his own tribe.

The trail had become a little narrow as they passed through the scrub pine trees and rocks. Finally stepping into the open, John and Lorenzo stopped to take in the sight of the craft that was about the size of an old Army Black Hawk helicopter. It had impacted the cliff about halfway up, split open like a melon, and then slid to the bottom.

Parts of it were scattered over a large area and from his guess, the scrub pines had been burnt in the fire at least five years ago. The sun-bleached bones of the crew had been scattered over the landscape most likely from coyotes, vultures, and desert wolves.

The vessel seemed to have been mostly round, like a ball, but it was hard to be sure, looking at the wrecked mess. Half of it was totally smashed into shards. The other part still held some of its original form, but was now partly covered in sand. What was left contained markings on the side, along with a destroyed window.

As they started to walk towards it, John cautioned his son to be very careful what he touched. Slowly walking into the center of the crash site, he recognized many parts on the ground. Large coils from the anti-gravity units, similar to the hover-helos of his day. Powerful force jets, utilizing ion force for thrust, crushed like old cardboard among the rocks. This was technology he could at least understand. Now if he could just find some hand tools and maybe some working computer parts.

As he walked, he realized Lorenzo was no longer beside him. Looking back, he saw that his son was bent down, looking closely at a skull in the sand. John stopped to watch for a moment. "It's not a pretty sight, is it?" John asked.

"May I touch it?" Lorenzo asked.

John turned around and set the butt stock of his rifle down on the sand. Resting both hands over the barrel tip, he spoke up, "Go ahead, pick it up and take a good look at it."

Lorenzo reached into the sand and pulled out the mostly sand-covered skull. It was larger than his, with very large eye sockets. "They are not like us, are they?"

John calmly responded back, "No, they're not, we have very little in common with them. Everything that is good in this world, they destroy."

Lorenzo slowly rolled it around in his hands, finally allowing it to roll out of his hands to hit the ground below. He looked up at his father with a disturbed look—something seemed to bother him at his very core. "Father, you can feel the evil. Even in the bones."

"I know Son. Remember that feeling. More than once, I have felt it around me as a warning that something bad was in the area. Learn from this moment," John counseled his young son.

With the most sober look this tall eight-year-old boy could give his father, Lorenzo looked at John, nodding his head in an affirming manner.

"Well, let's get looking around, I would like to gather up some parts that I can use," John remarked.

After an hour or so, John and Lorenzo fell into a simple pattern of work. John carefully worked inside the broken craft. Lorenzo accepted any parts his dad found and laid them together in a pile, away from the ship on the desert floor.

Lorenzo kept hauling the stuff out that his dad handed

him, taking a moment to look each item over, not knowing what he held. Soon John stopped and stood in the center of what was left of the small craft. Lorenzo dropped off his last item and walked back. John noticed him walking back and motioned for him to walk in.

"I think I've got everything of possible working value, but I wanted to show you something." John motioned for Lorenzo to walk over to him. "This is a chair, Son, you sit in it," pointing towards a simple chair that seemed to be made out of something like aluminum.

John indicated that Lorenzo should try it out, knowing that his son had never had the experience of sitting in anything like this before. It took a moment for him to figure it out. The arm and headrest seemed strange to him. But soon, Lorenzo relaxed into it.

"That is where the pilot would have sat as he flew this ship in the air," John commented.

Lorenzo took a moment to answer, "Would it have been hard to fly?"

John shook his head, "I don't know, this is my first time being inside one of these. But I don't think so."

John smiled as he watched his son take it all in, and after a moment, he spoke up, "Come on, let's walk around the site and see what else we can find."

The Present

A week had passed and the world was slowly turning into a new and deadly place. It seemed to everyone that the world was either deploying troops to the Middle East or were about to. With much of Washington's top brass now dead, the American military quickly promoted many officers upward to fill the empty spots.

The Brits and the American Navy did a "stare down" with the Chinese Navy. A lot of yelling, but in the end, no one fired a shot. Russia moved much of its military and Navy in positions along its southern border, "Just in case things went bad."

The fact that General Mullins' body went missing at the blast site was not lost on the government. As a result, a general order, at the highest level, went out to acquire the entire family. Mac moved Daniel and Wendy north to a remote fishing lodge in Canada. As a result, Daniel and Wendy, AKA Mr. and Mrs. Montcell, just became the new owners of the Alexander Mackenzie Hotel in Mackenzie, B.C.

Mac's public office in Washington had been raided, boxed up, and removed. But his hidden office remained untouched and served as a useful hospital for Henry Mullins as a small team that took care of his wounds.

Lying in his hospital bed, he slept less and less as he reduced his need for pain pills. Karen, the older black woman who was doubling as his nurse and wishing she wasn't, wandered in to ask if he needed anything to drink. "No, thank you, Miss Karen, I am just getting a little restless lying around here in this bed," Henry remarked.

"I understand, I had a few surgeries in my time, they're never fun. But trust me, I would like you out of here as fast as possible, myself. You're taking up room in my office, you know," Karen informed him with half a smile.

Henry smiled as he watched her turn to walk away with her clipboard. As she did, she found someone was coming in to the room at the same time. They politely excused each other as Jenny and a dark brown-haired woman walked in. Henry's eyes lit up, recognizing her familiar face.

"Jenny, I'm glad to see you," putting out his hand towards her for her to shake. "I am sorry to hear about your grandmother, she was a good friend. How was the funeral?"

Jenny swallowed and responded in an informative manner, "It was good, very little was said and I tried really hard not to cry as they played taps at Arlington. Took awhile to get out of there. Lots of shadows following me, so losing them took a while."

"Hmm, sorry to hear it. Who's your new friend, an agent in training?" Henry remarked.

Jenny's eyes lit up a little, as she looked at the woman beside her and then back at the General.

"You don't recognize her?" Jenny asked with a smile.

"Should I?" Henry asked.

The woman smiled and moved her right hand up and over one side and down the other of her head. Her hair started changing from brown to red as she pulled her sunglasses off.

The face was close to looking like his daughter, but Henry was still not sure. Finally he asked, "Megan, is that you?"

Megan really wanted to give her father a hug, but the desire to pester him a little bit in a fun way motivated her more. Putting a hand to her cheek, "What do you think? All the fashionable secret agents are wearing this new look now."

Looking at his daughter, Henry's only response was, "Hmm."

Changing her tone, Megan asked"And by the way, why didn't you tell me that Victoria Bond had a granddaughter?"

Henry was glad to see his daughter was normal, even though her face still looked a little off. Trying to pull himself up a little more in his bed, but feeling the pain of his broken ribs, Henry responded with a smile. "Well, I guess it just never came up."

Megan smiled a little more in hearing her fathers voice as Henry kept looking at her as he asked, "And what's with your face? You don't look quite like yourself."

Jenny spoke up in response, "It's the latest invention from Carol. Three-dimensional makeup—if properly applied, it can make subtle optical changes to a person's face. Making areas like nose, cheekbones, eyebrows, lips and that kind of stuff bigger or smaller. It's the new thing. Listen, I got a few things to get done. Megan, enjoy your visit with your father. You, however, might want to bring him up to speed." Jenny smiled as she stepped out the door.

311

Fading Starlight

Megan stood there for a moment looking at Henry, and then finally sat down next to his bed in a small wooden chair, a little more quiet and solemn. Henry just waited a moment for her to speak. She looked across the room at some picture for a moment and then spoke, "Command protocol, Starlight is in effect."

The news sent a bit of a cold chill down Henry's spine as he realized what that meant. Megan continued, "A lot has happened around the world and personally. This month, I got pressed into service into an underground organization and I found out you and Bond were the secret oversight directors for. I also found out this month that we have aliens looking like humans, humans working for aliens—what a mess. They tried to take Johnny and myself away, most likely to kill us. They did, however, manage to kill a lot of people in Washington and around the world, including General Bond, who I was just starting to learn to like. Our camp in Utah has been closed up and abandoned. A helicopter from the camp suffered a sudden power failure at 40,000 feet. Eight people died, including Dave Shaver and several family men; and... no one is investigating it. We found Watson's jeep empty at a local gas station. We don't know where he went."

Turning her head to look at her father, "This is starting to feel worse than Iraq, Dad. Everyone else, including Andrew and Daniel, are in hiding." Megan paused for a moment, "We lost Josh as well."

Henry slowly inhaled as much air as he could into his pain-filled rib cage. Silently exhaling it, as the new reality around him settled in. Watson had been a good friend over the years. It hit hard for him, but not as hard as hearing the complete report, including the fact that his daughter and grandson almost died.

"What about Danny and Wendy?" Henry asked in a calm tone.

"Mac moved them, gave them new names," Megan responded back.

Feeling the slow movement of emotions like anger, loss, and sadness settling in, Henry made a mental decision to set it behind him for now. He opened his mouth, "Where do we stand overseas?"

"It's a bloody mess, lots of dead. But cooler heads stopped some of it just short of an all-out nuclear exchange," Megan reported.

"And OMA?" Henry inquired.

"Relocating and rebuilding in hiding. Mac is creating a new base of operations out west. Team Six who helped bring you here, was just killed while in Maine. So Mac gave the order to have Jenny relocate you to the new base. That's why we are here, to move you out."

Megan paused for a moment and then changed her tone, as she turned her head to look right at her father. "By the way, you knew about Mac all this time. You pretended not to know him when you brought me to the Pentagon. That's why you so quickly jumped on board out in Utah, when you saw the Army logo. You've dealt with aliens before. And... is that why you had him take me away from the Pentagon?"

Pausing for a moment to look at Megan's face, "I'm not sure how to respond," Henry responded back, "Are you mad at me?"

Megan's eyes narrowed a little, "Only a little, the rest of me was surprised and a little proud. I guess this alien thing is not some random thing, it's kind of a family thing." Megan managed a brief smile before going back to staring across the room. Awkward silence settled in the room for a moment as Henry finally spoke up. "Strangely, I kind of expected a little more emotion when you said Josh died."

Megan slowly inhaled as she took a little time to think about it before responding. "Well, like I said, this is starting to feel like Iraq all over again. And, as an officer, I cannot cry in public. So... I reserve that kind of stuff for later."

Silence hung in the room for a moment and then Henry asked, "I guess it might be the medication but did I hear you correctly, the helicopter failed at 40,000 feet?"

Megan nodded her head as she responded back,

313

Fading Starlight

"yep!"

"Meg, helicopter don't fly that high…not enough air," Henry remarked.

Letting her eyes wander off Megan responded back with a sigh, "ya…ya, we know…but that was the report we given. It suddenly ascended, and then suddenly descended."

The Past

Deer jerky and dried fish for breakfast became part of the morning routine as the boys sat next to a scrub pine tree looking over the crash site. Lorenzo was still a little "star struck" by all of this. But not wanting to let his father down, in some boyish way, he mustered as much adult manliness as he could while participating in this project.

John was quietly impressed with how his son was doing. In all of this, it gave him hints of the man Lorenzo would someday be. But for now, a new problem presented itself. They had found way more, possibly usable stuff than John thought he would find so the looming question was how to get it back to the cave, by themselves.

Looking over the parts, he started to realize he could take the smaller anti-gravity ring that was mostly a composite of gold, palladium, and perhaps tungsten carbide and make a wheel out of it. The outer hull of the vessel seemed to be common aluminum sheeting. So he could beat it into any shape he wanted, making it possible for him to make something he had not seen in a long time.

This started to give him great hopes of building himself a primitive wheelbarrow. The way he figured it, when he was done with transporting his stuff. He could teach the tribe to use it for any building project back at the camp.

John took a stick and started drawing out his plans in the sand. Lorenzo watched, totally clueless as to what his father was doing as he chewed on a piece of fish. As he did, John realized that he was going to need to almost build a small shop first. Because of this, he needed Lorenzo gather as much firewood as he could to heat the metal, and find something to use as a hammer and a few flat rocks for an anvil.

It would be a strange mix of advanced and primitive technologies. But at least, in his mind, he thought it would work. Finally, Lorenzo spoke up, "Father, what is it?"

Without thinking John answered, "It's a wheelbarrow Son." As if Lorenzo should know what that was.

Not wanting to seem dumb in front of him, Lorenzo simply pretended he knew what a wheelbarrow was. In reality, the words meant nothing to him.

As the day passed, Lorenzo had collected a large pile of wood to put next to the fire. John had removed the pilot's chair from the ship and tossed it with a lot of the loose stuff outside. Feeling confident his makeshift shop was going to work. All the large scale sheet metal bending would take place over the fire. Smaller stuff would happen inside where he could utilize some of the corners and objects within the craft.

By nightfall, he had the main body banged out of the wheelbarrow. Lorenzo helped as much as he could, even though he understood very little. John had found items to use for the various under parts he would need. The assembly would happen in the morning, as well as setting the center axle. He had created two disks out of the sheet metal to hold the axle to the wheel. It would take heat to permanently mount them.

The next morning, John ate very little. His own boyish nature was taking over, as he was excited to see if all the effort he had done was going to work.

Lorenzo got a fire going and kept it hot. John got all the parts ready inside so that all he had to do was slide the hot axle in the center and slam it hard on both ends at the same time.

Fading Starlight

John rehearsed the whole thing with Lorenzo so that he would hold the right things at the right time. Finally, somewhere around mid-morning before the heat of the day, it was time. John made a makeshift jig to hold everything on a control console of the ship.

Carefully, they slid the glowing hot axle in place. John looked at his son and spoke up, "Here we go, hope this works."

Picking up a rock that he had tied to a stick to make a hammer, he hit the end of the shaft hard. Seeing that it needed to move more, John hit it several more times, harder each time than the last.

As he hit it the final time as hard as he could, the impact vibrations caused various parts of the control panel to light up briefly with various lights. The sight of it stunned both of them for a moment as the control board made a single beep sound. Then, as quickly as it happened, it stopped.

The boys looked at each other with a shocked look on their faces. Lorenzo opened his mouth first, "What does it mean Father?"

Totally perplexed and feeling a little anxiety in his system, "Well, I think it means it's time for us to move on. We might have just overstayed our welcome." John quickly mounted the wheel and loaded the parts he had, as Lorenzo kept a watch on the sky, "Just in case."

Present Day
Truck stop, somewhere in South Dakota.

This long and lonely stretch of the windy highway only had one semi-truck on it for miles. The white and blue Con-Way transport truck geared down as it approached the rest stop. The flat and open landscape of this part of the Dakota's felt the continual movement of the wind on the amber prairie grasses as it quietly shaped all life in that area.

The truck had a managed good time, with the tail wind it had received over the last eight hours. As it pulled into the rest area, a white semi-truck pulled out from between two other trucks, leaving a spot open in the middle next to a Red Knight and a Lynden transport truck.

The Con-Way truck slowly pulled into its place with barely inches to spare between them all. The driver never got out; he simply pulled out a sandwich and started eating it as he put his foot on the dash. Unseen by everyone, unless you were standing at the right spot, the side door of the Knight and the Con-Way trucks opened up. Carefully they passed their cargo between them.

After a few minutes, the doors closed and the red and white Knight truck pulled out onto the open windswept road.

The Past

It had been two days since the boys made their wheelbarrow. It worked good but lacked the bounce that an air filled tire would have had. The bumps and dips of the trail telegraphed up the handles to John's arms, causing him to totally forget the incident back at the crash site.

The two of them had a few conversations about things. Aliens and girls were mostly the topic as they traded off running the wheelbarrow. John was amazed and had no idea how much thinking Lorenzo did in his spare time. It seemed to him, his thoughts were profoundly deep for an eight-year-old.

To his surprise, John discovered his son thought a lot about building things. He learned this the night before as Lorenzo started asking a lot of questions about how to make bigger walls out of stone. Now this morning his questions rotated around why girls do the 'strange things' they do.

All of this made them forget to stop and eat something. Around noon, John laughed a little at his son's latest question about why girls are always cleaning themselves so much when their just going to get dirty again, when John heard a sound coming from his son. It was his stomach, apparently Lorenzo was hungry. John looked around and could see a nice place to stop up ahead with shade. It would be a good place to park the wheelbarrow.

"Lorenzo, I think we should find something a little better to eat. How about you?" John remarked.

The mention of food finally caused him to stop talking about girls for a moment. "Sure... what?" he asked as his eyes lit up.

"Well, I keep seeing deer tracks. So let's pull the wheelbarrow up there in the shade. We can spend the rest of the day here, hunt, and we should be able to rejoin everyone tomorrow," John explained.

A smile quickly came across Lorenzo's face, "OK." Lorenzo paused and thought about it, then with a sparkle in his eyes, he asked, "Can you teach me to use your rifle?"

Without even blinking, John quickly responded, "No, I don't think so." Seeing his son's face fall a little, John continued, "I need to save the bullets, I will use a bow today, just like you."

After stowing the wheelbarrow, pack, and rifle in the sandstone rock overlook, they hiked about an hour up a narrow canyon. Hoping to catch some deer, John and Lorenzo parked themselves on opposite sides of the deer trail.

The site looked promising—the spot opened up well at the place they chose. As a result, the deer and men would not be able to see each other until the prey stepped out of the dense underbrush. John had already decided he was not going to fire the first arrow. It was Lorenzo's time. John figured this whole adventure would give his son bragging rights around the campfire with friends for months.

The minutes seemed to have slipped into at least one hour. Nothing to do but wait. In John's mind, if nothing showed up in the next hour, he was ready to move. This place had far too many bugs and they all seemed to want to jump on him.

John looked over at his son and could tell Lorenzo's eight- year-old mind was starting to wander. He was starting to take his arrow and draw in the sand and dirt at his feet.

Seeing this told him it was time to move on. Just as he was about to motion his son that it was time to go, two things happened, one right after the other. First, a small long-nose leopard lizard with its red spots came out from hunting bugs to stop and look at him, as if to say, "you're in my hunting spot."

The second was after John admired this rare sight. He looked up to the hillside above towards his son. He could see a very familiar sight that he had only seen a few times in his dreams.

It was the same big buck that had talked to him in his dreams, and he knew it. The sight of him felt natural, but it almost seemed like a warning. As he realized what he was thinking that it felt like a warning, the buck quickly faded from view like a mist.

As the image faded, a cold chill started over his body in the early afternoon heat. Something was about to happen, he knew it, and every part of him felt it. Stress-filled pain that felt like needles started stabbing him in his jaw, as he realized all he had for a weapon was a knife and a bow. Lorenzo, unknowingly, kept playing with his arrow in the dirt, as something started stepping out of the brush into the open.

Two men, who looked a little like Egyptians but with modern boots and what looked like combat vests, stepped out into the clearing following the boys' tracks. They carried in their hands something similar to rifles with ammo clips.

This caused John not to fire his arrow as soon as they came out. One of the men stopped looking at the trail, and followed a set of tracks with his eyes up the gentle slope to where John was.

At that moment as their eyes locked, a second shock informed John what was going on. The otherwise normal looking man had eyes that were larger than they should be. His mouth and nose to the same degree were smaller than his head. Aliens, and John knew it.

Instinct took over, as John sent his arrow down the gentle slope impaling the Egyptian-looking alien. The arrow pierced his lungs, causing him to expel his air as he fell to his knees. The other alien, who had not yet looked up in time, only saw his comrade fall.

Lorenzo heard it as well. It broke him out of whatever fantasy land he was in to land him into the land of shock and fear as he slipped backwards to fall and hide behind a rock.

The alien watched his companion fall to his knees and then his side, dead with an arrow in him. Looking up, he saw John getting a second arrow ready. John saw him look up at the same time. At this point, John realized he would never get the second arrow ready in time.

With as much effort as he could, John jumped to the safety of a large rock as the alien opened fire with his rifle, spraying the brush in something like bullets.

Lorenzo was paralyzed with the fear as he watched. His father had the disadvantage and was slowly being hunted. Lorenzo watched in horror as his father jumped and slid from one large rock to another to keep away from his hunter.

The alien slowly walked up the hillside behind John. Deeper and deeper into brush, John moved as fast as he could, seeking cover. Finally, the alien changed the setting on his weapon. Now his bullets started to set all the brush around Lorenzo's father on fire.

A new level of fear gripped Lorenzo as he watched, knowing his father was about to be burnt alive. His eyes felt frozen to watch from behind the rock. But for some reason, his mind allowed him to look down to see the dead alien.

Without thinking, he bolted from his position and ran

down towards him. Very soon, he had the dead alien's weapon in his hands. Pointing it in the general direction of his enemy, Lorenzo's fingers seemed to have found the trigger.

He never expected the gun to push back so strong from the force of the bullets leaving the gun. Shocked, it soon felt like he had hold of a wild snake, bullets flying everywhere. They flew into the sky above, the ground below, into rocks and trees. The alien soon found he needed to take cover from this crazy, screaming Indian boy.

Soon the rifle fired its last shot as he emptied the ammo clip. Lorenzo's body was shaking from the adrenaline in his system as he dropped the rifle.

Seeing that it was now safe, the alien slowly stood up and smiled, bringing his rifle up to his shoulders as he prepared to kill Lorenzo.

Without a warning or a sound, John jumped through the fire. He launched himself from his position and jumped off the closest rock in front of him with his knife. The alien never heard him, but Lorenzo's tear and dirt-stained face watched, as his father sailed through the air to plunge a knife in the alien, just below the back of his head.

The smoke of the brush fire slowly rose up into the sky. As they both rolled together to the bottom of the slope, John lay there for a moment with small first-degree burns on his arms. Lorenzo soon fell on top of him in an embrace of emotion.

As John lay their holding his son for a moment, gasping for air, he slowly collected his thoughts. Pulling himself up, Lorenzo was not ready to let him go. But John needed him to let go for a moment. Sitting up, John grabbed his son's face with both hands to look him straight in the eyes.

"Son, listen to me. You did good, you did good. Do you understand?" he emphatically told him in an attempt to reassure him.

"I hid," Lorenzo responded.

John quickly rebuked his son's thinking as he shook his

head. "Son, no, don't go there in your mind. All warriors hide at some point, remember that. You did good, you did good... ok?"

Lorenzo nodded his eight-year-old head, showing he understood.

"We need to leave, more will be coming," John exclaimed. John then reached over and grabbed the dead alien's weapon as he got up. "I guess I will need to teach you to shoot after all," he remarked as he stood on his feet.

Father and son quickly made it back to the wheelbarrow under the rock outcrop. John grabbed his pack and dug out his can of spray-on bandage.

His burns were painful, but the soothing anti-burn agent in the bandage made the pain disappear. He took a moment to enjoy the feeling of the pain leaving when Lorenzo spoke up.

"Father, I see something over there, what is it?"

John looked to where his son was pointing. About a hundred yards away, John could see the aircraft the aliens came in. "It's one of their ships," he exclaimed. Pulling out his binoculars to get a closer look. The ship looked different from the last ship, it even had wings. The cockpit was open and he could clearly see the craft could only hold two people at a time.

Lowering the binoculars, he spoke to his son, "Lorenzo, take the wheelbarrow and head out, I will destroy the ship and start covering our tracks."

Lorenzo was a good hundred to two hundred yards down the path when John reached the aircraft. The side of it held an emblem, which puzzled John as he looked at it for a moment and then realized it was an Egyptian Cartouche. Unfamiliar with Egyptian hieroglyphs, the marking meant nothing to him, except that the bottom of it did resemble an electrical blueprint of a switch and a resistor.

Quickly glancing around the inside of the aircraft, it was obvious all the writings were a mixture of Egyptian and some sort of binary coding. Knowing he most likely had very little time and not wanting to accidentally activate anything within it, he stepped away.

Pulling a grenade out of his pack, he set the electronic timer under it for 20 seconds. Pulling the pin, he tossed it into the craft, turned and walked quickly away.

Soon the ship exploded in a fireball that burned for the better part of a half hour, creating a tall, thin smoke trail into the air as the two walked further and further away.

Fading Starlight
Chapter Ten
Pharaoh
Akhenaten

Present Day
Undisclosed location in Central Idaho.

The Red Knight transport truck backed up to a set of large doors in a hillside. Ever so slowly, the thick covering of pine trees that covered the hill swallowed the truck from sight. Then the doors closed, making it vanish from the outside world.

Inside, the halogen lighting made bright circles on the cement floor as a flagger directed the truck to stop. Max got out and stretched his back from the long drive once he stood on the ground. Tossing his jacket to a man passing by, he waved at Mac who stood on a platform near the back of the truck.

As the platform was being raised to match the height of the back door of the truck, Mac nodded his head back at Max to thank him. Then turning his head towards another man near him, he simply ordered, "Open it."

The back door of the transport truck opened to reveal two doctors, Megan, and Henry who was sitting in his wheelchair with a cast on his leg. His jacket was partly open, displaying the evidence of the rib wrap that held his ribs together.

Mac smiled as they looked at each other. "How was the trip, General? Glad to get out of bed?" Mac greeted him in a friendly, sarcastic way.

Megan started to push him forward as Henry raised his head to respond. "I've had worse, but I would have loved better."

Crossing over to the platform, they shook hands. "Our people made up a room for you so that you can recover.

When you have rested a bit, we will..."

Mac did not get to finish as Henry raised his hand to interrupt. "Nope, I don't think so. I've just 'rested' as you call it for the last 1800 miles in the back of that truck. So first things first, I need a real bathroom. And then, I would like to sit down with some real food, like a steak, while you and your team update me as to what kind of world we are living in."

Mac's right eyebrow raised upward as he looked at Megan and then over to a man standing near the door. Raising his voice towards the man, "Davidson, escort the General to my office so that he can use the bathroom. Then bring him to C2W when he's ready."

Davidson, who appeared to be an ex-Marine saluted, walked over and took charge of the General's wheelchair, wheeling him away.

Megan watched her father being moved down a hallway and then turned to face Mac. "Wow, this is a big base. How many people do you have in here?"

With a deep inhale, Mac folded his arms as he started to speak. "Close to a hundred, but we can hold way more than that. The cave was discovered late in the 1930s. The military kept the discovery silent for years. In the 50s, they packed it with all sorts of stuff for the Cold War. Then it was sealed and abandoned in 1972. We have been quietly restoring it for the last five years, just in case protocol Starlight ever got issued," Mac responded.

"Can't someone just start searching local records for places like this?" Megan inquired.

Mac slowly shook his head in a negative manner. He then unfolded his arms and motioned for Megan to follow him. "We burned the trail all the way back to the 30s. Even searched the local libraries for any reference to this place. Then we turned this land over to a fake landowner who lives in the South Pacific."

As Mac stopped talking, he walked up to an old phone that was mounted in the wall. Picking it up, he spoke, "Mess hall."

Looking over at Megan he asked, "How does he like his steak?"

Megan responded, "Medium to well-done."

Taking that information, Mac conveyed it to the person on the other end of the line. Along with the instructions to deliver it to C2W "as soon as you can."

A young man, in a mostly clean chef's coat, was rushing down the hallway with his food cart. He turned a corner towards the Command & Control Warfare room, otherwise known as C2W, and stopped in front of the door where the guard was posted.

The brass plate mounted on the wall identified the room as C2W, Command & Control Warfare sub-level, subsection four. He was expecting to be stopped and his food inspected. To his surprise, the guard opened the door as soon as he saw him.

The General was having a cold drink of water as Mac and Danny Connor got the last of the makeshift presentation ready. C2W was not that large of a room, far smaller than the Pentagon's, with only room for maybe six people to work in it. The chef moved the General's steak and pre-baked potato to the table in front of him. He then excused himself as Henry picked up the knife.

Rick Chen came through the door as the chef exited the room. Handing Mac a folder, Rick looked at him. "That should be the last of it, Mac."

"Thank you, and have a seat. Just in case I forget something," Mac spoke up to Rick as he motioned for him to take a seat.

Henry put the first bite of his steak in his mouth as Mac spoke up.

"Ok, here we go. Hopefully this will make sense... and I will provide you with documentation of everything for you to look over at your own speed. As you already know, we had an incident in Salt Lake with three people who wanted to take your family away. We never got the name of the woman or the men who were sent. After researching their images, we discovered that we cannot find them in any database. That also goes the same for the man who gassed up Major Watson's Jeep."

"So far, to date, almost everyone involved in operation Lorenzo in Utah has either been served discharge papers and sent home, or has died from some strange illness. I sent a team to interview some of the men who have been given an early discharge. We found a group of them in a burned-out car outside of Dallas. Therefore, we have tried to acquire and recruit as many of the others as we could find into OMA to keep them safe." Mac reported.

Henry raised his eyebrows as he picked up another bite with his fork. "Burned earth, they are destroying everything that leaves a trail. I assume this is what happened to Josh?"

"Carol drew a blood sample before he died. At first, we found an unknown chemical in his system. After analysis, Carol discovered massive amounts of a Nagalase protein in his system. It totally overpowered and assimilated any cancer drug given. Making the drug either useless, or the Nagalase would turn it into copies of itself, thereby, overpowering and blocking the body's natural production of the McMAF binding proteins." Mac reported as he flipped to the next page.

Henry leaned forward as he listened to Mac's report.

"This chemical, General, was altered into the perfect breeding ground for cancer to grow in. It was bio-engineered to attack and assimilate. As a result of all of these recent events, I have activated everyone on our reserve lists. Teams One through Seven have been called up for active duty. We are also in the process of recruiting as many high-level scientists as we can. It's a race to build a brain trust at this point. As far as we can tell, over ninety of the world's best and brightest in their field have disappeared or died in the last two weeks," Mac remarked.

"Seriously," Henry remarked as he opened his eyes a little wider.

"Seriously, General. Mathematicians, biologists,

robotics, chemical engineers, molecular scientists, genetic researchers, and molecular geneticists—the list goes on and on. They have all died from things like home invasions, drunk drivers, sudden respiratory failure, overdose, or snipers. Four of them were ruled a suicide after being found hanging with their hands tied behind them." Mac informed him.

Henry put his cup of water down after hearing the last one. "Suicide, with their hands tied behind them? And this ruling was issued by the police?

Rick spoke up to respond, "At less than an hour after being found, each time with no autopsy. Each body was cremated. They seem to have several pre-planned actions running at the same time around the earth. Burning the trail and destroying top scientists is only a part of it. It seems they are now moving towards propaganda control of the public thinking."

Mac reached down and picked up a remote and pointed it at the wall. Several videos came up on the screen. "These videos started popping up on the internet. They all follow the same disturbing pattern. A pretty girl, sexually attractive in her late 20s, dressed in a simple manner. She is interviewed, gives her testimony of how it's a wonderful and exciting thing to become abducted by aliens. Claims the gray aliens are from a place called Zeta Reticuli. Each girl states, however, that they are really humans from the future who need our eggs and sperm to restore the human race before it dies. The women on the videos basically put a happy spin on being forcibly raped and in many cases, according to the videos, being used as modern brood mares to carry hybrid humans for six months within them. Then they are taken back, the child is removed, and the cycle starts over again."

Henry's tension was growing into internal anger as he thought about it. "Gentlemen, this is highly disturbing. And what is even more disturbing is how this is being portrayed. Is there any way to verify these stories?"

Mac turned back to the video wall and selected one video with the remote. Enlarging her video so that

Henry could clearly see the kind looking blond-haired woman. "This woman here, Tara Jean Wallace, was twenty-four years old. She was en route to a speaking engagement in Reno. Her car hit a deer outside a small backwater town called Mesquite Wells, population seventy-five. We had one of our people respond and pretend to be from the Nevada State Coroner's office. We brought the body back and looked it over. She shows evidence of having been pregnant over eighteen times."

"My God," Henry responded. "So they have been active in this before my Grandsons books were found."

"I would say recent events have forced them to upgrade their timetable," Rick calmly responded.

Mac continued, "And that's not all. We found several micro-implants in her body all connected to her nervous system. The largest was connected to the memory center of her brain. We don't know how it works yet. But according to our people, the location suggests they could make her say and do anything they wanted. And she would have believed it was a good thing."

Mac paused for a moment, allowing Henry to process the information in his mind. Finally, commenting on what he was seeing, Henry spoke, "So, nothing is better for a slave master than to have a happy slave who recruits more slaves."

Rick leaned forward in his chair. "That's what we're thinking as well. People who have these implants are just as dangerous as the aliens themselves."

"Can the implants be removed and the people returned to normal?" Henry inquired.

"Not sure, but it's starting to look like the answer is no," Mac replied.

Henry started to slowly tap his index finger on the table as he thought about it. "And the hybrid children?"

"According to the video testimonies, it seems some of them go on to become the aliens themselves. We're not sure about the rest," Rick responded.

"Some of them," Henry responded back.

"It would be fair to assume that the ones that look the

most Human are raised on Earth," Rick spoke up as he turned his head to look at the General.

Henry calmly spoke up, "Parasites... they make their hosts believe it's a good thing."

"They do a good job of it, the videos are highly compelling, designed with empathy to make the viewer believe this is a good thing that's happening. Generally, this video and others like it are slowly gaining ground, becoming viral," Mac added.

Henry, who had eaten about half of his meal, lost interest. He pushed it forward and responded, "I feel like we are swimming upstream against a river."

Mac straightened up his back. "I'm sorry General, but this is just a tributary. We found more, a lot more."

Mac opened up the folder that Rick brought. "These photos are microscopic internal scans of the implants we found in Tara Jean Wallace."

Mac set them down in front of Henry next to another set of photos. "The photos on your right, however, come from a Japanese technology company. They just filed these with the patent office."

Henry looked up, "So they're sharing their technology, why?"

"Not sure. It's being introduced into a new drug. This new product is being promoted as a way to control chronic pain," Rick added.

Mac then moved back to the other end of the room. "It gets worse, according to a back channel from our insiders. Two days ago, secret meetings are now being held in at least fourteen countries. Our sources say these gray aliens are actively holding talks. It feels like they are getting ready for something big."

Henry closed his eyes, only to reopen them after a moment.

"As you know, General, OMA has a few secret satellites disguised to look like telecommunication satellites. We have always picked up a few unknown objects in space. But that has changed."

"How much?" Henry inquired of Mac.

"Over 200 percent and climbing. As a matter a fact, it's

so much that we can now track regular traffic routes. Common routes include the moon, Mars, some of the bigger asteroids, and one comet," Mac stated.

Henry carefully looked over the photos Mac provided. After a few moments, he spoke up, "Mac, you had more time to watch this unfold than me for obvious reasons. What are your recommendations?"

Mac stepped forward to emphasize his next point. "In that blast, we lost all of our oversight directors except you. I think it's time to change how we do things. If we have to do this stuff underground, then I say we should do it correctly. This is not a problem that's going to go away overnight. We need long-term realistic goals. My recommendation is that we walk away from directorial oversight. OMA needs to become a military operation as foreseen by our original founders. You take charge, General, in building an underground military and we will make plans to fight back if we can."

The words, "underground military," caused Henry to sit back in his chair and be silent for a few seconds as he thought about it. "Colonel Erik Bjornsen, where is he?"

"On assignment in Argentina," Mac responded.

"OMA is too small to take this on alone. Get him, we will also need him to make contact with other groups around the planet."

Henry's eyes slowly followed his own finger as it moved across the table. As it came to a stop he spoke up one more time, "Mac?"

"Yes," Mac responded back.

"That body you've got...Tara Jean Wallace, what is she?" Henry asked.

"Best guess General...her DNA show evidence of several generations of manipulation. Carol calls her a long-term planned Eugenic hybrid. It could be where they want to take us."

City of Akhenaten, Egypt 1335 B.C.

Fading Starlight

In the late afternoon light, a small sparrow hawk gracefully sweeps over the mirky waters of the Nile to hunt for her morning meal. Crossing over its reseeding banks from the most recent flood, the little hawk rounds the corner of the temple of Ra searching with her eyes for a small lizard displaced from the flood. Soon, she leaves this spot in the air behind as she glides her way north over the storehouse. Seeing a small lizard in the distance near the royal palace, she pulls her wings in close and quickly drops down to pin it against the palace stone wall.

Inside the palace, Pharaoh Akhenaten had just finished another meeting with his advisors. Irritated, he stood up from his chair with his tall crown and walked away from them leaving them in mid-sentence of another pointless explanation.

As the pharaoh passed from their sight, he entered one room and then another and walked to the balcony that overlooked the Nile. Horemheb, the Pharaoh's adviser, arrived in the room at the same time. Slightly shorter, this darker-skinned man who seemed to carry a special level of authority moved closer to the Pharaoh.

Akhenaten's eyes noticed him and inquired if he had news for him. Horemheb gently nodded his head to confirm that he did. Akhenaten stepped forward, speaking in an almost hushed tone. "Speak, what have you learned."

"I have learned many things, and have much to report," Horemheb gently spoke with a little glee in his eyes.

The Pharaoh's strangely narrowed eyes grew a little narrower as he asked, "Who is it that moves against our race, against me?"

Horemheb's eyebrows raised, "We believe it is Vos 26 of the grays."

Anger filled the dark eyes of Akhenaten upon hearing that name. "Hmm, grays... disgusting little hybrids of the Blues. Deceptive, parasitic race requiring human hosts to continue their own. Ptah 18 should have

332

destroyed the Blue race in the east sooner, then we would have been rid of the Blue's nasty little creations."

Horemheb spoke up, "Some say some of the Blues escaped far away to a distant galaxy."

Akhenaten spoke up, "Rumors without foundation. Told by the same voices that claim that I shall live forever. I, Ptah 56, may well be the last leader of the tall whites. Too many before me have loved the human females, contaminating our bloodline, and this will result in a new race that we shall leave here. They should never have allowed such an abomination to take place. As a result, we may soon need to leave this world to preserve the sky blood we have left. What of the sky ships?"

"Two have been built in orbit around Horus's red world. We are only mining the rest of the minerals we need to construct a third now," Horemheb informed him.

With a bit of pride and reflection in his eyes, Akhenaten responded back. "Paraduse the Red, fourth in this system, I will miss you." Pausing for a moment, as the Pharaoh looked into the sky towards the planet Mars, "So what all have you discovered Horemheb? What are Vos 26's fingers into now?"

"Many things, my Pharaoh, they have spoken lies to the human slaves that we planted on the western continents, driving them to rebel with lies of feathered gods. Soon, our workforce will totally oppose us. Also, they speak late into the night to the temple priests here in your city," Horemheb whispered.

"So they seek to overthrow me, even here. We must protect our race's interests here along the Nile. Perhaps in the future, our race will only live on the sky ships. Perhaps we will only visit this world and abandon it these lower races," Akhenaten said in response as he looked away from the outside world.

Horemheb smiled as he pulled out a small crystal. "Perhaps, my Pharaoh, we can look through a window to the future and make a plan."

Akhenaten's face acquired an inquisitive look as he

saw a crystal that Horemheb was holding out of his hand. Holding it out he dropped it into Pharaoh's hand to hold. Holding it up to the mid-morning light, Akhenaten spoke, "This is not a natural crystal. What am I looking at, Horemheb?"

Akhenaten handed it back to him as Horemheb started to speak, "It has very advanced technology, my Pharaoh, from the future."

Horemheb turned away from the balcony and started to walk over to a golden pillar about four feet high. Putting his hand on the outer ring, he pressed down and turned to the right. A small post of gold, about three inches in diameter, rose from the center. Stopping at only six inches high, as Horemheb continued talking. "Not long ago, a routine patrol picked up a short-lived signal from one of the grays' airships that they patrol and hunt the earth with. The signal started and stopped quickly. A ship was dispatched to investigate but was never heard from it again. After many days of searching, we found that humans had attacked, killing them and destroying their ship with some sort of explosive device."

Akhenaten's eyes grew concerned. "They are primitive, they do not possess the technology," he protested.

Horemheb nodded his head in agreement. "I know, so we decided we must learn more and expanded our search. That's when we found this crystal, my Pharaoh. Far from the battle site, a team found the sun-bleached skeleton of an unknown gray form we had not seen before. Animals had scattered their bones over the landscape. But within its skull, we found this crystal data recorder. It took our people a long time to build a computer program to read and operate the crystal. I transferred that program here in your room. Behold, my Pharaoh."

Horemheb placed a small device on the golden post and then placed the crystal on top of it. They both stepped forward away from the pillar to look at the hologram that was now being projected into the room behind them.

"According to the temporal time signature, these images are over three thousand years into the future. As you can see, the grays have a vast amount of ships, both on and inside the moon, as well as hidden cities on the earth. It also seems they are currently fighting a war with humans. There are many images of this war on the recorder. But the image, of this man, is seen many times. Especially near the end. Observe, my Pharaoh." Horemheb informed him.

They both watched as events played out like a video recording of the aliens' fight with John Becker in the cave. Then the image became highly distorted for a moment and even flashed a time or two. Soon, the last images recorded came from the ground level, as John rolled and pushed the alien off a small cliff.

"According to the internal date stamp within the recorder, the last images were just a few years ago. My Pharaoh, we believe this man traveled from the future and is the one who destroyed our patrol." Horemheb remarked.

Pharaoh Akhenaten was speechless for a moment as he stepped back. Lifting his hands, he removed his tall crown so that his elongated head could stop sweating from inside his crown.

Finally, he spoke up, "A time traveler—our people believed it was too dangerous to try this. With the knowledge this human carries, we could regain this planet and destroy all the other races that oppose us. Release the fleet—find him at any cost. He is our highest priority."

No sooner had he said this than the holographic image abruptly ended. Both Akhenaten and Horemheb turned around. In their horror stood a gray alien near the pillar who now had the crystal in his hand.

Turning from them, he ran and jumped off the palace balcony. The Pharaoh and his advisor ran behind him just in time to see him land on something flat, like a rectangular floating platform. The gray alien gave one last look at them from the platform, as it started to fly away.

335

Fading Starlight

Turning his head toward Horemheb, Pharaoh Akhenaten exclaimed, "Now it is a race, we must hurry."

Present Day

Megan had left the room with Johnny, as it was getting too late for him to be up. Henry watched the two exit his room, noticing the door failed to completely shut. With a smirk, Henry pondered if he should go to bed himself or get a little more work done. He sat there for a moment, thinking over the last two weeks since his arrival at the hidden base. Walking was now much easier with the help of his cane and from what Carol told him, he might not even need that in the future.

Picking up his cane, Henry got up and moved through the small apartment to the fridge in his office. He had been a water drinker for years, never really cared for the taste of other things until the world changed.

Rick Chen gave a light push to the door, walking in as Henry pulled out a can of root beer. Rick's right eyebrow raised as he saw it. "Never pegged you as a root beer drinker. I would think you would want something a little harder after everything you have been through," Rick stated with a smile.

Henry smiled as he turned around to look at Rick. Pulling the top open Henry poured it into a cup. "Call it the weakness of age, Mr. Chen. My grandson has got me hooked. I am finding at this point in life, some of the simple pleasures are just hanging out with my family. It's what Johnny likes to drink now, and he likes to share with his grandpa."

Henry tossed the empty can in the trash near him and leaned against the closest cabinet to speak with his guest. "How can I help you, or are you just dropping in before going to bed yourself?"

Rick smiled as he spoke up, "A little of both. I wanted

to let you know that all the activity we are picking up in Israel is the indication of something that I feel is about to happen. Several of the world leaders are quietly meeting in Ashkelon. Our insider says they will be meeting with alien leaders for a few days. The purpose is unknown at this point."

Henry was quiet for a moment and then spoke up, "Who is the closest team?"

"Team 15. It's made up of the remains of Teams Nine and Ten after last week in Africa. I assume you want them deployed?" Rick inquired.

Henry nodded his head to confirm the decision, then added, "Do not engage, just observe and learn at this point until I make better underground connections with other militaries around the world. We have lost too many people at this point." Henry ordered as he took a drink.

Rick had a slightly solemn look on his face as he thought about it. "Strange to be building a worldwide underground army."

"It's all or nothing at this point," Henry added.

"Generally, I have a few connections in Asia, namely China and Korea. They're weak. Do you want me to reach out to them?" Rick asked.

"Yes, I would. But I think you should wait until after we see what's happening in Ashkelon. It may answer a lot of questions for us," Henry responded back.

Megan quietly slipped outside the room that she and her son shared together. Johnny was asleep and she needed to walk around for a moment, to clear her thoughts.

Reaching the upper levels, Megan moved past the main control room offices to the loading and storage area. Looking around she noticed the old steel catwalk built along the edge of the cave. Enjoying the climb to the top of the cave, her hands occasionally touched the hard stone walls. Just before the small exit door on top, Megan glanced downward the hidden base below. With a simple push on the door above her it gave way to a hidden floor under the old watchtower that was built long ago on top of the hill.

In its day it was used to keep watch for forest fires before the days of satellite monitoring. It was a good place to be alone, think, and watch the skies. Wondering if the shooting stars you see are really stars or something darker.

Megan made her way to the top, after opening the door, and then up to the tower. Settling herself to be as comfortable as possible on the floor next to a support post, she looked out at the third phase of the moon that was high in the night sky. She admired the evening stars against the blackness of space, as the coolness of the night settled in around her. Megan just sat there, soon feeling the need to speak, to pray, to express the concerns of her heart.

Breathing in a bit of the night air, Megan slowly spoke out in a quiet voice. "You know, Lord, so many, so many mistakes I make. And yet that never seems to be a high concern for You. This world seems bent on a dark road and all I feel is You and Your heart, and... I love it. And even though You have covered my mistakes, here I am again asking for wings to fly. I am in the middle of this bazaar, strange war with family and some friends. Yet, with everyone around me, somehow, I still feel alone."

Megan sat there for little longer in the silence, watching the night sky as she thought about her next words. "Last night You gave me a another dream. I was dancing in that blue dress again. It was like another world, I really want that world, that place. I WANT HIM, Lord, and..."

Megan thoughts were suddenly interrupted by a noise from the hidden door below. Looking downward, Megan saw Max Lewis stick his head out to speak with her.

Looking upward into the tower, Max spoke loudly so that she could hear him. "Megan?" Max asked.

"Yes?" Megan replied back.

"Looks like you've got a mission in the morning," Max responded.

Puzzled, Megan answered back, "Mission? What, me?

I'm in communications. Not covert boom boom, bang bang. That's your world."

Max shrugged his shoulders, "Sorry, gal, I just heard about it. Saw you walk up here so I thought I should let you know."

The sound of it didn't set right with Megan. "Hmm. I guess I had better come back down and check into this," Megan quietly spoke to herself.

Getting back up Megan looked around at the dark outline of the north Idaho forest around her. The silence of the night was only interrupted by the lights of a car along a road far away. Megan took in a deep breath to leave when she noticed the head lights turned towards the hidden entrance to the base far below her. Megan raised her right eyebrow and started down towards the hidden door below her.

Working her way back down the catwalk she watched as security opened the large doors allowing a small, dark Ford Focus to drive into the base. More than half ways down Megan lightly grinned as she noticed Jenny get out of the car and hand the keys to a security officer. Raising her voice as she neared the bottom of the catwalk Megan asked, "Enjoy the trip?"

A little tired Jenny looked up and smiled for a second, "Ah, Megan. No not really, I wrapped up stuff in Montana." She remarked as she flung the strap of her bag over her shoulder. Walking towards Megan Jenny sarcastically asked with a grin, "It's getting late, I would think an 'elderly woman' like you would be in bed by now."

Megan's eyes narrowed at her comment, "nice to see you to princess smarty pants! I'm headed into the office, rumor is I have mission in the morning."

Jenny lightly snickered as she responded back, "I need to check in so I guess we will join you."

Finishing his talk with Henry and making a few other stops along the way, Rick walked into C2W at the same time Megan arrived. Mac was finishing up and getting ready to leave when they came in.

Noticing Jenny walking through the door first Mac

spoke up, "Your back, how was it?"

"Ah, the dude with the files in Helena was a jerk, so I got no with him. But then as I left I found out he had a business partner who lives in Missoula. He on the other hand was more than helpful and told me the whole story about the hostile takeover of their computer company." Jenny informed Mac as she pulled a thick binder out of her bag to plop it on a table. "In fact he gave me his entire financial report for us to look over."

"Nice," Mac responded back as Rick stepped over to look at the binder.

Jenny closed her bag and was getting ready to turn around when Megan stepped around her to ask. "Mac, I just heard I was getting a mission, I thought communications people don't go on missions. Especially ones who are 'enemy number one' with the Aliens?"

Mac set down a coffee cup he was holding to look at her, "Normally, you wouldn't. But in this case, you look like you need some fresh air. And I thought, in view of what this mission is, that you would want to be a part of it."

"Curious, what is it?" Megan asked.

"Just got word in from Andrew in Steamboat Springs. He says he's got new information for us about the cave," Mac stated with a smile.

"Seriously? You're right," Megan responded back. "When do I leave?"

"In the morning, with Jenny and this guy," pointing to Rick, who just became aware of the mission for the first time. "Their main priority will be your safety."

"I just got back," Jenny protested.

Surprised, Rick jumped in, "So this is just a simple in and out?"

Ignoring Jenny Mac turned his head to look at Rick, shrugging his shoulders, "So far, never know, it might turn into more."

Jenny sunk her head a little as she turned for the door, "I guess I better get some sleep then."

"I would," Mac remarked.

Rick nodded his head in confirmation, "Ok, well, I guess I'm ready for some fresh air myself ." With that, Rick turned and left, letting the door close behind him and Jenny.

Megan watched them leave and then turned back to Mac to look at him. After a moment or so of awkward silence, Mac spoke up in a slightly official tone. "Is there anything else?"

Any momentary amount of concern Megan perceived from him a moment ago had just evaporated. So Megan quickly panned her eyes over to see the man who was working the night shift station. His back was turned to them as he worked on his paperwork.

Stepping up to Mac in an official way as if she needed to speak something sensitive to him, she drew herself very close and looked him in the eye for a moment. She simply spoke, "Yes, sir, there is." Then, with both hands, she quickly grabbed his jacket and pulled him up to her level. Planting a strong kiss on him that lasted for a few brief seconds, she let him back down.

Shocked as she let go of him, Mac stepped back, a little unsure. "Megan, what the...?"

Megan's eyes narrowed as she looked at Mac with a stern look. "I'm right in what I've been thinking. You do like me, don't you?" she informed him.

More than just a little stunned, the only thing that came out of Mac's mouth was, "Ahh..."

Taking this as confirmation of her thinking, she raised her finger and pointed it in his face. With a slight bit of anger in her voice, she asked, "Then why in the world did you suddenly become so cold, as if you didn't care. In the little time that I have known you, you have always been solid and sure of yourself. You obviously still like me so what gives, my little man?"

Mac swallowed hard as he regained his confidence. In hushed tones as not to be heard by the night watch Mac responded back. "You're right, I do have feelings for you... to my surprise, strong ones for both you and your son. But as soon as everything hit the fan and we had to declare command protocol Starlight, everything changed, I no longer have that luxury. Now I have to think about the world. I need to treat you the same as any other person under me. Do you understand?"

Megan stood there for a moment, looking at him. Lowering her hands and putting them on her hips, Megan spoke up in the same hushed tone. "I understand your thinking, and I disagree. You've got some ridiculous idea in your head of standing alone against the world. That's bull, mister, and dangerous. Man was not created to be alone and I am not going to let you."

Mac looked at her with wide eyes and a bit of emotion in his tone. "I'm sorry, it's not about what you or I want. It's about what needs to happen—you should go now."

Megan was un-phased by his ending comment, narrowing her eyes for a second, Megan decided to give him his space anyway. In a very matter-of-fact tone of voice, she responded back with a finger in his face, "Fine, you don't want to see reality now, I can wait and in the morning, I'll go do this mission. But mark my words, this little talk is not over yet, Mr. MacWilliams."

A little more unsure about life and what he was feeling, Mac watched Megan turn and march out.

With their hair color changed, Jenny and Megan walked in with Rick into a local hardware and animal feed store in Steamboat Springs.

They made their way to a salesman in the rear of the store that had his back turned to them. Megan spoke up first, "Excuse me, can you help us?"

To their surprise, former Private Cameron Huckins turned around.

"Ah... Private Huckins?" a shocked Megan asked.

Stammering for a moment, and confused by what he was seeing, Huckins responded. "Captain Becker, ah... I mean Ms. Becker... ah, ma'am." Finally regaining his thinking, "Welcome, how can I help you?"

"Mr. Huckins, I was supposed to meet a friend here. Do you remember Lieutenant Hansen?" Megan inquired.

"Of course I do, and just to let you know, here in the hardware store, my employers prefer that we all use our first names. So please call me Cameron or Cam. They like to make it simple for the customers. And as for your meeting, Megan..." Megan cut him off in mid sentence.

"Mary, for now please use the name Mary," Megan insisted.

Confused, Cameron's eyes narrowed as he responded back, "Mary?"

"It's a long story, I hate it; just play along," Megan reassured him. "You were saying?"

"Ah... Ms. Mary, as for your meeting, please turn around." Cameron raised his hand, directing everyone with his index finger to turn around.

"Hello, Mary," responded a familiar voice.

Standing behind everyone was Andrew dressed in the same blue and red hardware vest as the rest of the store employees. Megan's eyebrows raised as she spoke, "You work here as well?"

Andrew smiled as he responded, "Well, after the Army gave us all the left boot of fellowship, I needed to find a job. So I came here, thinking I would start getting into the outdoors with a local job. I applied here and they made me the floor supervisor. That's when I ran into Cameron here."

Megan turned her head back towards Cameron. "You were here already?"

Cameron shrugged his shoulders, "I grew up here."

"Oh," Megan responded back as she turned her head back towards Andrew.

"Cameron here is the reason I contacted Mac. He has some information for you," Andrew spoke to the group.

Everyone except Rick, who was watching the rest of the store, turned their heads to look at Cameron. Cameron smiled in a slightly embarrassed way as he reached for his phone in his back pocket.

"Well, one of the reasons I never made it past my pay grade in the Army was because I sometimes got in trouble and disobeyed orders," Cameron spoke up to the group.

Pulling out his phone, he started accessing his picture app as he spoke. "I am sorry, but one of the times on duty, I snuck into the cave that you ordered off-limits. No one was inside so I took some pictures with my phone."

Megan moved around to see the pictures on his phone as he swiped through them.

"I don't understand, we took a lot of photos of everything. However, sense we no longer have them it is nice to have these." Megan stated as she looked up at Andrew.

"You did not have photos like this," Andrew insisted.

Cameron continued speaking, "At one point I thought I heard someone coming, so I turned to get out of there, slipped and fell on the floor. I did not realize it until later, but when I fell, my phone camera took a picture from the floor up. See, look at it."

Cameron held it a little closer so that Megan could see the odd picture. Part of the picture frame was covered by his finger, but you could clearly see some rectangular impressions on the walls near the floor.

Megan, who was a little surprised, looked back at Andrew who spoke up. "When you ordered Josh and me to clean the cave, we stopped below knee height. For some reason, we thought there was no need to go below that."

Megan looked at Andrew and then Jenny. "So there's more in the cave," she exclaimed.

Jenny spoke up, "Director MacWilliams will want a follow-up on this. I looked at my cell phone and I can't get any reception in here. I will need to step outside to text him with our change of plans."

Rick turned his head to look at her. "Go, we will stay here and wait for you."

Jenny turned and walked outside as Cameron spoke

up. "What's up, what's with all this cloak and dagger stuff?"

Rick turned his attention away from the rest of the store to answer Cameron's question. "Have you tried to contact any of your fellow servicemen that you worked with at the cave?"

"Yes," Cameron responded.

"Let me guess, no one is returning your call," Rick almost coldly responded.

"Yeah, but people often do that to me, it's kinda normal," Cameron answered back.

Bending his head a little towards him to speak, "Not normal, they're all dead," Rick informed him.

Megan responded to the shocked look on Cameron's face. "It's true, we have rescued or have hidden everyone we could find for their own protection."

Taking a moment to think about it, Cameron's asked, "What about me?"

"You disappeared so quickly we thought they already got you. So we stopped looking," Rick told him.

"And now?" Cameron emphatically asked.

Megan spoke up, "Andrew wanted to disappear into the background. You can keep your head down and join him or you can leave with us."

Cameron was a little unsure by the look on his face. Speaking up, he asked, "So who is hunting us?"

Without even thinking twice, Rick responded, "The aliens."

Both Andrew and Cameron spoke together at the same time, "What?"

Rick went back to scanning over the store with his eyes as Megan started speaking. "I know it's weird, but it's true. And as of right now, my family is enemy number one. So are you in or out?"

Cameron, who had lost a little of the color in his face, responded, "No offense, but I think I'll stay right here," pointing at the floor to make his point.

Rick looked over at Megan, "Time to leave."

Andrew looked at Megan, who spoke up to him, "Sorry, we can never stay very long in any place,

345

goodbye."

Megan smiled as they started for the door. Andrew paused for a moment and started walking with them, leaving Cameron behind who gladly stayed where he was.

"I'll see you to the door, at least," Andrew told his old friend. Megan smiled as they walked to the door.

"By the way, what's the deal with your hair? Where did the red go?" Andrew inquired.

Megan started to respond as they made it to the doorway, only to be interrupted by screaming from the back of the store. As a pain-filled sound filled the air, all the customers began to look around.

Everyone turned to run back to Cameron as customers scattered out of their way. They rounded the corner to find Cameron slumping to the floor as two men Andrew recognized dressed in black suits stood over Cameron.

"I know you!" Andrew remarked as he recognized Johnson and Davis who turned to look directly at him.

Without a moment's pause, Rick jumped into the middle of them. Utilizing his martial arts training, he landed in the mid-section of Johnson. The fight was on, as both men attacked Rick Chen. Andrew tossed himself in like a cannon ball as Megan put her finger up to the transmitter in her ear to call for help.

Megan then looked around and grabbed a can of foaming wasp killer spray and charged into the fight. Soon, she had Davis on the ground, screaming in pain, as he clawed at his face with his hands attempting to remove the foaming spray.

Andrew and Rick were effectively tearing up the store as they traded blow for blow with the men. Crashing through a display of wooden birdhouses, Jenny soon responded to Megan's call for help and produced a gun. Unable to shoot for fear of hitting the wrong person, she reached out and grabbed a framing hammer off a display and jumped in.

Rick then hit Johnson hard enough to send him backwards. Jenny kicked the legs out from under the Johnson as he struggled to get back up. Jenny then took the opportunity and hit the Davis in the kneecaps with the hammer. But as soon as she pulled back to hit him with the hammer again, Megan started to scream as Lopez entered into the fight from behind her. He held her with his left arm around her neck as his right hand shoved something against her side.

Whatever it was it was causing an immense amount of pain. She started violently shaking as if she was having an epileptic seizure. Both Jenny and Rick turned and attacked Lopez, pulling him off Megan.

Lopez let go of his device, as it was now melting part of Megan's jacket. She slumped to the floor, barely alive, with little holes burned in her her.

Megan was starting to pass out as she heard two gunshots and the sound of something hitting the floor.

Soon Megan was tossed over Andrew's shoulders like a sack of feed as Jenny and Rick quickly cleared a path to the double doors of the hardware store, leaving Cameron laying dead along with one dead stranger and two that were heavily bleeding on the floor for the local police to figure out.

Henry walked with his cane into the cafeteria to get some coffee and a sandwich. Meeting up briefly with Max, they politely exchanged a, "hello" as Henry's head turned to see Max motioning with his head toward Mac, who was sitting at the far table. With a slight grin Henry knew that it mean Mac had a new update for him.

Henry thanked him with a wink, collected his ham sandwich and then turned to make his way over to Mac. Placing his food on the table, Henry sat down in front of Mac while leaning his cane on the wall, Henry spoke up as he sat down, "Max says you've got an update?"

Mac wiped his mouth with a napkin as he responded back while still working his plate with his silverware , "Yep, several General."

"Ok, What?" Henry responded back as he noticed that

Fading Starlight

Mac was definitely not calm, almost angry.

"Got a short note from Jenny, she reports that they are moving towards the cave. Apparently, after the meeting in Steamboat, they discovered there were some possible items in the cave that they missed," Mac calmly stated.

"Good. What else?" Henry calmly inquired as he unwrapped his sandwich.

"I have a team in place at Ashkelon, they are sending me some disturbing news," Mac calmly stated once more.

A little perplexed, Henry stopped for a moment to look at Mac. "If you have something disturbing, then why are we sitting here?"

Without looking up, Mac started talking a little fast as he kept working on his food. "Because, General, I have had a lot on my mind in the last twenty-four hours. I needed to get away and think for a moment. And even though the news is priority one, I personally need a moment to clear my head."

Henry raised his right eyebrow as he picked up his coffee cup. "Hmm, sounds like something my daughter would have said. This must be serious."

Mac did not stop what he was doing, but only looked up briefly at the mention of Megan's name, driving a glare at the General.

"Somehow, I suspect my daughter is at the center of your issue," Henry calmly remarked as he drank his coffee.

Mac looked up once, as if to agree with him. But not wishing to discuss the subject, he decided to continue talking about his priority one problem. "Apparently, some aliens are conducting high-level talks with major world leaders in the city. I am being told by our people that they are developing a treaty," Mac remarked.

"A treaty, that is serious," commented Henry.

"It's being called The Treaty of Ashkelon. It calls for earth to give them several parcels of land around the world to build on, in trade for solving various earth problems. It sounds like they are going to start operating in the open around the planet. So I assume at some point soon, they will make themselves known to everyone," Mac stated as he cut his food up into increasingly smaller bites.

Henry watched Mac cut up his food, wondering what his daughter did. Finally, he spoke, "Is that it or is there more?"

"Our hidden satellite tracking network is picking up a lot of alien traffic between the moon and a deserted area in the southern Egyptian desert. We have no idea what it is," Mac stated once more.

Henry pushed his chair back and thought about it for a moment. "Mac, deploy a team to that location to investigate. Whatever is going on, I would like to acquire any tech we find. And if possible, destroy the site."

"Got it," responded Mac.

Henry watched for a moment longer and then started to collect his stuff to leave. As he did, he started to speak. "I don't know what happened between you and my daughter, but I can tell you two things. One is that you need to stop punishing that poor steak on your plate. It's already dead. And the second is, whatever she said to get you so riled up, you need to get over it and listen to her. I know the look on your face, son. Megan's mother did it to me often and she was usually right. I just didn't want to admit it."

Mac looked up, with a little anger behind his eyes. Speaking in a very matter-of-fact tone, "She kissed me."

The corner of Henry's mouth started to turn upward. Henry then stopped it before it could become a smile. "Hmm, if a kiss pissed you off this much, I wonder what would happen if it got serious?" Henry started to turn to leave, but stopped and looked Mac in the eye. "Like I said, get over it. Chances are, this will not be the last kiss. My daughter won't be giving up." Henry emphasized as he tipped the top of his cain at Mac's face.

Mac watched Henry slowly walk away with his sandwich and coffee balanced in one hand while the other kept hold of his cane.

Fading Starlight

Pausing for several second, Mac looked down at his mostly uneaten, mangled steak, seeing for the first time how he had already destroyed his meal. He then pushed it away in disgust.

Max who sat by himself in the corner of the room watched the whole thing with a big grin while holding his coffee cup.

The Past

Lorenzo was repacking his homemade leather pack, as he and his father sat along the banks of the Colorado River. He was proud of his pack and had worked hard to make it look like his father's. Within it, he carried everything of value that someone eight years old going on twenty would want. Food, extra clothing, his homemade sword, and extra ammo for the alien rifle his father had taught him to shoot, as well as some tools his father made for him.

He was feeling proud and a little stronger now that he had his own weapon. And in the last month, his father even allowed him to kill a deer with it for the tribe.

They were coming back down from the hidden cave after spending a few days binding his father's gold books, as well as chipping out places in the cave walls for them to rest. This would be their last stop to rest before reaching their village. Because they were so close to the tribe, John was halfway considering catching some fresh fish to take back to the village. But winter was now coming, John and Lorenzo would be making no more personal trips to the cave. It was now time to hunt, gather, and prepare food for winter in the desert. So John weighed out the wisdom of taking time to fish now, or just join in with everyone else's work.

Suddenly John heard Lorenzo's voice excitedly speak up. "Father, look up."

John raised his head. To this horror, John could clearly

see what Lorenzo was pointing at. Four large alien craft were sweeping down the canyon, just over the top of them. As they passed fast and low, John could clearly see the gray aliens near the windows of their aircrafts. Adrenaline and a cold chill traveled through his body, as he watched them round the high canyon corners of the river. Somewhere inside both of them, they knew everything had changed.

"Quick, we need to leave now, Son. We need to run to the village," John barked out.

Soon, both were running as fast as they could for home. After several minutes of hard running over rocks, sand, and through the tough river underbrush, both stopped with their hands on their knees as they sucked in the air.

In the distance, just a little louder than the sound of there own pounding hearts they could barely hear a noise. A noise that Lorenzo had never heard before. But to John's horror, he had—it was the sound of explosions from aerial bombardments.

John yelled "NO," as he took off running once more. Not caring about how he made his way through the brush, his arms and face were now getting cut up from the small twigs and branches. Many long moments passed as he pushed his body beyond what he should, just to get to his people. Finally he rounded a corner, bursting forth from the underbrush. About a half mile from his tribe, he collapsed to his knees as he took in the sight.

The gray aliens had pounded the village from the sky. Smoke and dust rose upward into the afternoon air to cast a shadow on the distant hillside. John's sweat, dirt, and now blood-covered face slowly filled with tears as he watched. In anger his fingers dug deep into the sand under his hands as he beheld the aliens now walking among the dead bodies as they searched them.

Lorenzo finally burst forth from the brush behind his father to fall on the ground next to him exhausted. As he lay there on the ground with his face downward, he heard for the first time a low moaning sound that was coming from his father. Looking up at his father's face first, the sight of it struck his heart.

John reached out, grabbed his son, and crushed him against him very tightly. Ever so slowly, Lorenzo turned his head from his fathers chest to see what his father saw. It was a sight that would endure with him all the days of his life.

Soon the last aliens boarded their aircraft and departed into the southern sky. Time passed as father and son slowly got up and made their way towards home one last time. Deep holes in the ground replaced the stone buildings John had built. They tearfully walked past the small fires of burning bodies and wood scattered over the site. The smell of the smoke stung their eyes as they made their way looking, hoping, but knowing better.

John had suffered loss before, but not like this, never like this. He could not turn his head from the left to the right without seeing the horrible sight of the destroyed body of someone he knew.

Lorenzo had quit looking, but simply buried his face into the side of his father as they walked. He had already recognized a hand that belonged to his grandfather. And had seen the face of Tablita at a distance.

John's well-trained military mind started to betray him as it cataloged everything he saw. Even in his peripheral vision, it... cataloged the dead. John kept one arm around Lorenzo as they walked. The other held his rifle. Never did he want his son to experience this kind of horror. He had seen it too many times in his life, too many.

Part of him was starting to grow numb as he closed in on the location where his home once was. Slowly, he sat down on the edge of a double crater. Saying nothing, doing nothing, he just sat down, watching the far side of it.

Lorenzo sat next to him, listening to the sounds of the fires around them. After a while, he turned his head, to see his father's tear-streaked face just staring across the crater.

After a moment he spoke up, "Shouldn't we find Mother?"

With his gaze unbroken, John's quivering lips simply responded, "I already have."

The words stunned Lorenzo as he turned his head to see what his father was seeing. To his shock, on the other side of the crater lay the burning, broken, half-melted body of a woman.

Lorenzo screamed and started to lunge towards her. John quickly reached out, grabbed him by his arm and yanked him back. Spinning him around to look at him face-to-face, John emphatically spoke to him. "No, don't do it. You don't want to see that, Son. You never want to see that. It will scar your soul like nothing you have ever seen before."

Shaking him with both hands, "Son, you need to remember her the way she was. Not as she is now. Got that?"

John closed his eyes and crushed Lorenzo to his chest once more.

Time passed as the afternoon shadows grew long. The tears had stopped as both sat silently in the dirt. John slowly raised his head to look at the sky. In the distance, he could see the first evening star starting to make its appearance against the fading blue.

Slowly, he spoke up, "Come, it's time for us to get up, we need to leave now."

A little confused, Lorenzo protested, "Leave? Shouldn't we do something?"

John slowly shook his head from left to right. "No, the only thing you can do for them now, Son, is remember, just remember them."

Looking at his son's face and then back up into the sky, "They will be coming back, they're hunting us. So we need to leave."

John started to stand up as Lorenzo tugged a little on him, protesting his decision to leave. Seeing the conflict in his son's face, John spoke up. "Lorenzo, there's nothing you can do for them now. Your mother would want you to live, she would tell you to go. Her soul and

Fading Starlight

Rebecca's are not here any more and we need to leave as well."

As they finally started to walk, Lorenzo put his hand inside his father's for the first time since he was six years old. They passed the ruins of one home when Lorenzo noticed the firelight reflecting off of something in the dirt.

He pulled his hand out of his father's hand to pick it up. John stopped to watch as Lorenzo bend down and pull out of the dirt the Captain's pin his father gave to Rebecca.

Handing it to his father, John's heart stuck in his throat as he held it in his hand. It was now bent from a blast or maybe a fall. Turning his head around, hoping to find some other hopeful evidence, he soon realized the hopelessness of the landscape around them.

She was only four months old. And it would be the only part of her he would ever have.

Slowly making their way back Lorenzo paused for a moment behind his father as his wet face looked over the smoking village once more, "Tablita?" He whispered.

John paused for a second and themed around to ask, "what?"

"We... didn't find her?" Lorenzo asked.

Closing his eyes for a moment John responded back, "its...probably for the best, come."

Sucking in his lower lip for a moment, Lorenzo turned and walked behind John, picking up all the items they dropped, they finally reached their camp. Pulling the camp deeper that night between the rocks and underbrush to remain hidden. Tonight, there would be no fire, food, or words—only silence and the sounds of the river.

With little sleep, John woke up early in the morning to hear Lorenzo tossing the biggest rocks he could find into the river. He was working off his aggravation and John knew it. He thought about telling him to stop. But in the end, it seemed better to just let him blow off some steam.

It was normally a quiet trip back to the cave. One step in front of the other; over one rock and around another. The two and a half day trip some how got an extra day and a half added to it as anguish and quietness filled the memories. Old campsites along the river held pleasant thoughts and laughter of the past. Kasa's laugh, Kaviu snoring late into the night. The time Lonan and his wife Malia got into a fight and fell into the river. And soon everyone was laughing at them. If these old places could speak.

It was the longest trip back to the cave John had ever felt. He had lost two families now and the hollowness in his heart felt bigger than ever. As far as John was concerned, the aliens had won.

If it wasn't for the fact Lorenzo needed him now, the thought of shooting himself seemed like a good idea. What else was there?

The Present

Megan was walking up a hill, wiping her windblown, curly red hair from the front of her face. She noticed an older woman with a kind look on her face at the top of the hill. As she reached the top of the hill, the spectacular backdrop of ice and snow covering the mountains around them seemed to highlight the older women's blue dress with green and white highlights.

The sight of the place took her breath away, as everything in her mind seemed to jump at the sight of it. Far away in the distance, she could clearly see a small village that looked almost Bavarian. It was framed with a very large stone arch behind it that a waterfall flowed through.

The sight of all of it made her stop. Slowly, she panned her head around until she saw the smiling face of the old woman once more. She was old and young at the same time. With her right-gloved hand, she gently motioned for her to come over to sit at a table.

Fading Starlight

As Megan moved towards the table, she happened to notice a large buck standing at a great distance. The sight of it was strangely comforting. "I love this place," Megan spoke up.

The old woman never stopped smiling, "It is a place of rest for anyone who needs it."

"Is this the place of still waters?" Megan inquired.

"No, my daughter, this is a way station. You must follow the buck to find that place. But it is close," she replied.

"How close?" Megan asked.

"Just as close as you need it to be, or as far as you make it," the woman spoke as she sat down.

Megan looked over at the buck for a moment and did not see him anymore —only some man standing far in the distance. "Who are you?" Megan asked the older woman as she turned her head to look at her once more.

"I am your helper, I have always been with you," the woman responded.

Feeling a moment of concern, Megan told her, "They hunt us at every place we go. They seek to destroy us and our world."

Leaning forward, so close that Megan could see her powerful, beautiful green eyes that almost seemed to changed colors in front of her. Laying her hand on Megan she spoke kindly to her, "When you lie down, you will not be afraid; your sleep will be sweet. Have no fear of sudden disaster or of the ruin that overtakes the wicked of this world, for He will be at your side and will keep your foot from falling into their trap."

Megan woke up in the back of the car as it traveled. Looking up, she saw Jenny's face smiling at her as she applied a bandage to her burnt side. It made her side twinge a little from the pain.

"You're awake. Good," Jenny spoke with a comforting tone.

Feeling the effects of the dream starting to wear off, Megan tried to roll onto her side. The pain of it made her quickly choose to sit up instead. Jenny grinned and put out her hand to help Megan transition to sitting up.

Her straight hair was now a mess as were her clothes.

She looked down at her side to see the damage. Most of her jacket and blouse on her wounded side were burned or melted.

Andrew's voice spoke up from the driver's seat, "Good to see you alive. Jenny's been working with you for a while. I was afraid we might be losing you."

Megan's eyes started to focus enough to see Andrew's face in the rearview mirror. The concern in his eyes told her that he was not joking. Megan stuck her tongue out for a moment as she tried to figure out what was in her mouth. "How long was I out, and what is that horrible taste in my mouth? It's disgusting," Megan announced.

Jenny opened a bottle of water for her to drink out of. "It's a complex cocktail of drugs that Carol invented. You're not the first person to be hit with that device. You're just the first person we have ever got to test it on. And I would say you have only been out for about fifteen to twenty minuets."

Megan took a drink, "Why am I the first?"

"We captured their device a while back. It releases a complex collection of neuro-drugs under a powerful electrical shock. Designed to quickly kill with as much pain as possible. You're the first we have used it on, because you still showed some signs of life," Jenny reported.

Megan stopped drinking for a moment to look her in the face. "Seriously?"

Jenny's eyebrows raised upward as she slowly nodded her head. "Yep, you were almost dead."

Megan held tightly onto her water bottle as she responded, "Well then, thank you for not giving up on me. Do you have a mint?"

Rick turned a little in his seat to reach back and hand her a breath mint. "Here, it's all I've got."

Megan accepted the mint as they drove along the highway.

After a little while, Andrew spoke up once more. "Better settle in, everyone, it's a five-hour road trip to Moab from here."

Carol walked into Henry's office with a folder in her hand. The General looked up as he noticed her entry. Handing off the folder to Henry, "Here's the preliminary report, General, on the meeting in Ashkelon."

Henry smiled and opened it. Looking it over, he noted the names of everyone in attendance. "Hmm, that's interesting."

"I thought so as well, General," Carol responded.

"Yes, it seems that only a quarter or so of the people in attendance are leaders of governments," Henry spoke with some concern in his voice.

"I looked up the names of the rest of the attendees. They are all major leaders, overseeing most of the major corporations of the world," Carol added.

It had been some time, but the quiet travelers made their way back to the cave. John and Lorenzo arrived and started hammering and rolling out the last of the gold. There was not much, just enough for two sheets. On them, he would inscribe the last of his journal notes in honor of all who died, and then place them in the nook Lorenzo was tapping out of the stone near his feet.

Lorenzo finished before John, who was having problems putting the words down. Admitting defeat and talking about everyone who died was not the way he wanted to end this story. It made him feel lifeless, numb like he had stepped into a vacuum.

Lorenzo sat down and watched his dad with his blank stare. John had only managed a few paragraphs on the gold. "Father, what do we do now? Once you're done writing, where do we go?"

John turned his blank stare outward towards the canyon walls on the far side. "I don't know, maybe north, far away. Where they can't find you. I need to be alone for a moment to finish this. Would you mind stepping out for a moment?"

Almost emotionless, Lorenzo got up with his backpack and alien rifle and walked outside. John watched him walk a ways down the slight hillside. As he did, John calmly reached over and grabbed his rifle. Looking down at it, he cycled the action.

Having not eaten in days Lorenzo pulled his pack off to see if he had anything as he walked along the primitive path. Stopping he pulled out the toy sword his father made him, somehow it made him angry; it was just a toy, a child's plaything, not real. The sight of it for some reason made him mad.

With the culmination of all his aggravation built within him, he tossed it as hard as he could. Watching it skip off a rock and into some brush, far away.

Inside the cave, his father watched him from a distance. The numbness within him had grown, as he could almost no longer hear the sounds of the world around him. Slowly, John moved the end of his gun barrel to just under his chin. Placing his hand on the lower assembly, he then moved his finger to the trigger.

Suddenly, as he was about to make his last move, John heard a voice suddenly shout, "No." The sound of it shocked him like an electrical jolt, as he thought it was Lorenzo. He scrambled outside to see Lorenzo sitting calmly on a rock in the distance.

The voice was so clear and direct, it sounded like it was in the cave with him. Turning around behind him, John did not see anyone in the cave. The event so shocked him to the core as he looked back at his son. Slowly, his eyes made out the silhouette of a buck standing on the canyon ridge high above his son.

Dropping everything on the ground, John put his hands over his face for a moment to think. He slowly bent his knees to sit down on the closest rock. Lorenzo looked up and saw his father.

It only seemed like a moment or two had passed, but John was startled as Lorenzo's hand touching his shoulder. "Father, are you ok?"

Using his dirt-covered hands, he quickly wiped the tears off his face. "Yeah, I'm fine. Just thinking, just thinking," John quickly responded.

Lorenzo had a concerned look on his face as he studied his father's face. "Do you realize we have not eaten in days?"

John sat there for a moment, thinking about it as he slowly rocked back and forth while sitting on the rock. Feeling totally exhausted, he realized his son was right. "You're right, we should go hunting one more time before we leave. Get a good meal in and leave in the morning."

The Present

Andrew and Jenny had stepped into the gas station in Wellington, Utah to pay for gas and some groceries. Megan sat in the back seat of the car and happened to notice that everyone was looking up at the TV screen inside the station wall.

She leaned forward and tapped Rick on the shoulder. "Hey, something's going on. I think we should get inside." Rick got out and helped Megan to do the same. She did not think she needed the help, but surprisingly, Megan found her body stiffer then she thought she would be.

Stepping inside the gas station, the local news channel was ablaze with information. The news ticker that zoomed by on the bottom of the screen notified the world that they had just reached a treaty with aliens from space. The Treaty of Ashkelon.

On the TV screen, a tall, lightly gray alien, which looked almost totally human except for his elongated head, was standing next to two world leaders. They introduced him as the leader of his race. The alien stepped up to the microphone to speak to the world.

"Greetings, fellow humans, from your fellow brothers and sisters. I am called Vos, leader of the Solipsi Rai and advisor to the court of the Maitre. One million years ago, the human race evolved into three races. The Solipsi Rai, the Maitre, and you. Due to conflict with two races, the Mazarek and the Indugutk, we had lost contact with you. Those days are now forever behind us. We now seek to know our brothers and sisters in this faraway island in space."

"To show our good intention, we have entered into a treaty with your leaders to provide you with a higher level of education and life. We will wipe away your diseases, and food shortages and you will be like us. Knowing the secrets of the universe itself."

"In return, your world leaders are procuring land for us to build on in various places around the earth. So that we may evenly distribute ourselves among you for your education and benefit." Vos smiled as he finished his speech.

Astounded at this announcement, the team simply looked at each other in silence. Andrew quickly finished paying as they got in their car to leave.

The Past

The dark night had fallen as John and Lorenzo finished their meal of cooked rabbit. The cooking fire that was on the edge of the cave danced firelight images all around the caves interior. For a brief moment, with warm food inside them, everything seemed normal, as the two sat on the ground near the fire. Then Lorenzo spoke up, "Father, last time we were here, I had a dream. I just remembered it."

John was licking his fingers as he responded to his son, "Oh, what was that?"

Lorenzo pointed inside, "You were standing inside, right over there next to where you work. I came in from playing and asked you if we could meet your grandfather."

John looked over at him and lightly chuckled, "Oh,

really?"

"You said, no problem, it's easy to go back to my land. All we need to do is make a flag so that they can find us and take us home." Lorenzo informed him.

John laughed, causing Lorenzo to laugh a little as well. "Well, Son, if it was as simple as that, I would gladly do it."

John tossed the rabbit bones into the fire as Lorenzo leaned back to look at the night sky. John then looked up as well at the glittering stars. Slowly, his face changed as he thought about his son's words.

After a moment or so, John picked up a stick and started writing in the sand.

Lorenzo watched him for a while, and then spoke up. "What are you doing, Father?"

"Oh, it's probably nothing. Just thinking about something an old friend, Doctor Healy, said to me once." John responded back.

Lorenzo watched his father work with his stick in the dirt and then wipe out his writing, only to repeat the process several times. It was one of the last things he remembered as his tired eyes pulled him off to sleep.

The marmalade-colored canyon walls gave way to the early morning light, slowly changing them to a brighter hues of red, as Lorenzo stirred from his sleep.

Lorenzo had rolled over during the night, facing away from the cave. His eyes opened to see the morning brightness of the canyon walls. He lay there a little depressed as he remembered his loss. His mind however, slowly focused on the sound behind him.

Rolling over to see what it was, Lorenzo could clearly see his father working in the cave. Curious, he pulled himself to his feet to walk in.

John heard him approaching, and turned his head to look at his son. "Good morning, did you sleep well?" John inquired.

Lorenzo flipped his long Indian hair behind him and started to tie it with his hands. "Yes, I guess. What are you up to? I thought we were leaving?"

"We are Son, we are." Turning his head back to the

stone cave wall, John continued talking, "One way or another, we are leaving."

Lorenzo was standing at the outer edge of the cave, slowly walking in the rest of the way as he talked with his father. As he did, his eyes opened wide, puzzled at the sight. Much of the alien technology they had acquired was spread out around the cave. Some of it had been dismantled. His father had been fast at work, covering the walls with strange markings from a piece of metal.

"What are you doing Father?" Lorenzo inquired.

John stopped and paused for a moment. Then turning around, he bowed down a little to Lorenzo to look him straight in the eye. With a little excitement in his eyes, he spoke, "I am taking a suggestion out of your dream. I'm planting a flag." John smiled at his son and slowly turned back to the cave wall to check what he had scribbled out.

Lorenzo stood there for a moment, taking in what his father had said. "I don't understand," Lorenzo remarked.

John kept working on a math formula as he responded back. "I realized a few things last night after I thought about your dream. There may be a way to open the door and step back into eternity once more. If that can happen, we should be able to travel back to my time. Or at least, some other time then this one."

Lorenzo's mind was slowly coming up to speed. "You mean we are going to leave this world and travel to my father's world?"

"Hopefully, yes. I spent all night working on it. Tearing apart all this equipment, trying to figure out if I have all that I need. When we made the first time jump, Doctor Healy made a lot of calculations just to move back a few years. He told me the Tow-Kef effect was simple."

"Dr. Healey said, 'In reality, it would be simple if we just had someone on the other end of this journey holding the door open.'" John laughed for a moment after quoting Dr. Healy. "We, Son, are going to get someone, at some other time to open the door for us. In effect, we have to plant a flag in the future," John informed him as he kept working.

Lorenzo stood there a little dumbfounded. After a moment, John quietly spoke once more, "Hopefully, the right people will open the door. You never know, there is a lot of history between my day and this one."

"Will it work?" Lorenzo inquired.

"Hope so, I am double checking my math now. Then I will finish assembling both the beacon for someone in the future to turn on. And then the Tow-Kef generator." Stopping for a moment to think about it, he continued, "Oh, wait, I also need to write out the instructions on the gold plates so that they know how to turn it on."

Crossing over the Gulf of Mexico from Africa were three alien airships with Egyptian markings. A troop transport and two fighters made a course correction over South Padre Island of Texas, heading northwest.

Acting under the orders of Ptah 56 aka Pharaoh Akhenaten, Horemheb stood in the doorway of the transport, giving orders as they made their turn. Turning his head one of the junior offers yelled out to him. "Satellite images say the Gray's have destroyed several villages in the area."

Nodding his head Horemheb responded back, "They can't find what their looking for, so they're destroying it all before we can find it."

Lorenzo sat for a good half hour and watched as his father assembled the generator. It was a strange collection of alien parts connected to his father's medical kit from the future.

After a moment or so of checking it over, John started assembly of the beacon that would send a signal that the generator could read. Once it read the signal, the generator would automatically calibrate and open the door, signaling that Lorenzo's flag had worked.

Lorenzo, who was growing bored, heard a noise outside. Getting up, he walked over to the opening to see what it was.

"No. Oh my God, Father, look." Lorenzo pointed in the far distance so that John could see. John came in from behind him. Seeing what it was, he quickly grabbed his son and pulled him back in.

John had not seen gray aliens like this since Madrid. The tall grays he saw were round like a weightlifter. He remembered them, strong and powerful. And now there were two of them carefully searching the area. The hunters had found them, and John was running out of time. John slowly and cautiously scanned the are around the corner. Jerking his head back, he looked at Lorenzo.

"Son, you need to be very, very quiet. These two are scouts and they're looking for us. I need to finish so that we can leave. So I want you to keep a careful watch on them. Also keep your rifle very close, do not shoot at them unless they see us or are about to find us. Understand? We need to stay as hidden as we can for as long as we can, got it?" John quietly, emphatically informed him.

Fading Starlight

Lorenzo emphatically shook his head, indicating he understood.

John moved back toward the unfinished beacon. But before he did, he looked in Lorenzo's eyes and said, "Son, no matter what happens. Know that I am proud of you and that I love you."

The Present

Andrew, Megan, Rick, and Jenny got out of their car in the desert near the old camp. Rick pulled a pair of bolt cutters out of the trunk for the newly installed lock at the gate. It was meant to keep people out of the area by the looks of all the government signage around. With a 'snip' Rick simply let the lock fall into the sand after it was cut.

Jenny pulled out a pistol from the trunk and handed it to Andrew. The plan was not to stay around long. A simple in and out operation of finding it, bag it and tag it, nothing more.

Soon they made their way up to the cave and started searching around the inside. "Well, Cameron's picture is a bit unclear, and I really don't see anything," remarked Andrew as he looked around the cave.

Andrew took his light jacket off and tossed it over to Jenny for her to hold as he got down on the floor. Jenny stood there, a little confused as to why she was holding his coat.

Seeing the look of confusion, Andrew spoke up. "Cameron's picture was from the floor with a light above. In my chest pocket, Jenny is a small halogen light. I need you to be the light source from above. Maybe I can see what the picture saw from down here?"

Several minutes went by as Jenny used the small flashlight to highlight the cave walls. Megan got down on her knees to start looking closely at the wall as well. Rick, however, moved away from them to watch the cave entrance. Digging in the dirt was not really for him—guard duty was a better fit.

Then came an announcement from Andrew, "Wait, back up your light for a moment, Jenny. I might have something here." Andrew started carefully running his hands along the stone wall until he found a soft spot of sand.

"I see this is my fault. When Josh and I cleaned up in here, I most likely kicked some of the sand out of my way, accidentally packing this cavity," Andrew remarked as he carefully started digging with his hands.

Megan moved from her spot closer to Andrew to see what he had found.

"Yep, it's a manmade hole, full of sand. I think it will only take a moment or two," Andrew commented as he continued digging. After digging several hands full of sand, Andrew suddenly remarked, "Wait a moment, I think my finger hit something."

The Past

John steadily kept working on the beacon. Hoping that it would not only work, but that it would also fit in the hole Lorenzo made. Outside, Lorenzo watched the two aliens move along the hillside below him, searching the ground. Then he heard a noise in the distance. Looking up, he heard something go boom, far away. It was similar, but different to the sound he heard when his village was destroyed.

The two aliens and John heard it as well. As John kept working, the aliens tried to move to a higher place to look around to see what the noise was.

Suddenly, over the horizon, an alien ship zipped into view. Hot on its tail was a second ship. One of Horemheb's attack crafts from Africa was advancing on a smaller airship from the grays.

Lorenzo quickly recognized the gray's ship as the same

kind that destroyed his family, but he did not know the other. Unfortunately, in his surprise and excitement, Lorenzo very loudly let out a yip-like noise that was heard by the aliens below him.

They turned to look upward, square into the eyes of Lorenzo. The combination of sudden events caused Lorenzo to freeze for a moment in fear. As the battle raged in the sky, the two below started upward towards the cave. Lorenzo, started to regain his mind as he fumbled with his rifle. Before he could get it to his shoulder, he heard a shot from above him. It was John standing above him, who kept his weapon trained on the advancing aliens.

The first one fell from the headshot. The second alien was surprised, watching the first fall. As he turned his head back to look at the cave, John planted the second bullet, this time between the eyes of the second alien.

John lowered his weapon and quickly looked around to see no one else approaching. Then in a controlled panic, John looked up into the sky. He could clearly see the two types of aircraft dogfighting out above them.

One was smaller, more saucer-shaped like the ones who killed his people. The second was way bigger, nearly twice the size. It looked like two saucers linked together on the main fuselage. It would have reminded John of their old hover-helos of his time, had he stopped to think about it.

John stepped back into the cave to resume his work. Then speaking up to his son, "When they get done fighting, they will be coming for us. So they are buying us some time."

Realizing he needed to somehow encourage his son, but having no time for it, John gave him a thumbs-up sign, winked and said, "Keep your eyes open, good work Son."

Totally confused, Lorenzo, who was holding his sister's Captain's pin in his hand, made the same thumbs-up sign with that hand. Wondering what the thumbs-up meant.

Andrew kept digging and then ever so slowly, he pulled out a single, thin gold plate. It was unlike the others they had found earlier —smaller, bent into a semi-circle to fit into the hole. Lying on his side as he extracted it, he slowly lifted it towards Megan.

Megan carefully took hold of this family treasure. Bringing it over to the stone table in the room, she laid it down to look at it.

Jenny moved the light from the wall to the treasure for Megan to examine it.

"Well, there is some more writing, but it's inside the roll. We will need to flatten it out," Megan remarked.

"We should keep moving," remarked Rick Chen. Megan looked down at Andrew in the dim light.

"Anything else?" Megan inquired.

"I don't think so," Andrew commented.

"Ok, I'll look at this later," Megan responded.

Explosions in the distance were growing closer as John kept working. One was big enough that it shook the dust off of the cave walls.

"Ok, I think I've got it. Let me run one final test." Setting up the generator next to the beacon, he turned them on for a moment. Looking it over, he then turned them back off.

"Ok, they're talking to each other. How's it going out there?" John inquired of his son.

"Well, they are still fighting in the sky. But now, some are fighting on the ground as well. And it looks like the tall ones are killing all the gray ones," Lorenzo remarked.

"Are they moving towards us?" John inquired as he folded up the beacon.

"No Father, they are not," Lorenzo responded back.

"Good," John commented as he slid the beacon into the hole near the floor. John got it all the way inside and then thought about it for a moment. Reaching up, John grabbed the gold plate. With the point of his knife, he started to write on it. Finishing his writing, he rolled the thin plate so that it would fit into the hole. Pushing it deep inside John then moved over next to his son to watch.

The two alien factions seemed like they were almost done killing each other. The tall ones were winning against the grays and John knew that meant they would soon be looking for them.

The crazy air battle had blown apart some of the rock formations, making a large amount of rock rubble in the area. John knew there was nothing else he could do at this point. So he tapped his son on the shoulder and motioned for him to follow him to the back of the cave.

Suddenly an explosion happened near the cave entrance from the air battle above. It caused Lorenzo to fly a couple of feet forward into his father's side. As he did, he let go of everything in his hands, including his rifle and his sister's Captain's pin that landed on a rock ledge near the cave opening.

John picked up his son's rifle and handed it to him. Silently, John sat down on the floor with his back to the cave wall and motioned for his son to do the same. Lorenzo did as his father wanted, even though he was unsure about it.

Lorenzo snuggled in close as John turned the generator on and set the device to open automatically once it received the beacon signal.

"Son, when they get done fighting, they're going to be coming in here. So we need to stay close to this generator. And keep your rifle pointed at the doorway. The first thing that comes through it, you kill it, understand?"

"Yes, Father. When the door opens, will your people find us?" Lorenzo asked.

John looked down into his son's eyes, "Hopefully.

There is a lot of time between now and then. Anyone could find it, we will know soon, I hope." Looking over at the hole in the wall, John had a thought. "Son, could you kick some sand into that hole? We don't want the bad guys to find it."

Lorenzo did as he was told and with his bare foot, he pushed some sand in.

Time passed by as the sounds of the air battle raged on. Outside, the tall whites from Africa had won the ground battle and started making their way to the cave.

In the sky, however, was a different story. One of the grays broke away from the main fight and turned towards the ground battle. He opened fire, strafing the hillside in an attempt to kill the tall whites on the ground.

This caused them to seek cover in the cave. However, as the first one rushed in, he was met by gunfire from John and Lorenzo.

Falling backward, he hit the ground and rolled out the door to the feet of his comrades. The gray alien pilot in the air recharged his weapon as he turned in the air and opened fire once more as he passed by.

Seeing they had no choice but to make a run for the cave once more, they took off running to the mouth of the cave. The airship from above overshot and missed its target. However, his overshot hit the canyon wall high above them knocking loose a major section of the stone wall above.

Inside, it sounded like the world was about to fall on them. John, without thinking, grabbed his son to cover his body with his own. The falling boulder from high above the cave entrance came rumbling downward and hit the ground on top of the aliens with a mighty crash.

Suddenly, the cave was filled with darkness and dust as the mighty boulder sealed them in. Lorenzo let out a panic-filled scream as his father lay on top of him.

371

Fading Starlight

The Present

Megan followed everyone out of the cave as she carefully kept looking at the gold artifact they found. Being the type of girl who was always peeking at her Christmas presents, she could not help but bend the corner of the roll a little to see what it said.

Megan suddenly stopped when she saw what it said. "Hey guys, I think we need to go back," Megan spoke as she looked at the bottom of the message.

"What's up?" Jenny inquired as she turned around.

"I think there's more inside," Megan responded.

Rick, a little aggravated that they could not leave yet, looked around and responded, "Fine, let's get this done quickly. I don't like standing around in the open."

Moving back to the cover of the cave, Megan used the stone table to unroll the gold. First, with Andrews's flashlight, she started to read, and then her eyes filled with water.

"Meg, what happened?" Andrew asked.

Putting her hand over her mouth, she responded, "The aliens attacked the village. They killed my Granddaughter Rebecca." She stopped reading for a moment, handing it to Jenny. Jenny looked down at it and decided to read it aloud for everyone.

"We came back from a trip, Lorenzo and I, to watch the gray aliens finish pounding the village from the sky. They are hunting us now, and because of us, they have killed everyone we know. My wife, Kasa, and daughter, Rebecca are dead. Lorenzo and I are now alone. I have suffered loss before, but not like this, never pain like this. We must move on, maybe to the north."

Jenny looked at Andrew's eyes for a moment and then back to the writing. "Hey, the second part is different. It says; 'They are coming for us, no place to go. We can't leave. Please find a device in the same hole as this message. Press the blue button.'" Everyone looked at

372

each other as they spoke in unison, "Blue button?"

Andrew moved away from everyone and laid back down on his side to resume digging. "There has to be more," he exclaimed.

After a moment, Jenny inquired as to his progress.

"Not sure, there is a lot of sand in here. I'm not sure, but I think it's empty." Andrew stopped and then looked upward, "Sorry, it's empty."

Jenny was about to speak when Megan got down. With tear marks down her face, she ordered Andrew out of the way.

"Move, soldier," she informed him in a harsh tone.

They traded places as she kept digging with her arm. The sharp edges of the stone hole cut into the side of her arm, making her bleed a little.

Then in a moment of victory, she expelled, "Ah ha! I've got you. You dug it out, but you did not dig downwards." Megan informed him

Soon, she pulled out a strange-looking device with folding tripod legs. Megan spun around in the dirt to sit on her bum. She looked closely at it. "It really does not look like anything from around here," Megan remarked.

Standing up so that everyone could see, Megan turned it around and found the blue button on the side of it.

"Now what?" Jenny asked.

Bending down toward the ground, Megan remarked, "I think we should do just as my son asked."

Megan discovered how to open the tripod and set it on the ground. Then touching the blue button, she slowly stepped back. Ever so slowly it came to life, powering a small ancient internal generator. The blue button started to glow a dark cobalt blue. Slowly, it changed to a lighter sky blue as the power increased. Suddenly, the beacon "popped" and released a small shock wave that everyone could feel but not see.

Everyone stared at it as it had now turned itself off, leaving the room silent once more.

Rick looked at Andrew and then the rest of the team. "What was that?"

"I don't know," Andrew responded.

Not sure if something else was to happen, Rick looked outside for a moment. Nothing out there; nothing in the sky. So he walked back in. Jenny reached down and picked it up. "Well, more questions without answers. Let's bag it and take it back."

Jenny started to turn when everyone began to feel the air within the cave change.

Megan was the first to respond to it, "Do you guys feel that?"

It was like the air was becoming clear and crisp. And the hair on the back of everyone's neck was starting to react from the growing level of static electricity around them. Then, near the floor, a slightly bluish haze started to form. It grew and became stronger in intensity before them. Jenny stepped forward, being the closest she could feel the skin on her face react to the blue light. For a brief moment, she thought she could see a man standing in the growing mist before her. The man walked up to her, put his hand on her shoulder, and spoke in her ear.

No one else saw it; they could only see what was happening on the floor. Then in a moment, it was all gone. Andrew tapped his flashlight which had suddenly died to get the light back on.

Megan's eyes grew wide in the light, overwhelmed by emotion as she watched a man rolling off of a young boy. Both were incredibly filthy, what little clothes they had were torn, half naked from living a primitive life. Their bony ribs and faces reflected a living with small amounts of food. His long hair and matted beard were packed with dirt from the explosion that just happened.

It was obvious that only moments before they were holding on to the time generator, rifles, and backpacks. As the man now rolled onto his bare back, his eyes struggled to focus on the people in the room.

Megan looked intently at the man, in whose face she quickly saw the image of her late husband, Thomas.

Filled with emotion, Megan asked, "Johnny, is that you?"

He had not spoken English in so long that the sounds seemed almost foreign to him.

Slowly his mind, reeling from the shock, started to make

sense of it all as he looked closely at her. Awkwardly opening his mouth to form the words, John asked, "Mother, am I home?"

For the first time in a long time, Johnny exploded in tears of relief and joy, as Megan and her son grabbed each other on the floor. Andrew, realizing what had happened, bent down to join the embrace of them as Lorenzo just hugged them as well, not knowing exactly who he was hugging.

Rick stood at a distance, watching it all happen in amazement. Then, looking at Jenny, a little puzzled, he approached her.

"What's up?" Rick asked.

Still a little in shock, as an emotional ball formed in the back of her mouth at the sight of everything, she spoke up, pointing with her index finger at the air in front of her. "Someone stepped out of the mist with them. And he talked with me," Jenny reported.

Rick's eyebrow raised as he carefully asked, "What did he say?"

> *"Hunted they are,*
> *for out of the darkness their pursuers come.*
> *Twisted and gray as the shadow they awoke from.*
> *Dark are the intentions of their hearts.*
> *Lovers of everything the Light despised.*
> *Good and pure is the cloak they wear.*
> *As they hunt for the souls*
> *of the sleeping.*
>
> *Behold, this tired and ragged sword before you,*
> *shall dream at the healing waters of the King."*

STAY TUNED

Book 2 ~ The Eugenics War is coming.

"When dark plans are set in motion can it end well?"

Questions to Ponder

This is a simple collection of questions for the purpose of creating dialogue.

1. In 1859 Charles Darwin released his paper, "The Origin of Species." The Body of Christ was unprepared. As a result, the Theory of Evolution became a "Gate of Hell," that has devastated many generations after this. Q. Do you think the Body of Christ is ready to deal with the issue of Aliens when the Government tells the world they are real?

2. Many people who have been researching this issue for decades have been warning people that at some point the Government will do a "soft disclosure" to get the public ready. Q what do you think?

3. On page 360 the government signs the Treaty of Ashkelon and Vos who claims that his race, Solipsi Rai and Humans are brothers. Q. If such an event happened today, and the leaders claimed to have the evidence that this is true, would you walk away or stay close to Jesus?

4. Q. Do you think Aliens are real? If so how do they fit within the biblical narrative? Can you provide scripture to back up your thoughts? Are they demons? Were they created by demons? Or are they something else?

5. Sense these creatures that we call Aliens have shown up sense the ancient times. Please reflect on Colossians 2:6-7 and ask yourself how open disclosure would effect your faith?

www.BreadstonePublishing.com

Robert A. Foster was born in the American Southwest,
raised in the Pacific NorthWest
And has been married for longer than he has not while
enjoying as much quiet life as he can. Farming, Science,
American archeology, dusty books that make you sneeze
have all been points of interest along the road for Robert.

Enjoying many Science Fiction shows like Star Trek and
Dr. Who in his younger years. Robert has at times
wandered off to other shows like Stargate (TV Shows),
Warehouse 13, and Eureka while trying to figure out if
Starwars will ever get its act together.

Coming to Christ after High School, Robert has been
influenced by many of the modern charismatic
movements of today while paying attention to the
shadows of older movements.

"Breadstone Publishing is a new ministry minded publishing company centered around identifying and raising up younger content creators in a Holy Spirit led Community. So that a new generation can lead the next.

Our intent is to give back to the Body so that the Body grows like a garden in the middle of this wasteland we all call home."